"Nothing's missing from my life," she denied hotly.

"No?" His voice went silky. "How about this?" His mouth covered hers in a ravenous, devouring kiss. Thunderous sensation made her blind and deaf and so weak she trembled like a leaf in the wind. At last he pulled away, and they both were breathing hard.

"Dammit, don't you get it?" he rasped. "Desire, passion, lust—I don't care what you call it. Between us, it's raw and it's honest, and, by God, it's real. But you're terrified of anything that strong . . ."

Her eyes glittered copper-bright with humiliation and unshed tears. "I hate you. How could I have forgotten that for even a moment?"

His lips pulled back in a grimace that was not a smile. "You only hate the way I make you feel."

OUTLAW HEART

SUZANNAH DAVIS

AVON BOOKS ◆ NEW YORK

OUTLAW HEART is an original publication of Avon Books. This work has never before appeared in book form. This work is a novel. Any similarity to actual persons or events is purely coincidental.

AVON BOOKS
A division of
The Hearst Corporation
105 Madison Avenue
New York, New York 10016

Copyright © 1989 by Suzannah Davis
Published by arrangement with the author
Library of Congress Catalog Card Number: 88-91351
ISBN: 0-380-75672-2

First Avon Books Printing: April 1989

AVON TRADEMARK REG. U.S. PAT. OFF. AND IN OTHER COUNTRIES, MARCA REGISTRADA, HECHO EN U. S. A.

Printed in the U. S. A.

K-R 10 9 8 7 6 5 4 3 2 1

For all my friends at NOLA

Special Thanks to Betty Lajaunie
of the Lexington, Missouri, Chamber of Commerce

The general belief is that of the group involved in the daring robbery, these six were present: Jesse and Frank James, Cole and Jim Younger, Clell Miller, and Jim White. No one, however, has been able to learn the name of the seventh man.

—News report, 1866

Prologue

Lafayette County, Missouri
April 15, 1865

Surrender.

The man known as Tuck grimly watched the boy-leader knot a ragged white kerchief on the end of a stick. Half a dozen other men mounted on stringy, hoof-sore horses looked on, the remnants of Quantrill's band, bloody Confederate guerrillas all, dressed in sweaty red wool undershirts and greasy, dirt-streaked butternut trousers. Slouch hats were pulled low over eyes that had seen too much death to worry overmuch about the possibility of their own now. Life was cheap, and there were no illusions when you rode under the black flag.

"Think it'll work, Jesse?" one of the men muttered.

The youngster with the killing blue eyes looked up, his beardless, old-young face a slate on which the brutal lessons of the war were written. His once-boyish mouth was thin as a knife slit, and his voice was cold.

"What's the difference? It'll all be over soon. Won't it, Tuck?"

Tuck's lips stretched over strong white teeth in a grimace that wasn't a smile, and his green-eyed gaze narrowed like a reptile's. Several men looked away from that devil's grin, their nervous horses tramping uneasily beneath them. He shrugged.

"Soon enough, young'un."

"Let's go, then." Jesse motioned, and the ragtag group fell in behind him on the wooded, beaten track leading

1

toward Lexington and the amnesty a Union President had promised a defeated army.

It won't ever be over for some of us, Tuck thought. Memories of the killing and destruction burned a bitter hole in his belly. Not that he gave a damn. He hadn't for a long time now, not since self-loathing and revulsion had filled him up, giving him a soul-sickness so deep, so bottomless that sometimes he knew he clung to his senses by only a hair. But he had one more thing to do, and though he'd accepted long ago that no one would wonder or care if he survived, stubbornly he remained dedicated to the mission that had given him purpose amidst the madness.

He pressed the outline of the small book in his shirt pocket, and its weight was as reassuring as the heavy Enfield revolver strapped to his thigh. Yes, he held the key to the treasure called the Golden Calf, and soon the man known as Moses the Prophet would be called to account for all his sins. When that day came, then there would be time enough and more to contemplate a future looming as black and empty as the gates of hell.

Hoofbeats shattered Tuck's thoughts. Ahead, Jesse lifted his makeshift flag of truce. Tuck saw the flag fall almost before he heard the shots. Jesse's horse shrieked in mortal agony and fell, taking the boy down with him.

"No!" Tuck roared, but his shout was lost among the gunfire and yells of the small Union advance party bearing down on them.

God damn it! It wasn't supposed to happen like this! Not now! Not this close to success! Tuck's fury raged, the stench of treachery strong in his nostrils. He knew he'd been betrayed. He wanted to bay at the moon like a mad dog, but instead, he drew his gun and returned fire.

The main body of the blue-coated cavalry appeared, sixty or more strong, and the remainder of Tuck's band put spurs to their horses and rode for their lives. Tuck saw Jesse struggling beneath the bulk of his dead steed. He kicked his horse forward, and felt something icy-hot sear through his leg. Setting his teeth, he ignored the gush of blood that soaked his trousers and slid from the horse as the bulk of the troop galloped past in pursuit. The panicky animal shied and darted away.

"Jesse!"

"Help me, Tuck," the boy cried. A crimson splotch blossomed under his right nipple, and pink spittle trickled from the corner of his mouth.

Tuck dragged the wounded boy from under the dead horse, and together they plunged into the undergrowth. A handful of mounted soldiers came after them. Gasping, they took cover behind a fallen tree. Jesse raised his pistol and fired with desperate savagery. The lead rider fell in a heap among the forest bracken. Tuck's shot nicked another in the shoulder, and the rest drew back.

"Run!" Tuck shouted, his voice harsh and heavy with pain. "Go, boy!"

Jesse coughed. "Good luck." He dodged off through the brush.

Tuck's feral grin was humorless. What had luck to do with anything? Someone had betrayed him, but he hadn't survived four years of war, prison, and worse only to have his luck run out in these backwoods.

He quickly knotted his neckerchief around his bloody thigh, grunting against the pain, his eyes searching out the best path of escape. He ran clumsily, dragging his injured leg, humped over to present a smaller target.

The hail of gunfire caught him near the top of a small knoll. A shell creased his temple, and silver light exploded in his brain, sending him tumbling blindly down the slope. Dazed and bleeding, he was driven onward by sheer animal will, crawling forward blindly, instinctively. He didn't know how long he'd been moving or how much farther he went before he collapsed beside a broken rail fence.

His breathing sounded raspy in his own ears. Looking upward through the dappled canopy of green buds, he saw woolly white clouds sailing across a China blue sky. The fresh scent of crushed grass came to him, and the sweet singsong of a wren warbled on the soft air.

God, it's beautiful, he thought in wonder.

He knew he was dying, and the vast ugliness and sterility of his existence mocked him. He'd lived a life that was a lie, shadowed by hatred and deceit and betrayal. And for what? Even his death would hold no meaning now as he took his secrets to his grave, unmourned and un-blessed.

His vision grew fuzzy, and a velvety darkness caressed him. Remorse mixed with relief that it was finally over. The universe receded, shrinking down to a tiny pinpoint of light.

I'd do it differently, he thought with an intolerable sadness.

The light winked out.

Chapter 1

Lexington, Missouri
January 1866

Dr. Sara Jane Cary considered herself an excellent judge of character. And when she gave her all to save a man's life, she made certain it was someone she approved of. She heartily approved of Johnny Tucker.

Sara stood with the other matrons and widows on the fringes of the lively crowd overflowing Eph Taubman's barn, idly twisting the thin gold band on her left hand and smiling affectionately across the crowded building at Johnny's familiar tawny head. He had a sunny disposition that matched his unruly golden curls, a willing nature, a gentle smile, and the greenest eyes she had ever seen. The fact that he was a man without a memory didn't matter at all.

Fiddlers on a platform at one end of the barn sawed frantically at their instruments, and couples bowed and promenaded through squares and reels in the open center. Overhead, children swung their legs over the edge of the hay-filled loft and tossed bits of fragrant straw down to fall unnoticed in the dancers' hair. A makeshift table of boards and sawhorses held food of all description, pies and cakes and sliced ham, as well as the punch bowls, one a sweet concoction for the youngsters, and the other laced with a nip of something stronger to help the adults ward off the chill on this late January afternoon.

Johnny circled the edge of the crowd, watching the festivities with Clem, the Negro boy, perched on his giant shoulder. Sara couldn't help but admire his imposing size and superb physique, feeling proud and even a bit smug that it was thanks to *her* skill he'd recovered physically from devastating injuries. He'd been bloody and battered, his face hidden under a beard matted with his own gore, when a charitable farmer had brought him to the Aid Society Mission during the last awful days of the War of Secession. Now he moved with an easy, shambling grace that reminded Sara of a great golden bear she'd once seen in a circus. Like the bear, Johnny was powerful, a bit untamed, and inexplicably attractive with his amiable ways and cuddly appeal.

But after nearly nine months of convalescence, he seemed no closer to discovering the truth of his identity than in those first terrible hours when she had been certain none of her skills could save him from death. Repeated inquiries had yielded no clues to his past, yet curiously Johnny never seemed troubled by his strange condition. His great gentleness, ready laughter, and willingness to work hard had forged him a place within Sara's household, and with this he was content. For the time being Sara was, too.

"Nightgowns and nanny goats, Sara Jane! I never thought a stingy horsetrader like Eph would put on a feed like this," a feminine voice remarked at Sara's elbow.

It was a day of celebration at the Taubmans', the christening day for the wizened baby who bore the ponderous name of Ephrim Jedediah Matthew Taubman, Junior, the first Taubman son born after six sisters. Dr. Sara Cary and her household were guests of honor, for she'd guided Elizabeth Taubman through a difficult birth, and the Taubmans were grateful. Like most of their neighbors, they had been skeptical at first of a female physician, and only an emergency had convinced them otherwise.

Sara cast a smiling glance at her sister-in-law. "A son is certainly a reason to celebrate, Pandora."

"Hmmph!" Pandora Cary sniffed, her ample bosom heaving under a formidable expanse of black bombazine. Sixty and a spinster schoolteacher, Pandora never missed an opportunity to make an acerbic observation. "And what are all those daughters of his, I'd like to know—curds and whey?"

Sara laughed, humor warming her fine brown eyes and wrinkling her straight, elegant nose. "I'm sure he's just as fond of them, Dorie, but he's busting his buttons over that boy. Anyway, the patronage of a prosperous merchant like Mr. Taubman can't hurt my practice. It might even encourage my esteemed colleagues to allow my membership in the County Medical Society."

"The Medical Society should be ashamed of themselves, Sara Jane," Pandora complained. She nodded toward Johnny and Clem. "Those two are shining examples of your skill. Reason enough, either one of them, for admission."

"No 'lady of breeding' would even *want* to be a physician, according to them," Sara said, shaking her head. "I'm afraid it's hopeless."

"Oh, those prejudiced prigs. It's their loss, I say." Pandora snorted disdainfully. Her gray-streaked topknot shook with indignation, and her jet earrings bobbed in time with her words.

This fight for acceptance was nothing new to Sara. She'd fought battles all her life, from her earliest days to her years as the very young wife of old Dr. Will Cary, then as that aberration against society—a woman doctor—and most lately, through the war as a Unionist in a town that was decidedly pro-Southern. Yes, she'd had her trials, and some of them continued still, but it was pleasant to bask occasionally in the warm glow of success. Nevertheless, her tone was rueful.

"Well, membership in the Medical Society might encourage more patients to seek my services. I never dreamed the practice of medicine for a woman would be so financially unrewarding. If not for your hospitality, my situation after Will died would have been dire indeed."

Pandora looked indignant. "And where else should my brother's wife have come, I'd like to know? Your half interest in an overgrown hemp farm, a ramshackle warehouse, and an old homeplace may not be much in hard times like these, but it's your inheritance, and Will would have wanted you here."

"Even when I plunked a bunch of strangers into your warehouse?" Sara asked with a mischievous twinkle.

"The Aid Society needed room to house that flood of unfortunate refugees," Pandora said. "Women and children, barefoot and hungry, driven out by the war. How could I begrudge them?"

Sara's eyes sparkled with affection. Pandora hid a soft heart under her bluff exterior, and sometimes Sara couldn't help but tease her. "And even when I demanded you transform your best parlor into a proper doctor's office?"

"Even then."

Sara dropped an impulsive kiss on Pandora's wrinkled cheek. "Oh, Dorie, what would I have done without you?"

The older woman's face was instantly grave. "Survived," she answered. "As you always have."

"Yes," Sara agreed. Somehow, she'd always managed to survive.

Even as a frightened child-bride, sold by her uncle to a stranger, she'd survived. Her only sister, Louisa, wasn't so lucky. Orphans, they grew up on the fringes, barely tolerated by a scabrous uncle and a host of misfit cousins until Louisa's budding beauty caught their attention. Louisa died in childbirth; and the baby, too but not before she extracted a vow from the kindly doctor, a promise to save her younger sister from a similar sordid fate. Uncle Quentin, that sanctimonious old bastard, granted the doctor's request to give Sara her freedom, selling her in marriage for a fifty-dollar piece.

That marriage, that act of compassion, was Sara's salvation, and she came to love her husband, gentle Dr. Will Cary, though he was so much older than she. She did her best to be the perfect wife to him. Their years together were full, and Sara completed her education under Pandora's expert tutelage. It seemed natural for Sara to help her husband in his medical practice, especially when his health waned; and it seemed only right when that apprenticeship finally led her to leave him for a time to seek her own medical education back East. But the War Between the States followed, and then Quantrill and his murderous horde put an end to her contentment, slaughtering Will and a hundred others one hot August dawn in a Kansas town called Lawrence. Yes, even when she hadn't wanted to, she had survived.

The fiddlers ended their song with a flourish amid much laughter and applause from the dancers. Sara gave herself a little shake, determined to throw off her suddenly somber mood. She would not allow introspection to spoil the party.

"Well, those two are certainly grateful that you've never wavered in your devotion to medicine." Pandora smiled broadly and waved her hankie at the odd pair across the room.

Johnny, a blond giant of a man, easily balanced Clem, the small-boned Negro boy, on his massive shoulder. Fair-haired and tanned, Johnny had a finely chiseled, expressive mouth and features too distinctive to be called handsome. A square, aggressive chin balanced a broad forehead, and fine lines etched the corners of his eyes with an outdoorsman's perpetual squint. Twin parentheses scooped unusual hollows under his high cheekbones, and his jaw was broad, the muscles taut beneath the bone so that sometimes Sara could judge his mood simply by watching the tension ebb and flow there.

Catching sight of the two women, Clem, a lad of about ten, grinned and waved back, his black eyes dancing with excitement and good humor. He leaned down to whisper something in Johnny's ear. The tall man scanned the crowd. His clear, green regard fell full on Sara, producing in her a peculiar jolt, unsettling her with the uncanny way he seemed to see right through her, as if he knew all her guilty secrets. Yet those unusual leaf-green eyes held a transparent gleam of innocence that belied such knowledge.

He raised a hand in brief salute, and the corner of his mouth tilted in a half-grin. Gently, he set the slender child on his feet. Clem's progress across the dance floor was awkward due to the brace on his twisted leg and club foot, but he walked. By God's mercy, thought Sara, he walked!

Yes, she acknowledged with a sudden lump in her throat, *there have been successes.* Most visitors passed quickly through the Aid Society Mission, taking advantage of a warm bed, a hot meal, and free medical attention. Only a few stayed to find a place in Sara's household, the spacious

home of Will and Pandora's childhood. That old house
was located well away from the rough river area, along a
quiet avenue in the once-elite South Street neighborhood.
It was there that Sara opened her home and her heart to a
few special, needy souls.

Like Clem, the hungry, lame, colored child no one
would claim, a former slave not worth his keep. And
Johnny, a wounded man, his character and loyalties uncertain, but his need of her help critical. Sara might be
called foolish or a "do-gooder," but the rewards were
many, and her need to serve was a powerful calling. Some
efforts, no matter what the cost, were for herself as well
as her patients.

"Look, Sara." Pandora chuckled. "Johnny's wearing
that awful sweater."

Sara's cheeks began to burn. The laboriously knitted
vest in question had been her Christmas gift to him, but it
left a lot to be desired in shape and fit. "He's trying to
spare my feelings," Sara murmured.

"I despair of your ever being a decent needlewoman,
Sara Jane. At least the stitching you did on his head was
neater," Pandora teased.

A bubble of laughter escaped Sara. "Oh, Dorie, you
scamp! For all your praise, you *will* keep me humble."

A pale girl of about eighteen with a golden halo of corkscrew curls joined Johnny and Clem. She was a pretty
sight in her plum-colored linsey-woolsey dress, but she bit
her lip shyly and hung behind Johnny.

"Maybe we shouldn't have insisted Lizzie come, too,"
Pandora said, a frown adding to the wrinkles in her forehead.

"No, it's time she stopped hiding from the world," Sara
demurred. "She can't stay in our kitchen forever. Look,
Johnny's going to make her dance with him. I knew this
would be good for both of them."

Lizzie was another of Sara's "successes," with her
pretty features, porcelain complexion, and culinary talents. But old horror still darkened her blue eyes, and the
ragged pink scar that circled her slender throat marked her
as another victim of the bloody border conflict between

Missouri and Kansas. Only Sara's intervention had preserved her life and her sanity. The violation Lizzie had suffered at the hands of Jayhawkers had taken her family, her innocence, and her voice. Lizzie was mute.

Johnny led Lizzie to a place on the dance floor just as the fiddlers struck up another tune. Sara and Pandora watched the dancers swing their partners with such gay abandon that Sara couldn't suppress a sigh of envy. Beneath the hem of her sedate, brown gabardine gown, her foot tapped in time to the lively music. After all, she was only twenty-eight. It hardly seemed fair that she should be relegated to the legions of wallflowers, even if everyone knew her as Will Cary's widow.

As Johnny and Lizzie circled the floor with the other couples, Pandora's words broke into Sara's thoughts. "Johnny's leg has healed well, too. That boy has come a long way."

"Scarcely a boy, Dorie. He's over thirty, at least," Sara guessed.

"Considering the state he arrived in, I'd say it's a miracle he's alive." Pandora shuddered at the memory. "Such a desperate, confused time. So much trouble and killing, and Johnny just another problem to add to our woes. I'll never know how you managed to convince the provost marshal to leave him in your care."

Sara gave a weak smile and looked away, twisting the slender gold ring on her left hand. "Father Yves helped."

"Where is Yves, anyway? You don't think he took it personally that the Taubmans had the Lutheran minister perform the christening, do you?"

"Of course not. He told me he was going to work down at the mission."

"I may have had my reservations about taking in a priest, but I have to admit he works hard. When he's able."

"He hasn't had an attack in months, Dorie."

"Yes, and thank God for that." She shuddered delicately. "The last one was so frightening. Shouting of snakes and bloody hearts—insane things. Why, it fairly makes my blood run cold to remember it."

Sara pursed her lips. "Delirium tremens causes hallucinations. You know that."

"Well, whatever causes them, thank God he was able to help you with Johnny. To think, the authorities would have sent that boy to rot in prison, and him with pneumonia and that horrible head wound." Pandora smiled proudly. "I still say no one can doubt your medical skills after bringing Johnny through such an ordeal."

"Fortunately, he had a man's strength to sustain him. But . . ." Sara shook her head and watched Lizzie and Johnny make another round. "There are those who would say it's my fault."

"Nonsense! Whatever the outcome, there's no denying you saved his life."

Sara's expression was troubled. "Yes," she said quietly, "but would he thank me for it?"

"He's happy, Sara Jane," Pandora replied, her voice snappish with impatience. "There are many worse things than losing your memory."

Sara patted Pandora's hand. "I know he's lucky to be alive. I just wish I could do more for him."

"You've done plenty. Why, he's as strong as a horse, and he no longer behaves in such a peculiar fashion."

"Peculiar?"

Pandora made an impatient gesture with her hand. "You remember. He'd get that vague look and then spend hours studying some tiny thing—a dandelion, or a bug, or the shape of a cloud."

"Yes, I remember. It was as though he was rediscovering the world, or finding beauty in places where others had forgotten to look. I thought it was important."

"Well, I'm glad he's stopped, and you shouldn't encourage him. As I said, we don't want him to seem too peculiar."

Sara repressed a sigh and didn't answer.

Peculiar? she thought. What made Johnny any more peculiar than the rest of their oddly assorted "family"? Crippled Clem; Ambrose Dodd, their one-armed, war veteran "handyman"; Lizzie, a voiceless rape victim; and Father Yves O'Shea, whose hellish "visitations" might be caused by drink—or madness. Even Sara and Pandora were subjects of speculation behind raised palms in the community. After all, a spinster schoolteacher with a secret penchant for port had nothing over an uppity female medic who collected human strays!

Yet Johnny was different, in a way no one but God could truly understand. Sara had healed his body, but she was unable to heal his soul. He was a man with no name, no past, no future, and only the present that Sara and her people had given him out of compassion and pity. Brought together by circumstances, but held together by mutual need and affection, they were a family, and the man they called Johnny merely its newest member.

Peculiar? she wondered again. Perhaps. An intriguing and mysterious medical challenge? Of course. But it was his need that touched her most deeply, and Sara could not help but serve anyone who needed her.

Pandora turned away from the dancing. "Come with me to the refreshment table, Sara. Minerva has been dying to tell me something all afternoon."

Sara obliged, following Pandora's portly figure through the crush and murmuring greetings to acquaintances. She sipped a cup of sweet punch while Pandora cornered her dearest friend for an exchange of gossip. Minerva Haskett was a woman of about Pandora's age, as tall and gaunt as Pandora was plump and squat. They squabbled like street urchins and were frequently on the outs with each other, but neither could have gotten along without the other for long, despite sometimes loudly-voiced assertions to the contrary.

"My dear, don't look now," Pandora was saying behind her hand, "but there he is."

"He certainly believes in insinuating himself into the affairs of the gentry," Minerva commented, looking down her long nose at the subject in question.

Sara followed their gazes, recognizing the man greeting Eph Taubman with a hearty handshake. "That's Captain Plunket."

"*Judge* Plunket now," Pandora corrected. "You remember he was Deputy Provost Marshal during the war. They say he's well connected with the Radical party in St. Louis, and now he's been appointed Lafayette County Judge."

"Social climber," Minerva commented disdainfully.

"An upstart outsider like that will never be accepted in this town."

Sara watched Plunket's hand-shaking, back-slapping progress through the guests. Handsome in a bullish, robust way, with extravagant muttonchop sideburns and a full head of wavy, ebony hair, Plunket had cut a dashing figure serving in Lexington with the Federal garrison. He especially enjoyed great popularity among the single female population, despite the town's decidedly pro-Southern leanings, and was found to be just as charming at the functions sponsored by the Union loyalists.

His recent appointment to the judgeship had followed Governor Fletcher's Ouster Ordinance. It was unfortunate that the incumbents in the Conservative stronghold of Lexington had refused to yield their offices readily, forcing the governor to call out a company of black militia to oust the recalcitrants. But that was no reflection on Menard Plunket, of course. Now it appeared he was doing his best to mend the social fences.

The new judge reached them and bowed. "Ladies, how nice to see you again, and looking so beautiful."

Minerva and Pandora made suitable murmurs that were nevertheless lacking in warmth. Uncomfortable with her companions' coolness, Sara strove to make up the difference, smiling and extending her hand. "Congratulations on your appointment, Judge Plunket."

"Thank you, ma'am," he said, beaming. "It's quite an honor. I intend to do my best to uphold justice in Lafayette County. And how goes your admirable work at the mission?"

"A few minor troubles now and again, but on the whole very well. I fear inclement weather will drive the freedmen who haven't settled on farms or found employment to seek shelter with us before long."

"You can count on my support." Plunket's ruddy face was jovial, and his eyes, so dark a brown as to appear black, shone with obvious approval. He bowed again. "Ladies, I look forward to meeting you again soon."

"Impertinent!" Minerva sniffed as he moved away.

"I find him charming," Sara said.

"Miss Sara?"

She turned to find Johnny standing at her elbow. Smiling, he looked large and masculine but rumpled in his white shirt and blue hand-knit vest. He shoved long, blunt-tipped fingers through his unruly curls, heavy and sun-streaked. His hair had a vibrant life of its own. It made him seem boyish and endearing, a thought that made Sara smile back at him.

"Would you care to dance?" he asked, his voice deep and velvet-toned.

"Oh, it's been a long time . . ." she began.

"Hop toads and horse apples, Sara Jane!" Pandora exploded. "You can't stay with us old women all evening. Of course she'll dance, Johnny. Go on now." She shooed them toward the other couples waiting for the musicians to begin again.

"I'm quite rusty at this," Sara said with a soft laugh. "I may tread all over your toes." Self-consciously, she smoothed her brown hair, checking the tortoiseshell combs that held the heavy rolls in place on the sides of her head, and running fingertips up her nape to tuck a few stray strands of hair into the knot there.

"You'll be fine." He took her hand as the music began and whirled her into the middle of the floor. Sara's hand rested on his shoulder, and she felt the damp warmth of his skin radiating through his thin shirt. "Who was that you were talking to?" he asked.

Sara was concentrating on her steps. "The new judge."

Johnny muttered under his breath.

"I'm sorry, what did you say?" She glanced up and was surprised to see the tension in Johnny's jaw.

"Watch out for that one. He's slicker than an eel's belly."

"What?" She laughed. "Wherever did you hear that expression?"

"Something my old . . . someone used to say . . ." He broke off, his steps faltering and slowing until they stopped altogether on the edge of the crowd. A frown pleated his brow, and there was a blankness in his expression that told her he was searching for . . . what?

"Go on," Sara urged softly. Her fingers tightened encouragingly on his hand.

He shook his head and gave a crooked smile. "Nothing. Just . . . nothing."

Sara let out a breath she didn't know she'd been holding and bit her lip in disappointment. Had he been on the verge of remembering something? On rare occasions he'd had flashes, but never any concrete remembrances. She knew she shouldn't get her hopes up. After nearly a year, it was doubtful that Johnny would ever regain his memory. Perhaps his head injury had destroyed that portion of his brain that held the key to his identity. At any rate, now was neither the time nor the place to push for answers.

"Let's get some more punch," she suggested brightly.

They were nearly back to the table when Sara noticed Ambrose Dodd coming toward them. The empty right sleeve of his sackcloth jacket was tucked neatly in the pocket over the stump he'd won at Chickamauga. Bitterness was never far from the surface in Ambrose, and he seemed older than he was because of it. Now his grizzled face was pulled into a grimace that indicated imminent disaster. Sara hurried to his side. "Ambrose, what it is?"

He muttered low in Sara's ear, and her expression changed from concern to anger. High color stained her cheeks, and her small hands clenched into tight fists.

Pandora joined them. "Sara Jane, what's going on?"

"It's that man. I've complained and warned for the last time. As if raw sewage and garbage of all description in our alley aren't bad enough, this is the very last straw."

"What is?" Pandora demanded.

Sara's lip curled in disgust. "Ambrose just pulled a dead rat from our well at the mission! The water supply is fouled, and it's all due to that wretched Cavendish dumping the waste from the Brass Bull Saloon right on our back doorstep."

"What are you going to do?"

"We'll just have to haul our water until the well is safe again," Sara said, her expression coldly furious. "In the meantime, I'm going over there right now to give Mr. Cavendish a piece of my mind!"

"But—but—it isn't decent!" Pandora spluttered. Her voice dropped. "You can't just waltz into a *saloon!* I declare, the very idea is enough to bring on my palpitations!''

"Then I'll leave your smelling salts with you before I go. Johnny, please bring the buggy around. Ambrose, will you make sure the others get home?''

"Sara Jane, you can't be serious!'' Pandora's hands fluttered over her ample bosom. "Oh, if only William were here!''

"Will would approve completely, and you know it. This is a matter of public welfare, not to mention the survival of the Aid Society Mission. You know this isn't the first time something like this has happened. I feared our being back-door neighbors with a tavern might cause problems.''

"At least being on opposite sides of the same block means we don't have to watch the comings and goings of his unsavory clientele,'' Pandora said.

"Embarrassment we could deal with, but this unhealthy situation has gone on entirely too long. I've written letters and complained endlessly to the sanitation authorities, and even to Cavendish himself, all to no avail. Well, Mr. Cavendish has ignored me long enough!'' Sara's soft brown eyes flashed with a molten copper glint of determination. "Now I'm going to take matters into my own hands.''

"But whatever are you going to do? What *can* you do?''

Sara's shapely mouth curled in a smile of mischievous anticipation. "I can make Mr. Cavendish *very* uncomfortable.''

"You can't be that daft, girl! Why, all manner of ruffians and hooligans loiter at the Brass Bull Saloon. A *lady* would never—''

"I'm not a lady,'' Sara interrupted. "I'm a doctor sworn to protect life. I don't have a choice.''

"But ladies of quality just don't make spectacles of themselves.''

"I've long since passed the point of caring what snobs and gossips have to say about me. Medical school gave me a thick skin. And if something shocking will get the results I want, then so be it.'' Sara's firm expression softened, and she patted Pandora's hand. "Don't worry, Dorie. I'll use the utmost decorum and behave in the most ladylike fashion.''

"You like being outrageous," Pandora accused, but she recognized the determination in Sara's voice. "Then at least take Johnny with you on this fool's errand."

Sara glanced at the tall man. "Well, Johnny? Or are you going to object, too?"

"You always seem to know what you're doing," he said easily. "I'll come."

"Very well, then," Sara said decisively, warmed by his faith in her judgment. "Let's go."

Within minutes, Sara found herself sitting on the tufted leather buggy seat beside Johnny, bundled in her winter jacket and velvet bonnet and holding her black umbrella across her knees like a crusader's standard. Of slender, medium stature herself, the top of Sara's head barely reached Johnny's chin. His long legs, encased in his Sunday-best wool trousers, brushed the fullness of her skirts in the confined space, and his broad shoulders shielded her from the brunt of the chill breeze. The sun hung on the western horizon as they drove away from the Taubmans' home on the outskirts of Lexington and headed for the center of town.

Old Nubbin's hooves clip-clopped on the brick-cobbled streets. The fifty-year-old town of Lexington was an outpost of civilization on the American frontier. A major shipping port on the Missouri River, it was situated on high bluffs, with docks and warehouses below, and was a jumping-off place for western migration. Outfitters were again making a tidy profit as people headed west to establish new lives, and the Santa Fe trade was booming. There were all sorts of opportunists and men of business swarming the streets of Lexington these days, swelling the population to more than five thousand souls, and there were fortunes to be made at every turn.

Sara and Johnny didn't speak as they passed the Court House. Years ago, an unexploded cannonball had lodged near the top pediment of one tall white column, and now it remained, a monument to the pitched battle that had occurred in Lexington during the early days of the war. The Confederate forces had won the Battle of the Hemp

Bales, but had been unable to hold onto the territory. Lexington spent the last years of the war under Union control and Union martial law, a fact that grated on the many pro-Southern sympathizers. For some, old grudges died hard.

Leaving the more prosperous section of town, they drove into the area nearer the docks and ferry landing. Here at the top of Water Street, all manner of businesses had sprung up to cater to the traveler—clapboard boarding-houses, impressive three-story brick mercantiles, hardware stores, feed and seed, Winkler's Furniture and Coffin Manufacturers, tradesmen's offices, and, of course, the brothels and saloons. The old Cary business office and warehouse, which had become the Aid Society Mission with dormitory and soup kitchen, was located in this section. Not a prime location, perhaps, but since Sara didn't have to pay rent, it meant the mission's meager funds could be used for other essentials, and Sara wasn't going to let the unfortunate location of the Brass Bull across the back alley jeopardize the Aid Society's charitable enterprise.

Johnny eased Nubbin to a halt outside the shoddy storefront that marked the entrance to the Brass Bull. He tethered the reins and jumped down, then offered Sara his hand. She wrinkled her nose at the colorful signs advertising beer and spirits and a five-cent shooting gallery.

She hadn't wanted to admit her nervousness over this enterprise to Pandora, but the thought of what she had to do was daunting, even under the impetus of righteous anger. Nevertheless, Cavendish had to be convinced. The health of all who found haven at the mission was at stake, not to mention the entire town. Sara knew the value of health reform and basic sanitation. Why, a cholera epidemic was possible unless things were changed—and soon. She drew a steadying breath. Gathering up her courage, she placed her hand in Johnny's large one and stepped down.

"You'll come with me, won't you?" she asked. "And stay close?"

"Of course, Miss Sara." Johnny's voice rumbled deep in his chest. "Don't worry. You can count on me."

"Then let's get this business over with."

Holding her umbrella at a militant angle, Sara strode

determinedly forward. Just inside the frosted glass doors, she halted, letting her eyes become accustomed to the dimness. The warm, grainy odor of hops and acrid cigar smoke assaulted her nostrils. She felt Johnny's reassuring bulk behind her and started across the table-strewn room toward the long oak bar where cowboys in long dusters and men in business suits quaffed their drinks from thick-bottomed glasses. An ornate, gilt-framed mirror hanging behind the bar reflected their progress. A man noticed her, nudged his neighbor, and a stunned hush swept over the room.

"Here, now! Lady, you can't come in here!" The young, flustered bartender with thinning yellow hair ducked around the corner of the bar and hurried forward. His pale brown eyes were the color of stale dishwater.

"Mr. Cavendish, please," Sara demanded in her haughtiest tone.

"He—he ain't here."

"Then," she replied, "I shall wait." She moved grandly to an empty table and seated herself in the straight wooden chair with the dignity of a duchess, smoothing her skirts over her knees and propping her wrists languidly on the handle of her umbrella. Johnny took a position directly behind her, legs spread wide and arms crossed over his chest in the attitude of a sultana's guard.

The unfortunate bartender's face blanched, then became mottled with bright red splotches. He sputtered a protest, but one look in Johnny's direction was all it took to convince him there was nothing he could do. He wiped his sweating brow with the towel tucked at his waist, then hurried toward the rear of the building. Sara let her gaze travel over the rest of the occupants, nodding regally at several men she recognized. They blushed and fidgeted, and one by one began to sidle toward the door. The rest murmured among themselves, turning their backs, but casting occasional uncomfortable glances in Sara's direction. Several more gulped the remains of their drinks and made an exit. Sara caught a comment about an "uppity female" and smiled to herself. Her coming here was working better than she'd planned.

She chanced a glance over her shoulder at Johnny. His

expression was inscrutable, but he caught her eye and one lid slid slowly down in a wink. Satisfied, Sara resumed her waiting attitude. Moments later, the object of her quest burst through his office door, followed by the nervous, perspiring bartender.

Sara studied the barrel of a man bearing down on her, his jowly face flushed with rage. Earl Cavendish was short, round, and balding, with an enormous bristly brush of a mustache that gave him the appearance of a bucolic walrus. He wore a brocade waistcoat that was the most revolting shade of puce Sara had ever seen, and his shirt-sleeves were rolled up to reveal muscular forearms that could no doubt handle a full beer keg with ease. Rumor had it he'd made his fortune during the war from profiteering, and he wasn't particular about which side you were on as long as your money was good. He stormed up to Sara and glared at her.

"You again!" he barked. "Cary, ain't it? Well, lady, you might be a Godalmighty doctor in your neck of the woods, but females ain't welcome in my place!"

"This is not a social call, Mr. Cavendish," Sara said calmly. "The time has come to end this feuding once and for all."

"What the hell you gettin' at, woman?" Cavendish snorted, his beady eyes suspicious.

"This afternoon my handyman pulled a rodent carcass from our well, an incident directly related to the filth in your alleyway. We've had words on this subject before. Now the water supply for the Aid Society Mission is contaminated due to your negligence. I want to know what you intend to do about it."

"Why, I think I'll have a beer to celebrate!" he declared. "It'll be great to see you bunch of Bible-thumping do-gooders go. Now get out! You ain't got no right coming in here disrupting a peaceable place of business."

"So you intend to do nothing?" Sara demanded.

"You're damned right. Now haul your ass outta my place, and take this half-wit with you!"

A low growl issued from deep in Johnny's chest, but Sara imperceptibly shook her head, then fixed an imperious brown stare at Cavendish. "Amiable demands seem to have no effect on you, Mr. Cavendish. You must clean up the premises adjoining the mission. I intend to sit right here until I have your assurance it will be done."

"The hell you say! You can't do that," Cavendish blustered, pulling his mustache in frustration.

"I assure you I can. And I might warn you that I am known as a stubborn woman. So unless you wish to see all your customers disappear like those going through the door now, I suggest you reconsider."

"I'll have the law down on you for this!"

"I would welcome such an event. Bring them on. Perhaps then true justice could be done. In the meantime . . ." She paused and gave Cavendish her most condescending smile. "Do you serve tea?"

"Tea!" Cavendish was thunderstruck. His expression couldn't have registered more surprise if Sara had suddenly decided to stand on her head and whistle "John Brown's Body." Johnny's involuntary snort of laughter seemed to be the signal for the rest of the patrons to let go as well, and the room suddenly rocked with guffaws of boisterous laughter. Mortified, Cavendish's face turned crimson.

"All right, by God! That tears it!" he bellowed. "Eustace, you and Moody drag that sot of a clergyman in here. We'll just see who's making threats then!"

The sweating bartender dipped his balding blond pate and scurried away, followed by a burly, six-foot cowboy who sported bushy black eyebrows, a vacant expression, and a low-slung leather gunbelt. Within seconds they reappeared from a rear room, hauling a small red-haired elf of a man between them.

"Lemme go! No-good hooligans!" The little man struggled, swinging his bony fist but connecting only with air. "How dare ye strike a man o' the cloth!"

Sara jumped to her feet, her mouth hanging open in horror at the sight of the inebriated priest. "Father Yves! Oh, no!"

Cavendish grinned and grabbed Yves by the scruff of the neck. He shook the little man like a cat would a mouse, laughing at Yves's futile, drunken efforts to protect himself. "Now, you damned interfering female, I think we can negotiate. What was it—oof!"

One of Yves's flailing fists had connected with Cavendish's protruding stomach. The saloonkeeper angrily slapped him across the mouth. Sara cried out in protest. Johnny surged forward, his fists raised, his lips drawn back over his teeth in a silent snarl.

"Hold it, you!" Moody snapped. A blue-steel revolver appeared in his meaty fist.

Faster than thought, Johnny swung his elbow under Moody's chin, snapping the over-sized cowboy's shaggy black head back with an ear-ringing blow. A fast punch to the solar plexus and Moody hit the sawdusted plank floor like a felled timber. Then Johnny had the gun, cradling it in his big palms, and for an instant he froze. Revulsion flashed across his rigid countenance, as though he held a rattlesnake instead of an inanimate piece of metal. He bit out a single explicit swear word, then hurled the pistol across the room. It crashed into the ornate mirror behind the bar, shattering the glass into a thousand spinning, silver fragments.

Cavendish gave a roar of fury and threw Yves to the floor. Timid Eustace raised a glass pitcher over Johnny's head. Sara screamed, "Johnny, watch out!" and smashed her umbrella into Eustace's apron-covered middle, bending him double. Beer sprayed everywhere, spattering Sara's bodice and cheeks. The pitcher bounced and crashed like a meteor against a bystander's booted toe, sending him howling and hopping into the fray. Cavendish took a swing at Johnny, who ducked, and pushed the unlucky bystander into a groaning, red-faced Eustace.

Yves struggled to his knees and grabbed Cavendish's leg, sinking his foxy teeth into the saloonkeeper's houndstooth-covered calf like a wolf on a rabbit. Cavendish howled an obscenity, kicked Yves in the chest, then fell forward, overturning a table laden with empty glasses and red and blue poker chips. Moody scrambled to his feet and caught Johnny with a terrific uppercut to the jaw that windmilled him into a group of patrons, shooting them across the room like billiard balls and spilling a couple out the front door into the muddy street.

Moody flung himself after Johnny, and they crashed to the floor, rolling and pummeling each other with their fists. Cavendish came to his feet with a roar, brandishing a broken chair leg at Johnny. Sara, enraged, shrieked at the top of her lungs and crashed her umbrella over his head.

And then all hell *really* broke loose.

Chapter 2

"Quiet!"

A babble of angry voices filled the high-ceilinged court-room with geeselike honkings. Judge Menard Plunket banged his gavel and shouted for order. "I said, be quiet!"

The turmoil hastily subsided, and Judge Plunket surveyed the battered group before his bench with beetled brows and a glowering expression.

"Mrs. Cary," the judge intoned sternly, "I am most astounded. I never dreamed we'd meet again so soon—and under such circumstances."

Sara swallowed uncomfortably and wondered how things had gotten out of hand so fast. Her bonnet was askew, its broken brim dangling forlornly. Rumpled and reeking of beer, she clutched the broken remnants of her umbrella and the scraps of her composure. Pandora would have a conniption fit when she heard they'd been hauled off by the constables for disturbing the peace and brought up before the new judge himself.

"Please, Your Honor, if I could just explain," she began.

"It was all my fault, Judge," Father Yves Armand O'Shea confessed brokenly. He stood small and forlorn, the vapor of strong spirits wreathing him like an invisible halo. The product of the union of a shantyboat Irishman and a New Orleans Creole belle, he had a checkered past that was as mysterious and confusing as his own heritage. His large gray eyes begged for Sara's forgiveness, and his voice was thick with melancholy and unshed tears. "It was just a wee bit of a tipple, Sara, lass. It helps to keep

25

that demon woman out of my dreams, ye know. I'm so sorry—for everything.''

"And well you should be, you old sot!" Cavendish growled. His waistcoat had lost all its buttons, and his face was beet-red with anger. Eustace and Moody, rather worn around the edges, nodded beside him. "And as for you, lady—''

"Don't you dare start in one me, you—you filthy heathen beast!" Sara retorted. The renewed babble of insults and accusations cut her off.

"Order in the court!" Plunket shouted, glaring at the lot of them with undisguised disgust.

Yves staggered unsteadily, and Sara put a hand out to support him, offering silent comfort and forgiveness. Johnny stood quietly beside her, gingerly fingering the puffy tenderness of a split lower lip. The underside of his jaw sported a rapidly darkening bruise. He stared into space, frowning slightly to himself.

"I think I've heard just about enough," the judge said. He pointed his gavel at Cavendish. "You have twenty-four hours to clean up your premises to suit Mrs. Cary or you'll be serving thirty days in jail."

"But, Your Honor!" Cavendish spluttered.

"Make that sixty days."

Cavendish peered narrowly across the bench at Plunket, then dropped his head, mumbling. "Yes, Your Honor. But what about my mirror and the rest of the damages?"

"I'll see that the mirror's replaced," Sara said hesitantly.

"Agreed, Cavendish?" Plunket asked. The saloon-keeper nodded. "Then get out of here."

The three men filed sullenly out of the courtroom, casting resentful glances at Sara. She gave a sigh of relief, straightened her shoulders, and looked hopefully at the judge. "If that's all, Your Honor, we'll be going, too."

"Just a moment, ma'am," Plunket said sternly, motioning her forward. Sara hesitated, then approached the tall walnut-paneled bench and the austere magistrate. "Mrs. Cary, what kind of assurance can you give me that the actions of your—er, charge won't be repeated?"

"You mean Johnny?" She was taken aback. "He was just trying to protect himself."

"Your charitable works are admirable, ma'am, but I have the safety of the town to consider. I realize this man has been placed under your care, but if this incident is any indication of his volatility, then perhaps the time has come to consider returning him to a military hospital or other institution."

Sara cast a quick glance at Johnny, but he appeared oblivious to the seriousness of this potential threat. She clasped her hands to conceal their sudden trembling, but her fingers worried nervously at her wedding band. Swallowing the sudden lump of fear that clogged her throat, she attempted to instill authority into her voice. "That's not necessary, Your Honor. He's as capable now as the next man. It was just the circumstances . . ."

Plunket sat back, and his dark eyes narrowed in speculation. He stroked the lush thickness of one raven-hued sideburn with his knuckles, then seemed to make a decision. He pointed to Johnny and spoke sharply. "You. Approach the bench."

Johnny stepped forward, his shoulders straight and his bearing unafraid. His green eyes were calm, giving away nothing of his thoughts.

"Do you realize I could remand you to jail for assault and battery?" the judge demanded.

"Yes, sir." Johnny was respectful but not cowed.

"A lot of you former Rebs seem to think you can get away with this kind of thing." Plunket's thick fingers drummed on the tabletop. "I'm not sure the government's policy of leniency is at all wise. I see that we have no record of your having made your loyalty oath. Perhaps you're harboring some resentment?"

Johnny shrugged, his impassivity an implicit refusal to be baited. "I'll take the oath."

"Johnny's case is quite unusual," Sara broke in, her cheeks pink with growing anger. "No one knows whether he was Confederate or Union, or even if he served as a soldier at all. No one," she stressed.

"I recall something of the circumstances, Mrs. Cary," the judge returned dryly. "A band of Rebs attacked one of my own advance parties shortly before this man was brought in wounded. I think it would be a safe assumption—''

"I beg your pardon, sir, but assumption is for fools," Sara snapped. "Major Rogers went all through this matter and accepted Johnny's parole. None of which has any bearing on what happened today. I accept full responsibility for the fracas at the Brass Bull. But if I had been able to receive any satisfaction regarding my complaints from the civil authorities, I wouldn't have been forced to attend to matters myself."

"Nevertheless—" began the judge.

"I said I'd take the oath," Johnny interrupted. His deep voice held just a hint of challenge.

Plunket's black eyes met Johnny's steady green glare. "I have my doubts about the sincerity of such an action, but very well. The clerk will administer the oath. Any breach of its restrictions and you'll find yourself in the Federal penitentiary—and it will be my pleasure to send you there. Is that clear?"

Johnny inclined his head in a mock bow. "Perfectly."

Plunket's sidewhiskers quivered. "You may go."

Johnny took Yves' arm and led him from the room. With a sigh of relief, Sara turned to follow, but Plunket called her back.

"One more moment of your time, Mrs. Cary, if you please."

Sara bit her lip in trepidation and returned to stand hesitantly before the high bench. What further restrictions could he require of Johnny? He had the power, literally, of life and death over those who could be labeled "disloyal." And there was no one but herself to defend Johnny. She drew a steadying breath and lifted her chin.

"Your Honor?" she questioned.

"No need to stand on formalities now that we're alone," Plunket said. He set aside his gavel and stepped down from the podium. His stern expression vanished and his lips twitched. A chuckle escaped him. "I have to know. Did you really knock Cavendish down with that umbrella?"

A fresh tide of color stole across Sara's cheekbones. "I'm deeply ashamed to admit it, sir."

Robust laughter burst from Plunket's thick chest, and he shook his head in reluctant admiration. "You misunderstand me. That lunkhead deserves it—and more."

Stunned, Sara could only stare. Plunket caught her hand and bowed over it. "I applaud your convictions, if not your methods, my dear. Only, the next time you have problems with your neighbors, perhaps you could come to me directly? I'm certain I could have saved you some embarrassment, although I must admit I've enjoyed the sport immensely."

"That's kind of you, Your Honor," Sara returned feebly.

"Please, Sara, call me Menard. I've long admired you and your work. In fact, I'd like to make a donation to the mission." He named a sum that left Sara gasping.

"That's extremely generous," she said.

"Not at all. I intend to take quite an interest in Lexington from now on. As you know, I've acquired an interest in the Alexander Mitchell banking firm, as well as in several other businesses. So, in addition to my judicial duties, I've an added concern for the quality of life here. I've recently purchased the Morrison house, and I'm planning an evening's diversion at the end of the week as a housewarming. Not so rough and uncouth an event as the Taubmans', but a musicale, a genteel and cultured entertainment I think you'd enjoy. I'd be honored to have you and Miss Cary join us."

"Why—why we'd be delighted, I'm sure," Sara stammered, more and more at a loss.

"Splendid! I'll hold you to it." He tucked her hand into his curve of his arm and led her to the door. "I hope the next time we meet will be under less—er, trying circumstances."

Sara was still trying to understand the import of Judge Plunket's actions when she and her companions finally returned to the pink-bricked Cary house on South Street.

Once the showplace of Pandora's hemp merchant father, the house suffered from the effects of time and neglect, but the roof was sound, and the rooms numerous enough for them all, including Sara's office in the front parlor, wide porches, and a jutting rear wing that contained the menfolk's sleeping quarters. The back yard wasn't large, but it was tidily arranged, bounded by the separate brick kitchen that was Lizzie's realm and a clapboard carriage house that also served as a barn. Behind that lay assorted sheds, the necessary house, and the remains of a garden and apple orchard.

It didn't take long for Pandora to voice her reaction to Sara's disastrous outing. "Hens and highwaymen! Oh, how could you, Sara Jane! Brawling in a public barroom. I just knew something like this would happen. Oh, the indignity!"

"I'm dreadfully sorry, Pandora. It just—happened, that's all." Sara lay on the parlor divan, utterly drained and mortified by the day's trying events. She applied a handkerchief soaked in rose water to her throbbing forehead and stifled a moan. Pandora went into new gales of agony, and Sara sighed, laying her aching head back against the embroidered cushion.

Her tired brain spun with bewilderment. Judge Plunket's understanding and subsequent invitation had been totally unexpected. She was grateful, but confused. Plunket was a powerful, enigmatic force, both personally and politically, and not the type of person she normally chose to associate with. But if his attentions and friendship would help safeguard Johnny, shouldn't she pursue them? The thought filled her with uncertainty, while Pandora's hand-wringing tirade made her head pound.

"However will I face Minerva? That old biddy will have the story spread all over the town by tomorrow morning."

Sara lifted the hankie and peered blearily at her sister-in-law. "I'm sure it won't be that bad," she began.

"And Yves stinking drunk! Oh, the shame!"

Sara made a futile attempt to rise. "Perhaps I should check on him."

"He's all right." Pandora snorted. "Fell into bed and is snoring like an old boar now. Whatever could have set him off? I was certain he meant it the last time he swore off the liquor."

"His intentions are always good," Sara murmured, her

heart heavy with her own guilt. She knew full well what preyed on Yves. A movement at the door caught her eye, and she sat up. "Yes, Ambrose? What is it?"

Ambrose Dodd paused in the doorway, his grizzled face the picture of doom. Despite his handicap, he was a much-valued male member of the household with his wealth of practical knowledge. He ducked his head respectfully at Pandora, but his grumbled complaint was directed at Sara, as was his faintly accusing stare.

"Threw a shoe. Horse. Whatcha want done?"

Sara's head throbbed even harder. Why did she have to deal with this problem now? Ambrose knew what to do, but he always made a production of asking permission before every chore—just to remind them all who *really* ran the homeplace.

"I'll need Nubbin should I get a medical call," she said, trying for patience. "See that he's properly shod, please."

"Cain't do it myself." He waved his stump as a re-minder.

Sara bit back a sigh. "Take him to the smithy. Or get Johnny to help."

"If'n he's here." Ambrose turned away.

"What?" Sara came to her feet. "What do you mean?"

Ambrose shrugged and scratched his whisker-stubbled chin. "Too much trouble. Time to get out. Said he was goin'."

"Oh, no." The hankie slipped unnoticed from Sara's hand, and the color drained from her face. Her voice was hoarse with panic. "He can't leave! Not yet!"

He needed to think.

There was so much he didn't understand. For as long as he could remember, it had been as though he floated on a nice, flat ocean. Now there were ripples on his per-sonal sea, ripples of blackness that became waves thun-dering on a distant shore, shattering his peace. And all he knew to do about it was run.

Johnny rubbed the curry brush down Old Nubbin's flank, flinching at the soreness in his swollen and scraped knuckles. The rhythm of the task had always soothed him in some indefinable way, but now the soporific magic was lacking. God, he needed to think!

But he couldn't concentrate, not with Clem stamping around in the dim confines of the carriage house, filling the hay-thick air with his magpie chatter. And Johnny was too fond of Clem to order him away, even though his brain swam with turmoil and his gut lurched with inexplicable panic. He couldn't be unkind to Clem, the boon companion who'd shown him how to find quail's nests and catch bullfrogs during his long spring days of convalescence. No, not when he'd soon be saying goodbye to perhaps one of the only real friends he'd ever had.

"Tell me again, Johnny," Clem begged, digging into the sagging pockets of his cut-down trousers for his treasures. He opened his palm and revealed a handful of colored stones. "Tell me like we was real prospectors. What's this one again? And this?"

Johnny pointed to each rock, reciting the lesson for Clem once more, hardly thinking of what he did. "Flint. Quartz. Ironstone, gritrock, greenstone."

"What about this one?" Clem poked a yellow rock under Johnny's nose. "Think it's gold?"

"Naw. Gold doesn't look like that." Johnny was faintly surprised by his own certainty. And there it was again, that niggling, itchy sensation, those questions that roiled inside him, forming a black knot behind his brain, threatening his safe harbor. He had to get the hell out, before . . .

A quiet sound of dismay made him whirl around, reflexes lightning quick, fists raised defensively. Sara took an involuntary step back out of the stall opening, her fingers pressed against her slender throat, a feverish, too-bright accusation shining in her brown eyes. Shafts of golden light from a kerosene lantern he'd hung from a hook illuminated the stall, and tiny dust motes danced around her, touching her hair with a halo of copper highlights. She'd removed her jacket, and her high breasts heaved under the cotton lawn of her white blouse. Her skirt bore the stains of the altercation at the Brass Bull, and her hair was loose, tendrils falling from the tortoise-shell combs she favored to soften the elegant planes of her face.

Johnny relaxed, a half-smile teasing his lips. Sweet Sara. He called her that in his head sometimes. She always smelled so good, like roses and honey. And she was sweet inside, too. Who knew that better than he did? She'd been there when he was sick. He could remember the way her cool hands felt on his feverish body, the way her sweet perfume made him dizzy when she leaned over him to plump a pillow or smooth the coverlet. But he hadn't realized what a scrapper she was until today. His smile widened. "Miss Sara."

Her voice was husky, and her lips trembled. "You're remembering."

"What?" Confusion made him shake his head.

She took a step toward him, her tone suddenly sharp. "The rocks. You know their names. Not everyone has such specialized knowledge. You're remembering from before."

"No, I'm not." The flat denial was out of his mouth before he could think. Deliberately, he picked up the curry brush, returning to the monotonous task of making slow circles on Old Nubbin's back.

Sara hesitated, noticing Clem's wide-eyed interest. "Go on up to the house, Clem. I must talk with Johnny. Will you check on Father Yves for me?"

"Yes'm." Clem visibly squelched his disappointment at being denied the pleasure of this fascinating conversation. Sara gave him an affectionate, encouraging pat as he went, but her gaze never left Johnny's broad back and the muscles flexing under the blue expanse of that ill-made vest. He groomed the old sway-backed nag's rusty coat with as much care as if he were the finest thoroughbred. The smell of horse mixed pleasantly with the musky odor of man.

"Why did you tell Ambrose you were leaving?" she asked.

"Because I am."

"But why?" Her distress was real.

Johnny sighed. "I've caused you enough trouble. If I stay, there will just be more."

"Because of what happened today?" Sara was incredulous. "That was my fault! And besides, it's all over now."

Johnny looked at her, shaking his head in a too-worldly assessment of her naiveté. The rough timbre of his words was distant and laden with weariness. "They don't forget things, Miss Sara. I owe you too much to bring trouble into your home." His attitude softened, and his smile was sad. "I wouldn't have left without saying goodbye."

Sara fought down a rush of panic, trying to keep her tone reasonable. "But where will you go? What will you do?"

"I'm not helpless—nor simple-minded," he said, suddenly brusque. The brush resumed its course of looping circles.

Sara swallowed harshly. "I know that."

"I'll get by." His currying stopped, and he leaned against Nubbin's rump, meeting Sara's disturbed gaze. The gentle sadness of his expression contained elements that mystified and baffled her. She also saw he was dead serious.

"But you don't have to go," she cried.

"All I can do to repay your kindness is leave."

"But we need you here," she said desperately. "Ambrose can't do everything, and Clem's too young. And Yves . . ." She trailed off, clasping her arms around herself as a sudden chill swept her slender frame. How could she stop him? How could she keep him here? There were ties that bound them, bonds he could not begin to understand, and it was not time to dissolve those fetters—not now, not yet. "Don't leave me, Johnny."

He winced, then stared down at his fist clenched around the brush. "I have to."

"Why?" she whispered. She saw his Adam's apple bob convulsively. His jaw bore a purplish discoloration, and she wondered distractedly if she should prepare him a compress.

"I'm afraid of what I might do," he muttered through clenched teeth, tossing the brush into the corner of the stall with barely restrained violence.

Sara didn't understand. "What? I don't see . . ."

"Dammit! Don't you realize?" he shouted. He held up

his hands, clenching and unclenching them before her staring eyes. "I'm strong. Strong as a bull. And this afternoon, in that place, when I used these on those men—" He shook his fists, and his voice was tortured. "It felt so God damn *right*, so good . . ."

"But it's all over now. Don't think about it," Sara urged.

The words seemed wrung from him. "What kind of a man am I, Sara? Why don't I remember?"

Sara's heart pounded. Here it was at last, the curiosity she'd been waiting for him to show. Surely it was a good sign, but she had not expected the turbulent ferocity that now engulfed him. She longed to take him in her arms and soothe him, offering comfort. Instead, her fingers tightened on her own forearms, biting into the soft flesh to stop from reaching out. He needed solutions, not solace, and she was helpless to supply them.

"Don't press yourself for answers," she said, her words husky and fervent. "They'll come when you're ready to accept them. I'll help you, Johnny. Until then, stay here where you're safe and needed. Running away won't solve anything. Please."

"You don't know what you ask." His tongue traced the tender, puffy split in his lower lip, and he grimaced.

He was afraid. Terrified was more like it, as if he was standing on the edge of a thousand-foot precipice with the rock crumbling beneath his feet. And across the black sky were occasional flashes of revelation that were more frightening than the fall that was certain to come sooner or later. And he was angry, too. He'd been happy. Wasn't that enough? Or had God tired of this cosmic play, discontented with the serenity He'd sent to him? So with each passing minute, the peace he'd known withered away, leaving—what? The unknown gaped before him, bleak and comfortless like an endless, barren desert.

Johnny's stormy green gaze met Sara's soft coffee-warm eyes. "How can you stand to have me here?" he demanded. "I'm a stranger, bound to bring you only grief for your kindness. Everything about me is strange. Even my name feels as if it belongs to someone else."

"Never deny your name. That much is yours. When I thought you would die and I begged for a name to mark your resting place, you gave it to me with the last of your strength. That and a thousand other things have shown me the kind of man you are.'' She tried to smile. ''So rest your fears. We all have our demons, but all I've seen proves you're a good person, kind and thoughtful. Your answers will come in good time. Until then you have a home with me—with us. If I trust you, surely you can trust yourself.''

Johnny's head whirled. She could make him believe—almost. The truth was he didn't want to leave. Sara and her family were his entire world, and he sought to protect them in the only way he knew. Still, perhaps he had been impulsive in his decision. Perhaps this was only a ripple, not a tidal wave in the making, and his ocean would once again be flat and calm, given a bit of time . . .

. . . *time. He has to give me time,* Sara thought, anxiously searching Johnny's tumultuous expression for a clue to his thoughts. She sensed his wavering, his indecision. ''Please, Johnny,'' she whispered again.

He raised a hand to her face, gently touching the wisps of dark hair at her temple. ''How can one little body hold a heart so large?''

Sara gave a tremulous laugh, guessing she'd won. ''I have my faults, too.''

He shook his head, and his callused palm cupped her soft cheek. ''I don't believe it.'' His strong face was serious. ''What if you don't like the answers I find, Sara?''

She trembled beneath his touch, and her breath faded into an uneven whisper. ''I—I have faith in you.''

''You should send me away,'' he warned darkly, a frown drawing his wheat-colored brows together in a formidable line.

''No. I won't do that. Never,'' she vowed. Her hand covered his as she made that pledge.

''Never? You're a brave woman to make such a promise.''

''I promise.''

Her words sank into him like the warming rays of the sun. Slowly, as if the muscles in his face were rusted like old hinges, he smiled. A low laugh rumbled deep in his chest, half amusement, half relief, and he tugged her, unresisting, until she rested against him, her cheek against the man-warm cotton of his shirt, her fingers tangled in the unevenly purled rows of the vest, her ear pressed against the deep hammering of his heart.

"Sweet Sara," he murmured over her head. "Then I'll stay, at least for now, and I pray you never have cause to regret it."

Sara caught her breath, and sudden pinpricks heralded unbidden tears. She blinked them back, refusing to give in to the wave of regret. What would she do when the time really came for him to go? What would he do when she finally told him the truth? Told him that to save his life, on a dark and desperate night those many months ago, she'd held his hand and pledged her troth and become his wife.

Sara Jane Cary's second marriage had been as much a rescue as her first. Only this time, Sara had done the rescuing. As a physician, she'd sworn to preserve life at all cost, and the idea to marry Johnny had been merely an extension of her oath. As a woman of tender compassion, she'd meant to ease a dying man's last hours. And as Will Cary's widow, she'd intended to pass on a favor. But there had never been any doubt, once the idea was sown, that it was something she had to do.

"No, ma'am, Dr. Cary," Major J. B. Rogers, the federal Provost Marshal, had said to her those many months ago. His face was lined with care, and his tone was abrupt. "Rebels viciously attacked Captain Plunket's patrol. Men were killed. Consider your patient under arrest, and we'll transport him to one of the prison hospitals immediately."

"I've worked too hard to save him to have the army kill him now," Sara retorted.

She sat in the Major's office in Lexington's appropriated Baptist Female College. Her face was pale with fatigue, but her spine was straight and her chin tilted at a stubborn angle. She'd performed surgery to remove bone fragments from her wounded patient's skull, a tricky procedure at best, and then a post-operative fever had kept her up all night. She was in no mood to quibble about what was best for the man they called Johnny.

"I'm sick to death of politics, Major," she continued. "It matters only that the man needs help. Haven't we seen enough bloodshed?"

"Madam, be reasonable."

"What's easy and what's my moral duty are two entirely different things, Major." Sara's voice was tight, and her expression brooked no opposition. "Moving that man will kill him. His chances are minimal anyway. Why not show him the same mercy as that other boy?"

The Major stirred uncomfortably. "That boy has a mother who's sent for him. The least I can do is let him go home to die. You've seen him?"

"Yes." Sara nodded, remembering her interview with the lung-shot boy of seventeen who coughed red sputum into his patterned handkerchief and looked at her with suspicious blue eyes. She'd come to the garrison to see him on learning another wounded man had been brought in, hoping that he could give her some clue to Johnny's identity. But Jesse Woodson James hadn't been much help, other than to mutter that, yes, he knew her yellow-haired giant. They'd called the big man "Tuck," and he was good around horses, but that was either all he knew or all he'd tell.

"I can make some allowances, doctor," the Major continued, "but Southern guerrillas face charges as outlaws and are subject to the penalties due their crimes. And a grown man has more to answer for than a boy. In the absence of some legal guardian—parents, wife—who could take responsibility for your patient's conduct in his incapacity, I must follow my orders. Good day, doctor."

Sara came away frustrated, her tired brain whirling, her spirits mired down with exhaustion and desperation. It was only when Father Yves came in that night, singing tipsily in French, that she realized how easily her problem could be solved. It took some wheedling, but Yves' thinking was a bit muddled, and he had no defenses in the face of Sara's determination. She'd taken Yves in, after all, when he'd been cast off a steamboat in the throes of delirium tremens, and had never questioned what had driven him from his order. He protested, but it was no use.

It was bizarre, marrying a man in that manner, Sara admitted, but desperation drove her. The groom was only marginally aware, but Sara held his hand and coaxed him until finally he whispered the wedding pledge. She guided his fingers, replacing on her hand the thin gold band that Will had given her. When Johnny lapsed again into that deep unconsciousness from which she had scarce hope he'd recover, she was reassured that at least the outward signs of a marriage had been fulfilled.

She dutifully noted the fact in the family Bible, stating that on this day Sara Jane Sartor Cary had married one John Tucker, and then confidently presented the evidence to Major Rogers. Flabbergasted, he could no longer deny her resolve to protect the man in her care. And if she perjured herself a bit in the telling, well, the Major was harried by more pressing duties than to question the legality of this ploy. At any rate, he made the necessary arrangements, and accepted Sara's request that her actions remain confidential, for as he knew, it was simply a way to let the man die in peace rather than in the squalor of a prison cell.

Except that Johnny refused to die.

Sara's thoughts whirled with these images and memories. Sitting across the supper table from her, Johnny frowned down at a pallid mound of mashed turnips in the center of his Blue Willow plate. His lashes were gold-tipped crescents that cast shadows across his lean cheeks in the soft flutter of light from the kerosene chandelier. At last he picked up his utensils. He approached the meal as he did everything, Sara thought, with care and deliberation.

Watching him surreptitiously, Sara remembered his struggle to live despite the devastating trauma inflicted on him, and the way his stalwart heart rejected death. When he'd finally come out of the coma, she'd been too glad to worry about a paper marriage, too relieved that her subterfuge had worked. It was meant to be a temporary solution, but when the true nature of Johnny's disability became evident, how could she turn him out, with no memory, no people, no home? The ancient Chinese philosophers believed if you saved a life you became responsible for it, and Sara could not deny their wisdom.

The normal sounds and smells of a family supper flowed around Sara. Clem brought a fluted serving dish of savory greens and pink ham to Pandora, who thanked the boy graciously, placed a spoonful on her plate, and passed it to Sara. Yves' place was empty, but no one remarked on it, and Lizzie pecked daintily at the meal she'd prepared. Ambrose preferred to eat in the kitchen where no one could notice that Lizzie cut his food for him, and Clem joined him there after performing his duties at table, one of the small chores he could accomplish easily and with pride. Silver cutlery clinked against china plates, and conversation was sporadic. Johnny stirred the pile of turnips with his fork, caught Lizzie's bright gaze on him, and hastily shoveled a lump of the hateful vegetable into his mouth.

"It's good, Lizzie," he said, swallowing, and the young woman beamed.

Sara's lips twitched, and she bent her head, rearranging the dinner on her plate yet again to disguise her lack of appetite. She smiled to herself. There was something special about a man who'd swallow a dish he loathed to please another. In Johnny's presence Lizzie had even lost some of her distrust of men. Yet, there was probably another family somewhere whose dinner table contained an empty place, and who mourned the loss of their Johnny.

Sara stifled a sigh. It was time—past time—for Johnny to reclaim his place in the world. From now on, she must take an active role, encouraging him to remember, questioning, jogging those imprisoned memories loose and releasing the man inside if she could. He needed—no, deserved—a name and a family of his own.

As for their "marriage," that would be easily enough undone with a quiet annulment. But that could be accomplished once Johnny had recovered and returned to his rightful place. For now, their marriage was still insurance against any meddling Radicals who couldn't remember the war was over.

Lizzie stood to clear the supper plates with Clem's help, and Sara served golden-crusted apple pie. Steam rose from each slice, and the spicy aroma of cinnamon and nutmeg drifted to her nostrils. She cut Johnny's piece extra large as a reward for eating the mashed turnips. He glanced down at the over-sized portion, then gave Sara a slow, conspiratorial grin. She made a decision.

"Johnny, will you come to my office after supper?" she asked. "I've something important to show you."

Chapter 3

"This stuff is important?" Johnny asked skeptically. He gestured to the assortment of items spread out on Sara's desk.

A few grubby coins. A spent cartridge. A leather pouch, half-full of aromatic tobacco. A folded scrap of paper, with faint, inky scratches on one side that might have been a map. A faded packet of untitled, unsigned letters filled with innocuous gossip. A bent and creased daguerreotype of a family group, the faces muddied and indistinguishable. A small pocket Bible with a few pencil notations in the margins.

Sara's breath left her lungs on a disappointed sigh. "Don't you know?"

"No."

"It all belongs to you. This is what you carried when you came to us. I was waiting for the right time to show you . . ." Her voice trailed off in frustration. "Isn't anything familiar? The people in the picture, perhaps?"

A troubled frown creased Johnny's brow, but he accepted the daguerreotype and studied it again. He shook his head, and his voice was anxious. "I've never seen them before. I'm sorry, Sara."

"It's not your fault. It was just a chance . . ." She hesitated, biting her lip. He'd carried one other possession, but revealing that might do more harm than good, especially considering his actions at the Brass Bull. Yet what if it were the clue he needed to open the door to his past? There was only one way to find out. She reached into the desk drawer, removed a heavy bundle covered in an oily rag, and pushed it into Johnny's hands. "This is yours, too."

He unwrapped the rag, revealing silver-blue metal. He stopped, the muscle in his jaw working, then slowly pulled the massive Enfield pistol free. He hefted it, testing its weight, and to Sara, the gesture looked practiced. The notion chilled her.

It was so easy to forget that Johnny had probably been a soldier, perhaps a guerrilla. She'd seen his gentle, sensitive side, but what kind of a man was he really? No, she told herself firmly, she wouldn't let his fears become hers. She knew him. The fact that he'd once carried a gun meant little.

"No," he said abruptly. He set the gun on the desk with a muffled thump. "It isn't mine."

"You carried it," she began.

"No, I said!" His mouth was a harsh, angry line, and his eyes were flat with denial. "It doesn't belong to me. None of it!" He shoved the collection of odds and ends off the desk with an angry swipe. Coins hit the floor and rolled like tiny cartwheels, and papers fluttered like birds with broken wings. "You can't make me something I'm not."

Alarmed, Sara grabbed his arm. "Johnny, it's all right."

"Don't do this to me," he warned, unconsciously echoing her earlier words. He glared down at her, his fists clenched.

Dangerous, Sara thought in sudden panic. *He looks dangerous.*

"Don't lie to me again."

"I wouldn't! Don't you know that?" Sara cried, then dropped her eyes in sudden, guilty realization. Hadn't every action she'd taken with him been based on a lie? Her words trembled. "I'm sorry. I was just trying to help."

"Why are you doing this to me? Don't you understand? I don't care if I never remember."

"Johnny, no." She gasped. "You can't mean that. What if you have a family? What about your responsibilities? There's probably someone out there sorrowing for you this minute, not knowing whether you're alive or dead. Don't you care?"

"I guess I don't," he said flatly.

She was taken aback, repelled by this callous dismissal of everything she held dear. To Sara, family was all important. How could he not care? She took in his arrogant, defensive stance, the aggressive jut of his jaw, so unlike what she'd come to expect from him. Yet in his eyes there was something vulnerable and—hurt. Then she understood.

"You know what I think, Johnny?" she asked softly. "I think you're trying to run away again. But soon you're going to have to face the truth about yourself—whatever it is. You're not going to have a choice."

"All I know is that you're making matters worse." He turned away and strode angrily from the office, leaving a trail of words behind him to torment Sara for her good intentions. "Next time, Miss Sara, don't *help* me so much."

A few days later, word came in the blackest portion of the night that Lacey Maguire was taken bad.

Sara pulled on a plain dark skirt and a shirtwaist and bundled her hair into a crocheted snood while Lizzie held the lamp. "Poor Mrs. Maguire. I feared the end was coming," Sara murmured, shoving her feet into her shoes and reaching for the buttonhook. "Tell Ambrose I'll need the buggy—"

She broke off at Lizzie's sharp gesture. "Oh, you're right. Nubbin still hasn't been shod. I'll have to send Johnny to the livery—no, that'll take too long." Sara bit her lip, grabbed up a candlestick, and started from the room, hustling Lizzie out ahead of her into the quiet of the sleeping house. "I'll go with him and we'll take a rig from there. Get my bag, quickly, Lizzie. I'll wake Johnny."

Lizzie padded down the front stairs, her feet quiet on the worn Oriental runner. Sara headed toward the rear service stairway. When she reached the landing, she nearly ran down the long hall that connected the men's wing of the house. She paused and rapped softly on the last door.

"Johnny? Johnny, wake up."

She cocked her head, listening. No answer came, but a

peculiar moaning floated through the paneled door. She knocked again, impatiently, then thrust open the door, in too great a hurry to worry about propriety. Johnny had been unusually tense and preoccupied since their visit to the Brass Bull, and he had avoided Sara. She thought it wisest not to press him, so had let him be, but now she needed his help.

The room was small, modestly furnished with a hand-made cherry bedstead and washstand. Johnny's few pieces of clothing hung from hooks on the far wall. In the dim glow of the single flame she saw the outline of his body thrashing underneath the patchwork quilt. His restless movements shook the multicolored hills and valleys in a Lilliputian earthquake. Setting the candle on a small table near the door, she hurried to the bedside and touched his bare shoulder.

His reaction was instantaneous. She had no time to register the warmth of his flesh against her fingertips, or to repeat his name. Cruel fingers locked around her throat, and she was twisted, turned, pulled down across the rumpled bed covers and held there by a powerful arm. No sound could issue from her constricted throat, no air pour into her tortured lungs. Surprised, she struggled, her hands pushing, but it was like trying to move iron bars. Her ears began to hum, a high-pitched whine shrilling a warning as silver spangles sparkled at the edges of her vision. Darkness crouched and leaped. Talons ripped her consciousness into black and silver ribbons. In that instant she was afraid.

He was afraid.

Darkness. Suffocating darkness, closing in on him from all sides. The cold, moist earth against his face, in his mouth, choking him. Escape. The perimeter of a cell in exchange for a grave in the bowels of the black Virginia earth. Digging like a blind mole, with the ever-present fear of entombment, or worse, discovery. Hands, pulling him back to that hell . . .

With a growl, he fought those hands, but the dream twisted, changed, and the demon under his hands became another face, softer, sweeter . . .

"Godalmighty!" Johnny loosed his grip with a mighty oath. She lay limp and still. "Jesus, Sara!"

Then she gasped, sucking in a ragged breath that lifted her rounded breasts against his hand. He gave a strangled cry and cradled her like a babe against his naked chest, the softness of her skirts nestling in the V of his thighs a contrast to the itchy wool of his long johns. She lifted the back of her hand to her forehead, her breathing shallow, her eyelashes fluttering like moths against her snow-white cheek. She moaned softly.

"Oh, God, Sara." He cupped his trembling hand under her nape and used his thumb to tilt her chin upward. "God, I'm sorry! Are you all right?"

She fought the dizziness of the swoon, forcing her eyes open, drawing another deep draught of air into her lungs. "What . . . ?" She frowned, making a supreme effort to focus her gaze on Johnny's worried face. Her hand fell, the palm trailing across his chest, her fingertips tangling in the soft blond hair on his torso. The edge of her nails scraped delicately across a bronze nipple, and Johnny stiffened, familiar but half-forgotten sensations heating his loins. "You were dreaming," she murmured.

"Yes." He gritted his teeth, relief that she seemed unharmed edged with growing anger. The fear, the inner forbidden stirrings, the tattered, bizarre remnants of the dream—all made him defensive. His hands tightened on her shoulders, and he shook her. "What the hell are you doing in my room?"

"I needed you," she muttered, her head still swimming. She felt him jump, and her gaze climbed upwards to meet his hot eyes. A blush changed her pallid cheeks to crimson. She was suddenly intensely aware of how she lay in the curve of his strong arm, her face pressed intimately against his bare chest. She struggled to sit up. "I—I mean . . ."

Johnny let her go and ran his hands through his thick gold curls. His low curses fell on her like hot coals. "Damnation, woman! I thought I'd killed you!"

"Don't you talk to me like that!" Recovery had brought a full return to her temper as well.

"Any female fool enough to disturb a sleeping man is liable to get more than she bargained for," he thundered.

She scrambled to her feet and flung an armful of bedclothes in his face. "Hush, you'll raise the house. I've a patient and no way to get to her," she said. "Someone must escort me to the livery, and you're elected. Now get dressed. I'll wait on the porch."

She stormed across the room, pausing at the door to bestow a haughty glance. "Duty is what drives me, sir, not some base and lustful fancy, so don't flatter yourself. Now hurry! My patient needs me."

Johnny gaped after her, open-mouthed. Jesus Christ! What had gotten into him? Nearly strangling Sara was bad enough, but then to insult her as well! He jerked on his trousers with angry movements, furious at himself—and her. Jamming his feet into his boots, he snatched up his shirt and sack coat and strode after her, buttoning as he went. Chagrin ate at his belly. He'd made a fool of himself, no doubt about it. It was only a sick call, nothing more, but that blasted nightmare had made him drag an innocent lady into the depths of his personal horror. He shook his head. Jesus, he should have left when he had the chance!

Lizzie held out a lantern to him when he reached the porch. Sara said nothing, merely swung her long dark cloak around her shoulders, picked up her heavy medical bag, and hurried down the steps into the cold, dark street. He had no choice but to follow.

He quickly caught up with her. The lantern light swayed drunkenly before them, illuminating the rough street curb with its feeble rays. Sara stepped over a dirt clod, straining with both hands to carry the heavy case. Johnny reached over and took the handle, but she jerked it away, glaring at him.

"I can do it!"

"We'll get there faster if you let me carry it."

She digested his words for a moment, her mouth compressed into a tight line. She couldn't argue the truth of his suggestion, so with ill grace handed over the bag. She walked faster, ignoring him, her head held at an imperious angle. Johnny smiled at the mass of dark hair bobbing in its net on the back of her head. Damn, what a tigress! She might be sweet and biddable on the outside, but inside she had a fiery streak. Why had he never noticed it before?

They reached the livery stable in short order, roused the drowsy attendant, rented a team and buggy, and within minutes were heading south out of town on the Old Independence Road. Sara gave terse directions, and they followed the Little Sni Creek. They spoke little. Sara was preoccupied with concern for her patient, but resentment against Johnny's startling and unexpected treatment still simmered. She gave another short directive, pointing out a turn.

"The Maguire place is about another mile."

"Is Mrs. Maguire ill?"

Sara gazed into the blackness at passing silhouettes. A few leafless trees poked skinny, stark fingers into the starless, navy-blue heavens. She sighed softly. "She's dying. It's tragic, for she's a young woman, with children. All I can do for her is ease her suffering."

"I'm sorry. Is there no hope?"

Sara shook her head. "She has a cancer—of a feminine nature." She gave a wry, sad smile. "At least I've offered some ease, and the fact that her physician is a woman has saved her needless embarrassment, she says. That is something. Turn here."

"How do you know the way so well? And in the dark?" Johnny asked.

She shrugged, pulling the cloak around her shoulders and repressing a shiver. The night air was a sharp reminder that winter was far from over. "My husband's family owns land hereabouts. Before the war, we came often to picnic on the creek and explore the caves."

Johnny said nothing, merely clicked softly to the horse. The wind blew his hair, and he tugged at his collar.

"Are you cold?" she asked, concerned.

"I'm all right."

"You'll need a warmer jacket before the weather gets worse," she said absently. "I must see to that . . ." She trailed off. The steady drum of the horses' hooves filled the silence between them.

The muscle in the side of Johnny's jaw twitched. Even

though he could tell she was still a bit angry at him, she cared. How had he come to deserve such acceptance? He knew somewhere deep in his gut that it was not something he was accustomed to. After another interval, he swallowed uncomfortably.

"I—" He stared straight ahead and frowned. His voice was gruff. "Did I hurt you?"

Startled, Sara raised her hand instinctively to the side of her neck. She pressed the tenderness where his fingers had squeezed. "No."

"I'm sorry I scared you."

She chanced a glance at his averted profile. "What were you dreaming about?"

"I don't remember." Now, why should he lie to her? Johnny wondered. He remembered well the smothering sensations of the nightmare, only he wasn't so sure it had been that exactly. Had he been dreaming of something that he'd actually experienced? Is that why the terror had been so all-consuming? And what instinct for self-preservation made him hold this information back from Sara? Still, until he had more to go on, the notion was little more than a hunch. Besides, a man was entitled to a few secrets about himself—even a man with no past.

The Maguire farmhouse was a block building of native stone. It hugged the rolling hillside with a fierce determination to endure despite the ravages of war and the caprices of nature. Specterlike figures moved across the faint golden glow at the windows. Death hovered here tonight, and there was no welcome for strangers.

"I don't want you here," Maguire said, blocking the doorway. His eyes held a wild light, and his hair stood up around his head, twisted there by tortured fingers. "You've been no help to her. I want her to die among decent folk—not at the hand of a shameless hussy who spends her time in barrooms."

"But Mr. Maguire," Sara protested. She bit her lip, aghast. How had word of her debacle reached even this remote location so swiftly? And would her patient suffer needlessly because of her well-intentioned actions?

"I sent for the doctor, Ethan. Let her pass," a reedy voice ordered. Lacey Maguire's aged, wizened mother stood erect and adamant behind him, holding a wide-eyed grandchild. "I'll not let you deny my daughter an easy death because of your stubbornness."

"She's my wife!" Ethan raged.

"And my daughter!" the old woman snapped. From the rear of the house came a low, agonized scream. She reached out and half-dragged Sara into the house. "Come, Dr. Cary. She needs you."

Lacey Maguire passed from life shortly before dawn. At the last, due to Sara's medicine and ministrations, she had no pain and was able to quietly kiss her children goodbye. Holding her grieving husband's hand, she merely quit breathing. Sara signed the death certificate and offered to help with the laying out of the body, but the old woman declined, tears streaming down her wrinkled visage.

"You did enough, thank the Lord," she said in a hoarse whisper. "God bless you."

Ethan Maguire, overcome with rage and grief, silently endured Sara's expression of sympathy, his body tense with resentment. Sara could forgive him that, though. A widower with six small children to raise would doubtless need someone to blame. She gathered her bag and left the deathroom. In the main room, a tumble of sleeping children sprawled on pallets near the fireplace, and Sara's heart twisted at the sight.

God had not blessed her with children. It was her secret sorrow and shame that she was barren. And oh, how she'd longed for just one child of her own! Perhaps when time had taken the edge off Ethan Maguire's grief, he'd allow her to contribute in some small way to these little ones.

A chair creaked, and a tall figure stood. Sara was faintly surprised by Johnny's presence. She'd all but forgotten him. Now he came forward and pushed a tin cup of tepid coffee into her hands.

"Is it all over?" he asked in a low voice.

She nodded and automatically sipped the bitter brew. It lay sour and acid in her empty stomach. Fatigue and a sense of failure weighed her down. Her tone was dull. "We can leave now."

The first faint streaks of gold and orange gilded the horizon on the ride toward town. There was no need for urgency now, and Johnny let the horse set his own pace. Sensing Sara's need for quiet, he said nothing, leaving her alone with her thoughts.

"Stop here," she said abruptly. He drew the buggy to a halt where the trees thinned and a triangle of undulating open land splayed away from the road toward the creek. In the distance, a peculiar rectangular outcropping rose like a giant's abandoned plaything, a child's block of immense proportions illuminated from behind by the cresting sun.

Sara scrambled down out of the buggy, dragging the hem of her cloak, then strode purposefully out across the field. A hard crust of frost made the dry grass crackle beneath her shoes. Shadows moved and streaked behind her, night diminishing, day arriving. She stopped at last, standing with her arms wrapped tightly around herself, staring at the rising sun.

Johnny's hands moved restlessly on the reins. What was she doing? he wondered. Why was she standing there, motionless? With a muttered expletive, he secured the reins and vaulted down. His boots crunched through the rough, dry grass. He came up behind her. Moisture glistened on her pale cheeks. *Oh, God,* he thought helplessly, *she's weeping.*

"Sara?"

She drew a deep, shuddering breath, and her lips trembled. "I wish Will was here."

A surge of pure, unreasoning anger caught him by surprise. What should it matter to him that she wished for a dead man? He knew nothing of her late husband, only that he had died in the war. But as Clem had once pointed out, "If Miss Sara loved him, he must have been a good man." He clenched his jaw and jammed his hands into his trouser pockets, hating his inability to be what she needed.

Sara gave a self-deprecating laugh, sniffed, and wiped her wet cheek with trembling fingertips. "He liked to come here to sketch. He was quite an artist, you know, but he never was satisfied with the Sugarloaf." She gestured toward the abutment. "You've seen the sketch hanging in my office? I thought it was his best, but he said the light changed too rapidly to capture it. But if you watch, it does

look like a loaf of white sugar, though we've seen little
but brown during the war and since—''

"Sara." He used her name to break into her babbling
tirade. He knew her real concern wasn't sugar or land-
scapes.

She buried her face in her hands, and her voice was
muffled. "He always knew what to say. I never do."

"You did all you could." His hands came up of their
own accord to rest reassuringly on her slender shoulders.

"But nothing to stay their grief. Those poor motherless
babies! Do they even understand?"

"Life and grief are synonymous, Sara. We all have to
face it sometimes."

"At least she wasn't alone." She sighed, raising her
head. "She was with those who loved her."

"And all they have now for their love is pain. Perhaps
I'm the lucky one after all, not to remember such." He
felt her jerk of surprise, and his hands fell away.

"Maybe you are," she said slowly. Her brown velvet
eyes held an element of sad reproach. "But that's a coward's way to face life. You are so alone, Johnny, more
than anyone. Are you a coward as well?"

Sara's words haunted Johnny for the rest of the day. He
went about his chores mechanically, trying to look inside
himself for the answer. Was he a coward? Had he been
purposefully holding a flood of remembrance at bay, pushing back hints and tantalizing flashes of his past because
he was afraid of what he might find? He couldn't believe
it. Sara was a good woman, but in a lot of ways she was
a damned busybody. Pushing and prodding a man, bedev-
iling him with unanswerable questions! No, a mind was a
tricky thing, as she'd said before. The head wound that
had nearly killed him was responsible for his lack of memory, not a willful desire to forget. Wasn't it?

Work was a balm. He took a load of donated vegetables
down to the mission and helped Father Yves, chipper and
cheerful as usual, distribute them. There was wood to
split and stalls to clean, and an endless series of chores to
be done, but he performed them with only half his attention, consumed by an inner restlessness. A part of him

waited, in anticipation of he knew not what, while another portion of him chafed at the delay. A nagging sense of unfinished business hovered in the back of his consciousness, and he itched for action, like a cougar on the prowl. Only his prey was unknown.

Later, Clem helped him polish the tackle and leads, chattering ceaselessly. The last bit of harness gleamed with oil and was carefully placed on its appropriate nail when a sound began to register. The ring of metal against metal. But something was wrong. It lacked rhythm, melody. Johnny tilted his head, listening, then left Clem in midsentence, exiting the tack room and following the elusive, discordant beat across the yard to the lean-to shed behind the kitchen. He thrust open the plank door, his shoulders tense.

Ambrose straightened, his expression truculent. A charcoal fire glowed orange in a small forge. He held a heavy hammer in his left hand and was clumsily attempting to straighten a horseshoe he'd clamped to an old anvil.

"Well, what the hell you lookin' at?" Ambrose snapped.

Johnny ignored him. There was something so familiar about the clean smell of the hot metal and the smoky charcoal. The echoes of hammer on anvil rang in his ears, singing a siren's song that beckoned him forward, almost mesmerized, into the Vulcan's den.

"Ain't you ever seen a one-armed man shoe a horse?" Ambrose demanded.

Johnny took the hammer out of his hand. His answer came from far away—another world away. "I'll help."

Ambrose stepped back, uncomfortable with the strange, preoccupied look in Johnny's green eyes. "Whatever you say."

Johnny gave the hammer a tentative swing. Somehow, this weight felt *right*. Far better than the gun Sara had tried to say was his. He looked around, found a pair of long-handled pinchers, and used them to plunge the smoldering iron horseshoe back into the coals. He reached around and gave the wheezing leather bellows a squeeze. The rush of air made the coals glow brighter and hotter. When the shoe was glowing, too—just right, he knew somehow—he quickly used the pinchers to pull it out and hold it against the anvil.

And then, with the hammer, he made it sing.

Despite her late night, and despite the growing gossip about the ruckus in the Brass Bull, Sara saw several pediatric patients in her afternoon clinic. The office had once been Pandora's front parlor, but now it held a large rolltop desk, a wooden examination table, and tall glass-fronted cabinets filled with tobacco brown and cobalt blue bottles of pharmaceuticals. Will Cary's landscape of the Sugarloaf hung in a gilt frame on the wall next to her diploma from the Woman's Medical College of Pennsylvania.

Sara had just written a fifty-cent prescription for Mrs. Becker's youngest, appeased the howling child with a sweet, and sent them on their way when Ambrose came in. She knew something was wrong instantly, for his normal scowl was gone and a look of—wonder? admiration? surprise?—smoothed his face, reminding her he was a relatively young man, and, some would think, a handsome one, as well.

"Ambrose?" she asked. "What is it?"

He shook his head, beyond explanations. "Johnny. See for yourself."

Moments later, they stood in the doorway of the makeshift smithy watching Johnny work over the anvil. The heat from the forge hit her face in a wave. She winced at the rhythmic hammer blows blasting her eardrums: BANG! Ting, ting . . . BANG! Ting, ting . . .

"Ain't hardly said nuthin'," Ambrose muttered. "Went to work. Like a man born to it."

"It's a good sign," Sara said. A tremor of excitement shook her. Johnny was obviously skilled in this work. Was it a clue to his past? "I'll stay and watch a while, Ambrose."

"Don't seem right. Kinda spooky-like." Ambrose grimaced and turned to leave, grousing under his breath. "Got things to do. Queer, if you ask me."

Sara had to agree. It definitely gave her a queer, fluttery feeling to watch Johnny. He hadn't acknowledged her presence by so much as a flicker of an eyelash, so intense was his concentration. He grimaced, grunting softly with each terrific blow of the hammer, molding and melding the hot, pliable iron.

He'd removed his shirt, and his broad shoulders were covered with a fine sheen of moisture. Rivulets of sweat trickled through the soft matting of hair on his chest and down his heaving, straining back to soak into the waistband of his rough denims resting low on his narrow hips. He thrust the horseshoe back into the fire, running his hand across his wet brow. His cheeks and arms were smeared with soot and ash, and every sinew of his muscular body stood out in high relief, an example of virile, masculine beauty.

He resumed his pounding, forging the horseshoe into shape until he was satisfied. He dropped it into a waiting bucket of water. Steam hissed, and a foggy cloud rose around him like a white mantle, shrouding him for an instant in a demonic cloak in this place of fire and brimstone.

Sara's ears rang with the sudden quiet, and her own breath sounded raspy and too loud. She shivered despite the heat. Sensing her presence at last, Johnny swung toward her, pinning her with his gaze, holding her still and motionless in her place against the wall. The light in his green eyes made her gasp.

"I remembered," he said softly.

"Yes." Her single word was a mere breath of hope.

"I've done this before." There was certainty in his tone. Suddenly he laughed, exultant, and his grin flashed white in his blackened face. "By God, Sara! I remember!"

"You do? What?" she demanded, laughing, reaching for him, her face joyous.

His hands caught hers, his rough and grimy, hers smooth and clean, and their fingers entwined. He bent to search her face, and she, breathless, stared up at his.

"The forge . . . I know . . . the war! I was a smith with a cavalry unit, following the action with that sonofabitchin' portable forge. God, the work was unending! Making repairs on guns, machinery, shoeing the horses. I've done it all before, Sara. I remember!"

Suddenly she was caught up in his arms, clasping his

thick neck, unmindful of the soot and sweat on his bare skin, spinning as he swung her around, both of them laughing and giddy, her skirts flying, her heels kicking air, his whoops of laughter bouncing off the walls, the roof. Gasping and lightheaded, Sara clung to him. Finally, the dizzy dance of celebration slowed, and her feet touched the floor, but their arms remained locked around each other. They grinned like fools. Slowly, Johnny's smile faded, and he looked at her with another kind of wonder. He bent closer, then his mouth touched hers, a soft, fleeting kiss that stunned her into breathless immobility.

He raised his head, and his voice was husky with emotion. "I've done that before, too."

Sara tried to say something, but nothing came. His eyes searched her startled, bemused expression, and his fingers threaded through the thick brown hair at her nape. He groaned, dragged her close, and kissed her again, a deep, soul-stirring kiss that melted all thought of resistance and all hesitancy in its sheer heat and sensuality.

Sara's fingers moved spasmodically over his slick shoulders, and her knees sagged. Johnny might have kissed this way before, but she had never—never!—felt such waves of sensation, rushing over her and crashing through all the reserves she'd spent a lifetime building. When his tongue gently traced the seam of her mouth, she gasped with the electric shock of it, and that surrender gave him access to even more intimate secrets. He stroked the sweet interior of her mouth with his tongue, evoking such carnality that she moaned wildly, and he answered her with a low growl of passion deep in his throat.

Sweet. God, she was sweet! And that wonderful woman taste! He pulled her even closer, delighting in the pressure of her soft breasts against his chest. It had been so long! He wanted to inhale her, to consume her, to take her softness and bind her forever to him. Desire coursed through him with such force he thought he might explode. How he'd missed her!

His golden-haired beauty. Everything, every sacrifice, had been made for her. Those hellish months in Titusville had paid off. He'd shower her with gold to match her golden locks . . .

He opened his eyes, and reality smashed into him with the impact of a careening cannonball. He held a small brown mouse, not his golden nightingale. Time blurred, slowed, speeded, rippled, stampeded, stopped . . .

And the pain and self-contempt nearly doubled him over.

A golden-haired wife. But she was dead. And a battlefield was a good place to hide when you had nothing to live for. Only he hadn't reckoned on becoming a damned hero. And then there was nothing else to do but volunteer again, to use the deceit and reckless disregard consuming him to undermine Quantrill's cause, to find the man called Moses, and to recover what had been stolen. It was the least a man could do for a country and a service that had provided him with what he'd wanted most—the opportunity to die.

The universe shifted for the final time, and the seconds, minutes, and hours of bitter existence flowed once again in complete and logical order. The soft lips beneath his own that had just seconds ago been so sweet were now the bitterest gall. He jerked away, breathing hard. He could almost smile at the pliancy in Sara's warm body, the bewildered flutter of coffee-colored lashes, the softly bruised mouth that quivered ever so slightly—had he not in that instant hated her so desperately.

Sara's passion-glazed eyes opened, and the soft brown depths shimmered with confusion. He pushed her away, his eyes blazing in a face she hardly recognized. He grabbed up his shirt and stalked past her to the shed door.

"Johnny?" Her voice was tremulous and stricken, but he couldn't hear it for the roaring memories in his own head. Green cougar's eyes snagged those of a wounded doe, and the fangs that pierced her heart left a mortal hurt.

"Damn you." His voice was vicious, acid with hatred. "God damn you to hell."

Chapter 4

It was a long time before she could move, before her lips stopped throbbing and the hot ache low in her belly subsided. The coals in the forge died and turned to gray ash, but still she cowered in the corner of the shed like a small, hurt animal searching for a place to lick its wounds.

Confusion paralyzed her. Johnny's kiss had rocked her to the very bottom of her soul with its sweetness and power. But what had made him curse her in the same breath as that token of love? His eyes had burned with loathing when only moments before there had been joy and discovery and remembrance. She shivered, chilled to the bone.

Movement was difficult. With the jerky motions of an old woman, she tried to compose herself, smoothing the rolls of heavy hair loosed by Johnny's questing fingers, jamming home the combs Will had given her, fastening the single button at the throat of her dark shirtwaist. She licked dry lips and nearly groaned aloud as the flavor of his mouth again exploded against her tongue.

It won't do, she chided herself, *it won't do at all!* She had no right to feel anything more than compassion for Johnny, no matter what a piece of paper said. He was her patient, and too many complications stood in the way of anything else. But since he was her patient, it was her duty to oversee his recovery, and he *had* remembered something—for better or worse.

Sara chewed her lower lip. That had to be it. She wasn't the true object of his contempt, merely a convenient target to lash out against in a moment of emotional flux. But what had he remembered that brought him to such a rage? She had to know. And she had to be sure he didn't really hate *her.*

When she had finally calmed sufficiently to leave the shed, she told herself it was concern for her patient that made her go in search of Johnny. But he was nowhere to be found. Neither Clem nor Lizzie nor Ambrose had seen him in the yard and outbuildings, and his room was empty. Sara felt a tingle of alarm. Just how upset had he been? Was he likely to do anything rash? She was in the hall, considering this possibility, consternation knitting her brow, when Pandora found her.

"Sara Jane, why aren't you getting ready?" Pandora demanded.

"Ready? For what?" Sara asked distractedly.

Pandora threw up her hands. "Sara Jane! Tonight's Judge Plunket's musicale! You haven't forgotten he's sending a carriage for us, have you?"

Truly she had, and it seemed of little importance at the moment. "Oh, Dorie, I can't go. I can't find Johnny. Have you seen him?"

"Not go?" Pandora's lower lip quivered, and her bosom heaved with disappointment. "Why, we just can't miss this! Lord knows we get few enough invitations as it is. Besides, a lady never reneges on an invitation she's accepted unless it's an emergency."

"But Johnny . . ."

"Oh, pooh! You worry about that boy entirely too much." Pandora drew a lace-edged handkerchief from her skirt pocket and dabbed delicately at the corner of her eye. "I don't suppose it matters to you how I've so looked forward to an evening's entertainment out."

Sara felt a stab of guilt. Their pleasures had been few and far between of recent years, it was true. And she knew that Pandora would never consent to going alone. Surely Pandora was right, and there was no need to worry about Johnny just because her own nerves were raw and frayed. No doubt he had gone to Father Yves at the mission and would return in due course. Upon consideration, she decided it would be prudent to let some time and distance

renew her objectivity before she put any questions to him.
She quickly pressed a kiss to her sister-in-law's cheek.

"Of course it matters. We'll go as planned."

Pandora clapped her hands in a gesture of girlish delight.
"Splendid! But do hurry, dear. We don't want to be late."

Sara did as she was told. A quick sponge bath did much
to restore her equilibrium. A splash of rose water on her
wrists and neck reminded her she was a woman. With
Lizzie's help she donned the underpinnings necessary for
a lady of quality, lace-edge chemmie and pantalettes, petticoats and steel-springed hoop, and boned corset.

Sara had long since denounced the evils of tight lacing,
choosing to forgo the ubiquitous corset for everyday wear,
but out of sensitivity for Pandora's sense of propriety, she
allowed herself to be tied into the contraption, cautioning
Lizzie to leave her room to breathe. She was convinced
that a goodly portion of female complaints of shortness of
breath and fainting spells were directly connected to in-
discriminate lacing to the point of injury, and she often
included this information in her lectures on hygiene.

Her good black silk gown was too simple to be fashionable, but its classic style was elegant, the figured fabric
rich, and with a bit of velvet ribbon and her cameo at the
throat, it would do. When she began to fashion her hair
into its customary roll, however, Lizzie protested, waving
her small white hands and shaking her head.

"Too plain?" Sara asked.

Lizzie's dark blue eyes sparkled, and she made imaginary curls around her forefinger, then formed a questioning expression.

"But I'm too old for that," Sara objected. Lizzie
grinned and again shook her head. Sara couldn't deny her
hopeful look. "Well, all right," she said doubtfully, "but
remember I'm supposed to be a respectable widow, not a
frivolous debutante."

Lizzie smiled again and went to work, heating the hand-
held curling iron in the flame of the coal oil lamp. Minutes
later, Sara peered into the mirror over her washstand and
admired the results. Lizzie had rolled her hair away from
her face as usual, securing it with hairpins, but the back
fell down her nape in a cascade of fat sausage curls. A

sprig of black lace knotted at the back of her head made a suitable accent. Sara dipped her chin, making the curls bob, and laughed with pleasure.

"You do have a way with you, Lizzie. It's very pretty. Thank you." She turned and smiled at the blushing girl. "Next time, we'll fix yours."

Lizzie wrinkled her nose with distaste and tugged at the mass of pale blond corkscrew curls framing her piquant face.

"I love those curls," Sara protested, gently touching a springy tendril. "Most ladies of fashion would trade their eyeteeth for them, and all the young beaux adore them."

Lizzie's face clouded, and she looked down, shaking her head. She touched her chest, then rubbed her hands together as though she were washing.

"That's not true!" Sara said. She laid her arm around Lizzie's slumped shoulders. "You're not dirty. What happened was not your fault. You have a lot of love to give, Lizzie. Someday you'll be able to show some lucky man just how much."

Lizzie lifted her troubled gaze, and a shimmer of moisture glistened in her eyes. She gave a helpless shrug, and her smile wobbled. From downstairs Pandora called to Sara that the carriage was waiting. Sara gave Lizzie a quick squeeze of encouragement.

"I have to go, but we'll talk again." She grabbed her embroidered mantle and looked for her reticule, then recalled she'd left it in her office. Casting Lizzie a quick farewell smile, she hurried downstairs, trying to quell her uneasiness. Any other time she would have looked forward to the evening's diversion, but she couldn't keep her thoughts from Johnny. No matter how late the hour when they returned from Judge Plunket's, she would have to talk with Johnny or face a sleepless night.

Pandora was allowing Father Yves to assist her with her fringed Turkish stole when Sara reached the foyer. The older woman looked imposing in black satin banded with rows of black velvet ribbon. A perky cap of lace and ribbons sat atop her graying chignon, and her cheeks were pink with excitement.

"Ready, Sara Jane?" she asked.

"Just a moment. My bag's in the office," Sara replied, crossing the hall. "Father Yves, have you and Johnny had your dinner?"

The slight red-haired priest looked surprised. "I haven't seen the lad since early this morn."

Sara came up short, her hand on the cool porcelain doorknob. "He's not with you?"

Yves followed her across the hall. "That he's not. I didn't see him around when I came in, either."

"Sara Jane, are you coming?" Pandora asked, her voice querulous.

"Go ahead, Dorie. I won't be another minute," Sara hastily assured her. Pandora nodded and stepped through the front door, descending the porch stairs toward the waiting carriage.

"Is something the matter, lass?" Yves asked, his puckish face creased with concern.

"Johnny. He—he seems to be remembering."

Astonishment lit Yves's gray eyes. "But that's a miracle!"

"Yes, but something—we had a discussion—" She broke off, swallowing, and her glance skittered away from Yves' questioning look. For an instant she relived the confusion of the moment when Johnny had thrust her away. Her stomach tumbled, and her nerves strummed. She forced herself to continue, pushing open the door. "I—I couldn't find him earlier and I thought . . . oh, my God."

Chaos littered her once-immaculate office. Cupboard doors stood open. Instruments were spilled across the oak examining table like used cutlery. Rolls of bandages, tossed carelessly aside, had unraveled in filmy white trails across the floor. Her letters and correspondence lay in white drifts like a snowfall of paper. Her desk had been ransacked. The drawers hung half-opened, and the pigeon holes were plucked clean.

"By all the saints!" Yves exclaimed. "Who would do this?"

Sara could barely breathe. "Johnny."

"What? Has the boy gone mad? Why, in heaven's name?" Yves stared at the mess and ran agitated fingers through his carroty mane. His mouth thinned, and his expression grew thunderous. "You'd better check your cash box, Sara."

Dazed, Sara sat down at the desk, reaching for the tin box that contained her meager receipts. After a minute, she raised her head. "It's all here," she said faintly.

"Then what?" Yves demanded. A thought struck Sara, and she gasped. With trembling hands she shuffled through the contents of the desk. She lifted a stricken face to Yves.

"He took his things. Letter, coins, his Bible."

"What else?"

She swallowed harshly. "His gun."

Yves exhaled, whistling between his teeth. "I see."

Sara's hands lay limp in her lap, and her voice was dull. "Do you suppose he's gone for good?"

"Nay, lass. He'll be back," Yves prophesied. "After all, where else can he go?"

Bread of deceit is sweet to a man; but afterwards his mouth shall be filled with gravel.

"Crap!" Johnny muttered under his breath. "What the hell does that mean?"

He shut the palm-sized Bible with a snap and stared morosely into the foamy, yellow beer in his mug. He lifted the glass, studying the ale thoughtfully, squinting through the pale gold liquid at the distorted silhouettes lining the bar of the Brass Bull Saloon. He'd gotten a few considering glances when he'd arrived, but it was a place like a thousand others found on the seamier edges of society, a place where no one knew your name or cared to ask, and just because a man had busted a few skulls was no reason to hold it against him.

The air was smoky and fetid with the stink of unwashed male bodies, the conversation raw and raucous, the flow of rotgut whiskey and bad beer unceasing as long as you had money in your pocket. You might even find yourself whiling away an hour above stairs with one of the "soiled doves." Johnny knew now that he'd been in other establishments exactly like this one, in anonymous, sophisticated cities and booming frontier towns, and they were all the same. He'd been here before, too. It felt like home.

He took a sip of the warm brew, letting the malty liquor

caress his tongue before it slid down his throat. Out of habit he'd chosen a small table in the far corner where he could see everyone and everything. Something about the grimness of his mouth or perhaps the fierce light in his eyes warned men off. Here was a man not interested in camaraderie. No one disturbed him as he nursed his drink and flipped through the tissue-thin pages of a worn Bible. He tucked the small book into his shirt pocket and ran a hand across his jaw, thinking hard. Hell, what was he going to do now?

Now that he'd remembered. Now that he knew his name. Now that he had the key to the stolen treasure in gold known as the Golden Calf. Now what?

He grimaced to himself. Good question. Damn good question.

Except for that first moment when it had all come rushing back, he wasn't as disoriented as he would have expected for a man who'd checked out of life for a while. This surprised him. His recent experiences had melted into the knowledge of his past history, two flat images merging into one solid reality. The edges might be blurred, but the main scene was clear enough.

Yes, he knew who he was, and the knowledge clogged his throat and soured the beer in his stomach. John Tucker McCulloch, privileged son of a Philadelphia scion, hero of a daring escape from a Confederate prison, intrepid geological entrepreneur, black sheep, widower, cuckold. He ground his teeth. No, he wouldn't think about Gwendolyn now.

He wouldn't think about what had driven him to accept an assignment perfect for his black mood and reckless character. He wouldn't think about his cold parents, or his rebellious childhood, or how he'd left college to apprentice to a smith, or even the success he'd made developing a process to extract petroleum from the earth. And he wouldn't think about that other woman, that damned interfering Sara, with her big brown eyes and soft mouth, who made him remember—too much. No, he'd only think about the war, the harrowing, exhilarating existence that had taken him to hell's edge and back again.

The fact that he held a commission as a major in the

U.S. Army didn't mean much. What did matter was that he'd been coming in after nearly two years as a spy with Quantrill's guerrillas, and that he'd had the knowledge, encoded in Quantrill's Bible, of the whereabouts of the largest shipment of gold ever lost to the Confederates. The fact that someone had tried—and nearly succeeded—to kill him for it mattered most of all. He'd been betrayed, and someone was going to pay.

It had taken all his skill and nerve to infiltrate the ranks of Quantrill's Raiders at General Philip Sheridan's orders. His mission was twofold: locate the gold before it was transferred to Confederate coffers, and eliminate a band of guerrillas that was running circles around the regular army. As "Tuck," he'd risked his life passing information about the raiders and matched wits with Quantrill's own informant, a mysterious contact in Lexington known as Moses the Prophet for his uncanny ability to foresee Union troop movements.

In the confusion of the last desperate days, there hadn't been an opportunity for Quantrill to lead them to the golden cache secreted in Lafayette County. They'd been forced to split up to avoid capture, but in the last minutes, with solemn, oath-sworn ceremony, Quantrill had handed Tuck a Bible. Insurance for the Confederacy, he'd said, in case he couldn't return for the gold himself, a book of Scriptures with the location of the Calf clearly stated—if one were clever enough to decode it.

With the Federals hot on his heels, Quantrill had headed into Kentucky, his band all but eliminated, his power waning. And Tuck had turned back for Lexington in the company of some Clay County boys, after sending word ahead to his own contact at the federal garrison, Captain Alex Thompson, that Tuck was ready to come in at last and that the Golden Calf was theirs.

He'd never made it to Lexington.

Why had Thompson failed to protect him? He couldn't believe it was betrayal. Thompson had been too loyal, too trusted. The possibilities made the hairs on the back of Johnny's neck prickle with apprehension. He drained the mug, then wiped his mouth on the back of his hand and considered his next move.

He was in a hell of a mess, caught between two worlds. That damned yokel Plunket wanted his hide because he was a "Rebel." But revealing his Yankee loyalty could be just as dangerous in this stronghold of former Confederates. His guerrilla friends wouldn't hesitate to slit his throat if the truth came to light. After all, the word traitor depended entirely on your point of view.

The only way to vindicate himself would be to complete his original assignment—locate the Golden Calf and bring it to the Union authorities. It wouldn't be easy, but he wouldn't ignore his duty, even at this late date. He knew something else: Whoever was responsible for his present situation was going to pay—and pay dearly. Revenge wasn't much when your life was as empty as his was, but it was better than nothing.

He stood up, feeling the cold, reassuring weight of his revolver beneath his shirt, nestled against his belly. No doubt Major John McCulloch was presumed dead. Well, let him stay dead a while longer. His family didn't care; he owed them nothing. He was in the right place, Lexington, and now he was going to make it the right time to recover a treasure and exact revenge.

As for Sara Cary, well, she'd wanted him to remember, hadn't she? Now she would have to live with the consequences of her probing into an old wound. The war might be over for some, but John McCulloch had some scores to settle, and one last mission to accomplish. He'd be damned if he let anything—or anyone—stand in his way.

He sauntered toward the crowded bar, a loose-hipped, long-legged man with the gleam of the devil in his eye. The first thing he needed was information, and for the price of a beer, it could always be found in a place like this.

The Misses Regina and Aimee Whitaker played and sang—badly. The exquisite grand piano was recently imported all the way from New York by Judge Plunket just for the occasion of his musicale, but Regina thumped it as though it were a recalcitrant child, while Aimee used her vocal talents to set everyone's teeth on edge. It was fortunate that the young ladies were more comely than they were talented; at least the audience could admire their beauty while praying that the recital piece would soon end. Sara sat demurely on a burgundy velvet-covered sidechair in the elaborately appointed parlor with a polite smile firmly anchored on her lips.

"Excruciating," Pandora whispered at Sara's side. She was thoroughly enjoying herself, silently critiquing each participant. After all, nearly thirty years as a teacher of music and deportment gave her some authority, especially over those young ladies who hadn't seen fit to avail themselves of her tutelage.

Sara gave a nod of agreement and stifled a sigh. The evening's entertainment had seemed interminable. Unwilling to upset Pandora, she'd followed Yves' advice, mentioning nothing about the state of her office and Johnny's apparent flight, and proceeding to the musicale. Yves promised to right the office before their return, but that was the least of Sara's concerns. She'd been forced to make polite conversation and sit through the recital while her stomach churned and her palms grew damp with anxiety.

Where had Johnny gone? Would he come back? Why had he taken his gun? What should she do if he returned? If he didn't?

The sound of polite applause startled her from her moody reverie, and she hastily added her approbation as the Whitaker sisters made their curtsies. The judge, resplendent in dark evening dress, paid them pretty compliments and bowed them back to their seats.

"Now, my friends," he said, "there's still a few minutes before the supper's announced. Surely we can prevail on another guest to continue the entertainment? Something light, perhaps? Who do you suggest?"

"Sara Jane sings for us at home nearly every evening," Pandora observed to no one in particular.

"Dorie!" Sara exclaimed, aghast. She enjoyed music and liked to sing, but leading a family chorus of "Yankee Doodle" around the piano was hardly the same as a public performance!

"Mrs. Cary," boomed the judge. "Would you be so kind as to favor us with a tune?"

Sara's color mounted, and she shrank back in her chair.

"Oh, no. No, I couldn't, really. I've nothing prepared—"

"Nonsense, Sara Jane!" Pandora reproved. "That Irish air will suffice. We practiced it just the other night."

"And you'll accompany her, Miss Cary?" the judge asked. His ruddy face glowed. "How fortunate for us. Do come, ladies."

Pandora rose with a gracious nod, and her skirts rustled as she made her way to the piano. The other guests looked at Sara expectantly, some with approval, a few with obvious reservations. She had no choice but to acquiesce with as much good grace as she could muster. She managed a weak smile as she passed Menard, and he beamed encouragingly.

Pandora seated herself and pressed a few soft chords. Sara took her place at Pandora's side and dropped an aggrieved whisper in her ear. "How could you do this to me, Dorie?"

"You hide your light under a bushel, girl," Pandora retorted cheerfully. The rippling introduction flowed from her fingertips, drowning out her low words. "It's time you let it shine again, especially when there are eligible bachelors around."

Sara's cheeks burned, but she had to save her objections for another time or miss her cue. She launched into the melancholy lyrics of "Sweet Thames," and her lilting words filled the room. Hers was not an especially strong voice, but Pandora's tutorship had seen that it was clear and tone-perfect. Despite her discomfort, her rendition held a particular poignancy tonight. The applause was enthusiastic, but as she and Pandora acknowledged it, Sara wondered if people were clapping merely because she and Pandora hadn't been "excruciating."

"Delightful, ladies!" Menard Plunket said. He gallantly offered an arm to each of them. "And on those notes, allow me to escort you to supper."

The dining room was aglow with gas lights, the gas manufactured right on the premises, Menard was eager to explain. Frothy syllabub filled a cut glass punchbowl, and the table held an array of almond cakes, marzipan and tiny mince pies, cold beef and chicken and ham, and bite-sized biscuits melting with rich yellow butter. Menard was the perfect host, pointing out the choicest morsels and seeing to their comfort in every way. He settled them on a low bench with their cups nearby.

"You've certainly done wonders with this house, Judge Plunket," Pandora commented. Her eagle eye noted with approval the elaborately swagged cornices and long brocade drapes puddling elegantly on the polished hardwood floor. From the ornate mahogany sideboard to the gilt-edged china, no expense had been spared.

The decor was almost overwhelming for a locality that had so recently been at war, Sara thought. On the other hand, perhaps it was time for a new prosperity to re-emerge. The old southern plantation life that had been adopted in this part of Missouri was gone forever. The decline of the southern cotton market and the abolition of slavery had led to the demise of the local hemp and tobacco plantations. A way of life was over, but it seemed Judge Plunket had attempted to re-create a gracious and luxurious atmosphere again, at least in his new home.

The Morrison mansion was set in the middle of several acres of landscaped grounds just a mile or so east of Lexington. Like so many others, the Morrisons had chosen to flee at the beginning of the war. The judge had probably acquired the place for little or nothing, but at least it would not be allowed to fall into disrepair.

"I'm glad you like what I've done, Miss Cary," Menard replied. He was flushed with the triumph of the evening, and his dark eyes sparkled. "And what do you think, Sara?" he asked.

"It's lovely," she murmured, ignoring the way Pandora's eyebrows climbed up her forehead at his familiar use of her name. Just then, Mrs. Whitaker approached and bore Pandora off to discuss piano lessons for the unfortunate Regina. Menard took Pandora's place beside Sara on the bench.

"You look beautiful this evening, Sara," he said, his voice low and intimate. "But . . . sad. I wonder why."

She glanced up, startled. Even Will had never called her beautiful. "I'm a bit tired," she said. "A patient of mine, Mrs. Maguire, passed away this morning."

Menard's eyes clouded sympathetically. "I'm sorry."

Her glance fell from the obvious warmth in his, and she gazed at the crowd of about fifty, an intriguing mix of old Lexington society and the new political and commercial elite. "You've made quite a success tonight."

"Yes, it's going well, I think." His tone held an element of smugness, but it disappeared with his easy, engaging grin that showed off brilliant white teeth. "I think it's essential to be accepted in a new locality in order to function effectively, don't you?"

"Yes, I suppose so."

"Coming to office as I have, almost a stranger despite my military tenure here, and from St. Louis, I thought it imperative to create a good impression with my neighbors and constituents."

"Your family's from St. Louis?" she asked curiously. A wealthy, influential background might explain his rapid rise in political circles and his apparent plenitude of funds. "Have they business interests there?"

"Oh, this and that," he said evasively. His expression sobered. "Sara, there is a serious matter I wanted to discuss with you. I hope you won't think I'm being impertinent."

"Of course not. Go on."

He drew a deep breath and smoothed his thick sidewhiskers with his knuckles. "Cash is in short supply right now for a lot of people."

"Yes, it is." She couldn't fathom what he was driving at.

"Cavendish has approached me regarding the damages you promised to pay. I know you own some property hereabouts, and I'd like to offer to buy it from you so that you can—"

"Thank you for offering, Menard, but that won't be necessary," Sara interrupted hastily.

She felt embarrassed at the direction the conversation had taken, but she wanted to reassure the judge, who had tried to be tactful in a delicate situation. She had a little savings, and it had taken only the sale of a small piece of her jewelry to complete the sum for Cavendish. Besides, she wouldn't sell Will's land for any reason. "I'll have the full amount for Mr. Cavendish in a day or two."

Menard cleared his throat. "Well, that's good then."

"I appreciate your concern."

He took her hand and squeezed it gently. "You'll let me know if you change your mind, won't you? I like being concerned about you, Sara. I want to help you in any way I can."

She didn't know what to say. Was Menard declaring his interest in her on a personal level? Sara's experience with men was limited, and the thought made her anxious, flattered in a way but unsure of her response. She smiled uneasily and tugged her fingers free of his grip. "You're very kind," she murmured.

"That fellow Johnny hasn't given you any more trouble, has he?" Menard asked. Sara jumped, and her glance was sharp.

"No," she denied. "Why should he?"

"He seemed rather unstable. I thought perhaps . . ." He shook his head. "Well, never mind. I'm glad to hear all is well. Just don't let him wander off without that loyalty oath in his pocket or he could be picked up by the militia."

"I'll remind him," she said faintly. Another guest called to the judge, and he excused himself, promising to return as soon as he could.

Sara set her untouched plate on a nearby table, suddenly too agitated to eat. Her head ached, and her blood pounded in her veins with new anxiety. Menard's words touched on a subject too close to her heart. She might never see Johnny again, much less pass on the warning. It didn't matter that he'd gone without a word; the habit of worrying about him was too ingrained in her. She couldn't even work up a little righteous anger at his apparent ingratitude. She only wanted him safe.

Helplessness and sorrow twisted her heart, and she knew she couldn't be cordial any longer. Pleading a headache to Pandora wasn't a lie, and soon, to Sara's immense relief, they were on their way back to town.

Pandora didn't notice Sara's unusual silence because she was so full of all the gossip she'd heard and the people she'd met. She kept up an uninterrupted diatribe on the music, the food, the furnishings, and that wonderful young man, Judge Plunket. The house was quiet and dark when they arrived home, and Pandora headed off to bed, well-satisfied with her evening.

Sara said good night, then went into her office for a headache remedy. She didn't light a lamp, but the one Lizzie had left burning on the marble-top credenza in the foyer cast enough light for her to find her way around the again tidy room. She found a paper of headache powder in the cabinet, mixed it with water from a pitcher she kept filled, and gulped down the bitter nostrum.

She was gazing out the window, staring at the silver-edged night, when she saw the flicker of movement around the corner of the carriage house. She was instantly alert. Could it be Johnny? Had he come back?

Sweeping her mantle around her shoulders, she moved through the silent house, letting herself quietly out the back door. Her feet crunched on the gravel as she crossed the drive. The carriage house door stood open a crack, and she craned her neck, peering into the enveloping darkness.

"Johnny?" she called softly. There was no answer, yet she sensed a tangible presence, a warmth, a disturbance in the air. He was here, she was certain of it. Stepping through the door, she called again. "Johnny, is that you?"

A large hand clamped tightly over her mouth. A steel-banded arm grabbed her by the waist and pulled her back, crushing her against a hard male body. Startled, but not really frightened because she'd been expecting Johnny to do something like this, she relaxed against him.

Beside her ear, a deep voice tinged with humor rasped into the darkness. "Hot damn, honey. You been expecting me?"

Sara gasped. It wasn't Johnny!

Chapter 5

"What's the matter, honey?" the voice said with a laugh. "Cat got your tongue?"

Sudden, unreasoning terror choked Sara. She couldn't breathe. His callused hand tasted faintly salty against her lips. She bit it.

"Ow!" He jerked away, cussing a blue streak. She struggled, gasping, but he merely swung her around, pinning her against the rough plank wall with such force that her head and back smacked the boards, bruising her spine and making her ears ring. "Dammit, you bitch!" he growled.

One large hand pressed against her breastbone, holding her against the wall, but she was too winded and shaken to move. She heard the snap of a sulfur match against a tough thumbnail, and a flame fizzed into life, blinding her.

"Let's see what we got here," he muttered, fumbling with one hand to light a lantern hanging from a hook. The wick caught, and a soft glow illuminated the barn. Her hands pushed futilely against the thick column of his arm. Rough fingers lifted her chin, holding her face up toward the feeble light. "Not bad. I thought a female medic would be an old horse-faced battleax, but you're not bad at all."

Sara blinked, forcing her frightened gaze to absorb the face leaning over her. He was surprisingly young, a handsome, red-haired beef of a man with sidewhiskers and a horseshoe mustache, dressed in rough outdoorsman's gear, slouch hat, and a long canvas duster. But it was his pale blue eyes that scared her, eyes that glowed with a vicious enjoyment of her terror.

"Who are you?" she said, gasping. "What do you want?"

"Well, now, honey," he drawled, running his hand insolently down to cup her silk-covered breast, "that all depends."

Sara drew in a breath to scream, but again his salty palm stifled her. "I wouldn't advise it, doctor lady. Just do what I say and I won't hurt you, understand?"

She nodded once, her eyes dilated with fear. Slowly, he removed his hand, but his other retained a painful grip on her shoulder.

"I'm looking for somebody," he said.

"Who?"

"You called him Johnny. Big fellow, yellow hair."

"He—he's not here."

"Where is he?"

She tried to shrug. "I don't know. Gone."

"You're lying."

"No, no!" She gulped, trembling. "He left, I swear. Why do you want him?"

"We got business. Do you know where he was headin'?"

"No. What—what kind of business?" she faltered.

"We're . . . looking for something." He grinned and tugged one of the fat curls falling over her shoulder. "Yeah, that's it. Looking for something."

"Well, he's not here." She fought her fear, staring at him with challenge in her brown eyes. He ran his hand up the slender column of her throat, and she couldn't prevent the convulsive shiver that racked her. He smiled again, leaning over her, crowding her against the wall with his body. His hot breath drifted against her cheek.

"It was a long ride, honey. And just so's it's not a wasted trip . . ."

"Let her go, Cole." Johnny's voice was quiet with menace. Sara went limp with relief. She'd never heard any sound so welcome.

Cole stiffened, and his hands fell away from her. Lifting them slightly from his body to show they were empty, he slowly turned around. "Hello, Tuck."

"Cole." Johnny nodded, his eyes narrowed, his thumbs

hooked lazily over the waistband of his pants. His shirt hung open, unbuttoned halfway down his chest, revealing shadowy whorls of hair. He walked toward Sara, and Cole backed away.

"She your woman?" Cole asked.

Johnny stared down into Sara's pale, frightened face. His eyes glittered. "Yeah," he drawled.

"Sorry," Cole said easily. "You know I don't poach on another man's territory."

Sara gasped, outrage pouring into her numb body. She was no man's woman! How dare they talk about her as if she were a horse or a dog! She opened her mouth to vent her wrath, but suddenly Johnny was there, smothering her protest with his mouth, catching her nape and covering her lips with his. It was a rapacious, devouring kiss, meant to be insulting and cruel, and it branded her. He lifted his mouth slightly, and his fingers squeezed her neck painfully in warning.

"Keep your mouth shut, understand?" he murmured. She was too stunned, too bewildered to even nod, but he seemed to sense her reluctant assent. He turned back to Cole, half-hiding Sara behind him. "How'd you find me?" he asked.

Cole tugged his horseshoe mustache and grinned. "Heard about a big, yellow-haired son of a bitch tearing up a place called the Brass Bull. Figured it had to be you. Still like your fun, eh, Tuck?"

"On occasion."

"All kinds of fun," Cole reiterated, leering in Sara's direction.

Hot waves of humiliated color flooded her face, but the brutality of Johnny's kiss left her swaying and cautious. Why had Johnny led this man to believe they were lovers? And what was this "business" they had together? Tension crackled in the air between them. Was Cole really a friend of Johnny's? Or an old enemy?

"Jesse'll be glad to know you ain't dead," Cole continued. "He thought you'd been kilt."

"The kid's all right?" Johnny asked in surprise. Sara's scattered attention focused on the name: Jesse. Why was it familiar?

"He's kinda poorly. Lung-shot, you know. But doing better, especially after being nursed up at his cousin Zee's place in Kansas City. You're not the only one found himself a little fee-male companionship."

Johnny grunted noncommittally, and Sara nodded to herself. The description of the boy's wound brought it all back. So that youngster she'd questioned about Johnny in the hospital *had* been with him. The old-young face flickered across her memory, and she shuddered. Both faces, Jesse's in her mind and Cole's before her now, contained the same element of cold ruthlessness. What truly frightened her was that she'd seen a flash of it in Johnny's face, too, just as he'd kissed her. There was a rigidity to his features she'd never seen before, a new, frightening facet of a personality she'd never guessed was as hard as diamonds.

Oh, God, she thought, staring at Johnny's back. *Who is he now?*

Johnny crossed his arms over his chest. "So what brings you visiting, Cole?"

"You got that Bible the colonel gave you?"

"What Bible?"

"Ain't done you any good neither, has it?" Cole laughed. "The colonel didn't trust anybody, Tuck. Jesse's got one, too."

Johnny's expression was blank. "So?"

"Neither one's complete. But Jesse thinks maybe together they'll lead us to the Calf."

"Us?"

"We're just about the only ones left. Jesse and Frank. Me and Jim. A couple more."

"What makes you think it's still out there?" he asked.

"Moses told us."

Johnny's eyes narrowed. "You saw Moses?"

"You know he don't work that way."

"So what's he want?"

"For the Calf to go to the right cause."

Johnny laughed in disbelief. "Feelin' a mite generous, ain't you, boys?"

Cole's face tightened. "I ain't forgot what side I was on, if that's what you mean. But there's no rush. When you decide you need what we got, come talk. Up Liberty way. You know where.''

"Sure."

''We'll be seeing you pretty soon, I'll wager.'' Cole half-laughed and turned on his heel to go. He paused and studied Sara, then reached out and chucked her under the chin, laughing again. ''But maybe not as soon as all that.''

Sara knocked his hand away. Her bruised and swollen lips pouted mutinously. ''Don't touch me!'' she exclaimed.

''You're doing good, honey,'' Cole said, his mustache lifting with wry mockery. ''Damn good to hold onto old Tuck here for as long as you have. Usually he don't take a shine to a skirt more than a day or two.''

She glared at him, her anger and confusion compounded with pride. What good would it do to deny anything to this man with his talk of calves and colonels? The villain could believe what he liked, if he would just go.

''Why don't you get the hell out of here, Cole?'' Johnny suggested. His tone was casual, but the coiled tension in his body allowed no dispute. Absently, as though he were accustomed to touching her, he slid his fingertips down the back of Sara's arm to cup her elbow. She shivered at the gooseflesh his action raised, transferring her angry stare to him, but his fingers tightened and she couldn't pull away.

''Sure thing, Tuck,'' Cole replied, smirking. ''Almost like the old days with Colonel Quantrill, ain't it? Killing Yankees in the morning and bedding their women in the evening.''

Sara's head snapped around. Time seemed suspended. Comprehension dripped through her brain like the thickest, blackest sludge. ''Quantrill?'' The name felt like the vilest filth on her tongue. ''You rode with Quantrill?''

''Ain't Tuck never told you?'' Cole asked. ''The damned Yankees finally killed him, but the colonel was the finest soldier that ever lived.''

Sheer horror made the small hairs on the back of her neck quiver. Her voice climbed the scales, seeking a register for a growing hysteria. ''Were you at Lawrence?''

''Yeah.'' Cole's expression blackened. ''We both was.''

"What of it?" Johnny asked roughly.

She lifted eyes gone bleak, their brown hue rusty with despair. Her face worked with the memory of death. She could almost smell the smoke, hear the cries, see the blood. "I was there."

She jerked free of Johnny's touch, and her breath rasped through her lungs as though she'd run a great distance. Her eyes darted between the two men.

"Did you hear me?" she screamed. She struck her chest with her clenched fist. "I was there! You bastards! I was there when you killed my husband!"

Cole shrugged. "That was war."

Something snapped inside Sara. How could he so casually and callously dismiss that atrocity with no apology, no remorse? Animal fury consumed her, and with a cry, she flew at Cole like a wildcat, snarling and spitting, kicking and biting, clawing and scratching, intent on meting out her own brand of justice.

Caught off balance, Cole stumbled backward under her onslaught, his arms raised to fend off her frenzied but puny blows. At the moment he lost his temper and raised his fist to strike her, Johnny caught her from behind, wrestling with her.

"Stop it, Sara!" he cried. Her low shriek of fury was the only answer he got.

"She's a crazy bitch," Cole muttered, touching his cheek where her nails had raked parallel rows. "Damn, if she isn't!"

Johnny had Sara in a bear-hug, easily controlling her wild struggles. Her eyes reflected a crazed light, and she sobbed harshly, dry, racking gasps of rage and hatred.

"Get out of here," Johnny ordered Cole.

"You bet." Cole moved toward the door, his eyes never leaving Sara. He flashed Johnny a sudden grin. "You get tired of trying to tame her, Tuck, give me a holler. I'd like to have a go at it."

"Just get the hell out!"

Cole disappeared back into the night, and Johnny loosened his hold on Sara. He grunted when her elbow punched his ribs, and his wrists stung where her nails tore his skin. "Dammit, Sara! I don't want to hurt you!"

"What do you know about hurt!" she shouted. "Will never hurt a fly, and they killed him. *You* killed him! Oh, God! If I had a gun, I'd shoot you dead this instant!"

He flung her away so hard she staggered on the hay-strewn floor. He pulled his heavy revolver from under his shirt and thrust the cold metal object into her hands. "Do it then," he ground out, his face livid with defiance. "Do us both a favor. What are you waiting for?"

Grasping the heavy gun with both hands, she raised the long barrel until it was on a level with his thick chest. A bullet would pierce the chest wall, then the heart. Muscle and tissue would be destroyed in a blast of steel. Death would be instantaneous. Her finger quivered on the trigger. God, he deserved to die!

His green eyes bore into her, silently willing her to do her worst. Only the flicking muscle on his broad jaw indicated any tension. That unconscious mannerism undid her resolve. This was Johnny, whom she'd doctored, and worried over, and almost loved. Her patient. Her friend. Her husband. The moment's fury faded as the bitter irony of her situation sank in. Married to her husband's killer! Better she turn the pistol on herself!

With a low, keening cry she pointed the gun away from him and squeezed the trigger. The hammer fell on an empty chamber, echoing hollowly, mocking her. Johnny's hands closed around hers, pulling the gun out of her nerveless fingers. She gazed at him in stupefaction.

"No guts, huh?" His grin was wicked, satisfied.

From far away, Sara knew she was falling, but she didn't care. He knew her, what she was capable of and what she was not, and she no longer knew him at all, this stranger with Johnny's face. Her overwrought system could find no relief to insurmountable pain and sought escape in a final, feminine defense. She'd dissected cadavers, set bones, performed surgery, all with no qualms, but now, for the second time, Sara Jane fainted in Johnny's arms, and she welcomed the rushing blackness like a lover.

She climbed from the dark, warm pit with reluctance. It was so hard to open her eyes. She murmured a protest, but consciousness would not be denied. She blinked, curious that she appeared to be lying on something flat and hard, with a sheet pulled over her. She heard the crackle of the fire and saw the flicker and waver of shadows falling on the brick wall. The odor of fried bacon and stewed apples and coffee hung in the air. What was she doing in the kitchen?

Turning her head, she looked up into a face she knew, met eyes the color of a new spring leaf. She smiled and, as if in a dream, lifted a hand to stroke his cheek gently, lovingly, the way she always wanted to. The stubble on his jaw rasped pleasurably against her fingertips. She tried to whisper his name, but he looked at her so strangely, with such intensity, that she stopped before the word left her lips. Her fingers trembled on his face, and he caught her slight wrist, curling his hand around it like a shackle. And it all came back to her.

"Who are you?" she whispered.

"You don't want to know." His voice was harsh.

She had to hear it. "Who *are* you?"

His jaw tightened. "They call me Tuck."

Silver tears pooled suddenly in her eyes, grief wrenched her heart. Johnny—her wonderful, loving, giving Johnny— had been a dream, and that dream was dead. Her voice broke. "I hate you."

He was unmoved. "You're not the first."

"I should have let you die." She felt his fingers tighten on her wrist, then he let her go and looked away.

"It would have saved us both a lot of misery."

She rolled on her side, realizing at last that she lay on top of the kitchen table wrapped in an old tablecloth. Curling into a ball, she let the hot tears fall unchecked. "Oh, God." She sobbed her disillusionment. "Why did you have to come back?"

His face twisted. "If I hadn't, you'd have ended up worse than Lizzie."

She gasped and struggled to sit up, pushing up on her elbow and shoving the enveloping cloth away with an angry motion. "You made me look like your whore. Am I supposed to feel *grateful?*" she cried, her tone scathing.

"Cole won't bother you as long as he thinks you're

mine. Yeah, gratitude might do for a start," he drawled. His eyes roamed over her.

Sara glanced down at herself and gasped in shock at her state of dishabille. Her gown hung open down the back, falling off her shoulders and sagging in front to show the edge of her chemise and the soft rise of her breasts. Her stays were unlaced, and everything hung so loosely she had to make a frantic grab to stay covered at all.

"What have you done?" she demanded, trying to swing her legs off the table. Her hoops and petticoats tangled with her skirts to impede her. She tugged at the neck of her dress and reached for the cloth. The sudden movements made her head spin dizzily and black starbursts spotted her fuzzy vision.

"Be still, Sara, you'll hurt yourself." He grabbed her with angry hands and forced her back down on the table. "You're not going to pass out on me again."

"Swine," she managed faintly, her teeth chattering.

"Why? Because I loosened that damned rig so you could breathe? Lady, that was a favor." His hands pressed her shoulders, and his fingers felt hot against her cool skin. The tension in his hands changed subtly, and his grip became almost a caress. His eyes were hooded, and a slow, knowing grin spread across his mouth. "Besides, we have no secrets between us, do we, Sara? Not any more."

She moaned and shut her eyes, turning her flaming face away. He let her go abruptly. "Lie there until your head clears," he ordered.

He turned his back, squatting in front of the wide arched fireplace and stirring the embers with the iron poker. He kept his face hard and implacable, but his mind careened in all directions.

Dammit! There was nothing like taking a simple objective and really fouling it up. It hadn't taken many rounds of beers to learn the whereabouts of Captain Alex Thompson.

"Sure, you can find him," the old geezer had said with a cackle, "up there in Machpelah Cemetery."

They'd found him in a ravine with his throat slit just after Appomattox. Those last days, even after Lee's surrender, had been rife with violence and uncertainty, with allegiances shifting back and forth so fast a man couldn't be certain who was friend or foe. Perhaps Captain Thompson had been a mite careless.

Careless or expendable? Johnny wondered. Both he and Thompson had been neatly eliminated by someone with something to lose. And that person was almost certainly Moses the Prophet. Moses must have discovered Thompson had a contact within Quantrill's band and feared he was compromised. That would explain why Thompson had been killed at such a crucial moment for Johnny. Instead of receiving safe passage, Johnny had run straight into an ambush arranged by Moses. Moses had sacrificed the Golden Calf to save his skin, but according to Cole, he was after it again. So now Johnny had a double reason to seek his revenge on the Prophet, and the recovery of the Golden Calf was more important than ever.

Johnny stared at the leaping flames and listened to Sara's ragged breathing. He'd intended to pursue the gold quietly from his trusted position within the Cary household. If only Cole hadn't brought Sara into it! And how the hell could he have known her husband died in the Lawrence massacre? Of all the damned bad luck. But what was he supposed to do? Deny he'd been part of it with Cole standing there ready to gun him down at such a confession?

He'd been on the fringes of the group a mere six days when they'd ridden toward Kansas, and he hadn't been privy to the grand plan until it was too late. Still, in the general melee he'd taken a desperate chance, fording his horse across the rain-swollen river to alert the Union troops stationed there, only to find the ferry boats were missing, set loose so that when the troops were finally able to cross they'd found only death and carnage in Lawrence. He'd been able to concoct a plausible tale, made believable by the fact that he'd nearly been captured by a party of Federals before escaping into the brush with a skillet-faced youngster known as Frank James.

Oh, he supposed he could tell Sara the truth now, but what good would it do? She already knew more than was good for her. Besides, he couldn't take the chance that she'd keep such a confidence, even if she believed him. So let her hate him. It was her fault he'd been thrust back into an existence he'd forgotten. He was furious at her for that, and for accepting so easily a history he couldn't and wouldn't explain. And he was mad at her for the way Cole had touched her, too. The woman was nothing but a pack of trouble!

And way down deep, it gave him a sick pleasure to know she believed the worst of him. He deserved it.

He made an angry sound, a low rumble deep in his throat, then set a blue speckleware coffee pot containing the remains of the supper coffee on the glowing coals. He stood up and turned back to Sara, meeting her apprehensive gaze. "You all right now?" he asked abruptly.

"Yes."

She didn't move, and he wondered if she was still afraid of him. He thought so. Good. It would make what he had to do easier. He clenched his jaw and reached for her, easing her into a sitting position. He tried not to notice the way she flinched away from him. Hand on her waist, he turned her slightly.

"What—what are you doing?" Her voice was faint.

"Putting you back together."

"No, stop." She clutched her clothing defensively across her breasts.

He muttered an expletive. "Save your breath, Sara. Unless you intend to go back to the house half-naked." He watched a blush climb from her neck to the crests of her cheekbones.

"I can do it," she protested.

"Shut up, woman! If I were going to take advantage, I'd have had plenty of opportunity before now, and I don't mean just tonight." His tone grew nasty, and he taunted her. "We both know that, don't we, Sara?"

She refused to meet his eyes. "I—I don't know what you mean."

"Sure you don't," he mocked. "But you're just fooling yourself. You were mighty fond of old Johnny, weren't you? Maybe too fond?"

"Stop it."

"Don't worry, Doc. Miss Sara's a bit long in the tooth for Tuck. He likes his meat a bit more tender."

"Damn you!" She buried her face in her hands, her words choked with humiliation. "How I hate you!"

When she said nothing more, he went to work at her back, concentrating on the task and ignoring the way her flesh shuddered at his touch. His hands were brisk, businesslike, tugging the strings of her corset, pulling the gown back into place around her shoulders, fastening the long row of buttons down the back. He worked as quickly and impersonally as possible, trying not to notice the silkiness of her skin or her sweet scent, trying not to recall how frantic his efforts to ease her of these same constrictions had been earlier.

Her swoon had startled him, and when she hadn't revived immediately, he'd picked her up, surprised at how small and fragile she seemed in his arms. Funny, he'd always thought of her as a sturdy female, but her curves were womanly, her weight a mere pittance as he carried her to the warmth of the kitchen. Now, for all his snide assertions to the contrary, his fingers tingled with the desire to explore the gentle curve of her spine, the sweet hollows of her nape. He grimaced and forced the last button home, inwardly cursing his clumsiness.

Oh, God, why couldn't he finish? Sara moaned to herself. She'd never felt so mortified, so humiliated in all her life. Her soul seemed to shrivel up inside. Yes, her secret self could admit, she'd been attracted to Johnny, but she'd never let him know it, never by so much as a look given him any indication, had she? The epitome of propriety, that was Sara Cary. Always a lady. Always seeking to help the unfortunate. But just see where her good intentions had gotten her!

She'd taken him into her home and affections, like an asp to her bosom, and her faith in her own judgment was badly shaken. She couldn't stand it. Married to this man—this Tuck, a vicious killer, one of Will's murderers! Thank God she'd never been tempted to confess their union, even if it was in name only! She had to undo that legal tangle immediately. She might not be able to change what he was or what she'd unknowingly done for him, but she didn't have to stand for it any longer!

He finished and moved away. She dropped her hands

into her lap and gathered her composure. Then she slid from the table. She had to grab the edge to keep her balance, and was surprised at her own weakness.

"Here," he said, thrusting a mug of black coffee into her numb hands. "Drink that. It'll make you feel better."

Her weakness disappeared in a white-hot flash of rage. With a furious cry, she threw the cup at him. It missed, crashing into the brick hearth behind him and shattering, splashing hot coffee across his boots and the plank floor.

"God damn it!" he roared. He slammed his own cup down on the table and grabbed her shoulders. "What the hell's wrong with you, woman?"

Sara's hands were clenched into tight fists, and she glared at him with hate burning in her eyes. *"You're* what's wrong with me! And nothing's going to make me feel better until you're gone—out of my sight, out of my house, out of my life!"

He took a step back, watching her carefully. "That would make you happy, huh?"

"Immensely!"

He paused, as if considering, and reached for his abandoned cup. He took a swallow, then smiled at her. "No."

She was dumbfounded. "No? What do you mean? I want you to leave. Now!"

"And how do you propose to make me? Appeal to my better nature?" He was laughing openly at her now.

Sara saw red. He barely had a chance to set his cup down before she flew at him, beating on his massive chest with her fists, screaming her rage and impotency. He controlled her easily, shaking her hard. Her head snapped back, and he held her wrists still in one large hand, the other holding her nape. His words were a snarl, his teeth drawn back over his lips as he spoke.

"Listen to me! I'm not going anywhere until I'm damn good and ready, do you hear?" He smiled again, a taunting, evil grin that chilled her to the core. "I like it here," he said softly.

"God, no! You can't!" she cried, frantic. She was so close to him she felt suffocated. "You can't stay here!"

"What about your promise? Remember you said you'd never send me away," he goaded.

Her eyes widened with disbelief. "But that was before. You can't mean to hold me to that. Don't you understand I don't want you here anymore?"

"It doesn't matter to me what you want. I've got business to see to before I leave, so get used to the idea."

"Business," she spat. "Oh, yes, you and that ruffian friend of yours. I can imagine what kind of business engages a brigand like that. Luckily, you managed to recover your memory just in time for his visit—or was that all a pretense?" she demanded.

He slid one hand to the small of her back, but he didn't release her hands. He shook his head, and a flicker of pain etched his expression. "No, that was real enough."

"But now you remember."

"Everything." His face was hard, his eyes like green marble.

"Then there's no reason for you to stay. Go back to wherever you came from. Go home or go to hell, but just leave us in peace."

"When I'm ready."

His complacency infuriated her. "I—I'll go to the sheriff, the judge. *They'll* make you get out."

"What do you think they'll say when they discover you've been harboring Quantrill's right-hand man all this time? Your whole family will be held 'disloyal.' Do you know what that means?"

Sara blanched and tried to pull away, but he held her fast. "No. I don't—"

"They'll confiscate everything. You'll have nothing. You might even go to jail. They probably wouldn't send Pandora, but Yves, Ambrose . . ." He shrugged.

"You ingrate! You despicable bastard! You'd do that to people who took you in, befriended you, and saved your rotten hide!"

"Whatever it takes, Sara."

She stared at him, her expression stony. She knew he meant what he said. He was that kind of man. How could she risk the safety of her family by defying him? How could she stand to have him here any longer? She licked her lips, and her voice was cautious. "What do you want?"

He smiled and let got of her wrists. "Now you're beginning to see reason."

"Don't bandy words with me."

His expression stiffened. "No, by all means, let's get it straight. I intend to stay right here for a while. When I finish my business, I'll leave, but not before. Is that clear?"

"How long?"

"Not long. A month, maybe two. In the meantime, no one but you and I need to know that I'm not still good old simple-minded Johnny."

"And if I try to turn you in to the Federals, you'll swear we've been involved all along."

"You got it." He chuckled at her thwarted expression and reached out to touch her hair. She jerked away, and his mouth hardened. "You behave and you'll have no trouble out of me. In a few short weeks, I'll be gone for good. What do you say?"

"I say I'd rather make a pact with the devil himself than deal with the likes of you."

"But . . . ?"

She glared at him, and a single tear dripped down her cheek. She brushed it away angrily. "I don't have much choice."

"No, Sara." His voice was soft. "You don't have any choice at all."

Chapter 6

Five-year-old Willis Stokes had a bad case of tonsillitis and not the "diphthee"—the diphtheria his nearly hysterical parents had feared. It was satisfying to Sara to reassure them that Willis would recover in due course, provided he was plied with doses of hot lemonade and Sara's fever-reducing palliatives. They were disconcerted by her adamant refusal to purge and bleed the child, and her explanations of her eclectic medical training had taken time and tact, but at least she'd been able to put her intolerable predicament out of her mind for a moment.

Now, sitting beside Ambrose as he drove her back into town, all of the previous night's trauma swirled through her brain with the force of a hurricane. The cold crept into her bones despite her bulky winter petticoats and enveloping cloak, and the gathering dusk shrouded her thoughts with despair. How could she have agreed to accept Johnny's ultimatum? Her conscience screamed in protest. How could she pretend nothing had changed, that Johnny was still the fond friend of months past? Will's memory reproached her, begging her to deny the truth, condemning her for harboring a man who had her husband's blood on his hands.

But what else could she do? For the sake of the people who depended on her, she must endure the situation, no matter what it cost her. This thought did nothing to comfort her as Ambrose pulled Nubbin to a halt in the drive, especially when she caught a glimpse of Johnny disappearing around the rear of the kitchen after Lizzie. Something about the furtiveness of his movements alarmed her.

Sudden fear tightened her throat, and all her protective instincts shrieked a warning. Lizzie was a pretty young woman. And Johnny was a virile man whose sensual needs had been neglected. Would he . . . ? The thought curdled half-formed in her brain.

She scrambled from the buggy before Ambrose pulled it completely to a halt. The cold wind held a promise of snow, and her dark cloak billowed around her. "Leave the horse and come with me," she ordered and hurried after the retreating figures, her heart pounding in her chest.

The old shed was a private place. She knew to her shame how easily a woman could lose herself in the sensual onslaught of Johnny's embrace. Rosy color suffused her cheeks and then receded, leaving her face stark. Would Johnny take advantage of a mute girl? She couldn't even cry out for help! Sara rounded the corner of the rear shed at almost a dead run, afraid of what she might find, and came up short.

Two blond heads lifted in surprise, one angel-fair, the other tawny gold. They held a bundle of dried and withered evergreens between them, the browning mistletoe and red-berried holly and crisp, once-fragrant cedar branches that had adorned the parlor over Christmas and New Year's. That happy time seemed like another life to Sara now.

"You need something, Miss Sara?" Johnny asked.

She drew in a deep, shuddering breath. "I—what are you doing?"

Johnny frowned. "Miss Pandora wants all these old decorations gathered up for her bonfire this week. Something about Candlemas Day." Lizzie nodded, gracing them with one of her beautiful smiles, and tugged her knitted shawl closer about her shoulders. Ambrose appeared behind Sara.

Candlemas Day! Sara thought. She'd nearly forgotten. Pandora celebrated the old holiday on which all the church candles for the coming year were blessed with a ritual bonfire, her festivities nearly as gay as Christmas itself. All the withered greenery was burned with high ceremony, for every leaf left over meant a trouble in the house. Pandora insisted on it with a child's superstitious fervor, and now, looking at Lizzie's and Johnny's inquiring faces, Sara felt a shivering chill of premonition. There was something more sinister than mere trouble within her house. She might have felt foolish about her suspicions if she hadn't been so frightened. Instead, she counted herself lucky that this was an apparently innocent meeting and Johnny had done no harm to Lizzie—this time.

"Let Ambrose do that," Sara said abruptly to Johnny. "You come unhitch Nubbin."

"Can do it myself," Ambrose muttered, his hackles rising. "Ain't no cause to—"

Sara's tenuous control snapped. "Just do what I say," she shouted. "All of you!" She stomped off, leaving three bewildered people behind. Lizzie touched Ambrose's arm for reassurance, and he cleared his throat uneasily. Johnny shrugged.

"Guess we'd better do what she says," he remarked, and sauntered after her.

Sara grasped Nubbin's harness with trembling fingers. She was urging the horse forward into the carriage house when Johnny joined her. Brushing off her near-ineffectual efforts, he led the animal into the opening of the barn and began to unhitch the buggy with quick, efficient movements. He slung the harness onto its hook and turned Nubbin into his stall. Sara watched him narrowly, her heart thumping. Johnny shot her a curious, mocking glance.

"What's stuck in your craw?" he asked. "Something rile you in particular or is it that time of the month?"

Sara sucked in an outraged breath. It seemed Tuck had none of Johnny's gentler qualities.

"Never mind me," she said. "From now on, you stay away from Lizzie."

"Lizzie? What about her?" Johnny's brow puckered, and his face grew dark. He stepped closer and his voice was a low snarl. "Just what the hell were you thinking out there?"

Challenge and contempt radiated from Sara's uptilted face. She would not be cowed, not in this! "Just stay away from her."

Naked fury twisted his mouth and made his eyes burn like flames in the dimness. His fists clenched, and for a moment she thought he was going to strike her. His throat worked, and the words rumbled from him. "You think I could do that . . . to Lizzie?"

"I don't know *what* you're capable of," she snapped. "But then, you've given me a fair idea, haven't you?"

"She's a child." His tone was disgusted. "I've lived in the same house with her for nearly a year and never laid so much as a finger on her. You think things like that change overnight? Lady, you're unbelievable!"

"I'm not taking any chances. She's suffered enough. I won't let her end up like Louisa!" To Sara's utter horror, her voice broke. Pressing a white-knuckled fist to her mouth, she spun around, but Johnny caught her arm, preventing her retreat.

"Who's Louisa?"

She averted her face and refused to look at him, blinking rapidly against tears. She'd never intended to reveal so much. The pressure of his hand made her flesh shudder. "Let go."

"Tell me, Sara." His words were a surprisingly gentle coercion, but they held a hint of steel.

"My sister." She lifted her chin, glaring at him with hate and defiance. "They used her like a whore. She's dead. Will tried to save her, but it was too late."

Johnny swallowed. Understanding quelled his indignation. No wonder she'd leapt to Lizzie's defense like a tigress protecting her cub. "I'm sorry."

She laughed, a painful sound. "Of course. You didn't know, did you, that Louisa and I were raised like that? Like wild animals, really, scratching for survival. She was all I had, and she stood between me and those rutting monsters who called themselves our cousins, and Uncle Quentin, too . . ." Her torrent of tortured words trailed off, her expression unfocused as she gazed on an old horror trapped within her memory. She blinked, staring up at him again, and her mouth hardened. "They were men like *you.*"

He didn't wince, didn't even attempt to deny her judgment, though his eyes darkened. Her words were forthright and honest, and her vulnerability shamed him. "You have no cause to fear for Lizzie because of me. I swear it."

She searched his expression for something of the old Johnny, something she could believe in. "How can I trust you? You're Tuck now." The name slipped from her lips with an effort. "And I must protect my own."

She looked pointedly at his hand on her arm, and he released her slowly, reluctantly, torn by a response he scarcely recognized.

But regret was useless to him. He knew himself for what he was—ruthless, driven by revenge. It did no good to remember the sweet pliancy of her mouth under his, given freely. She'd never repeat a mistake like that again, and neither could he. He'd frightened her badly the night before, but, scrappy bit that she was, she still had the courage to come after him when she thought one of her charges was threatened. That kind of bravery deserved respect. His voice was gruff.

"As long as you keep your end of our bargain, no harm will come to you, or any of your people. Just forget everything that's happened and go on as before."

"I can't," she whispered miserably. "You can't ask it of me."

"You can and you will. Nothing's really changed."

Sara's eyes were bleak as she turned away. "You're wrong. *Everything's* changed."

It was a brittle peace.

But then, a bargain based on deceit could be little else. In the following days, Sara wished a thousand times she'd had the courage to defy Johnny, for she was hard pressed to play the part he demanded of her. The frigid weather was no colder than the icy hand that held Sara in thrall. She knew she waited in the eye of the storm, in an uncertain limbo of emotional paralysis.

Johnny's behavior was unobtrusive, circumspect, and innocent as he went about his duties. But Sara knew the difference, and the waiting nearly killed her. She counted the minutes, jumping at shadows, her nerves stretched taut, trying to work at the mission and her clinic as usual, and waiting for Johnny to complete his sinister and mysterious business. She prayed for the day of her deliverance,

knowing that if it did not come soon her fragile control
would surely shatter.

"He's not sick, Mrs. Wiley. Not yet," Sara said to the
young Negress dressed in shabby cottons and a faded head
kerchief. The main office of the two-story brick mission
was chilly despite the small coal fire that burned in the
black iron stove. The only furnishings were a table, a few
chairs, and the tall beaded plank counter over which Will's
father had once conducted his business. Sara quickly
folded the frayed blanket around the squalling, naked in-
fant lying on her lap, softly crooning a wordless lullaby.
She gently handed him back to his mother. "He's just
hungry."

"Yes'm. My milk is poor . . ." Daisy Wiley's lower lip
trembled, and she clutched her child closer. His shrieks
diminished to muffled whimpers. Her dark eyes were anguished in her thin, dusky face. "My man cain't find no
work. We got no place to go."

Sara touched her shoulder kindly. "Little Benjamin isn't
the only one who's been going hungry, I know. But we're
going to change that. There's a place for your family here.
You'll have coal and food, and we'll try to find your husband a job, too."

Some of the desperation in Daisy's expression abated,
and her eyes lit up. "Oh, Dr. Cary, ma'am. I'm beholden
to you! I'll clean and I can cook some. Whatever you
want . . ."

"There's always plenty to do." Sara smiled, wishing all
life's problems were as easily solved.

The front door rattled, then swung inward on a burst of
cold air. Sara rose in time to see Clem, bundled to the
earlobes in an oversized coat and knitted scarf topple forward into the room, a strong gust of wind fairly flinging
him inside. He caught himself on the doorknob and
grinned at Sara.

"Clem!" Sara scolded. "Don't you know it's too cold
out for you?"

Clem's brow puckered anxiously. "Miss Dorie said there
was a new family come and I thought . . . I thought . . ."

Sara's heart gave a peculiar lurch. Clem had played this
scene many times before, searching for his parents. He

had become separated from them in the confusion of invading armies, and he'd never given up hope that one day they'd come for him. She hated to dash those hopes yet again.

"This is Mrs. Wiley, Clem," Sara said as gently as possible. Daisy gave Clem a tentative smile, but the boy's face registered his disappointment. "Close the door, dear," Sara urged softly. She swallowed on the wave of emotion that seemed all too near the surface. What would become of Clem should Johnny's threats become reality? She had to hold on, no matter what.

'Yes, ma'am." Shoulders slumped in dejection, Clem began to close the door, then held it back deferentially as a second visitor materialized in the opening.

Menard Plunket cast his dark gaze over the sparsely furnished room. His face was ruddy with cold, and his stiff white shirt collar looked even whiter against his swarthy neck and bushy, coal-black sidewhiskers. He wore a tall beaver hat and a richly tailored navy wool topcoat. His smile was wide when it lit on Sara, and his voice was so hearty it warmed her immediately. "Mrs. Cary, I was hoping I'd find you here."

"Judge Plunket." Sara suppressed her surprise and went to meet him, offering her hand while Clem closed the door. "We're honored."

"I hope you'll pardon my intrusion. I could not contain my curiosity any longer about your excellent enterprise," he said, bowing over her hand. "I wondered if I might be allowed a look around?"

"Of course. Your generous donation alone gives you that privilege," she replied. Self-consciously she smoothed her hair and settled the folds of her plaid wool skirt. "We'll be able to accommodate many more needy due to your generosity. We can't express our gratitude sufficiently."

"Nonsense. It was the least I could do."

Sara gestured to Clem. "Will you show Mrs. Wiley to her room, Clem? Top of the stairs on the left."

"Yes ma'am, Miss Sara." Clem hobbled forward.

"Admirable help you have there," Menard observed. He dug in his pocket. "Here's a shinplaster for your trouble, boy. Buy yourself a licorice whip."

Startled, Clem shot a questioning glance at Sara. She nodded, and he accepted the piece of paper money. "Postage currency" was still widely used due to the shortage of coins. The thin piece of colored paper, issued by a bank, was only worth a few cents, but to Clem it was a fortune.

"Thank you, sir." He gulped.

Menard waved aside his thanks and turned back to Sara. Clem scampered toward the rear door, and Daisy Wiley followed, her mouth open in wonder. Sara heard their feet on the wooden staircase and Clem's voice, high and excited. This was a day he wasn't likely to forget soon. She allowed herself a small smile.

"You've made him think you're Father Christmas, Menard."

His laugh boomed through the tiny office. "A holdover from the holiday season, I suppose."

"Pandora and I want to thank you again for your hospitality. Your musicale was most enjoyable."

"The pleasure of your charming company was the height of the festivities, my dear, and I hope we can see each other often. In fact, I'd like to invite you to join me for a drive this evening. If it snows, we'll inaugurate my new sleigh which just arrived from Chicago. I've been longing to try it with a suitable companion."

"That sounds adventurous." Sara laughed, flushed at the invitation. "But Pandora has plans for her annual Candlemas bonfire, and I couldn't disappoint her."

"Another time, then."

Sara smiled and became businesslike. "Would you care to see how your money is being spent?"

"With pleasure, ma'am."

Sara led Menard on a brief tour of the converted warehouse at the rear of the office, showing him the men's dormitory, the women's and children's quarters, the partitioned rooms for families, the makeshift kitchen. Black and white alike were welcome at the mission. Some stayed a few days before continuing on their way, but others with no place to go looked on the mission as a semi-permanent home. They paused in the common room, where Father

Yves was reading from the Bible to women sewing around the fire.

"Very impressive," Menard said. "I can see your able hand here, Sara."

"There is much to be done," she replied. "We lack bedding, for example. Some have only straw to sleep on. But the most pressing need is work for those willing and able to accept it."

"Hmm. Then perhaps we can do each other a further service. I confess a need for strong laborers to work the land I've acquired in the area. May I send my overseer to hire on workers? Housing and credit for supplies against next year's crop are included, of course."

"Oh, Menard, that would be an answer to my prayers!" She beamed.

Menard launched into a discussion of details. Sara listened eagerly while in the background Yves read melodically from Proverbs. A sudden movement over Menard's shoulder caught her eye, and the smile froze on her lips.

Sara shivered at the cold warning in Johnny's implacable expression. He stood in the doorway of the common room, a loaded coal bucket in each hand. It was as though no one else was in the room, and his message was unmistakable: Be careful what you say or else . . .

Sara blanched and tore her eyes away, sudden panic churning her stomach. What was he thinking? Did he believe she'd gone to Judge Plunket? Had she jeopardized them all with her courtesy to an unexpected and—she realized now—potentially dangerous visitor? The angry rattle of coal being dumped into a scuttle jarred her scrambling thoughts.

"That's fine, Menard," she interrupted hastily. She took his arm, guiding him swiftly out of the room in that feminine way known to all charming women. She hardly registered the surprised and pleased look he gave her, or how his thick hand carefully folded over hers. "I'm sure everything will be perfectly acceptable," she told him, rather desperately.

"I'm glad we're in such complete accord, Sara." They paused in the chilly front office, and Menard regarded her closely. "Do you feel well, my dear?"

Sara forced a bright smile and sought to still her trembling fingers by burying her hands in the folds of her skirt. "I'm just excited over the prospects of your idea. I can hardly wait until I tell the others."

Menard settled his hat back on his dark head and smiled. "I'm certain it will be profitable for all concerned. Good day, Sara. I'll call again soon."

"Good day," she echoed, closing the door after him. Her relief fled before the realization that she'd have to explain everything to Johnny—to Tuck . . . Oh, she didn't even know what to call him anymore!

She wrung her hands, resentment warring with a sense of grinding loss. She missed Johnny—the old Johnny— badly. She had no one to confide in now, only this stranger, this Tuck, to torment her. Simmering animosity began to boil. It was high time she stopped acting like a coward! Why did she owe him any explanations? She was tired to death of treading on eggshells. Her brain whirled with possibilities—all bad. Who could predict the actions of a man who had absolutely no moral scruples? With a groan, she leaned her elbows against the tall countertop and buried her face in her hands.

"What the hell did he want?"

The rough demand made her jump and swing around, her face chalky. Johnny made an irritated sound. "For God's sake, will you quit that!"

"What?"

He crossed the room in long strides, a big blond bear of a man in a bulky shearling jacket, and threw the contents of the coal bucket into the stove with an attitude of leashed violence. His temper was foul, but he didn't care. He knew he was spoiling for a fight, and who better to fight with than the only person who really knew him?

He'd carefully questioned every no-account and ex-soldier in this God-forsaken town and fruitlessly studied that damned Bible until he thought he'd go blind, with absolutely no success. The Golden Calf might as well have been on the moon for all the good it did him. Frustration made him edgy and explosive. And now Sara had that patronizing dandy of a judge panting after her. It was just too damn cozy for comfort.

He ground his teeth. Dammit, she brought his wrath down on herself, the little fool! Standing there, her high breasts and lithe form snugly outlined by that demure schoolmarm dress, looking defenseless and alone. Every time she flinched it made him madder than hell, especially since he had no one to blame but himself. He knew he deserved her hostility, but he found himself missing their previous open and easy friendship. But he couldn't let her undermine his purpose with that kicked-kitten look of hers. He shoved the stove's small square door shut with the tip of his boot and glared at her.

"You jump like a scalded cat every time I come around."

She lifted her chin belligerently. "What else do you expect?"

"I expect you to act normally. That's the whole idea, remember?" His tone was silky. "We wouldn't want anyone to start getting awkward ideas, now would we, Sara?"

Her gaze dropped away. "I'm trying."

"Well, try harder. The last thing I need is your acting so tight-assed around me that everyone thinks I'm bedding you every night and twice on Sunday."

She gasped sharply, and twin flags of color blazed in her cheeks. "You're insufferable!"

His laugh was a taunt. He bent over her rigid figure and ran a knuckle along the delicate line of her jaw. "Not that the idea hasn't crossed my mind," he said softly. His gaze caressed the outline of her lips. "I haven't forgotten how sweet your mouth is. Like candy."

She knocked his hand away, but he caught her wrist and held it, his lips twisted into a devilish, mocking grin.

"Stop it! How can you treat me this way?" she cried. "I've done everything you wanted. How much longer do I have to endure your detestable presence?"

"Until I've found what I'm after. And don't think that ass Plunket is the answer to your prayers, either. What did he want?"

Her lips thinned mutinously, and she tugged at her captured wrist. "Nothing," she said sullenly.

"Sara . . ." He jerked her arm, pulling her closer. Her shackled hand lay against his chest like a snared dove, and her skirts brushed his boot tops. She shivered at the familiar male scent that filled her nostrils, a mixture of wind and shaving soap and warm skin. She told herself it was revulsion, not excitement evoked by his provocative words that trilled along her nerve endings. Forcing her chin up at an angle, she met the glitter in his eyes with a haughty stare.

"It was just mission business. Menard gave me a donation, and he wanted to see about hiring some men."

"So it's Menard now, is it?" Anger and a surge of unreasonable male possessiveness hooded his gaze. He wasn't jealous, he told himself, he had no right to be, but he had to protect his back from a scheming woman. They were all alike. "I want you to stay away from Plunket, do you hear?"

"He came to me," she protested.

"Sure, and you were making sweet eyes at him for the good of the mission, right? I can't take any chances. If he comes sniffing around again, you get rid of him, understand? Tell him he's not welcome or something. Turn on that icy bitch routine of yours. It doesn't work on me, but it might on him."

"I can't afford to alienate Judge Plunket," Sara said angrily. "His support is important to the mission, and I'll need it long after you're gone."

"No, you can't sacrifice your charity cases, can you? You enjoy being Saint Sara too much."

"You dare to talk. Every mouthful you eat and every rag you wear, I provide. And this is the thanks I get, you loathsome, ungrateful pig!" She was incensed, her face flushed with lovely color and her sweet breath wafting across his face in angry puffs.

Her accusation ate at his pride, and his jaw tightened. Even the heavy jacket he wore against the bitter cold was her doing. He'd found it on his bed, left without a word, her kindness to him undiminished even by the ruthless bargain he'd forced her to accept. He wondered how long she'd deliberated before leaving it. It must have gone against the grain, but she was too soft-hearted to leave even a dog suffering in the cold. A gnawing feeling of guilt made him even angrier.

"So that's what you want?" he said. "Gratitude? Is that what Plunket gives you?"

"No, he treats me with respect like the gentleman he is. And I find his courteous attentions flattering. He invited me to go for a drive, and if I choose to, I will, no matter what *you* say."

"First your charity, now you." Johnny's lips stretched in a sneer. "Better watch out, Miss Sara, that kind of bastard is always after something." He gave her a look that stripped her naked and laughed in derision at the hot confusion that rouged her cheeks. "Maybe it's not your virtue he's after. But what else have you got? Land? Family jewels? A trunk full of Confederate bank notes?"

"Ohh!" She struggled to free her hand, but he held her easily. "You're despicable! He likes me. Why is that so hard to believe?"

"Not unbelievable. Just—unlikely."

"You . . . you . . ." She spluttered and her eyes flashed. The tendrils of hair that softened her temples quivered in her feminine outrage. "Why shouldn't a respectable man court me? I've got a good head on my shoulders, and my face won't crack a mirror. Why shouldn't a man find me attractive, even desirable?"

He swept his other arm around her, crushing her against his rock-hard length so fast she gasped. "Find you desirable?" he said. "Like Cole did? Like Plunket does? Like I do?"

He pulled her imprisoned hand down between their bodies and ground it against his groin, letting her feel the turgid hardness of his sex bulging against the rough denim of his trousers. Sara gasped, shocked to her core, her palm burning with the rigid evidence of male arousal. Sensations like lightning zig-zagged from every extremity to lodge full and heavy and aching deep in her belly. Johnny rubbed himself against her, the movement of his broad chest startling her breasts into throbbing, puckered arousal. He thrust his hips against their joined hands in an erotic mimicry of lovemaking. Sara's knees went weak, and her protest sounded faint to her own ears.

"Don't . . . Johnny . . ."

"Hell, woman," he said huskily in her ear. "It'll grab

you and turn you inside-out, but it doesn't mean a thing. It never does." He released her abruptly, and she staggered back, reaching for the counter for support. Confusion, humiliation, and the distant shadows of passion lingered in the brandy-dark depths of her eyes. They were both breathing heavily. "You understand me yet?" he taunted.

She shook her head in denial of his words, of *him*. "No, and I don't *want* to."

His laugh was harsh. "That's right, hang onto your delusions. You might see something no *lady* wants to see. You might even learn that appearances can be deceiving, and truth is a matter of perspective. Take that as a warning from me."

She went livid. "I don't want anything from you. I know exactly what you are—a murdering outlaw, the lowest scum that ever crawled on the earth. You're wonderfully brave against a lone woman, aren't you?" Johnny took a threatening step toward her. She kept right on, her voice rising. "I've had all I can stand. Go on, get out! Tell your lies. I don't care what happens any more."

Her eyes held a wild, frantic light, and he knew suddenly that she was near the breaking point. He'd pushed her too far with his damned nasty temper. She was the only thing standing between him and discovery, and he wasn't ready for revelations of any kind. Not yet. Two steps and he had her by the shoulders, forcing her to focus on him. He felt her shiver and automatically ran his hands up and down her arms to warm her.

"Stop it, Sara." His voice was low and firm. "You know that would mean disaster. And you don't want that, do you?"

She closed her eyes and took a deep, shuddering breath. "No."

"That's more like it. You're the only thing I can count on in this whole damn mess, honey." He released her, picked up the coal bucket, and strode toward the door. He gave her a brief smile that showed white teeth, but no humor. "You *do* care, Sara, too much for your own good. So stay away from Plunket."

Sara shivered in the empty room. She was appalled at

what had passed between them and angry, too. Angry at Johnny, but mostly furious at herself for her weakness, both physical and moral. She couldn't endure this situation another moment. There had to be something she could do. Sitting meekly by and letting things continue indefinitely according to Johnny's pleasure was an intolerable situation.

So he thought he knew her, did he? So he believed her completely cowed by his threats? More the fool he! There had to be a way to reduce his threats to mere emptiness, and she *would* find it, she vowed. Her chin firmed with determination and resolve.

The undemanding companionship of a dumb animal was comforting when a man needed to think. Johnny rubbed the curry brush over Nubbin's flank, letting the warmth of the horse's velvet hide seep into his fingertips. The barn was warm against the gray February chill, and the air smelled pleasantly musty with hay and feed. The snow had stopped an hour earlier, and he could hear Clem's occasional shriek of childish delight as he played behind the kitchen. The work was soothing. Or it should have been.

The near hysteria Johnny had seen in Sara's eyes earlier preyed on him. He knew instinctively that she'd reached the end of her rope, and his cozy refuge was about to go up in smoke. It was time to get the hell out, before she decided to do something rash that might land him in a whole pile of trouble.

He was going to have to admit it, it looked as though Cole was right. He couldn't find the Golden Calf by himself. And he'd thoroughly worn out his welcome with Sara.

Ambrose appeared bearing a bucket of mash for Nubbin. He poured it into the trough, then settled in companionable silence on the woodpile beside the stall. He fumbled in his shirt pocket for a small drawstring sack of tobacco and proceeded to deftly roll a limp cigarette, using his mouth and one good hand.

Johnny tossed the brush aside. "Give me one of those, will you?"

Ambrose looked at him, his stubbled face dubious. "Miss Sara won't like it."

Johnny's expression soured. "I'm not a kid."

"Nope." Ambrose passed Johnny the cigarette and a match, and began to roll another. "Guess you ain't, at that."

Johnny lit the cigarette and puffed, coughing slightly, the flavor harsh and familiar against his tongue. The smoke warmed his throat.

"What you doin' hiding out here? Miss Sara lay into you about somethin'?" Ambrose asked. Smoke drifted about their heads.

"None of your damn business." Johnny half-smiled to take the edge off his reply.

"Yeah. She did." Ambrose nodded agreeably, his hazel eyes crinkling at the corners. "Woman's tongue can flay a man alive. Lizzie's the only one I can stand to be around for long."

"Did you know Will Cary?" Johnny asked abruptly.

"Some."

Johnny spit a flake of tobacco off his tongue and ground his teeth. Ambrose's laconic replies were beginning to annoy him. "What was he like?"

"A good man. Good doctor. Couldn't ever figure how he come to hitch up with Miss Sara, though. But they were what you call dee-voted, even with him being old enough to be her Paw."

"That a fact?" Johnny frowned thoughtfully and ground out the butt of the cigarette beneath his heel.

"Yep. Reckon she ain't never gotten over his death, seeing how it was her idea to move to Lawrence and all. Wrong place and time when Quantrill came—for a lot of folks."

"Yeah."

Ambrose stood up, the cigarette dangling from his lower lip, grumbling. "Miss Pandora's about ready to light the bonfire. You coming?"

"In a minute," Johnny mumbled, his mind churning. An attack of conscience was hardly what he needed now, but even a man whose soul was little more than rubble couldn't help but feel a twinge of guilt now and then. It had seemed so clear cut when he'd made his bargain with Sara. He'd thought himself beyond guilt and remorse. For him, softness like that could be dangerous, even fatal.

Unbidden, the memory of her mouth came to him, soft and quivering with a vulnerability that belied the resolute tilt of her chin. And the feel of her sweet woman's frame pressed against him, her hand cupping him intimately. He cursed under his breath. God, he was so damned horny he was about to explode! That was it. He needed a woman, any woman, and prissy Miss Sara was the nearest target. Damn, it was past time to leave when he started having fantasies about a self-righteous do-gooder like her!

Hell, he wasn't getting anywhere around here anyway! He was faced with two choices: either forget the idea of locating the Golden Calf or join Jesse and Cole in the search. Both were equally distasteful, but stubbornness and an ingrained loyalty to duty wouldn't let him give up. And an arrogant assurance in his own shrewd abilities made him confident he could handle those vicious boys.

Hell, yes! He'd get on with it. Things had been at a standstill long enough. Cole had said Jesse was with his pretty cousin, Zerelda Mimms, in Kansas City. It was time to go see his old compatriots. Lexington's docks were always busy. It would be no trouble to hop a riverboat headed west tonight.

The decision pleased him. He was itching for action. Sara would be glad to see the back of him, and he'd be free of her sanctimonious condemnation and tantalizing mouth once and for all. She'd have her charity cases, Yves and Clem and the rest, and maybe even that jackass Plunket coming 'round, and he'd go on alone, as always—and that's the way he wanted it, he told himself.

He stepped out of the carriage house, right into the path of a skillfully thrown snowball. Clem's high laughter made him grin, and he scooped up a handful of the powdery substance and fired his own missile. The boy dodged, pitched another one at Johnny, then disappeared around the back of the building. Johnny dusted the snow from his jacket, laughing softly to himself. Yeah, he'd miss Clem.

The orange and gold flicker of Pandora's bonfire caught his attention. He could see the outlines of bundled figures circling the blazing pile of stripped limbs and tattered wreaths as it crackled and burned merrily in the front yard. They were all there—Miss Pandora, Lizzie, Father Yves, Ambrose, and Sara, wrapped in her voluminous blue cloak. Their faces were illuminated by fitful bursts of yellow light, and sparks shot up over their heads, drifting on waves of heat toward the overcast heavens. Johnny smiled wryly. He could even afford to be a little nostalgic, now that he was leaving them all behind.

There was a sudden cheerful jingling of bells and thud of hooves, and an elegant white sleigh hove to a stop at the edge of the street. Johnny stiffened, recognizing the driver. Plunket!

Johnny's eyes snapped back to Sara. A cherry-red muffler covered her dark hair, and her face was a pale oval highlighted with gilt by the bonfire. Her expression was all too easy to read. She cast a furtive look toward the group, and he could see the momentary hesitation, then the instant of decision. He could almost feel her set her shoulders, then she walked swiftly, with purpose and determination, toward the waiting sleigh.

Johnny cursed, knowing as sure as the devil what she meant to do. She was going to tell Plunket everything!

Chapter 7

I'm going to tell him everything, Sara thought. Her feet crunched over the crisp crust of snow toward the edge of the street where Menard Plunket's sleigh waited. It was the only thing she could do. Surely if she told Menard the truth of her situation, he'd believe her over some cock-and-bull story from Johnny. Then, with the teeth taken out of his threats, Johnny—or Tuck—would be forced to leave her in peace.

"Good evening, Sara," Menard called. His face was ruddy with the cold air and good humor. The team of matched bays stamped and snorted, the bells on their harness jingling cheerfully, a silver presence in the darkening evening air. "Could I tempt you with a ride?" he asked.

"Menard, I—"

"Godalmighty, Miss Sara! Come quick!" Johnny's voice made Sara jump guiltily.

Oh, my God! she thought. *He knows!*

He loped across the yard, bareheaded, sliding to a halt on the icy ground beside her. She took an involuntary step backward.

"It's Clem, Miss Sara," Johnny said urgently. "He's sick, bad sick. Upchucking everywhere. And there's blood . . ."

"Oh, no!" Sara gasped. She cast a helpless glance at Menard. "I'm sorry . . . I can't . . . I'm sorry!"

Johnny took her arm, half-carrying her across the messy yard, hurrying her toward the house. Menard shrugged philosophically, clicked to his team, and drove away. The group around the bonfire gave them a mildly curious look, then turned back to their festivities. Dr. Cary often got calls at the strangest hours. Sara and Johnny clambered up the porch steps and burst into the foyer.

"Where is he?" Sara asked.

"Your office."

She rushed through the door, dragging at her muffler, looking for the sick boy. "Clem!" The door slammed shut behind her. She whirled around, saw Johnny's expression, and took a breath to scream.

She never got it out. Johnny's hand dammed it against her lips, and he thrust her against the wall, holding her still with the weight of his body, a harsh sneer twisting his handsome features into an angry mask.

"Don't try it," he ordered. She nodded frantically. He lifted his hand from her mouth slowly, and she sucked in a ragged breath.

"Clem?"

"There's nothing wrong with Clem."

"You lied!"

"You're damned right. To keep you from spilling your guts to Plunket." Hot, guilty color swept up her throat, and he laughed harshly. "I knew it."

"No, I wouldn't—"

"Save your breath, Sara. You don't lie worth a damn. And the hell of it is, I'm leaving tonight anyway."

"You are?" Hope surged through her, making her giddy. He was leaving. At last! Abruptly, he released her, stepped to her desk, and pawed through the meager contents of her cash box.

"Take as much as you need," she said. The inanity of her words struck her as humorous, as if she were pressing him to accept another slice of pie or cup of coffee, and she fought back a hysterical giggle.

"And good riddance, right, Doc?" he taunted. He reached out again, fitting his hand around the nape of her neck inside the collar of her cloak. "It'll do for a stake, only what do I do with you, now that I know I can't trust you to keep your word?"

"I won't tell anyone, I swear!" Her words were a ragged whisper. "It would serve no purpose."

"Except revenge." His fingers trailed down her throat,

pushed aside the cheerfully red muffler, and settled in the V in the hollow of her collarbone where the pulse jumped erratically. "You think I killed your Will; you know I've used you. You'd have the law on my tail before I got ten miles down the road."

"No, that's not true, I won't—"

"It's no good, Sara," he said, eyes narrowing. His fingers tightened around her neck. "There's only one way to guarantee your silence."

Visions of her own lifeless body flashed behind her eyes, and she swallowed. "What is it?"

His smile was wicked, satisfied. "I'm taking you with me."

Sara woke in a narrow bunk, the bed hard and unfamiliar, the heavy warmth of her own cloak pulled over her shoulders. She'd fallen asleep in her clothes, of all things. For a moment, she lay immobile, mystified. Where was she? The low throb of powerful engines and the sibilant whisper of water teased her consciousness. Memory returned with a jolt, and she moaned in protest.

She threw the cloak aside and sat up abruptly, narrowly missing bumping her head on the low overhead. A glance around the tiny cabin proved she was alone. Another look out of the tiny porthole confirmed that she was on the steamboat *Alice,* in the middle of the muddy Missouri River, the distant banks shrouded in early morning fog. She went to the door, tried the knob, then kicked the footboard in frustration. Locked! Johnny! He'd done this to her!

Seething, she threw herself down in the spindle chair and clawed at her tangled tresses. She pulled the combs out to free the waist-length mass and tried to think.

Her cowardice made her cheeks burn with shame. After Johnny's startling pronouncement the night before, he'd had only to show his gun to clog her vehement protests in her throat. He'd made it clear that while he probably wouldn't use it on her, he'd feel no such compunction for anyone else who tried to stop them. Jamming a few of her things and his own belongings into her battered old carpetbag, he'd then hitched up Old Nubbin and calmly driven her away.

They'd stopped in the yard long enough for her to concoct some story for Pandora. Sara wasn't even sure what it was now, something about a call down Concordia way, and perhaps taking a few extra days to consult with old Doc Turner, too, regarding Johnny's condition. Sara had been astounded at the ease with which Pandora accepted the tale. They hadn't driven south toward Concordia, but instead, straight to the docks at the bottom of Tenth Street where the river bustle never abated. Johnny had taken one look and then chosen the river steamer *Alice,* picking her for the feverish activity on deck that indicated her imminent departure upriver. Quick instructions to a loiterer sent the horse and rig toward the livery. A hard hand clamped around her arm and the weight of his pistol bumping her hip through his coat pocket carried Sara on board, all without her able to utter so much as a word of protest or a single cry for help.

"Make yourself at home, Sara," he advised on reaching their tiny stateroom.

She stood as rigid as a pole in the center of the cabin, her fear abating now that he'd released her, and her anger building in its place. "You can't do this!" she cried, enraged.

"It appears that I am," he said mildly. He shucked off his jacket, revealing his coarse chambray shirt. A ruffle of pale chest hairs peeked out at the open throat over the edge of his winter underwear. He seemed suddenly very large and virile, a man who was a law unto himself, answerable to no one but his own indecipherable inner code.

"Pandora will worry," she warned him. "She'll send for the sheriff."

"Why should she?" he asked. "You've spent days away tending to patients before. If necessary, we can even send her a letter from Kansas City explaining you've been delayed."

"Wha—what do you intend to do with me?" Her eyes darted nervously between him and the stateroom door, but his bulk was an impenetrable barrier to any escape.

"Relax, woman. This isn't exactly my idea of a romantic tryst," he drawled. "Since I can't trust you to keep your mouth shut, you'll just have to stay by my side for a few days while I finish some business."

"And then what?"

He smiled, his eyes thin slits of speculation. "And then . . ."

She swallowed painfully and waited.

He shrugged and laughed. "I'll send you home."

"Oh." She sat down on the edge of the narrow bunk, her knees suddenly weak. He enjoyed terrorizing her, the bastard! She glared at him with hostility and resentment, but she couldn't prevent the telltale quiver of her lower lip. He made a sound of disgust.

"You brought this on yourself, you know. Look, Doc, the more you cooperate, the faster you'll be on your way home, and the sooner I'll be out of your life forever. So no hysterics, no surprises. You behave yourself, do what you're told, and nothing will happen. Cross me and . . . well, your imagination can fill in the rest. Understood?"

She nodded and swallowed. She could well envision what punishment he would mete out should she attempt to thwart him. He sat down in the thin-spindled wooden chair in the corner, and she watched him warily, her fingers twisting the gold band on her left hand.

"You might as well undress and try to get some shut-eye," he advised.

Sara jumped. She might have to suffer the enforced intimacy of his company in this small cabin, but she was no fool. "I'm not tired."

The corners of his mouth twitched. "Suit yourself."

Stretching out his long legs, he pulled his enormous Enfield pistol from his coat pocket. Sara stiffened, but he ignored her, merely spinning the chamber and polishing the steel-blue barrel with his handkerchief. Outside, the activity on the deck and docks increased until, with a blast of her steam whistle, the *Alice* got underway. Sara listened to the deep throb of the engines and the strident calls of the deckhands with growing dismay.

Every second took her farther and farther away from the ones she loved, in the company of a man she had no reason to trust. She continued to fume, but there was nothing in the room to break the heavy silence other than the occasional click of metal against metal. She leaned against the bunk wall, watching Johnny with antagonism she did not attempt to veil, until fatigue and tension and monotony eventually took their toll.

Sitting in the small chair now, with the thin early morning light peeping through the porthole, Sara was incensed to realize she'd fallen asleep under Johnny's watchful eye. It made her feel vulnerable and defenseless to know he'd watched her slumber. But where had he slept?

Her startled gaze jumped to the rumpled bunk. She shook her head. No, he hadn't joined her there. She'd have known that, no matter how tired she was. A happy thought struck her. Perhaps he'd left her and gotten off at another port. Or maybe he'd fallen overboard. No, nothing so timely would happen to her. No doubt he was prowling about the ship, seeing what kind of mischief he could find. Well, this was an opportunity she couldn't miss.

There had to be a steward who would answer her calls and knocks. It might be embarrassing to explain at first, but surely she could expect some sympathy for her predicament. And if Johnny were, indeed, still aboard, she'd have the captain of this vessel clap him in irons for his crimes. The melodramatic image did much to lighten her spirits.

Determination reasserted itself. She swept her hair over her shoulder and made a moue of impatience at her appearance. Wrinkled and slept-in skirts and tumbled-down hair made her look like a wanton. No one would take her seriously, much less believe she was a lady and a respected physician, until she'd repaired the ravages of an uncomfortable night.

Rising, she dug into the carpetbag in search of her brushes. It gave her a peculiar sensation to see Johnny's shirts and shaving articles tumbled so intimately with her own dainty things. With a sound of annoyance, she fished her brush from the bottom of the bag. Pulling the boar's hair brush through her unbound locks, she sought to bring the springy, vibrant mass of hair back into some semblance of order.

The scratch of a key in the lock made her swing around,

a cry of distress on her lips. She'd missed her chance to elude Johnny, all because of a rumpled skirt and tangled hair! The door swung inward, and Sara gaped.

"Good morning, darling."

It was Johnny, but he'd undergone a transformation. He was freshly shaven and had even had his hair trimmed, though it still had a will of its own, curling in beguiling ringlets over his broad forehead. Gone were the rough clothes of a humble laborer. He wore a fitted frock coat and pants, starched white linen shirt and striped cravat, and a gold brocade waistcoat. He was the epitome of cultured manhood, handsome and debonair, brash and magnetic. Sara was stupefied.

"I thought you'd be up," he said cheerfully. "I hope you're as hungry as I am. I've ordered breakfast."

A smiling black steward entered, carrying a tray loaded with covered dishes. The aroma of fresh bread and hot coffee tantalized her nostrils. The steward quickly set the tray on a folding table and drew the chair forward, then backed away. Johnny slipped a coin from his waistcoat pocket and pressed it into his palm.

"If'n you need anythin' at all, Mr. Tucker, sir, and ma'am," the steward said with a wide smile, "you all just call on me."

Johnny closed the door after him and looked at Sara. She watched him, open-mouthed in amazement. He stepped toward her, caught a long curling lock between his fingers, and tugged gently.

"Very pretty," he murmured, then grinned at her dazed expression. "It's not considered polite to stare, Sara." He urged her into the chair, sat down across from her on the bed, and poured two cups of steaming black coffee. "Perhaps some coffee might help?" he suggested solicitously.

Sara closed her mouth with a snap. "How easily you change your colors," she said, her voice scathing. "As if anything could disguise who and what you truly are."

"And are you so sure you know what that is?" he asked. "Careful, Doc. You've been wrong before. What makes you certain you know the truth even now?" He watched the flickers of uncertainty chase across her face and laughed low in his throat.

Her chin tilted at a belligerent angle. "I know the scoundrel you are. You drag me off without so much as a bonnet, then masquerade as a prize peacock. Did my money pay for this new finery?"

"No, and I'll buy you ten bonnets when we get to Kansas City if you like." His face took on the bright look of a boy with a secret too good to keep. He pulled something from his coat pocket. "Look."

Sara gasped. Fanned out in front of her was a crescent of greenbacks, more money than she'd ever seen. Her voice was shaky with accusation. "You've robbed someone at gunpoint."

He laughed. "Don't be tedious, Sara." His hand went back to his pocket and flipped a pack of cards onto the table. "I won it all—with these."

"Gambling?" Sara was incredulous. "You won all that playing cards? I thought you were a blacksmith."

"I'm a man of many talents." Johnny smirked. He removed the dish covers and served two plates with hot biscuits dripping with golden butter, shirred eggs, spicy sausage, and peach jam. "Eat, Sara."

Slowly, she picked up her fork, watching him out of the corner of her eye while he tackled his loaded plate. The demands of her own hunger wouldn't be denied, but her mind whirred in confusion.

How could she deal with a man like this, who constantly changed, chameleonlike, to blend with a new background? And who was he really? Sweet Johnny, or ruthless Tuck, or this charming, smooth-talking stranger? Each version held a peculiar fascination, yet she felt she saw only a portion of the puzzle that was his complex personality. Were there other pieces still missing? Would she ever know the complete man? Even if he would allow her that privilege, would she dare to look? Or would complete knowledge of his nature turn her heart to stone, like a single glance of the ancient Medusa?

Her appetite waned at the turn of her thoughts, and she set aside her fork. Johnny pushed his plate away and unfastened the bottom button of his waistcoat, giving a contented sigh.

"I don't know anything about you really, do I?" Sara murmured.

Johnny's tawny eyebrow lifted. "You never asked," he pointed out.

"I am now." She picked up her coffee cup, amazed at her own temerity. But Johnny's mood seemed expansive.

"Such as?" he asked.

"Where you're from."

"Pennsylvania."

Her interest piqued. "I took my medical training in Philadelphia. Do you know the city?"

"You might say that. I grew up there."

"Family?"

The planes of his face became harder, granitelike. "Not so you would notice."

"Is John Tucker your real name?"

He straightened abruptly. "It'll do."

"But . . ."

"You know all you need to know right now. It would just hurt you to know more, Sara."

"Oh." She thought of Will, and of all the terrible, unspeakable things that men did in wartime in the name of God and country, and knew he was right. Curiosity about Johnny would only lead to further trouble, and more heartache.

He watched the array of emotions flicker across her face and looked away, his mouth grim. A giant yawn surprised him, and he stretched his arms overhead, flexing them. "God, I'm beat," he muttered.

"You were up all night, playing cards?"

"Yeah. It was thanks to your stake I did so well. I'll see that you get it all back in good time. I might even get in another game tonight, seeing as how we probably won't reach Kansas City until tomorrow due to the ground fog." He looked at her, his eyes narrowing. "Are you finished?"

She nodded.

"Good. Go lock the door."

Slowly, she rose, giving him a doubtful glance that became wide-eyed when he stripped off his coat, vest, cravat, and boots, then threw back the blankets on the bunk.

Her hair swayed as she approached the door, but her back was stiff with tension. She reached for the knob.

"Don't try it, honey," he warned. She vibrated like an overwound watch spring, and he laughed. Defiantly, she twisted the key in the lock and whirled around, glaring at him.

"Don't what?" she demanded, all haughty innocence. For answer, he merely smiled and crooked his finger at her.

"What do you want?" she asked, pressing her hands against her fast-tripping heart. She was supremely conscious of his size and the sensual gleam in his eyes. Johnny curled his finger again, and his voice was a gravelly vibrato.

"Come here, Sara."

She stamped her foot. "No! Just because you force me to share a cabin, I won't . . . won't . . . My reputation will be in shreds as it is, but that doesn't mean—"

"Your reputation is intact *Mrs.* Tucker," he said. "And don't get any ideas. The steward's already been alerted to my *wife's* sometimes eccentric behavior and has pledged his silence for the price of several greenbacks." He studied the stubborn, frightened jut of her lower lip, then suddenly tired of the game. With a swiftness that caught her off guard and made her squeak with surprise, he grabbed her and tossed her none too gently onto the bunk.

Sara scrambled against the opposite wall, sucked in an outraged breath, and prepared to vent her wrath on him. His irritated words plugged her tirade unspoken.

"For God's sake, Doc, your virtue's safe with me. All I want is sleep. I want you where I can keep an eye on you, that's all."

She was amazed when he lay down beside her, folded his arms, and closed his eyes with a tired sigh. Deflated, she subsided warily, lying down as far away as possible, her skirts tucked modestly, her hands folded under her cheek.

So he'd led the steward to believe they were husband and wife. How ironic! If Johnny knew the truth, would he be lying so still, ignoring her? she wondered. Would he demand his husbandly rights, or would he even care that legally they were his to claim?

She studied the man beside her, trying to glean some understanding of what he was. How could she know him, yet not know him, and why did she feel such a strong fascination for a man who more deeply mystified her with each passing moment?

He was so close in the tiny space that she could see the fine texture of his skin and smell the crisp bite of his shaving soap. His chest rose and fell in a deep, soothing rhythm. He was so big, so solid. She could feel the heat radiating from his body and, in spite of herself, began to relax. She knew she ought to feel threatened, yet she experienced an incongruous sense of safety and protection. It would be so easy to sleep in this man's arms.

The thought crept in under her defenses, startling her with its force. But it was a betrayal of Will, of her Hippocratic oath, of her sense of decency! She made an involuntary movement of protest. Johnny's hand reached out to make soothing patterns on her knee.

"Be good, Sara, love," he murmured in a drowsy voice. "Pretend this is a pleasure trip. We'll visit the salon or take a turn around the texas deck later if you want. All right?"

"Fine," she whispered.

"That's my girl." He gave her knee a squeeze. Her skin burned where he'd touched her.

Sara didn't answer, suddenly afraid that what she really wanted was something she could never have, a sweet temptation that could lead her to heaven—or to hell.

Kansas City was a revelation. It rose from teeming docks, the bustling streets leading uphill in a topsy-turvy staircase of buildings. The boisterous town appeared to have tripled its size since the last time Sara had seen it. Wagons and drays clogged the muddy streets under gray February skies. Pedestrians hurried about their business, dodging horses and carriages, and disappearing into the lines of business establishments sandwiched together in rows upon rows. Garish painted signs in red and yellow graced the tops of buildings two, four, even five stories tall.

The advertisements boasted of the finest dry goods, the most productive feeds and seeds, workman's clothing at bargain prices, iron stoves and metallic coffins. If Lexington were a bastion of graciousness and culture, Kansas City was all ambition and scrambling upheaval. Johnny drank it in like an elixir.

He established Sara in a room at the finest hotel, ordered her lunch and a bath, and suggested she get some rest while he saw to a few matters. She refrained from reminding him that sleep was all she had done aboard the *Alice,* except for a few excursions among the passengers in the main salon. There, she'd been able to see firsthand Johnny's charming ways, his easy jokes, and ribald humor. He'd become a favorite among the other travelers, and even those whose purses were lighter for having met him seemed to bear the handsome, laughing scoundrel no ill will.

She supposed she was Johnny's prisoner, yet so far it had been a gilded cage, and surprisingly, she believed him when he said he'd send her home if she cooperated. So she dutifully ate her lunch, reflecting that she had little choice, and pondered her unusual situation. The chambermaid took away her rumpled gown to be sponged and pressed, and then Sara bathed in the painted tin slipper tub behind the tapestried changing screen, singing softly to herself and luxuriating in the sensual pleasures of hot water and fragrant soap. Afterwards, she pulled on a thin dressing gown she found balled in the bottom of the carpetbag. Her hair she'd put into a slapdash ball on the top of her head, and springy tendrils escaped and trailed down her nape and temples. She dug into the bag yet again for her brushes, and her fingers closed on a small book in the bottom that she recognized.

The Bible was a strange thing to associate with Johnny. Idly, she flipped through it, wondering if any of the underlined passages could help explain the enigma of the man. She took the book over to the window. Patterns of light and shadow fell through the lace curtain to dance across her face and the tissue-thin pages.

. . . *the weight of gold that came to Solomon* . . .
. . . *and gavest them bread for their hunger* . . .

. . . wandered in deserts, and in mountains, and in dens and caves of the earth . . .

Johnny followed the sturdy chambermaid into the room, his arms filled with packages. Sara stood by the window, holding a small book. His words of greeting dried up in his throat at the sight of her slender form outlined against the sunlight spilling through the sheer drapes.

She lifted her head at his entrance, and something elemental arced between them. Desire slammed into him with the force of a fist, and he stared, his mouth gone bone dry, his blood strumming in his veins. The maid chattered cheerfully, first hanging Sara's newly pressed traveling dress in the mirrored armoire, then moving to dip the cool bath water out of the tub into cans.

"Leave it," Johnny said, his voice strangely hoarse to his own ears. The maid bobbed a curtsy and disappeared, and still Sara did not move, the light falling on her pale, startled face, glistening on the damp curls and dewy skin. He set his packages down on the brass bed's damask spread, and moved stiffly toward her. His eyes glinted when he saw what she was reading.

"Snooping, Sara?" he asked, his voice thick. She smelled of roses and honey, and the heady scent made him dizzy with need.

"No."

He pulled the Bible from her unresisting fingers and tossed it into the middle of the bed. She gave a gasp of surprise. The movement drew his avid gaze to her breasts, rising and falling rapidly beneath the thin batiste dressing gown, then trailed upward across her slender throat, touched the aureole of her hair, and dropped to the trembling fullness of her lower lip. He nearly groaned aloud. He had to taste her. Nothing, not the Calf or Moses or even his own immortal soul was as important to him at that moment.

He caught her shoulders and bent his head, capturing her mouth with his own, sliding his lips across hers in soft invitation. She made a small sound, half protest, half pleasure, her hands fluttering against his shirt front. She drew back, and he allowed her to pull away—for the moment.

"Don't," she murmured, shaking.

"I've been wanting to do that again ever since that day in the shed," he confessed.

"Why?"

"To see if you were as good as I remembered." He smiled down at her. "I was wrong. You're better."

He took her mouth again, using his tongue to woo her, breaching her defenses with gentle persuasion, then taking her breath, making it a part of his own. He stroked the sweet and secret recesses of her mouth while his hands pulled her close, learning the indentation of her hip, and the rounded fullness of her breast with its hard and exciting center pearl. He felt her tremble against him and knew he trembled with need as well.

She dragged her mouth free, gasping. "Please, Johnny, no."

"Why not?" His tone was husky with desire. "We both want it."

"No. I can't . . . I never . . ."

A sudden absurd thought struck him. He put her a little away from him so he could see her face. "You aren't telling me—you're still a virgin?"

Hot color flushed her cheeks. "No, of course not. But I . . ." She paused, struggled momentarily, then blurted the words, their clinical coolness at war with the burning blush suffusing her neck and face. "As a doctor, I know that for some women the act of procreation is welcome and enjoyable . . ."

"But not for you," he finished.

She hung her head in embarrassment. "No."

Johnny inwardly cursed her dead husband. What had he done to her to make her doubt herself to this extent? "I could teach you, Sara, love," he said, most tenderly.

"I suppose you could try. You'd be disappointed."

He laughed. "Oh, no, honey, I think not. I think, in fact, that for the first time you may be really coming alive."

She lifted her head, and her words were raw. "It wouldn't serve any purpose except to make me hate you more."

"I didn't think that was possible," he said. The muscle in his jaw twitched.

"You'll be gone soon, and this would just be something else for me to regret." Her mouth quivered, her eyes were large and luminous with pain. "I have enough of those already."

He searched her expression and knew she was right. But damn, it was hard to separate his rational mind from the deep gut-ache that made his body throb. It wasn't in him to be noble, but somehow he knew if he took her now, he would regret it even more than she did. He set her slowly from him.

"For an intelligent woman, Sara, in some areas you're woefully ignorant—or innocent." He grimaced. "I guess it has its rewards." He turned away, then paused at the bed, snapping strings and tearing into brown paper. "I brought you something."

Rolling out the contents of the package with a flourish, he turned and spread the forest green alpaca gown across Sara's shoulders, studying her for effect. He pushed her in front of the mirrored door of the armoire, watching her trace with hesitant hands the graceful draped overskirt and the bodice fichu. "I wanted red, but I think this will do," he said.

Amazed, Sara nearly smiled. "I've never owned anything red in my life."

"It would suit you." He was offhand. Turning back to the bed, he returned with another gift, gingerly settling the matching green bonnet on her hair, then standing behind her, draping the sheer lace ribbons beneath her chin. It was a fashionable creation, with a tiny brim that rolled back becomingly from her face, and a small, iridescent bird whose tail feathers swept back over the crown. Johnny's eyes met Sara's in the mirror. "I couldn't find ten bonnets that I liked in this town, so this one will have to do. What do you think?"

She turned her head this way, then that, in a feminine preening. "I think," she said slowly, "that you have excellent taste in women's fashions, indicating a too fine familiarity with such services, perhaps from dressing far too many inamoratas." His appreciative chuckle made her smile. "I also think that Pandora would have a screaming fit if she saw this outfit. A lady never accepts so intimate a gift from a gentleman.''

''Hmmph. I'm no gentleman, as you well know, and from the way you scrapped at the Brass Bull, I'd say you're no lady, either.''

Sara laughed, a gay sound that trilled along his heartstrings. *She should laugh like that all the time*, he thought. How fortunate the man who had her trust.

''No,'' she said ruefully, still laughing, ''thanks to you, nothing about me these days remotely resembles a lady.''

''Why don't you get dressed? We have an afternoon appointment with some friends of mine.''

She paused halfway to the dressing screen, and her sunny expression clouded. ''Friends? Outlaws, you mean.''

He shrugged. ''Judge for yourself.''

''Why must I go?''

''I think you'll enjoy it. Besides,'' he said, ''nothing sets off a man's image like having a beautiful woman on his arm.''

''Compliments, Johnny?'' Sara peered around the edge of the screen. ''If I didn't know better, I'd say you were still trying to seduce me.''

Johnny rocked back on his heels, hands jammed deep in his pockets, and grinned engagingly. ''If I didn't know better, Sara, I'd say you were right.''

Chapter 8

Sara sipped her tea and nibbled the iced cinnamon cake that pretty Zerelda Mimms had made. The fire behind the brass firedogs in Zee's well-appointed parlor crackled cheerfully. Johnny and the boy named Jesse sprawled on antimacassared easy chairs, their booted feet stretched out toward the warmth, chatting desultorily about horses and politics and hunting. Zee gazed at Jesse with adoring eyes, then offered Sara another cake.

"No, thank you, but they're delicious," she murmured.

"Helping Papa run the boardinghouse has made me a passable cook," Zee replied. She cast a longing glance at Jesse. "It will be an asset when I become a wife."

Sara smiled and made some reply. She was amazed at the devotion the girl, who was no more than twenty and very attractive, exhibited toward the pale and painfully thin boy. Sara supposed he looked rather well for a youngster who'd survived a wound that should have killed him, but there was something disconcerting about him.

He'd exhibited no surprise or emotion at being reunited with his friend Tuck, and he'd practically ignored her own presence, though she knew he recognized her from their interview of nearly a year ago. Was such calculated dispassion something left over from the war, or an intrinsic part of his personality? It was hard to gauge the young man behind those continuously blinking, pale blue eyes. Such habitual winking was due to granulated eyelids, she diagnosed privately. It was nothing out of the ordinary, certainly nothing denoting a sinister nature, yet why did she feel so uneasy in the presence of Jesse James?

The afternoon had taken on a slightly unreal, nightmarish quality. Sitting in this genteel parlor, discussing the weather with men who'd ridden with Quantrill was an affront to common decency. Sara made polite conversation with Zee, while she tried to guess Johnny's plans. He looked dapper and self-confident in his gambler's finery, contrasting sharply with Jesse's farmboy best of starched blue shirt, wool trousers, and suspenders. What sort of "business" could these two seemingly disparate individuals have together? Whatever it was, no good would come of it, she was certain.

The front door reverberated with a knock, and Zee went to answer it. She returned shortly, her pretty face stiff with displeasure. "Cole's here," she said shortly.

Sara's cup clattered against her saucer at the appearance of the raw-boned, red-haired man. He stood in the doorway behind Zee, smiling from under his horseshoe mustache, idly twirling his battered slouch hat in his hands.

"Well, well," he said softly. "Ain't this a surprise."

"Cole." Johnny rose, and they assessed each other with measured stares.

"Yessir, I knew you'd come sooner or later," Cole said. He walked into the room and paused before Sara's chair. "And the lady doc, too, looking pretty as a picture. You must be going soft, Tuck. But it's mighty good to see you, ma'am." He caught Sara's hand and bowed mockingly over it. She repressed a shudder and jerked her fingers free, her glance cool and haughty.

"You're late." Jesse's soft words interrupted Cole's theatrics. He swung around and grinned expectantly at the younger man.

"It's getting nasty out there. Smells like a blizzard."

Jesse sat up and beckoned Zee. She came forward hesitantly, and he took her hand, smoothing it between his own. "Honey, why don't you ladies excuse yourselves? We menfolk have private matters to discuss."

Zee glanced at Cole and Johnny, her reluctance written on her dainty features. Surprisingly, she nodded. "All right, Jesse. Mrs. Cary, would you mind helping me clear the tea tray?''

Sara was only too glad to comply. She followed Zee into the large and neatly arranged kitchen at the rear of the frame house. Zee took the tray and began to deposit the dirty plates and cups in the metal sink.

''Have a seat, Mrs. Cary,'' she suggested, nodding at the scrubbed kitchen table. ''We're not fancy, but we normally don't make our guests sit in the kitchen. I'm sorry.''

''I'd rather be in here with you than out there with that Cole fellow,'' Sara confessed.

''I know what you mean,'' the girl replied grimly.

On impulse, Sara removed her bonnet and wrapped a dishtowel around her waist, then joined Zee at the sink. ''I'm not fancy, either, so let me help, please?''

Elbow deep in sudsy water, Zee smiled her thanks. ''Sure.''

Sara dried the plates Zee handed to her. ''You don't like Cole much, do you?''

''I—'' Zee hesitated. ''He's not good for Jesse. Every time he comes around, all they talk about is the war. Terrible tales.'' She shuddered in remembrance, and her voice dropped. ''He bragged once about executing sixteen Union soldiers. Stood 'em in a row and shot 'em with a new rifle to see how many it'd kill at one time.'' She shook her head. ''Things like that. It fetches the viciousness in a man to keep remembering such. Makes him restless, dissatisfied with a normal life. I wish Jesse would have done with Cole and the others, but he says they're his friends. I suppose I'll have to accept that.''

''But why?'' Sara asked.

''Why?'' Zee turned a surprised face toward Sara. ''I love him. I nursed him when he came here so weak and hurt. That's reason enough to stand by a man, I guess. You understand that, don't you? Why else are you here with Tuck?''

''Not for any reason that makes sense,'' Sara replied, shaking her head. Who could believe the wild tale she could tell of lost identity and rash decisions? She found it hard to believe herself. She dried the last cup and neatly folded the towel. "Do you suppose I could have another cup of tea?"

They were sitting around a steeping teapot, talking fashions, when Johnny and Jesse appeared in the kitchen door.

"We're going out for a while," Jesse announced. "I'm lending Tuck your Paw's dappled gelding, all right?"

"Oh, Jesse, you're not going to the saloons, are you?" Zee protested faintly. "You know it don't do you any good."

"Don't worry so, Zee," he returned, annoyed.

"Might be late," Johnny warned. "Could you put Sara up for the night?"

Zee glanced at Sara's stupefied expression. "Of course. We'd love to have her. Jesse, I'll help you with your coat."

They left the kitchen together. Johnny prowled around the room while Sara clenched and unclenched her hands beneath the table.

"What are you doing?" she demanded. "Don't leave me here!"

"You'll be safe and comfortable while I see to a few things."

"I won't ask what, but don't expect to find me here when you get back."

"Don't provoke me, Sara. Not now. And don't make things bad for Zee, either."

That made Sara pause. She liked the girl and had no wish to bring her grief, knowing there'd be enough of it in her life if she chose to spend it with Jesse. "I don't understand anything that's happening," she said slowly. "I'd like to go home."

"Soon. One night more."

It sounded like a promise, but she knew how worthless it could be coming from him. Helplessly, she nodded. "For Zee's sake."

Johnny smiled, and his hand stole across the nape of her neck in a fleeting caress. "Sweet Sara. I can always count on you to care."

"You mean there ain't a piss ant's worth of difference between 'em?" demanded Cole.

Jesse tossed two identical Bibles on the table. "The

Colonel was a scholar. Appears he may have outsmarted himself this time, huh, Tuck?''

Johnny shrugged in reply and took another sip of his whiskey. It seared a raw streak down his throat, but he held himself impassive. It had been a calculated risk, sharing his copy of Quantrill's Bible with Jesse, and he was as disappointed with the results as any of them.

His gaze flickered over the group seated in the back room of this run down, one-horse, no-name saloon. They'd met here, north of Kansas City, and the drink and the talk had lasted well into the wee hours. Besides Jesse and Cole, there was long-faced Frank James, Jesse's silent and morose older brother, a sad flicker to Jesse's brilliant flame; and Jim Younger, the baby of the Younger clan, but just as wild as his older sibling. Johnny knew any show of weakness and these men would fall on him like a pack of jackals.

Cole cursed, the obscenities low and disgusted. "Hell's bells! Then how are we going to find the gold?"

"Better ask what should be done with it once it's found," Johnny interjected.

"I can think of one or two things to do with sixty thousand dollars worth of minted Colorado gold." Jim Younger snickered.

"It ain't ours to do nothing with," Jesse said. His voice was soft but carried the cold steel of undisputed authority. "Jimmy Reynolds captured it as a prize of war and turned it over to Colonel Quantrill on that basis. The Golden Calf belongs to the Confederacy."

"Well, in case you ain't noticed," Cole said with a sneer, "there ain't much left of the Confederacy."

"But there's another war going on in Mexico, and an old ally of the Confederate States could use that money," Jesse stated.

Johnny carefully lowered his glass. What was this? he wondered.

"You mean Emperor Maximillian? Hell's bells, Jess! He's Napoleon's puppet," Cole said.

"Yeah, but France stood by the Confederacy."

Cole looked skeptical. "I dunno. How long has Maximillian been emperor of Mexico anyway? Two, three years? He ain't had nothing but trouble from the republicans ever since.''

"That's the point," Jesse replied.

Archduke Maximillian of Austria had accepted the crown of Mexico at Napoleon III's insistence, Johnny knew, over the opposition of the Mexican nationalists. French troops kept Maximillian in power, but the republican forces led by Benito Juarez were challenging the emperor's reign.

Cole reared back in his chair, eyes belligerent. "Yeah, but what's Maximillian got to do with us?"

"I don't know about you, but I'm hankering for action," Jesse said. "A lot of former Rebs have already volunteered to serve in the Emperor's army. I don't fancy spending my life following a mule or shucking corn from daylight to dark. There ain't nothing left in this part of Missouri but Jennison's monuments anyway.''

Several men around the table murmured in agreement. In retaliation for the Lawrence raid, federal troops had ordered the entire populations of three border counties to leave the area, causing much hardship. All that was left in the "Burnt District" was the charred chimneys of burnt-out homes, blackened sentinels named for the bloodthirsty Kansas Jayhawk leader, Jennison, who, with the Union officer Ewing, was responsible for the infamous "Order No. 11.''

"If we come calling on Maximillian with a gift like the Golden Calf," Jesse continued with growing enthusiasm, "he'll make us officers and probably give us the whole damn army to command. Think of it, boys! Union troops are helping Juarez. We'd be fighting the Yankees again!''

"You know, Jesse," Cole said slowly, "I think you might have something." The others nodded their agreement.

Damnation! Johnny thought. He fought to keep his expression as blank as Frank's. The United States wanted Maximillian out of Mexico, fearing such close ties to France and Austria in the western hemisphere. The Golden Calf was a substantial sum that just might turn the tide in the Emperor's favor over the freedom fighters working for a democratic Mexico. Suddenly, the necessity of recovering the Golden Calf had taken on even greater, more ominous, even worldwide, proportions.

"I say we go to Mexico even if we don't have the gold," Jim Younger proposed recklessly.

"It takes money to get that far." Frank James's rare comment surprised them all. He looked at his younger brother for guidance. "We're all busted flat, so what we going to do?"

"Well, we ain't giving up on the Calf, for one thing," Jesse replied. "We all know Quantrill hid it himself, somewhere 'tween here and Lexington. Moses told us that, too."

"How did Moses know?" Johnny asked sharply.

"The Colonel must have told him," Jesse replied.

Cole drummed his fingers against the scarred table. "I'll bet Quantrill meant to turn the Calf over to Moses, but things happened too fast there at the last. Now Moses wants a piece of our action."

"I'm not interested in Moses," Jesse snapped. "Except for what he might be able to tell us."

"That's a good idea. How do you contact him?" Johnny's voice was casual.

"Nuthin' to it," Cole said. "He used a drop in a watering hole in Lexington. Fellow name of Moody is the go-between."

Johnny suppressed a start of surprise. Moody! He rubbed his jaw. The bruise had lingered a week there following his fist fight with the burly cowboy in Cavendish's saloon. Yeah, he knew Moody all right. And the path leading to Moses had been right in his backyard all this time. The Calf might come first, but Johnny hadn't forgotten that Moses owed him and Alex Thompson a debt, and he fully intended to collect it.

"I still don't understand how we're going to find the gold," Jim Younger said.

Jesse calmly pushed aside an empty beer glass. "We'll retrace every step the Colonel took those last days."

"Hell, Jess, he could have stashed it anywhere," Jim said. "There's too much countryside to comb."

"I still say the key is still right here." Jesse tapped the two Bibles. "Right, Tuck?"

"It's got to be, unless the Colonel was having the last laugh," Johnny agreed.

"Then swear on the Colonel's Bible." Jesse held out the Holy Books. "Swear to look for the Golden Calf, and swear to hold it for The Cause when it's found."

Hands reached out and touched the black covers with unusual reverence.

"I swear."

"Swear it."

"On my honor."

Johnny echoed the words, self-deprecatory humor making him smile inwardly. What a perfidious lot. And he no better than the rest to foreswear himself without a qualm. To whose cause did these men swear their oaths? The Confederacy's? Or, like himself, to their own private causes, including the filling of their own greedy pockets?

"We're still gonna need some cash," Frank complained in his slow way. "We ain't got whiskey money, and I'm tired of eatin' cornmeal and fatback."

"It's nearly dawn," Jesse said. His thin mouth twisted in a sly smile. "Let's go roust out Clell and Jim and maybe some of the other boys. I have a feeling we can find just what we need up in Liberty today."

"We gonna do it, Jesse?" Jim asked eagerly.

"Why else you think we been hurrahing the town so often, you lunkhead?" Cole retorted, giving his brother a punch. "Everyone knows to keep inside when they hear our guns and the Rebel yell."

"Something going on I should know about?" Johnny asked lazily. His eyelids were hooded, masking his vigilant expression.

"We've been planning a little visit to the Clay County Savings and Loan Association, Tuck. A timely withdrawal will finance our expedition to Mexico," Jesse said. The other men chuckled at his wit, and he became expansive. "Nothing to it. We ride in, shoot up the town a little, me and Cole relieve Cashier Bird of his deposits, then we all hightail it out of there. No trouble, no killing. Simple. In fact," he said, grinning, "you might say downright inspired."

"Nothing like an original thinker," Johnny agreed dryly.

Jesse seemed to think it was a compliment. He offered one of Quantrill's Bibles to Johnny, and his meaning was clear. "Well, Tuck? Are you with us?"

Johnny felt a muscle jump in his jaw. For an instant he thought of Sara. So this was how it felt to have no choices left. But what was robbery added to his growing list of misdeeds? He'd long ago decided to live and work by the Machiavellian axiom of "the end justifies the means." And finally the end was in sight. His fingers closed over the limp black binding.

"Yeah. I'm with you."

Sara peeked again through the lace curtain draping the Mimms' parlor window. The somber daylight was fast dying, even though it was not much past midday. To the west, dark gray, snow-laden clouds built up over the prairie, whipped by gale-force winds into frothy crests. Snowflakes whirled and dipped, and the visibility was fast diminishing to nothing.

"It's snowing," she announced.

"Papa will be coming home soon, then," Zee said. She hummed softly under her breath, working at the cherry writing desk with red foil and white paper lace, cutting and pasting, creating a love-offering to present to Jesse on the morrow, St. Valentine's Day.

Sara wondered how Zee could be so philosophical. The waiting was intolerable, though Zee had been kindness itself during her overnight stay, even sending back to the hotel for Sara's meager baggage. Everything was comfortable physically, but mentally Sara felt as turbulent as the brewing blizzard. She was anxious to return home. She worried that her patients, few though they were, might need her. Johnny's half-promise to send her home had kept her placid until now, but the later it became, the more she was convinced he'd been delayed by some nefarious scheme, or else had finally deserted her. In either case, she was to the point of taking the matter into her own hands, but, since Johnny had left her without a cent, she would have to borrow the boat fare from Zee. She was trying to find a way to broach the subject when a movement in the distance caught her eye.

"Someone's coming," she said. Zee joined her at the window. A horse and rider appeared through the swirling flakes, picking their way slowly forward. Both man and animal slumped with fatigue.

"It's your Tuck," Zee said. "And half-froze by the looks of him, too. I'll go warm him a toddy."

Zee went off toward the kitchen, and Sara hurried to the door, flinging it open before Johnny could knock. He stomped the caked mud and snow from his boots on the narrow wooden porch, shook his shoulders like a slumberous bear, and swept off his hat before stepping inside, all without a sound. When Sara saw his face, her greeting died on her lips, and she gasped out loud. He was haggard, red-nosed with the cold, and gray around the mouth. His clothing was wrinkled and speckled with mud, and his jaw was covered with a day's growth of golden stubble. But it was his eyes that alarmed her, for they were wild and possessed.

"What is it?" she cried. "What's happened?"

"Get your things," he said in a harsh voice, ignoring her question. "We're leaving."

"Someone's dead." Her voice was flat with terror and certainty. "It's true, isn't it? Who? Jesse?"

"No, not him." The answer was nearly a snarl. "But God damn, it should have been."

"Then who? Tell me!"

He rounded on her, full of fury. "How the hell should I know!" he shouted. "No killing, Jesse said. And it went slicker than goose grease, until he shot down that kid in cold blood. An accident, he said, but he liked it, and they won't forget him the next time he comes around. Jesus Christ! Changed a bank robbery into murder—and now half the countryside's after us."

"Oh, God." Her hands covered her trembling lips. The words seared through her brain. Robbery. Murder. Death. Abhorrence rose in her like bile. She stared into Johnny's face and suddenly realized that his expression mirrored all her feelings and more—the rage, the horror, the repudiation. And behind the hard outer façade, behind eyes gla-

cial and green with repugnance and fury, there was sorrow
and regret and a humanity Sara had never thought to see
in him again. Moved by instinct, she reached out to him.
He hesitated the tiniest fraction of a second, then dragged her against himself, burying his face in her hair.

"Sara." His voice was ragged, and he shuddered against
her, holding her tight, as though he could absorb something of her essence.

Her cheek lay against the cool, snow-damp front of his
jacket, and her hands clutched his sleeves with the same
fervency with which he held her, willing him closer. She
smelled the fresh clean scent of snow and the warm, pungent odor of man and horse, and burrowed against him,
caught in a tangled web of need, unsure which was more
potent, his desire to be comforted or hers to comfort. His
breath rasped unevenly, and she wondered if he wept, but
his fingers held the back of her head, and he would not let
her look at him. She sensed his torment and felt her own
tears rise in response.

"Tuck?" Zee's voice was timid, but it served to drive
a wedge between Sara and Johnny, and they broke apart.
"You should come warm yourself," Zee urged. She stood
in the opening to the parlor, heating her hands around an
earthenware cup. "I've got a hot drink ready."

"I can't stay." Johnny's words were gruff, unexpectedly
thick. He forced a half-smile at the young girl. "But I'll
take that drink."

Wordlessly, Zee passed him the steaming cup and
watched him down coffee laced with whiskey in a single
gulp. Her expression was timorous, yet hopeful. "Jesse?"

"He said to tell you he'd be calling after Sunday dinner,
same as always," Johnny said woodenly. He rummaged
inside his coat pocket, then pressed several bills into her
hand. "For the gelding. That's enough for your Papa to
buy two replacements. Probably wouldn't want him back
now anyway, hard as he's been ridden today."

"You really mean to go on?" Zee asked, her pretty face
concerned. "The weather ain't fittin'."

"It's time for Sara to go home."

Zee glanced at Sara, who appeared anything but composed, then back at Johnny. "I'll get her things together."

When Zee had disappeared, Sara's agitation turned to concern for the girl. "You must tell her about Jesse. She has a right to know what kind of man he is."

Johnny's face was grim, as though his moment of weakness had been nothing more than an illusion. "She knows. Or can guess. Stay out of it, Sara."

She knew he regretted revealing anything to her, yet he'd let her glimpse behind Tuck's ruthless personality to the place where Johnny still lived, someone who could be sorry for his actions. Old affection and compassion were not dead in her after all, and for the first time, she wondered if some mitigating circumstances had led Johnny into his career as a guerrilla. The thought smacked of betrayal to Will's memory. Her confusion grew apace, so she forced herself to concentrate on Johnny's most important words: She was to go home.

Fast and hard on that understanding came the knowledge that she would soon bid Johnny a final farewell. She was surprised by the pang that accompanied the thought, knowing she ought to be grateful that this ordeal was coming to an end. She fought down the traitorous feelings. He no longer meant anything to her, could be nothing more than an object of hatred. She must focus on that and not allow any other emotions to cloud that all-important issue.

Zee reappeared with Sara's bag and heavy cloak. Johnny waited impatiently for the women to bid a fond and tearful goodbye. Zee followed them outside.

"You take care of her, you hear, Tuck?" Zee admonished. She pulled her shawl closer and shivered against the bitter wind and biting snow.

Johnny lifted Sara into the saddle sideways, threw the carpetbag over the saddle horn, and climbed up behind her. He carefully tucked the folds of the cloak around her and pulled her into the crook of his body. "I'll do it," he called. "Thanks again, Zee."

The tired horse responded to Johnny's nudges and clicks, carrying them off into a world filled with fat, floating snowflakes. They landed on Sara's lashes, and she licked them off her lips. The blurred edges of the other houses on the Mimms' quiet street were barely visible. Despite her awkward position, she was warm and protected from the brunt of the wind by the bulk of Johnny's body. She didn't suppose the horse would last long under his double burden, but the docks weren't far. Johnny could let her board a boat headed down river, and then what became of the poor animal and his new master would no longer concern her.

They were silent until they finally reached the dock area. Only one shabby freight steamer was taking on cargo, but Sara was in no mood to be choosy. If it were headed down river to Lexington, she'd have taken a raft, canoe, or rowboat.

Johnny halted the gelding near the base of the dock. The wind was milder here, but the snow brushing her face made Sara shiver. She sneezed and caught at Johnny to keep her precarious perch.

"I'm sorry to bring you out in such a storm," he said, frowning. He swung down and reached for her, setting her on her numb feet. "But it's the best thing that could happen."

"Why the best?" She sneezed again.

He groped for his pocket, pressed a handkerchief into her hand. "Weren't you listening? There's a posse after us. The snow will cover the trail."

"Oh." She swallowed. "What will you do?"

"The only thing I can do. Hide out someplace safe. Someplace no one would ever think to look." Sara was silent, and he peered down at her averted face, his lips twisting. "Well, Doc," he goaded softly, "don't you want to know where?"

"No. I only want to go home as you promised."

"I did promise, didn't I? And so you shall. Wait here while I arrange passage." He was back in just a few minutes. "It's not as luxurious as the trip upriver, but it will have to suffice."

"I'm sure it will." She hesitated, straightened her shoulders, and lifted her chin. She studied the rugged contours of his face for a long moment. After all they'd been through, it felt strange to be leaving him this way. "Goodbye, Johnny. I—I wish you well." She was surprised when he began to smile, a slow, wicked grin that hinted of mischief.

"Oh, Sara, honey." He chuckled, shaking his head. "You are such an innocent babe. Haven't you figured it out? The only safe place for me is back home in Lexington. You aren't shut of me yet. I'm going with you."

Chapter 9

"Cartwheels and camphor oil, Sara Jane! You shouldn't be up." The letters and papers Pandora were reading lay forgotten in a pile beside her breakfast plate. "Two days in bed is not enough. You'll take the ague for sure."

Sara sat down at the claw-footed dining table. She touched an embroidered handkerchief to a nose that was only faintly red. "I'm fine, Dorie. It's just a cold."

And soul-weariness, her mind whispered. Even the comforting familiarity of home brought no relief, for she could not forget for even a moment that everything she held dear was at risk due to her.

Pandora studied Sara's pale visage carefully. "I still say that trip was entirely too hard on you. I can't think what Dr. Turner was about, letting you and Johnny return in the middle of that storm."

Sara's gaze dropped. Her hands were hidden in the lap of her navy grosgrain skirt, and she twisted the thin circlet of gold on her finger in a flurry of agitation. It was so hard to lie to Pandora, even though her life now seemed one subterfuge and deception after another. "It seemed important that we get home," she murmured.

"Well, I'm sorry Dr. Turner had nothing helpful to offer on poor Johnny's condition, but at least the shopping was worth it. A fine horse to relieve Old Nubbin and a new dress, too. I still can't believe you found that gown and cunning little bonnet in Concordia. Seems like something you'd be more likely to find in St. Louis or Kansas City."

"Yes, doesn't it?" Sara replied inanely. She took a hasty sip from her water glass, her guilty gaze focused anywhere

but on Pandora's lined and caring face. The striped burgundy wall paper that usually gave her a headache had
never been more fascinating. She was glad when Lizzie
appeared with a loaded breakfast plate. "Thank you,
Lizzie," she said with a weak smile. "I'll try to do justice
to your cooking today."

"Bring her peppermint tea, too, Lizzie," Pandora in-
structed. "That seems to do better than any fancy tonic."
The girl nodded, smiled, and touched Sara's arm in an
unspoken message.

"Yes, I'm glad I'm home, too," Sara said with real
feeling. Lizzie bustled away, and Sara applied herself to
breakfast.

"Look what came for you," Pandora said. She passed
Sara a small bundle wrapped in green tissue paper. The
tiny jet earrings Pandora wore swung from side to side in
her anticipation, and her tone held a pleased, conspiratorial note. "Judge Plunket himself brought it by. He
couldn't stay to pay his compliments because he's been
called out of town on urgent business."

Sara unwrapped the paper. "Violets! Where did he find
violets in February?"

"They must have come from a St. Louis hothouse.
Lord, what an extravagance! What does his card say?"
Pandora asked excitedly.

Sara unfolded the note and scanned it quickly. "Just his
best wishes for a speedy recovery." She buried her face
in the purple nosegay and breathed in the scent of spring.
Deep within, her flagging spirits stirred to tentative life.
"How thoughtful. He's such a charming man."

"You could do a lot worse, Sara Jane."

Sara looked up, startled. "I've no wish to leave you,
Dorie. Marrying again seems an impossibility to me."
She suppressed a wild desire to giggle hysterically. If only
Pandora knew the truth of that!

"Oh, posh and pussy willows! You're still a young
woman. Will certainly would understand, and I confess
I'd feel easier if you were settled with a fine husband. I
wouldn't want you to turn down a perfectly good proposal
out of some misplaced loyalty to me." Pandora smiled
and arched her thin brows. "Menard Plunket may be a

newcomer, but he's up and coming, and quite a catch, and he's obviously interested in you.''

Sara felt heat rushing to her cheeks and busied herself re-folding the note. ''He's just being gracious. It's his way. Now, not another word, Dorie. You're making me blush.'' Sara was grateful Lizzie returned at that moment with the cup of mint tea. She thanked the girl and sipped the hot brew.

''He'd be a lucky man to win you,'' Pandora said, determined to have the last word on the subject. ''Especially since you'd bring to him a good family name and a profession, not to mention a sizable property, what with the lots in town and the land out by the Sugarloaf. A hill full of caverns isn't worth much, I know, but there's considerable timber, and the grazing is good—''

''Oh, do stop, Dorie,'' Sara begged. ''You make me sound like a mare up for auction.''

''Oh, very well. That's all I'm going to say, Sara Jane, but at least keep an open mind on the subject.'' Pandora reached for the newspaper at her elbow, unfolding it with crisp movements, and gave an exclamation of dismay. ''My goodness! Whatever is the world coming to? Some desperados have robbed the Clay County Savings and Loan. Why, it's unheard of! A bank has never been robbed before—and in broad daylight, too.''

''What—what does it say?'' Sara asked, her throat suddenly dry.

''They got over sixty thousand dollars.'' Pandora pulled a finger down the columns of black print. ''Well, about fifteen thousand in gold, it says, and the rest in bonds worthless to the thieves and a few greenbacks. Hmmph!'' She sniffed, looking up at Sara. ''A lot of good it will do them. No one has gold these days. They can't spend it for calling attention to themselves.'' She returned to her perusal of the story. ''And, oh dear! A young man attending William Jewell College, George Wymore, was killed, shot by one of the gunmen as they left town.''

''How awful,'' Sara murmured. She reached for her cup, gulping the aromatic drink while her conscience plunged and reared like a wild mustang colt.

''They're still looking for the men that did it. A posse

is being formed," Pandora continued, then glanced up. "I wonder if Judge Plunket went to join them." Shrugging, she began to read again. "It says witnesses have tentatively identified six as local men, but no one knew the seventh man, a dandy on a dappled horse. They think he headed toward Kansas City, and may be traveling with a woman. Imagine that!"

Sara choked and dropped her cup, spilling the pale fluid over the starched white tablecloth. She came to her feet with an unnatural awkwardness. "Oh! I'm sorry. That was so clumsy of me," she said, breathless and agitated. She blotted the spreading moisture with her napkin.

"Calm yourself, girl. It's of no consequence," Pandora soothed.

"Your mother's best cutwork cloth." Sara's voice was tearful.

Pandora frowned. "Sara Jane, are you sure you're feeling all right? Lizzie will get that. Perhaps you should go back to bed."

"No, I just need a little air, that's all," Sara said hurriedly. She smoothed her hair, touching Will's combs for comfort, and squared her shoulders. "I've work to do, the mission . . . where's Johnny?"

"I believe he and Yves went to the barn to check the new horse . . ."

Panic made Sara's blood race as she scurried through the entrance hall. She grabbed her tattersall wool shawl from the coat tree, threw it over her shoulders, and went outside into the early morning sunshine. The snow left by the storm was already melting, and the emotional numbness that had encapsulated Sara since returning home was melting, too, in the heat of fear for her loved ones. What if the search for the seventh man led to her doorstep? Johnny's presence could bring disaster down on them all!

She met Johnny and Yves leaving the carriage house. Johnny, chameleonlike, was again dressed in rough togs and a heavy jacket, appearing a simple laborer to the casual eye. But she knew better now and could see past the rugged features and tawny masculinity to the calculating intellect and villainous character. The priest was tucking a small Bible into his frock coat pocket, and Sara's instincts sharpened. What was Johnny up to now?

"It's quite a puzzle, laddie," Yves was saying. "I've always enjoyed deciphering Biblical passages, though. I'll put my thinking cap on for you." Yves noticed her then. "Sara, *cherie,* are you recovered?" he asked, his elfin features creasing with delight.

"Yes." Her voice was tight. "Johnny, I'd like a word with you."

Johnny nodded, his expression placid. "Sure, Miss Sara."

The cold breeze ruffled Yves' cockscomb of red hair, and he shivered. "I believe I'll see if Lizzie has something to warm these old bones. I'll give this some thought, my boy," he said, patting his pocket. He walked toward the kitchen, humming something gay and French under his breath.

Sara edged around the carriage house door, waiting until Yves was out of earshot. "What do you think you're doing?" she demanded of Johnny.

His eyelids drooped, hooding his gaze, and the corner of his mouth twisted in a mocking way that infuriated her. "You must be feeling better if you've come to sharpen your tongue on me," he observed.

"How can you make jokes?" She cast a furtive glance behind her and continued in a lower voice. "They're looking for the Clay County bank robbers—including the seventh man, on a dappled horse. That's you! You've made me an accomplice to robbery and murder by buying my silence at the price of my family's safety," she cried bitterly. "And now you're trying to make Yves a party to your wicked schemes, too. I won't have it! That I'm involved is bad enough, but I won't let you make any more of my people a part of this!"

His face grew hard. "It's too late for you to make conditions," he said harshly. "You made me a part of your damned menagerie of freaks. Now you'll just have to accept the consequences."

"Freaks!" His words shocked her, and she went livid with anger. "How dare you use such a vulgar word! We took you in, protected you—if I had only known!"

"That's the chance you took. But it was worth any cost to surround yourself with all these helpless, grateful souls, wasn't it, Sara? You feed on their gratitude like a vampire."

She gasped, stricken. "That's not true."

He took a step toward her. "Isn't it?"

"No!"

"You've gathered all the freaks together so Saint Sara can minister to them. You pour yourself out for them because they take but never make any demands emotionally. You're afraid to really experience life on your own, without the insulation of all your damned good works."

"Stop it! That's not true." Her face was white.

"Oh, it's true. But you miscalculated with me, didn't you? I'm not grateful for what you did. I never asked for it. And you don't know how to deal with that, or with me." He grabbed her shoulders and glared down into her pale, pinched face. "Admit it, Sara. You've substituted those poor, strange people for what's missing in your life."

"Nothing's missing," she denied hotly.

"No?" His voice went silky. "How about this?"

His mouth covered hers in a ravenous, devouring kiss. His tongue plunged through the frail barrier of her lips, taking her breath. He explored and stroked rapaciously, and a heavy ache built deep in her womb. Thunderous sensation made her blind and deaf and so weak she trembled like a leaf in the wind, buffeted by emotional gales she had no hope of withstanding. At last he pulled away, and they were both breathing hard. Sara tried to focus, to will away the spiraling dizziness.

"Dammit, don't you get it?" he rasped, his voice as rough as crushed glass. "Desire, passion, lust—I don't care what you call it. Between us, it's raw and it's honest, and, by God, it's *real*, not some lukewarm pap! But you're terrified of anything that strong. You want it thinned with gratitude. A man who's expected to feel *grateful* is no threat to that ivory tower of yours—but don't lie to yourself and say nothing's missing."

Her eyes glittered copper-bright with humiliation and unshed tears. "I hate you," she said, her voice uneven. "How could I have forgotten that for even a moment?"

His lips pulled back in a grimace that was not a smile. "You only hate the way I make you feel."

She slapped him then, putting all her rage and strength into the blow. Her palm stung like fire, and the imprint of her hand bloomed pink across his cheek. "I loathe you! God help me!"

He touched his cheek with a look of surprise, then began to chuckle, a harsh, dry sound that was chilling for its lack of humor. "You know, Sara, I'm beginning to think you're right." Still chuckling, he turned away. "But you'd better hope I find what I'm looking for before the law finds me—for all our sakes."

"Johnny!" His name seemed wrung from her. He paused at the door but didn't turn around. Her question was a tortured whisper. "What *are* you looking for?"

He shook his head, and the thick, tawny curls at his nape tumbled over the collar of his jacket. His tone, muffled by the broad curve of his shoulders, held elements of bitterness and self-mockery. "Would you believe me if I said my salvation?"

Mystified, she shook her head. "No."

"I suppose not." He swung around to stare at her, his eyes pale and blazing. "Call it revenge, then. That you can understand."

"I only want to understand that you're leaving and that my family is safe again," she cried wretchedly.

He released a long breath, and the muscle in his jaw worked. "Soon, Sara. I promise."

She felt like crying then, but she wouldn't give him the satisfaction. What were promises worth from a man like him? He saw the skepticism in her face, acknowledged it with a rueful shrug, then left her alone.

Sara pressed trembling fingers to her cold cheeks. How cruelly his words cut! She felt lacerated, pierced through, torn by pain in each vital organ. Perhaps Johnny's brutal assessment of her character was right. Her early rearing under Uncle Quentin's abusive hand could be blamed for part of it, but what about her failures with Will? Failures of intimacy, failures to conceive the child they'd both wanted, failures that had eventually driven him from her bed altogether. Maybe she had substituted service to others for what was lacking in her life, but it was because all she'd ever wanted was to love and be loved.

Her breath caught on a sob. Until Johnny had come into her life, she'd been content. Now that contentment was shattered beyond repair by his callous words, his unfeeling arrogance, his masterful kisses, and those distant, tantalizing flashes of pain and vulnerability that drew her to him even while everything he did drove her away.

But there was something she could do about it. She knuckled the moisture from her eyes, and her mouth firmed. Her foolish compassion for the wrong man now tied her and Johnny in a sham of a marriage. That, at least, she could change. Will had dealt with a St. Louis attorney who could be trusted to treat an annulment with discretion. The letter would go off today. It wasn't much, but at least that action would symbolize her resolve to free herself from Johnny once and for all. And if worse came to worse, and the authorities learned of her complicity, that action alone might prove her innocence.

"Well, Father Yves? Might there be a story in these markings?" Johnny asked. He tapped the cover of the small black Bible.

"Oh, aye," the man agreed. He sat at the simple table that served as both desk and altar in his austere bedroom. Afternoon sunlight slanted through the windowpanes, highlighting a polished crucifix set on the wall above the desk and the silver chain of a worn ebony rosary that Yves worried with his bony fingers. "There might, indeed."

Johnny struggled to contain his impatience. Seeking the help of the only Biblical scholar he knew was a tricky thing, but the best alternative he could think of, considering the short time left to him in the wake of the Clay County holdup. Jesse had given orders for the scattered band to regroup at Excelsior Springs in a week's time. There, they'd divide the profits and decide what to do with the remaining gold before continuing the search for Quantrill's lost cache.

Jesse counted on old loyalties and the natural reticence of the country people to keep any information of the band's whereabouts from the authorities, but Johnny knew a posse

of mounted deputies had left this very morning from the
Lexington Court House to join the hunt. There was no
doubt that similar groups from other towns had followed
suit, making a confrontation only a matter of time. Johnny
knew he'd have to locate the Golden Calf before then, or
else show up at the appointed time and place to keep his
cover intact with the James and Younger brothers.

Something had changed in Jesse since the war. He'd
always been deadly, but now that deadliness was unfocused, striking without plan or emotion on innocent citizens. And Johnny had no intention of getting involved
with that murderous boy again. His jaw set in grim determination. Once was quite enough.

Johnny felt Yves' gray eyes studying him. The little man
sighed, then rose and went to the narrow cot that lined
one wall. He reached under the corner of the mattress and
pulled out a flask of amber liquid.

Johnny frowned. "Where'd you get that?"

"I've gotten to be great friends with Eustace over at the
Brass Bull," Yves replied. "He's a solitary lad, but we
talk." He poured two fingers' worth in the bottom of a
tooth glass he took from the washstand and handed it to
Johnny.

"Drink up, my boy," he said, then tipped the bottle to
his own lips and sipped the fiery whiskey as though it were
nectar.

Johnny swirled the liquor in the bottom of the glass. So
that's how Yves got his whiskey. Sara would be hurt to
know it. He grimaced at the turn of his thoughts. Always
back to her! "What shall we drink to?" he asked harshly.

Yves sank down on the edge of the cot and wiped his
watering eyes. His smile was sad. "Why, to impostors, of
course. You and me. Two of the sorriest creatures ever to
take advantage of a kind lady's heart."

"Yeah. I guess I can drink to that." Johnny swallowed
the rotgut. "When did you guess?"

"That you've regained your past?" Yves shrugged.
"Not long ago. Ah, but that you were running away from
something—that I knew from the moment I laid eyes on
you, lad. As one lost soul to another." He lifted the bottle

in mock salute, but Johnny caught it and wrested it from Yves' grasp before he could drink again.

"Enough." He corked the bottle and set it down on the desk, ignoring Yves' reproachful look. "Why do you drink that stuff anyway? You know what it does to you."

Yves gray eyes were tortured. "I'd rather be known as a drunkard than a lunatic," he muttered.

"It's the whiskey that brings on those visions of yours, man," Johnny said irritably.

"Nay, laddie. The lady that haunts me is as real as you are. She beckons to me with a bleeding heart in her hand—my heart." Yves shuddered and passed a hand over his eyes. "It's terrified I am of her. Tell me, do you think I'm a madman?"

"No, Father," Johnny said, his mouth twisting wryly. "You're probably one of the few sane men I know." He clapped Yves on the shoulder. "Just stay away from the booze. It's bad dreams, that's all, and we all have those."

"Aye, that we do." A mocking light made Yves' gray irises nearly transparent. "So what is it you want, now that we're agreed I'm no madman and you're no wastrel?"

Johnny's jaw grew taut. "Never mind what you know or think you know. Things are—difficult with Sara. She wants me to leave, but I can't until I find what I'm after. It's here, somewhere in the area, from all I can guess. And the key—the map—is locked in those Scriptures. Did any of it make sense to you?"

"Maybe." Yves sat back and crossed his arms in a stubborn gesture. "And maybe I'll give you the benefit of my expertise—if you let me help."

"It's none of your concern," Johnny snapped.

"You know what drives a man to drink?" Yves asked abruptly. "It's looking into the mirror and hating what you see."

This brought Johnny up short. "Yeah."

"I failed a man who called me friend. My cowardice cost his life. It cost me my faith. Now you know why the she-demon is after me—to make me pay for my sins."

"I'm sorry." Johnny found that he meant it.

"Tell me what you're looking for."

Johnny searched the older man's face, reading the immovability in it. Hell, he thought, what's the difference? "I told Sara it was my salvation, but it might just as easily be my damnation. Unfinished business from the war, one last duty. It's a graven image, my own devil-god. Gold, Yves, a treasure in gold known as the Golden Calf. And believe it or not, I want to return it to the rightful owners, to keep more men from dying. Now, can you help me?"

"A worthy cause, and a chance to prove myself again," Yves murmured. "Your salvation could be mine as well, my son. We join the search together. Agreed?"

Slowly Johnny nodded. "Agreed. What can you tell me?"

Yves took the Bible from the desk and flipped through it, his face ruddy with his success and building excitement. "It's simple, really. I'm surprised you haven't figured it out yourself, but perhaps it's because you're not familiar with the landmarks hereabouts, and I've made a study of them. . . ."

"Yves! What?" Johnny demanded. Exasperation made him run both hands through his thick hair.

"A number of the marked passages bear a similar theme," Yves said. He flipped through the book. "Listen: *. . . did eat manna in the desert . . . hid them by fifty in a cave and fed them with bread and water . . . true bread from heaven . . . And this one especially, Stolen waters are sweet, and bread eaten in secret is pleasant . . .*"

"I don't get it. Bread?"

"And sweetness." Yves' eyes lit up. "You see? Bread. Manna. Loaves and fishes. And sweet. Honey and—"

Johnny snapped his fingers. "Sugar! By God, that's got to be it. Will Cary's masterpiece—the Sugarloaf!" He began to laugh.

"It must be the place to start. There are other things, too. Water repeated over and over, and references to gold, and cedar trees, and caves."

"Caves?" *Oh, Jesus! Not that!* Something scaly and terrifying set its icy claws into Johnny's spine. He forced down a shudder. He'd allow no weakness, not this close to success. He concentrated on Yves' voice.

"The Sugarloaf is riddled with caves. Which one is the right one? It might take some time," Yves warned.

Johnny cursed softly. "I haven't got any more time."

"I've been there, but I'm not familiar with the area, like—"

"Sara is," Johnny said abruptly. "She told me once that she and the family explored those caves quite often."

"Now wait a minute," Yves protested. "You can't expect her to—"

Johnny laughed, a bitter sound that echoed in the room. The memory of the cruel things he'd said to her that morning flitted through his mind like evil specters. What a perverse bastard he was, to torment her for the very qualities he admired, all because he wanted her and knew he couldn't have her. "Don't fret, Father Yves," he said. "She'll help. She'll do anything to be rid of me."

It was the last thing she expected, Sara thought, to be leading Johnny on a spelunking expedition through the Sugarloaf in search of God knew what. But then, she'd do anything to be rid of him. It was a thought she clung to.

"Where do we go in?" Johnny asked.

They stood on the bank of the Little Sni Creek, the scene of countless summer picnics. Now the branches of the shrubs hugging the banks were bare and lifeless. Spring would bring lush grass and shade and wildflowers, but that was yet to come. Now crushed bracken and dead leaves littered the rocky ground.

"There are several openings," Sara muttered. She shifted from side to side in her heavy walking shoes, glad that she'd chosen her heaviest wool petticoats. The February chill was sharp in the shadow of the hill, and she knew from experience that the caves would be colder still. "Does it matter?"

"Would there be an entrance near a cedar tree?" Yves asked.

Sara cast him a sharp glance, still unsure what his role was. It appeared her protests to Johnny to keep Yves out of this business had been fruitless, yet she wasn't certain what Yves knew. She wasn't going to be the one to tell him, either. But how did he know abut the cedar grove? "There is a way in close to some cedars," she said.

"Good. Let's go," Johnny said. He picked up the lanterns and a sack of candles they'd brought. His expression was unreadable, but there was a sense of leashed excitement in his movements. Did he really think he'd find what he was looking for here? Sara couldn't believe it.

"This way," she said, picking up her skirts and beginning to climb.

The going wasn't hard, but the stunted grove of cedars was on the western side of the abutment and halfway up. They paused for breath when they reached the group of shaggy evergreens. Johnny looked for any sign of an opening into the rockface.

"Are you sure this is it?" he asked skeptically.

Sara didn't answer. She moved to the largest, oldest tree, whose branches draped to the ground like a lady's skirts. Pushing aside one of the lowest limbs, she revealed the dark maw of a tunnel no bigger than a bushel basket.

"That's it?" Johnny asked, dismay in his voice.

"It doesn't stay that small for long," Sara explained. "About eight feet in it begins to widen, and then you can stand up."

"Jesus!" Johnny muttered.

"Perhaps this isn't the opening we want," Yves said hesitantly. "There are also some references to water . . ."

"It's the only one I know near cedar trees," Sara replied. "And there's a stream that follows the corridor to a small pool farther along the way."

"It's got to be the right one." Johnny's face was pale and tense. He squatted and lit both lanterns, then handed one to Yves. "Ready?"

"Wait." She pulled a ball of twine from her skirt pocket and tied the end to the cedar tree. "You can't be too careful. The farther you go, the more everything begins to look alike. It's easy to get turned around."

"Sensible idea," Yves praised. He glanced at the hole, and his features twitched like a rabbit's.

Sara looked at Johnny, then Yves, both hesitating. "Oh, for goodness sake. Give me that," she said, snatching the lantern from Yves. "What a bunch of babies. This was your idea, so let's get it over with. I'll lead. Just watch where you step; it's probably damp, and we may rouse a critter or two."

"Cr—critters?" Yves faltered.

Sara cast an impish smile back over her shoulder, amused in spite of herself. Imagine—both of them afraid of a little walk in the dark. She couldn't resist a bit of fun at their expense. She made her tone unconcerned. "Probably just a bear or two. Or maybe a bobcat. Stay close."

Hitching up her skirts, she ducked into the opening, scrambling forward on all fours, agile as a cat. The lantern illuminated the uneven rock wall with its variegated stripes of minerals and sparkled on the moisture seeping across the floor. She ignored the faint brush of cobwebs and pushed forward, letting the ball of string unravel between her fingers. It was colder here, and the stone seemed to suck the heat from her bones. The tunnel broadened, and she was able to stand upright. She lifted the lantern to illuminate the rest of the corridor. From a distance, she heard the trickle of water over stone. It had been a long time since she and Will and Pandora had explored here, but nothing had changed.

A scrabbling sound alerted her, then Yves crawled into view. He rose and began dusting off his coat with nervous movements, his eyes flashing the whites as he tried to see in all directions at once. The second lantern appeared, and Johnny joined them, pushing his bulk through the narrow opening with some difficulty. His breath rasped with exertion when he finally stood next to them.

"The pool's not far," Sara announced. Her voice echoed back and forth. "Let's go."

She took confident strides, smiling to herself at the disconcerted looks the two men gave each other. They walked for a while, Sara cheerfully pointing out formations she recognized. She explained that this was not what Will had called a "living" cave, with such wonders as stalactites and stalagmites, but rather a series of crevices and tunnels. When she grew tired of this travelogue, she began to sing, marching onward while snatches of "Amazing Grace" and "A Mighty Fortress" echoed back in a resounding chorus to remind her companions exactly how deep under the surface of God's green earth they were.

The corridor was uneven, littered with rocks and loose gravel, and it made countless twists and turns. Occasionally, side shafts joined the main corridor, but she ignored them, leading the group closer and closer to the sound of dripping water.

"A moment, lass," Yves said at last, gasping. "I need to catch my breath."

"Of course. I'm sorry." Sara came up short, her physician's ears attuned to the difficulty of Yves' breathing. "Are you all right?"

"Just a bit—winded," Yves said.

"Maybe you should go back," Sara suggested, studying his pinched features in the wavering light.

"Aye, I believe you're right," he agreed, puffing. "Perhaps I can just wait for you here?"

"You go back," Johnny said abruptly. He paced restlessly, trailing his fingers across the rough rock wall. "We're going on."

"But . . ." Sara began. He caught her arm, and she gasped.

"I said we're going on!"

Sara stared at him. Sweat poured from his brow, even though the air was chilly, and his skin was pasty. But his mouth was determined. She shrugged and passed Yves the lantern she held. "All right, Yves?"

"Certainly, lass. I'll just follow your guide string."

"Let's go." The pressure of Johnny's hand urged her forward. She cast a final glance back at Yves.

"It won't take long, Yves," she assured him. They went around another turn in the corridor and lost sight of Yves. Sara pulled free of Johnny's grip and cast him an irritated look. "You know, it would help if I knew what you're looking for."

"Gold."

She jerked, startled, then laughed. The sound echoed hollowly. "There's no gold here! A little coal, maybe . . ."

"A fortune in coal, unless I miss my guess. There are seams of it, high quality stuff, all through here." He was talking fast, frowning in concentration, as though he was fighting to hold some nebulous threat at bay by sheer force of will. "You could be a very wealthy woman if you developed it."

"I don't know anything about coal mining," she

scoffed, scrambling over a small pile of loose rocks and taking another turn. The tunnel narrowed, became little more than an alley, and closed in overhead.

Johnny kept near her, his breathing rapid, his words jerky and disjointed. "I do. I studied mineralogy. Made my father mad as hell. He wanted me to push numbers around a ledger like him. It might take shaft mining, but the technology is being used back East. Anybody tries to buy this from you, you be sure to get a fair price. That's professional advice, Sara." He chuckled to himself, and the sound raised the hairs on the back of her neck.

The passageway opened abruptly into a larger area with a sloping floor and a distant ceiling. Sara stopped at the entrance. "This is it."

Johnny raised the lantern, and light sparkled on an uneven basin of murky water. A thin trickle of moisture ran down the opposite wall, feeding the pool.

"God damn it," he said in a low, strangled voice. "Why isn't anything ever easy?"

"What's wrong?" she asked. He didn't answer, his gaze locked on the darkness overhead. Sweat dripped from soaked curls clinging to his temples and forehead, and his expression reflected a tremendous inner struggle. His chest heaved, and his breath hissed painfully through clenched teeth.

Abruptly, she felt his claustrophobic terror, sensed with him the weight of the rock surrounding them, pressing down, down. Some people could not endure closed-in places, but it had never occurred to her that someone as strong-willed as Johnny could suffer such fears.

He swayed and staggered, stumbling backwards on the loose gravel. With a cry, she reached for him, but it was too late. The lantern flew from his grasp, shattering against the rock floor. It flared for one bright instant, then all was dark.

Chapter 10

Buried alive.

The darkness pressed down on him like a suffocating hand, choking the life from him. In that moment he would have welcomed death as a merciful relief, but it did not come. Blood thundered in his ears, and he knew he cried out his terror, but he couldn't hear his own voice. He had to get out, to find the air and light again. But which way? Oh, God, which way!

He moved blindly, stumbling, falling, clawing at the walls like an animal, his panic crowding out everything else from his mind. He had no identity, no purpose other than escape, and, as the blackness surrounded him, he knew with a certainty there was none.

Something, some demon of the dark, touched him, and he fought it off, lurching and shoving. Words floated through his head, but he couldn't get the gist of them.

"Johnny, stop! Don't move! Johnny! Listen to me!"

The urgent tone and dulcet syllables made him hesitate, and the demon was upon him, soft and warm and sweetly fragrant of roses. So sweet . . .

"Sara." He couldn't catch his breath, and the name was nearly a sob.

"Yes, it's me. Hold onto me, Johnny," she said. Her hands moved over him, touched his face, pulled his cheek against her own.

Gratefully, as though she were a lifeline, he wrapped himself around her, and they sank down together on the cold and rocky floor. He could close his eyes now, and he pressed his nose into the warm and fragrant hollow of her neck, breathing in her scent, focusing on the softness of her skin, the delicious floral bouquet of her hair.

"It's all right, Johnny," she murmured, stroking his face. "Hold on."

He shuddered uncontrollably, mumbling between harsh gasps. "It's worse than a prison cell. We were almost through, had dug until our nails bled, and then the tunnel collapsed. Dirt in my nose, my mouth—I couldn't breathe! I knew I was dead, but they dragged me out, and we escaped anyway."

"That's all over. Nothing is going to happen to us. We're safe." She searched his pockets, patting him all over until she found the candles and matches she'd known he carried, but in his irrational panic had forgotten. It was clumsy work in the dark, with the weight of Johnny's arms around her, but finally she managed to strike a match. She lit one candle and another before the match spluttered out, then set them on a rock ledge. Her hands cradled his cheeks, gently urging him to look at her.

"I lit the candles, Johnny. We can find our way back outside," she promised.

His eyelids fluttered. His eyes seemed pale and colorless in the frail light, as if fear had bleached them. Focusing on her face, he let the delicate oval fill his vision and spurn the creeping blackness. Her fingers touched the vibrant curls over his forehead, traced the curves of his ear, trailed along his jawbone, reassuring him with the warmth of human contact. He took a deep breath, exhaled, then covered one of her hands with his own and pressed a beholden kiss into her palm.

"Let's go now," she said softly.

He swallowed. There was nothing he wanted more. But he would not succumb to an irrational fear when success was nearly in his grasp. "No. I haven't found the Calf yet."

"For God's sake, Johnny," she cried. "Enough is enough! You can't—"

"I will." He gritted his teeth, controlling himself by willpower alone, though his face was still blanched. His mouth was a pinched, stubborn line. "I must."

Was he being courageous or merely foolhardy? Sara

couldn't be sure. His bullheadedness made her furious.
"You—you stubborn *mule!*" She struggled to her feet.
"You do what you want, then. I'm going back."

"Sara." He rose, swaying drunkenly, his limbs unnaturally shaky, sapped physically by the ordeal. His voice
was low. "Doc, I need you."

Her lower lip trembled. She bit it, hard, and stared over
his shoulder in mute resistance. Damn him! He knew she
could scarcely resist an appeal like that.

"Please," he said.

She took a deep breath and frowned fiercely. Her gaze
snagged on an incongruous irregularity on the cavern wall.
"What—what's that?" she asked, pointing behind him.

Johnny turned, scouring the rockface in the tricky light.
A piece of thin rope, or cord, dusty and discolored, dangled from the sloping wall slightly above eye level, held
in place by a scrabble of loose rocks. He touched it, certain it held some significance. His fingers dislodged a film
of dirt, revealing the bright gold of regimental cords, a
Confederate colonel's insignia of rank.

"Quantrill!" he exclaimed.

Johnny grabbed the cord and pulled it free, sending a
shower of loose rock to the floor. Dust rose everywhere,
and Sara coughed. He dislodged more rock, uncovering a
small indentation in the face of the wall. His fingers
touched something smooth, and he redoubled his efforts,
scraping with his nails, heedless of the damage the
sharp, flinty shards inflicted. Grunting, he pulled at the
heavy, oilskin-wrapped bundle, finally freeing it from its
resting place and dropping it with a thud onto the floor.
He glanced at Sara, his face limned with rock dust and
animated with feverish excitement. "This is it, Sara!"

"But what is it?" she murmured, perplexed.

He ripped the wrapping, uncovering a duo of worn
leather saddlebags. "The Golden Calf. Quantrill's treasure. By God, Yves was right!" He fumbled with the reluctant buckle of one bag, opened it, dragged forth a small
canvas drawstring bag that bore the lettering, "U.S.
Mint." Tugging the string, he spilled the glittering contents into his grimy palm. Bright, brand-new coins, small

but perfect ten and twenty-dollar pieces, jingled in his hand. "Look at it, Sara!"

"Blood money." She picked up one of the candles, her shadowy face stiff with contempt and disappointment. The gold symbolized everything she hated in that part of Johnny he called Tuck, and when she looked at it, she saw only the bright glimmer of pain, crushed hopes, and shattered dreams. Her voice was bitter. "Congratulations. I hope it makes you very happy. Can we go now?"

She didn't wait for him to answer, but swung away, bending to pick up her ball of string, winding it around her hand and walking toward the slit of an entrance.

Johnny stared after her, stung in spite of himself. It wasn't hard to imagine what she was thinking, and, surprisingly, her condemnation hurt. He was abruptly conscious again of the walls closing in on him. Jesus, he hated this place! He'd gotten what he came for, and now all that mattered was getting the hell out. Hefting the heavy saddlebags, he grabbed the other candle and hastily followed her.

They backtracked in silence, each deep in his own thoughts. Johnny's elation at finally having possession of the Golden Calf was tempered by a steady throb of regret. The United States government would be grateful for his completion of his final orders, but that couldn't erase the fact that he'd used Sara Cary unmercifully in order to carry them out. She deserved better. She deserved . . . an explanation.

He nearly laughed. What could he say? "How do you do? I'm Major McCulloch. I couldn't tell you the truth because I didn't know who to trust and I'm too much of a loner to change. Sorry I deceived you, but I'm just that kind of bastard." Hell, she'd just abandon one set of reasons to hate his guts for another! The prospect was sobering.

Sara had always been able to see through him, down to his core. Maybe she couldn't unravel the tangled web of lies that surrounded him, but on an instinctive, emotional level, she knew him. It wasn't like him to show his vulnerable underbelly, but somehow she'd managed to touch a needy spot down deep in his soul. He might revile her for her kindnesses and compassion, but he was hypocrite enough to lap up everything she gave him just the same. And for the first time in a long while, he was willing to admit he cared what another person thought of him. Sara had always been honest with him. The least he could do was return the favor. Maybe she wouldn't accept it, but he had to tell her the truth before he left her life forever.

They reached the final stretch of the tunnel. To his relief, he could see a faint shimmer of daylight down the narrow mouth. Sara glanced back at him.

"You may go ahead if you need to," she offered.

Again, he was struck by her innate kindness. "Sara, I—"

"No, don't," she said, shaking her head. "I don't want to hear anything you've got to say. I just want to see you go, now that you've gotten what you wanted."

He shifted the heavy bags. "We have to talk."

"Are you going or shall I?" she demanded, her voice high with tension.

He could see it wasn't going to be easy to say what he had to say. But he wasn't going to give up that easily. She'd listen, even if he had to drag her to the nearest federal garrison to watch him hand in the Calf and reclaim his commission. "You go ahead."

Sara grabbed her skirts and ducked down, scrambling forward out of the hole. Determinedly, Johnny gritted his teeth. This narrow squeeze was the worst part of all, so closely resembling the escape tunnel he and his fellow officers had dug to escape that hellhole of a Confederate prison. One last hurdle. He concentrated, going down on his knees and pushing the weighty bags ahead of him. The pale circle of light at the end beckoned him, and he saw Sara's hems disappear through the opening. Inch by inch, he moved closer to the freedom of the light and air, his brow damp with sweat, his heart hammering against his ribs.

He scrambled into the open, pushing through the scratchy, pungent fronds of cedar, his lungs expanding in a grateful breath—that clogged in his throat.

"Well done, Tuck. Well done," Jesse James said. His

pale, reptilian gaze swept over Johnny. "You've done a great thing for our cause. It is our cause, ain't it?"

Johnny blew out his lungful of air, scanning the scene. Yves sat in a heap, his hands bound behind him, Cole Younger's blunt fist clamped on his shoulder. Jim Younger negligently pointed his pistol at the helpless priest. Frank James held Sara, one filthy hand pressed over her mouth. Her velvet brown eyes were wide with fear in the fading light. Cursing inwardly, Johnny knew the only way to win now was to continue to play the game. He threw the saddlebags at Jesse's feet.

"I swore it, didn't I?" he returned arrogantly. His steely gaze pinned Frank. "Get your hands off my woman."

Frank swallowed and removed his hands in haste. Johnny reached for Sara and drew her to him. He gave her a look that silently asked if she were all right. For answer, she dropped her forehead against his shoulder, quivering like a frightened dove. "Cut him loose, too," Johnny ordered, pointing toward Yves. "You boys did some fine detecting to be just one step behind me, and I had the good father, there, to read the Scriptures. How'd you do it?"

"Jesse sent a few of the passages to Moses," Cole said with a wide grin. "Shoulda done it months ago. The message he sent back made a few suggestions. Led us up here. Kind of you to leave a guide for us, too, Tuck." He drew a large hunting knife from his belt and began sawing on the rawhide thongs binding Yves.

"That wasn't real smart, Jesse," Johnny said, frowning. "Now Moses will want the Calf."

"What he wants ain't necessarily what he gits," Jesse drawled. "Things stand as before."

"Moses will come after you," Johnny warned.

"Hell, him and two-thirds of the damned countryside." Cole laughed. "So what else is new?"

"You're on the run? What about Excelsior Springs?"

"Too populated with lawmen to suit my health," was Jesse's laconic reply. "Never seen so many deputies so fired up over an accidental killing. Think it might be smart to make ourselves scarce until this blows over, eh, boys?"

"They've kept our tongues hanging, that's fer sure," Frank interjected.

"Yeah, we come looking for a place to rest up a few days, lay in supplies, and make plans. Cole's got some ideas." Jesse walked closer and smiled at Sara. "Figured Mrs. Cary might put us up a spell."

Her head jerked up, and she gasped in dismay. "What? No, I can't! You—"

"Shut up, Sara," Johnny ordered. His mind raced. Damnation! He'd been so close to pulling it off! Now, somehow, he had to get the Calf away from Jesse and manage to keep his own hide intact. Buying some time here before they headed for Mexico might give him a chance to figure some way out of this new mess. He formed his mouth into a welcoming smile and squeezed Sara's hand to ensure her compliance. "I think these fellows would enjoy a taste of Lizzie's cooking."

"Moonbeams and marmalade, Sara Jane!" Pandora exclaimed. "Whatever were you thinking of? I'd wager my last hairpin those men are up to no good."

"They were hungry," Sara said stonily, hating herself for lying to Pandora. She dipped the last of Lizzie's stew into a serving bowl. A raucous laugh from the dining room made her flinch. "And homeless. What else could I do? The mission is full, so I promised them a meal and a place in the barn to bed down for the night. They'll be gone in the morning, I promise."

Pandora's face pursed in disapproval. "Well, I think you've made a serious error in judgment, bringing them here. Have you seen the way that red-headed one looks at Lizzie?"

Sara frowned, and her lips tightened. Yes, she'd seen Cole's lecherous gaze on Lizzie, as well as Lizzie's nervousness. This group must seem very much like the men who'd attacked her. "I've sent her with Ambrose to the mission," she muttered to Pandora. "Clem, too. I told them to stay the night."

"So you do have some sense. My lands, my heart's pounding like a drum. This is just too much for me. I'm going to take my sleeping drops and go to bed. You make Johnny and Yves deal with those ruffians, do you hear?''

"Yes, Dorie.'' Pandora disappeared up the back stairs, and Sara carried the bowl into the dining room, her face set. It seemed almost obscene to have this murderous group sprawled in gluttonous contentment over Pandora's elegant furniture. Greasy plates and empty glasses, broken bits of bread and dribbles of gravy, gave mute evidence to the recent repast. Yves and Johnny sat with her other "guests," but she could not meet their eyes. "There's more stew," she offered.

"None for me, ma'am," Cole said, grinning and patting his flat stomach. "But I'd like to tell that pretty little gal what I think of her fine cooking'.''

"I'll tell her. She's gone on an errand.''

Jesse grabbed Sara's wrist. She bobbled the bowl of hot stew, and it hit the table with a clatter.

"What kind of errand?" he asked. There was a threatening light in his blue eyes.

Sara glared at him, her mouth tight. "Things to take to the mission, that's all.''

"You sure?''

Johnny's deep voice interrupted before Sara could make a reply. "She's sure, aren't you, honey?'' He sat with indolent ease beside Jesse, but there was a thread of steel in his tone. Jesse released Sara's wrist.

She jerked her hand back and rubbed the red marks, staring at Johnny for a long moment before nodding. "Yes.'' Johnny jerked his chin toward the door, giving a silent command. Her mouth cinched stubbornly. "I'd like to clear the table now, please.''

"Say, Tuck," Jim Younger said. "You got anything to wet a fellow's whistle around here? I think we got cause to celebrate tonight.''

Johnny lifted his sandy eyebrows at Sara. Reluctantly, she went to the breakfront and removed a bottle of Pandora's favored port wine and a decanter of brandy. She set them on the table, and her voice was flat. "I'll thank you to do your drinking in the barn.''

"Suits me," Jim said with a cocky smile. There was a general scraping back of chairs. Cole picked up the bottles, and Jim flung an arm around Yves in a companionable fashion. "Come on, *padre*. Have a drink with us to show there ain't any hard feelings."

Yves, much subdued by the events of the afternoon, shot Sara a quick, sheepish glance and hastened after Jesse and Frank. Discouraged and resentful, Sara cleared the dirty dishes, trying to ignore Johnny's eyes on her. Her thoughts tumbled like a squirrel in a cage. She hated him and all he stood for, yet why was she always so conscious of him, as if they were connected on a level neither could understand?

"I wanted to thank you," he said at last.

Her head snapped up, and silverware clattered against a plate. "For what?"

"For what you did for me in the cave."

"Oh." She swallowed and reached for another plate. He laid a hand on her shoulder.

"Sara, I wish I could make you understand . . ."

"Don't touch me!" She whirled away from him, her face working. "Don't ever touch me again. Nothing you can say will ever make up for what you've done."

A knot of frustration and guilt swelled in Johnny's chest. She was so small and defiant and desirable—and beyond his reach, like a dream. She was right. Nothing he could ever say or do would make up for the things he'd put her through. He'd taken advantage of her innocence and her compassion, and it was too late for explanations and excuses. A brooding sense of defeat clouded his mind and showed in the shadows crossing his face.

"Whatever you say," he muttered. He shoved his hands into his trouser pockets and moved toward the door.

"I want them out—before I wake in the morning. Is that clear?" she demanded. "If the law finds them here, with your blood money, then we'll all go to jail. Make sure they're gone—and you with them, or . . ." Breaking off, she stacked plates with a vengeance that threatened to shatter the Blue Willow patterned china.

He frowned at her implied threat. "Or what?"

She lifted her chin in defiance, but the copper glint of trepidation in her eyes hinted of false bravado. "Or I'll go to the law myself."

"You won't need to. I'll see to it." His face was grim with determination. At least he could spare her that indignity. It was just a matter of convincing Jesse that a new plan of action was in order. He stared at her, and his gut twisted at the skepticism on her lovely, strained features. He wished he could take her in his arms and kiss away that hurt look, but he knew it was impossible.

"Good night, Sara," he said quietly.

He picked up his jacket in the foyer and let himself out of the house. Crossing the backyard, he paused to breathe in the cool night air and gaze up at the star-riddled heavens. There was no tranquility there for him. He knew that his quest was even more dangerous than before. That danger must not extend to Sara.

He paused, staring at the windows of the house, watching the flicker of movement behind the curtains. One by one, she extinguished the lamps, plunging the lower floor into darkness. The glow reappeared upstairs behind the drapes of her corner room. His chest felt suddenly tight with regret and longing. Sadly, he turned away.

The carriage house was warm with the body heat of horses and men. Frank, Cole, Jesse, and Jim sat around in earnest argument, sprawling on piles of hay, leaning on saddles, propping against empty wooden boxes. A flickering coal oil lamp hung from a cross brace, casting eerie shadows on their young-old faces. They passed the decanter of brandy back and forth between them. Yves sat in a morose heap a little way apart, nursing his private flask of whiskey. Johnny approached the circle, snagged the bottle, and let a trickle of brandy burn down his throat. He wiped his mouth on the back of his hand and handed the bottle to Jim.

"I say it's the only way," Cole said. "The others want their split. When I was down in Texas I heard tell of this here Señor Gonzales. He'll take the gold coin we got in Liberty and trade it for greenbacks."

"Yeah, but won't he charge a discount?" Jim countered.

"So? We can't use the gold. Be like waving a red flag in front of a bull. Law would be down on us faster than a duck on a june bug."

"San Antonio is a long ride," Jesse offered mildly.

"Well, hell!" Cole snorted. "When we got there, we'd be nearly to Mexico. And that's where we're headed now that we got the Golden Calf, ain't it? We get Gonzales to discount the Liberty take, and send a share back to Clell and the rest. Then we just sashay over the border with cash in our pockets and the Calf for Maximillian."

"It suits me," Jesse said. "What about you, Tuck?"

Johnny shrugged, his face inscrutable. "I'm ready to get the hell out of this hick town. Been ready. And with the law breathing down our necks, I expect we'd better make tracks by first light."

"That's what I thought," Jesse said, and the others nodded their agreement. Although barely eighteen, Jesse maintained his leadership of his rowdy band with powerful personal charisma and the reputation he'd earned at Quantrill's side.

Cole snickered and dug an elbow into Johnny's ribs. "What's your hurry, Tuck? The new worn off of your lady friend already?"

Johnny fought back the sudden anger that clouded his vision. "Don't be an ass, Cole," he advised softly, his voice deadly.

"I don't blame you." Cole laughed. " 'Bout this time, they start getting clingy. Talking about wedding rings and babies and such. Well, never mind. Maybe you can find you a pretty dark-eyed *señorita* in San Antonio to ease your . . . er . . . mind. I know I will."

The others laughed congenially. Johnny gritted his teeth and grabbed the brandy again. The liquor burned a hot circle through his middle, but it was better than thinking. They continued to discuss the proposed journey, wrangling over details and passing the bottle until their speech was slurred and the conversation degenerated into wild war tales and overblown sexual exploits.

Johnny eventually left the circle and sat down next to Yves, his back against the wall, listening with half an ear, plotting his own moves. Surely during the ride into the wild country, there would be an opportunity to relieve this group of boasting boys of the Golden Calf. He'd see to it that there was.

"It's sorry I am, Johnny-boy," Yves muttered, his words barely understandable over the boisterous laughter and raucous jibes of the others. His eyes were red and bloodshot, and his nose was fast turning the color of a ripe cherry. "Couldn't even give you and Sara a warning they'd come. What a weak, sniveling coward I am! You can't mean to give it to them?"

"Quiet," Johnny warned under his breath. "You did your best. I'll take care of it, never fear."

"You'll be leaving with them in the morning, then?"

Johnny nodded, pressing his thumbs to his eye sockets in a gesture of weariness. He could not forestall his next words. "Take care of Sara."

Yves' head fell back against the rough plank wall, and he giggled drunkenly. "Oh, that's a royal one, that is. Me, feinting at shadows and demons. Why, I can't even take care of myself. And you've got the right to watch over Sara, more than anyone, you know."

"What do you mean?"

Yves tried to focus on Johnny's face, blinking owlishly with the effort. "She never told you, did she?"

Exasperation thinned Johnny's lips. "Told me what?"

"How she came to save you. Barely breathing, you were, and the Union soldiers set to drag your carcass off to prison."

"I know that. But she convinced them otherwise, didn't she? She couldn't resist another charity case." His mouth twisted with bitterness.

"Is that . . . You think . . . ?" Yves spluttered, straightening. He raised bony fists belligerently. "Ye *canard!* Worthless, ungrateful fool! I've a mind to thrash you myself!" He struggled to get up. Johnny placed a hand on his chest and pushed him back. Yves sprawled to his seat on the straw-strewn floor, his face crumbling.

"Stop it, Yves," Johnny ordered in a low, mystified voice. He risked a glance toward the other men, but they were engrossed in another high-flown tale and, thankfully, paying them no mind. "What are you driving at, old man?"

"Oh, aye, she convinced them—the only way she could," Yves said, blubbering. "Bartered herself for you, she did. And made me say the service over you both, spineless wretch that I am.''

Johnny tried to make sense of Yves's babbling. Had Sara—chaste, upright Sara—given herself to some lecherous soldier to buy his freedom? The thought made him nauseous. He twisted a fist in Yves' shirt front and shook him. ''God damn it, man! What are you talking about?''

Yves's drunken laugh was a bit malicious, a bit triumphant. ''Why, she married you, laddie.''

Johnny was thunderstruck. He shook his head dazedly, as though he'd been poleaxed. ''That's impossible.''

''Is it now?'' Yves' grin was foxy with relish. ''Remember it all, do you?''

''You know I don't remember a damned thing.''

''Surely you remember how she held your hand and coaxed the vows from your own lips, then said her own, knowing she'd be twice a widow when you died?''

''No.''

''She sacrificed herself to ease your death, then worked so hard she saved your life. Why do you think she's taken care of you all this time, you dunderheaded dolt? Duty— that's why!''

Johnny shook his head in denial and released Yves in disgust. ''It's not legal.''

Yves shrugged. ''As an ordained minister of the cloth, I say the marriage was sanctified in the eyes of God. And the Provost Marshal himself accepted it. Gave your wife custody, made her responsible in your incapacity. Saved you, she did, or else you'd be food for worms this very minute.''

''And she kept it a secret all this time,'' Johnny muttered.

A deep, soul-searing rage began to burn in him. Irrationally, he felt a sense of betrayal. He'd thought her honest and innocent, but she'd kept just as many secrets as he did, pawning him off with words about gratitude and honor and duty. The bitch! What right had she to moralize to him when she'd trussed him and laced him up like a bird on a spit? Married! After Gwendolyn's betrayal he'd sworn never to fall into that trap again, but look at him now!

A low, feral growl erupted from his throat. And how

well she'd played her female games on him! He'd had the chance to take her in Kansas City, and she'd put him off, the little cheat, though he'd had every right. Frustration boiled over in his veins. Cursing vilely under his breath, he stood up.

"Where—where are you going?" Yves gulped. A tremor shuddered through him.

"Drink your whiskey, old man," Johnny said. He pulled an old horse blanket from the wall of the stall and dropped it over the sodden priest. "You've earned it tonight. I've got questions to put to Sara, and I'll have answers one way or the other."

Yves' eyes dropped to half-mast. He slumped back against the wall in a torpor and muttered incoherently. "She meant well . . ."

Johnny stepped over Yves and strode toward the door.

"Hey, Tuck!" Cole's laughing voice caught him in mid-stride. "Goin' to say goodbye to your lady friend? Give her a kiss for me."

I'm going to kill that sonofabitch before this is over, Johnny thought grimly. He pointed a finger at Cole, then at the pile of saddlebags. "You keep your mouth shut and your eyes on *that,* understand? And it damn well better be here when I get back."

He didn't wait to hear Cole's reply. In the temper he was in, he'd have been tempted to beat the bloody hell out of him. But at the moment, there was another person who interested him more.

Re-crossing the yard, he let himself into the dark, silent house. He took the back stairs, heretofore forbidden to all men, two at a time, not bothering with stealth. He was too angry to care. His footsteps were muffled by the worn Oriental runner as he approached Sara's door. Boldly, he turned the knob. He'd have kicked it in had it been locked, but the door swung silently inward. A startled gasp rose to his ears, and he knew she hadn't been asleep in the high, carved bed that dominated the room. She sat up, her silhouette a lighter gray against the darkness. He shut the door behind him, and the latch caught with an ominous snap.

"J-Johnny?" Her voice was breathless with surprise. "What is it? A patient?"

He laughed his disdain. "Not this time, Sara, love."

The bedclothes rustled in the darkness, and she fumbled with the lamp, finally lighting it. Her hair fell in a long plait over the shoulder of her virginial, high-necked nightgown, and her face looked like a little girl's, puzzling out a problem. "What are you doing here?" she demanded.

He took a step toward her, and his voice was a low growl of a hunter scenting prey. "It's time to end the deception, *wife*. I've come to claim my rights."

Chapter 11

"Your what?"

Sara's voice was weak with shock. One look at Johnny's ferocious expression froze the blood in her veins. His eyes were emerald with fury, and a high, angry color dotted his cheekbones. This was Tuck—dangerous and unpredictable and enraged. She clutched the bedclothes to her chest in an involuntary, defensive gesture. "I—I don't know what you're talking about."

"Yves told me everything. I know all about our *wedding*." His tone scalded her nerve endings.

"You must have misunderstood," she said desperately. "He's drunk."

"That explains it."

Johnny shook his head. "Uh-uh. *In vino veritas.* I believe him."

"Wha—what do you want?"

He smiled, and she had never seen anything so frightening. "Guess."

He took a step, and she moved, rolling out of the far side of the bed with the agility of a monkey. Her bare feet hit the cool wooden floor, and she poised warily for flight. "Stay where you are."

"The truth, Sara," he demanded. The bed lay between them, but the door was behind him. A game of cat and mouse would not last long.

Sara swallowed hard. There was no one to call for help with Yves drunk and Pandora deeply asleep. She'd never meant for him to find out, but surely he could understand . . . He took another threatening step forward,

167

and she held up a placating hand. The dull gold band on her finger glinted in the wavering light, its purity a mocking reminder that the vows they'd made were a mere hoax, a bit of desperate chicanery, and not the sacred pact they should have been.

"All right. It's true. But it was just an expedient, that's all."

"Then we *are* married." His face was implacable.

"I—I suppose so. But it doesn't mean anything. It was a means to an end. I certainly never intended to hold you to it. Why, I've already contacted a lawyer to have it annulled."

Somehow, that made him even angrier—as if he'd lost all control over his own life. "How very commendable of you," he said through gritted teeth, moving to the foot of the bed.

"Johnny, be reasonable," she pleaded. "It had nothing to do with us. I was desperate, and it seemed the only way to save your life. Surely you can see—"

"I see the fine hand of Saint Sara at work playing God. But this time you've gone too far." He moved toward her, his voice husky with rage and a too-long suppressed passion. "You chose the role. It's time you learned how to act like a wife."

Sara gave a small, startled cry and scrambled back over the bed, hitting the floor at a dead run in her dash toward the door. Johnny's reflexes were lightning-quick. He grabbed a fistful of nightgown and drew her up short, swinging her around by her own momentum and throwing her onto the bed. Following her down onto the cushiony feather mattress, he covered her squirming body with his massive form. Sara beat at him with her hands, struggling frantically.

"Let me up, you sorry—"

He cut her invective short by covering her mouth with his own, muffling her screams of rage against his lips. Her fists flailed wildly about his head, and he pinned them to the rumpled sheets. His purpose was to punish, and his mouth was all-consuming. His tongue probed between her lips in a carnal mimicry of lovemaking until her cries diminished to faint whimpers of protest. The sound sliced into him like a knife.

He pulled back, rocked by the bruised and swollen outline of her lips. Her mouth was like a flower, and he couldn't get enough of her nectar. Melding her mouth with his, he kissed her again, with no less hunger, but the tenor of the kiss changed, softened, became a supplication and a seduction.

When he finally broke away, his heart was pounding like one of his own hammers against the anvil of his chest. He tested the tender curve between her neck and shoulder, nipping and tasting her velvety skin like a feasting predator. Her breathing was ragged, and her soft breasts pressed in erotic rhythm against his hard chest, driving him mad. He moved his knee between her thighs and nearly groaned aloud at how good she felt.

Sara gasped under the onslaught of flooding sensuality. His kisses were dizzying, masterful invitations to a world she'd never dreamed existed. He tasted faintly of brandy and wholly of himself, and she felt as drunk as Yves on a three-day bender. But it wasn't right this way, with no affection between them, a lustful mating fired by hatred and revenge. She fought the seductive pleasures of his lips and hands, her words breathless.

"Johnny, think! You're mad because of a paper marriage. But if you—we—do this, there'll be no grounds for an annulment, and—and this lie will become the truth."

He looked down into her flushed face with hooded eyes, considering. Her captured hands trembled in the manacle of his fingers, and he loosened his grip but did not release her. His voice rumbled deep in his chest, and his half-smile was sly.

"Clever, Sara, very clever. But here's something else to think about—a wife cannot be forced to testify against her husband. So, what's it to be?" He moved against her, allowing her to feel the hard tumescence of his sex pressed against her thigh. Her eyes widened, and he laughed softly, teasing her wickedly. "I think you know."

"No." She groaned, bucking against him, but to no avail. He held her firmly, enjoying her struggles with a devilish glint in his eye.

"This bridegroom has waited too long for his wedding night already, Sara, love," he taunted. He nibbled the delicate shell of her ear, and his hot breath carried a whispered promise. "Time to make amends."

"I can't! I told you . . ." She nearly choked on the words, her voice thick with fear and humiliation. "I can't."

He frowned and hesitated. "Your old man of a husband must have been a damned fool."

"He loved me!"

"Love? Spiritual love doesn't hold a candle to a good—" The word he used was graphic, shocking, and undeniably erotic.

Her eyes glistened with moisture. "Why are you so angry? It's just a paper marriage. What kind of pain makes you want to hurt me this way?"

His face darkened, and he dropped his head until their lips were only a breath apart. With one hand he stroked her from shoulder to hip until she quivered. "Am I hurting you, Sara? Or are you hurting yourself by denying what you want?"

"I don't want you."

"Don't you?" he murmured. His lips trailed a path of fire across her face, down her neck, across the soft swell of her breasts. The thin lawn of her gown grew damp from his hot, moist breath and clung to her fevered skin. His tongue flicked out, wetting the sheer fabric, slicking it down against her flesh, revealing the puckered outline of her fully aroused nipple, but not touching it.

She'd stopped breathing. It was impossible to draw air when his mouth held her captive. Her hand rested on his shoulder, her fingers digging into his shirt, but she had no strength to push him away. His breath wafted across her skin, cooling where his tongue had made the fabric wet. Her breasts tingled and felt heavy, swollen. His tongue laved the rounded mound, then he took her into his mouth, suckling strongly on the pulsing tip right through the fabric. Sara's back arched, and her heels dug into the mattress.

Her response moved him unbearably. Somehow his anger had disappeared, and now there was only this burning need to touch her, to know every inch of her, to love her until neither one of them could deny this thing between them that had been building for as long as he could remember. His voice was thick with desire. "Am I hurting you now, Sara?"

She moaned and gasped. "Damn you."

"Very likely." His fingers worked swiftly on the buttons at her throat, opening the front of the nightdress, revealing her ivory skin to his heated gaze. His eyes blazed at the delicate pink of her nipples. He trailed the backs of his fingers across her chest, down her breastbone, circling the creamy globes. "But I'll risk perdition for just one taste of you."

Sara cried out at the waves of overwhelming sensation as he again made hungry forays against her nipples. He suckled and bathed each breast with his tongue, playing mischievous games with the hardened nubs until she was writhing with the pleasure of it. Her fingers twisted into his thick hair, but to her shame she found she was pulling him closer, not pushing him away. The shock made her inhale sharply. Johnny raised his head, alerted by her sudden stillness. Her eyes were clenched shut, and a single tear trickled from the corner of one eye down into her hairline.

"Sara." His lips caught the tear, carried it to her own lips and placed it there with a soft, tender kiss. "Look at me."

Her eyelids fluttered, revealing the confusion in her coffee-brown eyes. "What are you doing to me?" she whispered, stricken.

"Oh, God, Sara," he murmured. He closed his eyes and rested his forehead against her temple in defeat. "How can you not know you were made for this? You're so beautiful to me, and I want you so damned much."

Somewhere, the line between good and bad, right and wrong had been blurred in Sara's mind. Her body sung with need, a deep, life-long hunger that transcended anything she'd ever felt with Will. She knew Johnny was offering her something she might never otherwise experience. He would be gone soon and with him, the chance to feel heaven in his arms. It was wrong. It was sin—or was it? She was too confused by the muddled legalities to care. He wanted her. *Her.* Suddenly it was clear that she, too, was willing to risk the pains of hell for an hour's pleasure—with this man.

Hesitantly, her fingers tested the crisp texture of his sideburn and trembled on the beard-roughed plane of his jaw. Johnny raised up on one elbow, his expression startled. A tangle of curls fell over his forehead, rakish and utterly irresistible. His green eyes held a question. Sara lifted her hand, gently pushing his hair back, liking its vibrancy and silkiness between her fingers. She met his questioning gaze shyly.

"I guess you'll have to prove it to me," she whispered timorously. "Please?"

The corner of his mouth twitched, and his eyes softened with tenderness. He bent over her, and his voice was gruff. "It would be my pleasure, ma'am."

Sara's involuntary laugh was breathless. "Oh, no, not entirely."

She reached for him, wrapping her arms around his powerful neck, and their lips met in a tender, tentative seeking. Sara melted in response, freely giving him what he'd once taken by force. Groaning, Johnny tightened his arms around her and sat up. She half-lay across his lap, easy prey for his questing, stroking, tantalizing hands.

He tugged the ribbon on the end of her braid and released the disciplined strands. Her rich brown hair spilled over her shoulders and down her back in a riot of sienna-highlighted curls. He buried his nose in it. "You always smell so sweet," he murmured.

Sara's hands were busy, too, unbuttoning his shirt, allowing herself to explore the forbidden expanse of his massive, muscular chest, letting her fingers glide through the bramble of silky blond chest hair. A bronze nipple caught her attention, and she dallied with it, thumbing the center and laughing softly when Johnny jumped at the shock. He retaliated by shoving his hand under the hem of her gown and stroking her thigh and bare hip.

"You're so smooth and soft," he said. His mouth nibbled delicately on her shoulder, pushing aside the garment. "I want to see you—all of you."

Sara's inflamed senses were burning too hotly for her to feel shy any longer. She helped him slip the gown free, then tore at his shirt. Throwing his garment to the floor, he kicked off his boots, all the while kissing her lips, her eyelids, the sensitive angle of her jaw. He laid her back on the bed, his thumbs rubbing sensuously over her hipbones. His head dipped, and he ravaged her navel with his tongue, making her gasp.

He left her for a moment to shuck out of his trousers and underwear, then he lay down beside her. His face seemed harsh in the glow of the lamp, but Sara felt his tension and understood its source. They lay side by side, exploring each other with hands and lips.

Sara couldn't touch him enough. Everything about him excited her, filled her with powerful, unforeseen longings. The rounded muscles of his arms were as tight and hard as a green Lexington apple, and she longed to take a bite. His lean flanks and long, horseman's legs seemed perfectly formed, an anatomist's delight. But her interest wasn't strictly clinical. Perhaps even from the first moment she'd found him beautiful and known instinctively his physical attraction for her would be a potent, dynamic force that could change her irrevocably.

His deep chest and wide shoulders constantly drew her attention. Her fingers explored his belly, flat and hard, and lightly dusted with sandy hair that arrowed down, then thickened and darkened into the nest surrounding his flagrant virility. Her mouth went dry, and she lifted suddenly apprehensive eyes to find Johnny watching her with a passion-hooded gaze.

"You're a beautiful man," she said shakily.

"And you talk too much, Sara, love." Catching her chin, he held her still for his kiss. The sweeping exploration of his tongue robbed her of breath. His hand trailed downward, dipped into her navel, tangled in the black curls shrouding her femininity. He explored the mysterious depths and found her dewy and ready. It was almost too much for him. He groaned and rolled her beneath him, spreading her thighs with his knee. He knew the instant she stiffened, and poised above her.

Lifting his head, he braced himself on his forearms and

stared down at her. His voice was hoarse with need.
"Sara?"

"I'm afraid, Johnny," she whispered, distraught.

"No, love, no. Not of this. Not of me. I won't hurt
you," he murmured against her lips. "Trust me."

She wanted to, but she didn't know how to begin. Nothing had prepared her for this intensity of desire. For so
long she had denied her own needs, but now they flared
out of control. She was afraid of such selfishness. She
wasn't comfortable taking, yet she knew how to give. And
she wanted—oh, so badly!—to give herself to this man.
She clasped his neck and pulled his head down for her
kiss.

A gasp escaped her lips at the first touch of him, hot
and hard as steel, probing between her thighs. He took
her breath into his mouth and made it his own. Sweat
shimmered on his brow, and she felt his constraint, the
iron control that let him ease inch by silky inch past the
threshold of her womanhood, allowing her body to adjust
with tiny shock waves to the magnificent fullness of him.
She'd never known such total pleasure. His restraint was
so complete she became impatient for him, lifting her hips
at last, taking all of him so that he was buried completely
within her. His mouth explored the hollow beneath her
ear, and she smiled in feminine triumph at his low, nearly
inaudible groan.

They paused, breathing heavily, adjusting to each other
and to the surges of rampant sensuality that flowed over
them like a moon tide. It wasn't clear who moved first.
As one, they strove together, from the first slow, breath-
stopping glide to the wild and plunging final ride toward
mutual oblivion. She clung to him, tracing the powerful
muscles channeling his spine, feeling them contract and
flex as he moved. Her nostrils were filled with the smell
of his skin, the pungent scent of sweat, and the unique
muskiness that was all male, all Johnny.

He palmed her bottom, lifting her to take his powerful
thrusts, and she welcomed him gladly, joyously. Her consciousness was filled only with him, just as her body was,
and she whispered his name over and over in a lover's
litany.

"Johnny . . . Johnny . . . Johnny!"

With a gasp of surprise, Sara felt her body explode, shattering into a million shining pieces with the force of her completion. Johnny saw it and threw back his head to laugh for joy. Then his face contorted in the throes of his own exquisite climax, and he gave a ragged cry, plunging into her up to the hilt. Ripples of sensation washed over her again and again, her inner convulsions tightening around him in the most intimate of embraces that went on and on and on . . .

She came to herself finally, still shaking, still a part of Johnny's body. His weight was a welcome and familiar rock in a world turned topsy-turvy. Eventually, he raised himself up on his elbows, grinning down at her with an expression of blatant male satisfaction. He pushed the tangled strands of her hair back from her sweat-dampened face and kissed her lightly.

"Sweet, sweet Sara. Jesus, woman! You're wonderful!"

Her breath caught on a sob. "I never knew . . ." Her face crumpled, and she covered it with her hands.

"Jesus, honey. Don't cry." He pulled away, rolling her over in his arms so that she lay against his chest. "Sara, please . . ."

She wiped her damp cheeks, raising herself up to shower kisses on his mouth, his blond-stubbled cheeks. "You don't understand. I never knew it could be like that."

His large hands cupped her face, his thumbs sweeping away the wetness from her cheekbones. "Never?"

She shook her head and bit her lip. "No."

"Your husband never—"

Her fingers against his lips silenced his question. "Don't. He was a good man in every other way."

"But you're so sweet, so responsive . . ."

"Will was a lot older than I was," she said, avoiding his eyes.

"Even so—"

"Ours wasn't a . . . a normal marriage. He wed me to take me away from Uncle Quentin when Louisa died."

Shock jolted him. His brow knitted in a frown. So her first marriage hadn't been a love match after all, but a goddamn rescue. Was it any wonder she'd used the same tactics to save his life?

"Then you never loved him," he began slowly.

"Oh, but I did. I loved Will for what he'd done for me. He was the kindest man who ever lived, but he wasn't a man of great physical appetites and we . . . we . . ." She broke off, flushing.

"He never satisfied you." Johnny sought to assimilate that. He could not prevent the primitive satisfaction that he had been the one to bring her to fulfillment for the first time.

"I didn't think it was possible for me," she admitted in a voice that was barely audible. Her luscious mouth trembled into a crooked half-smile. "I guess I should thank you for that."

She moved away from him, her embarrassment palpable. Yet she was too full of emotion to deny the miracle that had happened to her. She'd never expected to find such joy, and Johnny had made it possible. It seemed only right to tell him.

A lump of tenderness caught in his throat. He'd come to exact a punishment out of pride, and she had taken his worst and given him the best of herself, body and soul. From the elegant curve of her spine to the tremulous fullness of her soft mouth, she seemed so vulnerable and proud and honest, and in that instant he wanted to protect her above all things. Only he knew the thing he should protect her from most of all was—himself.

He couldn't give her up, not just yet. He reached for her, despising the things that separated them. At least he could hold her for a while longer.

"Good God, you're even polite in bed," he said in mock disgust, forcing a lightness into his tone, but the puff of male pride was hard to hide. He lightly slapped her bare bottom and pulled her next to him to snuggle, which she did, happily. Reaching out, he doused the lamp and tugged the covers over them. Folding his arms around her, he gave a satisfied sigh and kissed the top of her head. She felt wonderful next to him, her curves complementing his angles. She fit perfectly under his heart. After a while he spoke into the darkness.

"It would be easy to pretend with you."

"Pretend what?" She was drowsy, sated.

"That the world's not a rotten place. That things are different. Why didn't we meet ten years ago?"

There was such a wealth of sadness and regret in his voice, Sara felt tears prickle. She had similar questions, but the answers could wait until dawn. She slid her leg over his muscular thigh and trailed her fingertips over a bronze nipple in invitation. Her voice was soft.

"Can't we pretend we did?"

She came awake suddenly, tense and listening. Her room was suffused with a gray pre-dawn light. Something felt wrong. She was naked. A large tanned hand clasped her possessively around the waist. Her breath caught, and she closed her eyes again, willing the flood of returning memories away.

But the warmth and bulk of the nude man sleeping beside her could not be denied. Neither could the slight soreness between her thighs, the ache of muscles unaccustomed to intimate activities. She suppressed a groan of dismay. Dear God, what had she done?

Her eyes raked Johnny. He lay on his stomach, the tangled bedclothes twisted around his legs. Asleep, he lacked the fine-tuned ferocity that had so often terrified her, yet he was no less wickedly attractive. The fine sandy down that covered his legs and hard flanks glinted in the dim light. His back and buttocks seemed carved out of living stone. The planes and angles of his face were softer, relaxed, incredibly handsome and intoxicating. He filled the bed and her mind with his presence, obliterating everything but the power of their shared intimacy.

A hot blush of shame climbed up her neck. What had seemed so right and good in the depths of the night was revealed by the day in all its lustful sordidness. She was guilty and appalled at her wantonness, remembering how they'd both pretended, over and over again, inventing a dream that captured the glories of the flesh but ignored the dictates of heart and conscience. His seductive sweetness, talented hands, and inventive mouth had pushed her past remembrance into ecstasy time after time. But she had to forget his generosity and his delight in her cataclysmic releases, and remember what kind of man he really was. She'd succumbed to temptation and sacrificed every virtue she possessed, as well as the means to dissolve the legal ties of a false marriage. The knowledge made her want to weep.

The distant echo of a knock on the front door vibrated through the house. She threw off Johnny's hand and slid from the bed—Will's bed, in Will's house, her brain taunted—and grabbed her plain wool dressing gown.

"What is it?" Johnny asked, suddenly alert but his voice still husky with sleep and satiation.

She ignored him, pushing her hands into her robe and belting it tightly, then throwing her tumbled locks over her shoulder. The room held a chill, for the fire had burned down in the grate, but it wasn't the cool air that made her shiver. Pushing aside the drapery, she peered from her window. Her heart stopped. A group of mounted men on lathered horses milled in her front yard, and the unmistakable badge of a sheriff glinted on the chest of one of them.

"Oh, my God!" Her heart flip-flopped in a crazy rhythm. Were they after the bank robbers and satchels of stolen gold to be found in her carriage house? Would it mean shooting? Arrest for all of them?

"Find out what they want," Johnny ordered tersely. He stood beside the window, just out of sight, completely and unabashedly naked. His features were harsh with tension in the gray light. She hesitated, and he gestured sharply. "Go on."

Sara flung up the window sash and leaned out over the sill, clutching her robe to her throat. "Yes? Can I help you?"

The sheriff looked up over the slope of the porch roof to her window, and gestured to a deputy who'd been pounding on the front door. The sheriff was an older man with a weather-beaten face and a droopy mustache, and he expertly tightened the reins to still his jumpy horse. Tipping his dusty hat politely, he introduced himself. "Sheriff Ramsey, ma'am. You be Dr. Cary?"

"Yes. Is someone hurt, Sheriff?"

"No, ma'am. I need to ask you some questions."

"Get rid of him," Johnny whispered.

"It's very early, Sheriff," Sara began, "and, as you can see, I'm not dressed . . ."

"Are you in the possession of a dappled gelding, ma'am?" Sheriff Ramsey interrupted.

"Why, yes." Sara swallowed and tried to keep her face impassive. "If you could just tell me what this is all about?"

"We've been tracking some men we think are part of the gang that robbed the Clay County Savings and Loan. Followed 'em from around Liberty down to Kansas City, but we lost the trail 'tween here and there. Informant tells us one of 'em was riding a dappled horse. Where did you get yours, ma'am?"

"Lie," Johnny ordered in a low voice. "And you'd better make it convincing."

"I'm sorry for all your trouble, Sheriff," Sara called down. "And I certainly hope you catch up with those ruffians, but my horse came from Dr. Turner down in Concordia. Our old Nubbin is due for retirement to pasture, you see, and—"

"You got a bill of sale, ma'am?"

Sara didn't have to force the look of consternation that crossed her face. "Why, I'm sure I do somewhere. I'm afraid my bookkeeping isn't all it should be. Would you care to come inside while I look? And I'm sure your men would enjoy a cup of hot coffee, too."

Ramsey shook his head. Both his and his animal's breath made white streams of vapor in the cold air. "Thank you, no, ma'am, we haven't got the time. We got to meet up with a local posse down to the Court House. Rumor has it at least four of them came this way, and we was hoping, leastways I was, that they'd sold you that there dappled horse."

"Did you say four, Sheriff?" Sara asked. Beside her, Johnny stiffened. Thinking furiously, she leaned farther out of the window, her hair whipping around her face. There had to be some way to protect her family from being caught up in this mess. She had to buy some time.

"At least four, ma'am. Why?"

"I make a good many calls outside town, and I wondered . . ." She gave a girlish laugh. "No, you'll just think I'm being fanciful."

"Dr. Cary, if you know anything at all that could help us track these killers down, we'd be extremely grateful."

Sara chewed her lip in an imitation of deliberate thought. "Well, I did notice four strangers, just yesterday, in the neighborhood of the Sugarloaf." She heard Johnny's swiftly indrawn breath and muttered oath. "You know the place, down the Old Independence Road? But they were young, hardly more than boys."

"Was one red-headed? And the youngest peachy-cheeked and blue-eyed?" The sheriff's voice had risen with barely suppressed excitement.

Sara set a finger to her mouth in feigned concentration. "I believe so."

"Headin' toward Independence?"

"Yes."

"Thank you, ma'am! All right, boys, let's go!"

The sheriff led his posse out of the yard, and Sara backed out of the window. She reached up to pull down the sash, and then she began to shake, her knees knocking together like tambourines. She'd made herself an accomplice by her own lies! Johnny's deep chuckle infuriated her. She slammed down the window and turned to glare at him.

"Damn, that was impressive," he said, laughing in admiration. He leaned indolently against the wall, arms folded across his chest, to all indications oblivious to the fact he had on nary a stitch. "You could even give Belle Boyd a lesson in coolness. A spy after my own heart. I'll say this for you, honey, you've got nerve."

His approval of what was to her a despicable, illegal act only fueled her ire. She swung away from him, her breathing uneven due to a humiliating mixture of chagrin and involuntary arousal at his blatant nudity. She struggled for control and jumped when his hands captured her shoulders from behind.

"A performance like that deserves a reward," he murmured, pushing aside her hair to nuzzle her sensitive nape, something he'd discovered she liked during their hours together.

She shrugged out of his grasp and snatched up his trousers from the floor, flinging them in his startled face. "Get dressed," she ordered. "God help me, I didn't do it for you or your slimy friends, but to protect the ones I care about."

He frowned and stepped into his pants, but didn't bother to button them. They flared in a vee that led her eye inexorably to the bulge of his maleness. "What's the matter with you?" he demanded. "Got a case of the morning-afters? I would have thought you above such petty guilt, especially after last night."

She sucked in an outraged breath. "Only a cad such as you could be so indelicate . . ."

He laughed again. "What did you expect? Flowers? A thank-you note? As I recall, you've got a helluva lot more to be grateful for than I do. How's it feel to have the shoe on the other foot for a change?"

A pain so fierce it made her cry out pierced her. So the pretense was down. She'd made love to this man, and in her mind he'd been the old Johnny she'd caressed and cherished, but in the harsh early morning reality, it was horrid Tuck who taunted her for her weakness. Their dream, like all dreams, faded away to nothingness in the bleak light of day.

"Get out." Her fists clenched at her sides. She could hardly breathe it hurt so much. "Go, damn you! And take those filthy, detestable friends of yours with you!"

"All in good time, my dear."

"What?"

"Where's the last place a posse will be searching for us?" He caught a handful of her hair, twirling it sensuously through his long fingers, waiting for her answer. She shook her head, and his slow smile was faintly pitying. "Where they've *already* looked."

"Here?" she squeaked.

He nodded. "Here."

"No!" She gave a feline snarl of sheer hatred. Hands curled into claws, she flew at him, intent on tearing him to ribbons. He controlled her easily, shaking her until she subsided in a heap against his chest, racked with dry sobs of fury.

"Listen to me, you hellion," he growled in her ear. "I've got my reasons for this, so spare me your outraged sensibilities. You're in this so deep already, a few more days won't matter now."

"Sara Jane?" Pandora's sleepy, querulous voice drifted from down the hall. "What was all that ruckus outside just now?"

Johnny released her abruptly. "You'd better go to her. Tell her your guests have found they can extend their visit a little longer."

Sara stumbled toward the door, her reproachful gaze full of impotent fury.

His voice was as cold and icy as his green eyes. "Remember, Sara, the law could find a *wife* just as guilty as a husband."

She took a deep breath, her eyes too bright, and flounced from the room, hurrying to Pandora's side. The older woman was propped up in her tester bed, her nightcap askew, her faded blue eyes still drowsy. Sara was making some muddled explanation about Sheriff Ramsey and wondering fervently what she could do now when Clem knocked on the door.

"Got your morning tray, Miss Pandora," the boy called.

"Come in, Clem. Coffee ought to help clear my head," Pandora said.

"Yas'm." Clem beamed, hobbling in with the tray. "We're all back, and Lizzie'll have breakfast ready in two shakes of a wooly-lamb's tail."

The vision of Lizzie and Cole Younger's brazen interest brought things to a thundering conclusion for Sara. She couldn't allow this shoot-the-chute ride into calamity to continue. It was becoming more and more dangerous each minute she delayed. Her lack of action, her spineless inability to deny Johnny's initial plans, had led her to this pass, and she must do something before more murder or worse befell them all—no matter what it cost her. She moved to Pandora's dressing table and reached for pen and paper with hands that shook.

"Clem," she said, writing rapidly, "you must carry a

very important message for me to the Court House. Tell no one. There's a man there, a Sheriff Ramsey. Give him this.'' She pressed the hastily scribbled note into the boy's palm. "And tell him . . . tell him . . .''

"What, Miss Sara?''

Her face twisted with pain. "Tell him I know where to find the seventh man.''

Chapter 12

"That was too damned close for comfort," Cole said.

Johnny stepped through the door of the carriage house. "I have to agree."

Four pistols cleared holsters and belts, and hammers clicked back in threatening unison.

"Easy, boys." Johnny chuckled. He held up a smoke-blackened coffee pot and a handful of tin mugs. "It's just me."

"Where the hell have you been?" Cole demanded. His beefy face was flushed with temper and the after-effects of too much liquor. Strawberry-colored stubble sprouted from his cheeks, and his mustache pulled the corners of his mouth down in a scowl.

His brother Jim snickered. "Don't you know it ain't polite to stick your nose into a man's private affairs?"

Johnny's jaw set, and he wordlessly tossed each man a cup, then passed the pot. He wasn't going to talk about Sara, not with the taste of her still in his mouth and her scent still clinging to his skin. Damn the woman! She'd turned him inside out, sweet and giving one minute, spitting and scratching the next. How could a woman who'd reached the ultimate satisfaction be so full of regret and recriminations afterwards?

Having the damned sheriff show up on her doorstep, demanding answers, hadn't helped the situation, he admitted ruefully. But he couldn't waste time fretting about Sara's offended sensibilities. He was anxious to assess the possibilities and make quick adjustments. These developments might just put an end to this charade, if he could turn them to his purpose and regain Quantrill's gold. He hated threatening Sara, but there was no time for niceties—he had to have her cooperation. Jesus, what a mess! Making love to her—to his *wife*, for God's sake!—had just complicated matters, but for the life of him, he couldn't regret it.

"Quit picking on Tuck," Jesse chided Jim. His calm manner showed no ill effects from the previous night's drinking. A pale fuzz of mustache frosted his upper lip, but he was brushed and dressed and in charge. The others were less alert, still pulling on boots and dusters, obviously shaken by what must have seemed their imminent capture and arrest. Yves snored softly in the far corner, oblivious. "Did you get a look at 'em, Tuck?" Jesse asked.

"Ramsey and his men, asking questions. And he had too many damn answers to start with. Somebody's been talking. If it hadn't been for Sara's quick thinking, we'd all be sitting behind bars right now," Johnny replied. He took a drink of the black coffee and raised an expectant eyebrow. "Got any ideas?"

"Nobody's been talking," Jim protested.

"You were in the clear there for a while. Why's the law back on your tails all of a sudden?"

Jesse looked up. "Moses."

"Yeah." Johnny nodded. "Has to be. I told you he'd come after the Golden Calf—any way he can."

"And us, too." Cole's curses were vile. "We gotta get the hell outta here."

"With a posse 'round every turn?" Frank objected in a flat voice. He looked into his coffee cup, and his long face was morose. "Don't like them odds."

"There's time to think about it," Johnny said easily. "You're safe enough for now, and I think Lizzie's cooking up a batch of flapjacks for breakfast."

"Yeah, Lizzie." Cole's expression softened into lascivious anticipation, and he licked his lips. "I'll bet that ain't all she can cook, either."

"Leave her be, Cole," Johnny warned with a black look.

''That ain't neighborly of you, pard, wanting 'em both for yourself,'' the red-haired man said angrily.

''We ain't got time for none of this,'' Jesse interjected. ''Quit thinkin' with your crotch for just one damn minute, Cole! We got more important things to decide. What's it going to be? Take our chances and make a run for it, or hole up here for a spell?''

''Sara sent Ramsey on a wild goose chase toward Independence,'' Johnny said. ''They won't come looking here again.''

''Yes, they will.''

The five men swung around. Sara stood in the doorway, demurely dressed in a blue wool gown, her crocheted shawl around her shoulders. Her hair was once again in a restrained chignon, and Johnny felt an absurd stab of disappointment, even while the hairs on the back of his neck prickled with foreboding.

''They'll be back,'' she announced, her face pale but composed. ''I've seen to that.''

Cole grabbed Sara before Johnny could intervene. ''God damn it, woman!'' he roared. ''What the hell have you done?''

She glared her defiance and contempt. ''I sent for the sheriff. I told him you were here.''

Cole's backhand caught her across the cheek, the force of it throwing her to the straw-covered earth. Tears of rage and shock glittered in her eyes, but she blinked them back, showing her disdain in the belligerent tilt of her chin.

''They'll be here soon. Take your filthy lucre and go.''

Cole reared his hand back to strike her again, but Johnny's giant fist closed over it, stopping the blow in mid-air. An intense battle of wills filled the narrow space between them with a vibrating tension. Johnny spoke softly, his eyes narrowed, his voice deadly cold.

''Don't.''

Cole's blue eyes flickered with the sure knowledge of his imminent demise, and he eased back a trifle. ''Hell, Tuck!''

''She's mine. No one touches her but me.'' Abruptly, Johnny pushed Cole aside. He grabbed Sara's arm and lifted her to her feet, pushing her away from the group until her back pressed into the rough plank wall of a stall. His broad shoulders shielded her from the hostile eyes of the four. He held her shoulders so tightly she winced, and the red outline of Cole's hand marked the creamy skin of her cheek like an obscene sign. The muscle in his jaw worked, and his face was a taut mask, though his voice remained quiet. "In God's name, what are you doing?"

Her features were stony, fixed with a mutinous and triumphant defiance. "Protecting myself the only way I know how. Now you'll have to leave."

He felt as though he'd been kicked in the gut. Was it betrayal or punishment? "Is that what this is about? Or is it something else?"

Her gaze flicked across his face, and she drew a shuddering breath. "Be grateful I decided to warn you."

He shook her. "You sent a message? With who? Clem?" She nodded, her head bobbing like a daisy on its slender stem. He cursed deeply. "He's back? He gave the note to Ramsey?"

Her gaze fell away, and she answered reluctantly. "He'd already gone south. But Clem gave it to a deputy, who'll pass it on to Sheriff Ramsey when he returns, so . . ." She faltered to a stop, struck by the strange, wounded light in Johnny's eyes.

"Why, Sara?" His words were barely audible.

"I meant to turn you in—all of you. I sent the message; all I had to do was wait for them to come for you, but . . ." Suddenly her voice broke, and her eyes flooded, overflowed with a helpless, undeniable anguish. "I couldn't. After everything . . . I just couldn't."

He stared at her, feeling unmanned and growing angrier by the second. If only he'd told her everything. But it was to late for that. "Sara . . ."

She shook her head, her fingers clutching his forearms in desperate urgency. "Oh, hurry, Johnny! Go quickly before they come. Go somewhere I don't have to *care* about you anymore."

"You've got a damned funny way of showing it, woman."

Her eyes were as big as saucers. "Just go," she whispered. "It's the only way."

He knew she was right, now that her actions were forcing his hand. If he were arrested along with the others, with the amount of circumstantial evidence against him, there was a good chance he might find himself at the quick end of a noose before he could explain. And the entire situation was exacerbated by the meddling and sinister hand of Moses the Prophet.

Cole's strident voice sounded over Johnny's musings. "That about tears it, then," he shouted. "Thanks to that bitch, we'd better make a run for it."

"We'll have to split up." Jesse's calm voice quieted the angry mutterings. "Saddle up."

"What will we do, divide the gold?" Jim asked, reaching for blanket and bridle.

Jesse blinked furiously, thinking. "No. If any of us are caught with it, we're done for. Alone, carrying nothing, anybody stopped might have a chance to bluff his way through."

"What happens to the Calf, then?" Cole demanded.

Jesse's pale blue gaze probed Johnny, then flicked to Sara's tear-streaked face. "They take it."

"What?" Jim's and Cole's voices mingled in virulent protest, and even Frank muttered and shook his head. Johnny frowned, seeing at once the direction of Jesse's thoughts and disliking the idea intensely.

Jesse walked across the wide middle aisle and patted the frame of Sara's shabby buggy. His firm words overrode their objections. "No one will be likely to look in the lady doctor's buggy. We'll even include the coins from Liberty. She and Tuck can make a call out of town. What could be more innocent?"

Aghast, Sara shook her head. "No. I won't help you."

Johnny swung back to her, grabbing her nape with hard, punishing fingers and making her gasp aloud. "She'll do it," he said grimly.

Jesse nodded. "Once we're out of town, away from all these nosy lawmen, all we'll have to do is meet up again. *Rendez-vous*, the Frenchies say. What about Baxter Springs, down near the Indian Territory, in four days time?"

"You trust these two? You're crazy!" Cole bellowed.

"We can count on Tuck, and he'll hold the woman in line. Once we're on our way to Mexico with the Calf, it don't matter what she does," Jesse said. "Besides, Tuck knows if he don't show up on time with the gold, we'll come back—here."

Cole grinned in evil anticipation. "Yeah, we'll make it a little Lawrence. There'll be nothing left but ashes and dry bones when we get through, and I'll make sure I get a piece of that little Lizzie gal before we kill them all."

"Don't get your hopes up, Cole," Johnny said. "I'll be there. Four days. Baxter Springs."

Jesse picked up the heavy saddlebags and lifted them into the floor of the buggy. "Better find something to put that in, Tuck."

"I expect Sara has a traveling trunk."

"Good luck to you, then." Jesse took the reins of the saddled horse Frank brought him. He nodded to the other men. "Go one at a time. Head east and double back. No hurrahs, neither." Jim and Frank cast dubious glances at each other, shrugged, then took their own mounts outside.

Cole scowled at Johnny, hawked and spit in the earth at his feet. His words were for Jesse, though his eyes never left Johnny's face. "I still think you're crazy as hell, Jess."

"You'll get to have your fun—if I'm wrong."

"Yeah." Cole's hate-filled gaze flicked over Sara and made her shiver. He grinned, then left, too.

"Four days, Tuck," Jesse said.

"I'll be there."

"See that you are, else the lady's family will pay." Jesse blinked, scratched his chin, then swung into the saddle. They could hear the placid hoofbeats of his horse trotting away.

Johnny exhaled harshly. "Sweet Christ! You've really done it this time," he said to Sara. He raked a hand through his hair, his expression grim.

She slumped weakly against the stall. "They're gone, aren't they?"

"God damn it, woman. Don't you realize your interference has sealed my fate as well as your own?"

"You don't have to do it," she cried. Her hands lifted

in a pleading gesture. "Please, Johnny, stop it here. You can turn yourself in. I'll explain. It won't be bad—"

"I can't do it, Sara. If I don't show up as promised, they'll come back to kill *you*. Not even the U.S. Army could stop them." Reaching out, he slid his hand up her throat, pressing lightly at the base of her jaw. His voice was a gravelly mixture of menace and exasperation. "And as badly as I want to throttle you at this moment, I can't let that happen."

"Never tell me you actually have a conscience," she scoffed.

"What else would you call it?"

"I don't know. Self-interest? Wickedness? I can't guess—you never let me close enough to find out."

His arm swept around her waist, pulling her against him, and his hand caught the back of her head, forcing her face up to meet his. "We got pretty damned close last night," he said, his warm breath fanning her cheek.

"A mistake I'll regret to my dying day."

Her arrow shot home, taking him by surprise. He wasn't immune to her darts after all. He'd thought she'd found something beautiful in their joining, something beyond the physical, at least for a while. But she was no different from Gwendolyn, no different from all women. A lump of white-hot rage because he'd so thoroughly deceived himself burned through his heart like a glowing coal.

"The trouble with you, Sara," he snarled, "is you never learn anything from your mistakes." He savaged her lips for a brief, fierce moment, then thrust her away. "But you're finally getting your wish. I'm leaving, and this time I'm not coming back."

"Shall I pack for you?" she asked, her tone sweet, her eyes hot with outrage.

His laugh was rife with self-mockery. "Hell, why not? Isn't that what a wife does? Then you and I are going to take a little ride."

"Just saddle the horse and go. You don't need me."

Johnny's mouth twisted, and he jammed his clenched fists into his pants pockets. "Jesse's a shrewd campaigner, and his idea to use you as camouflage is right on the mark."

"Why should I help you? I've done all I intend to."

"Because you're going to have enough to explain to Ramsey as it is. And because if you don't, and I'm arrested, I'll cheerfully implicate the lot of you. Remember, aiding and abetting a guerrilla means risking a 'disloyal' sentence. You'll forfeit everything, and on top of that, you can count on Cole coming back to do his worst."

Sara shuddered. "You heartless blackguard."

"Whether you like it or not, if you care about your family, you're going to help me get out of town." He smiled, and it was a parody of kindness. "So come on, Sara, let's take a little trip. Only this time, I'll let you put on your bonnet first."

"Why are we going toward Independence?" Sara demanded sometime later.

Buttoned securely into her heaviest wool short coat, with her good winter bonnet tied securely under her chin, she sat spine-straight and belligerent on the worn leather buggy seat beside Johnny. Old Nubbin plodded forward, and the buggy jounced over a pothole in the rutted dirt road near the outskirts of Lexington. There was a steady stream of other vehicles, wagons, and horsemen, and no one remarked on their progress.

Although the air was crisp, the bright sun was warm on Sara's face. It was a perfect day for an outing, except for the presence of her small traveling trunk strapped securely to the back of the buggy. Quantrill's stolen fortune and the golden proceeds of the Liberty bank robbery filled the trunk, hidden beneath a jumble of her petticoats and other assorted items Johnny had confiscated for the purpose. The knowledge made her jumpy, especially since Johnny seemed intent on searching out the nearest posse.

"You know Sheriff Ramsey went this way," she said when Johnny made no answer. "I said, why—"

"Did you ever read a story call 'The Purloined Letter?' " he interrupted. "By a fellow name of Poe."

"Well . . . yes," she admitted. "But what has that got to do with anything? You should be headed east like the rest."

"Not necessarily." Johnny pulled the wide brim of his

felt hat a little lower over his eyes and scanned the rolling
countryside.

He'd taken time to shave, and in his rough working-
man's clothing he looked fairly harmless. Sara knew better, and she hoped fervently no one else would notice the
bulge of his pistol under his jacket. His bundle of possessions were stashed under the seat along with Sara's black
leather satchel of medicines and instruments.

"The thing is," Johnny drawled, "sometimes you can
hide something a lot better right out in the open."

"You have no right to take such a foolish chance," she
snapped, incensed at his arrogance. "There's more at stake
here than just your precious hide."

"Relax, Sara. I'm not likely to forget it, especially with
you carping in my ear all the livelong day."

Her lips tightened resentfully, and she closed her eyes
on a wave of remembered passion, seeking to deny the
traitorous feelings. It was hard to pretend indifference
when Johnny sat so close, tantalizing her, seducing her
again with the promise of sweet desire. There was no value
in useless regrets. What was done could not be undone,
but she'd have to deal with that after he was gone and her
life returned to normal. *If that's ever possible*, a tiny voice
whispered.

She felt Johnny's sudden movement and heard his muttered curse. Her eyes popped open. "What?"

"Looks as though we're going to get to test out my
theory sooner than I expected." He nodded ahead, drawing her attention to the fast-approaching party of riders
coming at them over the low crest of a distant hill. The
posse!

"What can we do? Try to outrun them?" There was a
thread of panic in her voice, and she unconsciously
clutched his arm.

"They probably won't even stop us," he said. His hand
covered her kid-gloved one and squeezed encouragingly.
"Just remember you're out on a call to see a sick patient."

She snatched her hand away, embarrassed to realize
she'd automatically sought his comfort and reassurance.
"Yes. Of course."

She took a deep breath, hoping the pinkness of her

cheeks could be attributed to the brisk air. Her feelings for Johnny were so turbulent and confused she didn't know what she was doing half the time. She should be concentrating on his treachery, but, strangely, it was the memory of his tenderness that colored her moves.

The riders got closer, and Sara sat in tense apprehension. Despite the coolness of the weather, she felt a trickle of perspiration drip down her spine. The first rider trotted past, raising a cloud of thin dust, then the second, the third. Sara began to relax, nodding awkwardly at the hats tipped her way. Johnny kept his eyes strictly ahead, his large hands loose and agile on the reins. Occasionally, he clicked to Nubbin, but the horse merely continued on at his own placid pace. Another knot of riders flitted past. Before Sara could draw a sigh of relief, one of them circled back.

"Damnation," Johnny gritted under his breath. "Here comes your beau."

Menard Plunket pulled his prancing black stallion alongside the buggy. "Sara," he cried, delighted. "Well met!"

"Good—good day, Judge Plunket," she replied. Reluctantly, she waved Johnny to stop. He called a low "whoa," and the buggy rolled to a halt.

"Now, now, I thought we were well past those formalities," Menard replied, a large, teasing smile splitting his broad face. He wore a thick-piled overcoat and dapper beaver hat more suited for city business than a trail ride. Despite the richness of his tack and the splendid breeding of his mount, his seat seemed awkward, and the stallion danced nervously in place. "I'm delighted to see you fully recovered from your indisposition."

"Yes, thank you. And thank you, Menard, for the violets. They were lovely," Sara said.

"The least I could do to express my concern and affection, my dear."

"Yes, er—well." She blushed and stammered like a schoolgirl. Feeling the tension radiating from the man next to her, she sought to make her excuses. "I have patients to see. I really must be on my way."

"Myself as well. I hope it's nothing serious that's called you out?"

"Ah, no. Just the—er, Maguire children. Croup and red throats, every one of them," she invented.

"Ethan Maguire? Funny he never mentioned it. He's been riding with us this last couple of days."

"Oh, they're much better now," Sara amended hastily. "Just a check, really." She smiled brilliantly and changed the subject. "Pandora mentioned your urgent business. Have you joined the posse pursuing those dreadful bank robbers?"

"I've been leading it," Menard said proudly. "Unfortunately, the clever culprits have run to ground. But don't worry your pretty head, my dear. We'll capture them yet."

"I don't doubt it," Sara murmured. She shot Johnny a quick glance from beneath her lashes and was appalled at the gleam of humor she saw sparkling there. Her attention was captured by the appearance of another contingent of riders. "Is this more of your party?"

"Why, I believe it's Sheriff Ramsey. Good Lord! What's happened to him?"

The sheriff approached on his dusty horse, the side of his face obscured by a blood-stained handkerchief. Two of his men followed him. They slowed their mounts to a walk as they approached the buggy.

"What happened, Sheriff?" Menard demanded. "Did you catch up with those outlaws?"

"No, dammit!" The sherriff growled, squinting at Plunket with his one good eye. "God damn incompetent let a limb slip and walloped me a good one. I've sent the rest of the men on toward Independence, and . . ." He noticed Sara. "Oh, begging your pardon, ma'am. It's Dr. Cary, isn't it?"

"It is, indeed," Sara replied. "You need that tended to. Get down, Johnny, and get my bag." Johnny moved carefully, his eyes narrowing, but Sara ignored him. Her medical calling came first, no matter what. She clambered down and spoke imperatively to the sheriff. "Come down from that horse and let me have a look at that face."

"It's nothing, ma'am. Just a thorn tree."

"All the more reason. You don't want it to turn to septic poisoning and risk losing that eye, do you?"

"No, ma'am." Ramsey swung down from the horse and shrugged in resignation.

Sara took her bag from Johnny and ushered the sheriff to the rear of the buggy, pushing him down to sit so she could reach his injured cheek. Johnny went to stand at Nubbin's head, and Plunket and the other men dismounted and gathered around to watch. She stripped off her gloves, then gently released the stained handkerchief and peered closely at the torn flesh.

"It's not too bad, Sheriff Ramsey, but it looks as though there are a couple of imbedded thorns. They'll have to come out."

Ramsey grunted his acquiescence, and Sara went to work with antiseptic and cotton wool.

"Did you see any sign of those robbers, Sheriff?" Menard asked.

"Not yet. It's damned hard—excuse me, ma'am—to get information out of folks hereabouts. They're as closed-mouthed as a Missouri snapping turtle, especially when it involves former guerrillas. Old habits die hard 'round these parts. You can't convince them these fellows are now preying on *them* instead of the Yankees."

"I believe more leads will come of questioning patrons of the lower-class saloons and taverns," Plunket said ponderously. "I suggest we seek out informants in such places as Zelby's and The Brass Bull." Menard cast a sparkling black glance at Sara, his lips twitching. "Why, even Mrs. Cary can testify to how rough those places can be."

Ramsey flinched and yelled, "Ouch!"

"It's all over now," Sara soothed, holding up a pair of tweezers with an inch-long thorn between the pinchers. She didn't look at Menard. "You'll be good as new in a few days, Sheriff Ramsey. Just let me cover this with a bandage and a piece of sticking plaster."

"I'm much obliged to you, ma'am."

Sara swiftly bandaged the wound. "Do you think the booty will ever be recovered, Sheriff? I can't help thinking about the poor people who entrusted their savings to that bank."

"They're being damned elusive, ma'am. But we haven't given up, not by a long shot. I have a feeling the clue we need to bring those scoundrels to justice is right under our noses."

Sara caught a glimpse of Johnny at the front of the buggy. His shoulders were shaking. Was he *laughing?* Her puzzled glance swept back to the sheriff. He stood up, dusting his hat on his thigh, and she was seized by a sudden wild desire to giggle.

Under their noses, he'd said? Poor Sheriff Ramsey! He'd been sitting on her trunk with its fortune in gold the entire time. She struggled to keep her face straight, though her voice was strangled. "I have every confidence in you and your men."

"Thank you, ma'am. Let's go, men." Sheriff Ramsey went to his horse. "You comin', Plunket?"

"I'll be along," Menard replied. The others mounted and rode off. Menard took Sara's hand and raised it to his lips, kissing the back. "You were wonderful, my dear."

"I—" She tugged her hand. "I really must go, Menard."

He stepped closer, pulling her nearer and placing her hand against his chest. His dark eyes were fervent and eager. "Sara, I've been so concerned for you during your indisposition. My esteem for you is as deep as the ocean, as high as a mountain. Surely you've guessed my humble affections are centered in your loveliness?"

"I'm extremely flattered, of course, but—but—" She flicked a glance toward Johnny, who rolled his eyes, then turned his back to admire the judge's mount.

"Tell me that there's some hope you might someday return my regard, and I'll go away the happiest man in Lafayette County," Menard begged earnestly.

"Well, of course, I like you very much." Sara foundered. Who would have guessed Menard would chose a time like this to become an ardent swain?

"So chary with your affections," he admonished lightly. "You really intend to break my heart, don't you?"

"No, of course not. I—I—" She gave him a confused, bemused look that spoke volumes, and he laughed softly.

"The indomitable Dr. Cary at a loss for words. Surely

I must—'' The stallion nickered shrilly, and Menard swung around. ''Here now, man. What are you doing?''

Johnny gently released the hoof he'd been examining and straightened, his face a bland mask. ''He's favoring that leg. Shoe's all right, so it might be an inflamed tendon.''

''That's an expensive piece of horseflesh, and I'll thank you to keep your hands off him. Really, Sara, how can you abide . . .'' He turned back, but Sara was already climbing into the buggy seat.

''Come, Johnny,'' she called. ''We must be going.''

''We'll continue our discussion later, if that's agreeable?'' Menard suggested at her side. Johnny climbed into the opposite side, his weight tilting the seat on its springs and hampering Plunket's conversation. ''I'll—come by—this evening—if I can.'' He broke off and glared at the blond man.

''Of course, Menard,'' Sara murmured, dragging on her gloves. ''We'd be delighted to receive you any time. Goodbye.''

Johnny picked up the reins, and they rolled off. Sara sat back against the seat, trembling.

''Thank God that's over!''

''What a performance,'' Johnny drawled nastily. ''You really enjoyed that pantywaist playing up to you for all he was worth.''

''And why shouldn't I? He's a gentleman.''

''He was pawing you.''

''He was not.'' Sara glared angrily at Johnny, but he stared straight ahead, gnawing sullenly on his lower lip. She was at a loss to explain his anger. Hadn't she done everything he'd expected? Why, he was acting like a jealous husband. The thought made her inhale sharply. Was that it? But he had no right, no claim—no matter what had happened between them.

''Where does that lead?''

His abrupt question made her jump. She recognized the turnoff he indicated, little more than a rutted wagon track. ''It goes south to Lone Jack.''

''What's there?''

''A little community. A few stores, a livery.''

He chewed his lower lip thoughtfully. "How far?"

"Twenty miles or so."

"It will do."

"Do for what?"

"We'll never get to Baxter Springs at this rate. We'll do some horse trading and get faster mounts in Lone Jack."

"We'll . . . ?" A horrified suspicion slithered through her mind as Johnny clicked to Nubbin and made the turn.

"Wait, I'm not going to Lone Jack. Let me off here and I'll walk back to town."

He gave her a look that showed what he thought of such an idea and slapped Nubbin into a clumsy trot.

"Johnny, what are you doing? You're free and clear. So let me off here. You said—"

"Forget what I said. Since our conversation with Ramsey and Plunket, you're going to have some awkward explanations to make. I think I'll spare you those."

"What do you mean?"

"You know too much for your own good, Doc, and on more than one occasion you've proven less than trustworthy. I'm going to take out a little insurance policy to guarantee a clean getaway."

Sara's voice was suddenly hoarse with apprehension. "No, Johnny."

"Yes, Sara. A wife's place is at her husband's side, and that's where I've decided you're going to stay." He smiled at her shocked, open-mouthed expression and gently chucked her under the chin. "I think you're going to like Mexico."

Chapter 13

Mexico!

The threat galvanized Sara into desperate flight. With no thought to the consequences, she jumped from the moving buggy. She landed hard, in a tumbling flurry of white petticoats, her hands and knees taking the brunt of the landing on the weed-choked roadside. The iron buggy wheels passed her with only inches to spare. Johnny's curses brought her to her feet, gasping and shaken, and intent only on escape, stumbling, half-running, knowing the futility of it even before his strong hands closed on her shoulders.

"Dammit, woman! Are you crazy?" he demanded, swinging her around. His eyes raked her, and a curious whiteness ringed his mouth. "You might have been killed!"

She struggled, bonnet askew and breathless, vainly trying to free herself from his punishing grip. "Let me go! You can't do this! It's—it's kidnapping!"

His expression was grim. Jerking her left hand up in front of her face, he pointed at her ring. "No jury would convict me, because this says you're my wife." Abruptly, he bent and, picking her up, strode with her back to the buggy, plopping her unceremoniously onto the bench seat. He leaned over her, hands braced on each side, his furious face inches from hers. "You're staying with me."

"I won't!" She was pale but defiant, ignoring the ache and sting of kneecaps and palms to glare her resentment. "I'll fight you every step of the way."

"No, you won't. First, because there's nothing you can

199

do that I can't beat. I'm bigger, stronger, and a lot more stubborn. And second, because if I have to waste my time arguing with you or running after you every ten seconds, then we'll never make it to Baxter Springs in time. You do remember what Cole promised to do if I wasn't there, don't you?''

Her eyes were wide and troubled, her reluctant reply a husky whisper. ''Yes.''

''Bright girl. Now you're making sense.''

Sara's lower lip trembled, and she bit it hard to control the betraying quiver. Once again, she was between the proverbial rock and a hard place. But she had to make her position clear. ''I don't want to—'' She swallowed uncomfortably. ''To be with you.''

He drew back, his expression unyielding. ''Tough.''

''You black-hearted monster! You—''

''Stow it, Doc!'' His index finger poked the air before her face. ''And if you ever try a damned dangerous stunt like that again, I swear to God I'll turn you over my knee and paddle that pert bottom of yours until you learn better. Are we clear on that?''

She crossed her arms and glowered at him. ''You wouldn't dare.''

''Don't bet on it, honey.'' His grin was slow and wicked. ''The idea has—possibilities.''

''Oh!'' Her cheeks burned. ''You're insufferable!''

He vaulted into the seat beside her and picked up the reins. ''Yeah. But you'll suffer in silence, because for the next four days, the most important thing in your life had better be getting us both to Baxter Springs.''

He whistled to Nubbin, and the buggy jerked and began to roll. Sara, in a high dudgeon, did not deign to answer. After all, what was there to say? He had her, and he knew it. She straightened her bonnet and for the following hours of jouncing, bone-jarring travel, fumed in resentful and apprehensive silence.

The prospect of spending even one more night in Johnny's company, much less an arduous trip all the way to Mexico, was more than daunting. That Pandora would be beside herself with worry went without saying. And what would Johnny require of her? Would he expect a continuation of intimacy despite the open hostilities between them? Or was he merely safeguarding his escape, using her as an inconvenient but necessary hostage?

She couldn't allow these worries to overshadow the necessity of their journey. Even a few hours' delay could be disastrous, should they miss their rendezvous with Cole and Jesse. Regardless of her trepidation, Sara knew she wouldn't attempt anything else that might jeopardize Johnny's timely arrival in Baxter Springs with the gold. She was equally determined not to allow him any further liberties. She had betrayed her conscience and herself once, but it would not happen again. She'd be prickly as a cactus, sharp-tongued as a fishwife. By the time they reached Baxter Springs, Johnny would be only too glad to let her go.

They made Lone Jack in good time, traveling the twenty miles in less than four hours. The community was merely a straggle of weathered clapboard buildings, but they were able to make a quick meal of German sausage and boiled potatoes at the general store. At the livery, Johnny swiftly obtained suitable mounts and tack, a large bay for himself and a smaller, sure-footed mare for Sara, complete with sidesaddle.

"You can ride?" he asked on an afterthought.

She stood inside the livery stable, stroking Nubbin's velvety muzzle in sad farewell. Though tempted to deny it, she nodded. "Of course. I'm no great horsewoman, but I get by."

"Good. Let's get our—er, cargo packed. I've laid in a few supplies and bedrolls. We'll take the lap rug from the buggy, but we'll have to leave everything else."

"Not my bag."

"I said everything. The horses—"

"If my medicinals stay, then so do I." Her tone was soft, but adamant. "You've had everything your way, but you can't change the fact that I'm a doctor."

In the end he relented, stymied by her stubbornness. Out of sight of the livery owner, Sara helped remove Quantrill's treasure from her trunk and distribute it evenly in the bottoms of the saddlebags. She abandoned the worn leather physician's satchel, carefully packing instruments and medicines on top of the gold, wrapping them in the dainty underthings Johnny had used for camouflage in her trunk. She was almost able to see the humor in leaving home with only a change of drawers and her doctor's bag—almost, but not quite.

They were ready at last, blankets rolled around Sara's puny scraps of clothing and Johnny's riverboat garb and securely lashed behind the saddles, packages of supplies stashed in the bags, and a new graniteware coffee pot bouncing on a thong against the bay's flank. Johnny lifted Sara into the saddle. She tucked her right knee around the curved support, settling her skirts and feeling for the stirrup with her left foot.

"We have to travel fast and hard," Johnny warned. He guided the toe of her walking shoe into the stirrup loop and swiftly adjusted the buckle on the stirrup leather. Squinting against the lowering sun, he turned a questioning face toward her, his hands resting familiarly against her ankle. "We can make a few more miles before sundown, but I intend to go in the dark as far as we can. If the weather holds, well and good, but if it doesn't, it'll be close getting to Baxter Springs. The time we gain now could make all the difference. Do you understand that, Sara?"

"You don't have to keep reminding me," she snapped. "I'm as anxious to arrive as you are. I won't make trouble."

He gave her one last considering glance, then mounted his bay. "Let's ride."

Johnny set an easy but mile-eating pace out of Lone Jack, heading south following the rutted cart track called a road. The undulating countryside, still covered with winter's brown mantle, held a sameness about it that was mesmerizing. Hillsides of rough prairie grasses alternated with bottoms lined with the naked, leafless silhouettes of scrub oaks. There were occasional homesteads on distant slopes, the gray-blue curl of smoke drifting skyward from native stone chimneys and the faint barking of yard dogs marking their boundaries.

They paused once, near sunset, to stretch their legs and drink water from the canteen, then pressed on. The temperature dropped as the sun did, but by that time Sara was too numb with fatigue to feel the cold. Stoically, she voiced no complaint. Her bent leg protested its cramped position, and her spine screamed with each beat of the mare's hooves, but she gritted her teeth, focusing on Johnny's back as night fell around them. When the half-moon rose, the path became easier to follow, but Sara was swaying in the saddle, not even fully conscious, when sometime after midnight Johnny finally called a halt beside a stream.

For a moment, she could not fathom what he wanted when he reached to lift her down within the small copse of trees. It was like waking from an endless dream.

"Oh!" she cried with a gasp, wincing as stiff, abused muscles claimed victory. She staggered when Johnny set her on the ground, clutching his coatsleeve for balance. Her feet tingled from lack of circulation.

"Walk around a bit," he suggested gruffly. "I'll get a fire going and see to the horses."

She did as she was bid, limping slowly around their campsite. The moon and stars gave icy-blue light to the navy night sky, but soon the yellow flame of Johnny's fire drew her like a moth. Johnny threw down the bedrolls on a flat piece of ground, dropping the lap rug over Sara's shoulders as she crouched before the fire, hands outstretched. She took off her bonnet and bent her head, wearily rubbing the back of her neck. Johnny thought it looked delicate and fragile, like porcelain, and his fingers ached with the need to touch her again. Mouth set against the need, he dug into one of the bags for a cold sourdough biscuit.

"Here, eat," he ordered, passing it to her.

"I'm not hungry."

"Eat anyway."

Obediently, she began to nibble at the crusty edge.

He had to hand it to her, Johnny thought as he unsaddled the horses. She'd proven she was a real trouper today—and not a peep of complaint out of her. There weren't many women who'd have done as much, but then her motivation was strong. She loved the people at home, those misfits who depended on her. It was as simple—and as complex—as that. That once she'd counted him worthy of being a part of her family was a poignant memory, over-laid with treachery on both their parts, and clouded by the knowledge of shared passion.

Johnny shook his head in self-mockery. Keeping her with him was an exercise in foolhardiness. No matter what his stated reasons for his impulsive decision, he knew that more than expediency, more than revenge, more even than simple lust kept him near her. Her feisty temper and open, compassionate nature completed him, and he was loath to lose that feeling, reluctant to give her up even though holding her drove yet another wedge of enmity between them. Making love with Sara had changed things irrevo-cably, and he wondered with forlorn hope if they would ever recapture the easy friendship that had once been theirs. Would she ever look at him with her old warm affection or relax enough to sing her little ditties again? He shrugged impatiently. With some things there was never any going back.

Recovering the Golden Calf was a goal muddled now by the need to protect Sara and the ones she loved. Some-how, he had to do both, and in such a way that Jesse and the others wouldn't blame her and turn on her in a desire for vengeance. How he was going to do that was beyond him at the moment, but the less Sara knew, the better, for her own safety. So he firmly squashed the impulse to tell her everything. He could bear her contempt if he knew she was safe.

Johnny gave each horse a handful of grain and tethered them for the night. Sara was coming back from a trip to the woods when he turned back to the fire. Her feet were dragging. She'd removed her coat and wrapped the lap rug around her like a shawl. Painfully, she lowered herself to the edge of a bedroll. Raising her knees, she bent forward and began to unlace her shoes.

She sucked in a painful breath. "Ouch!"

Johnny went down on his knees in front of her, con-cerned. "What is it?"

"Cramp. In my leg." She bit her lower lip and rubbed her right leg through her skirts. Johnny made a small noise of irritation and flipped back the hems, grasping her calf between his large hands and massaging it forcefully.

Sara gasped, falling back on one elbow. "What—ahh!—do you think you're doing?" She grimaced and moaned as his deft fingers found the hard, contracted muscle beneath her stocking.

"Helping you." Johnny's expression was unreadable in the golden glow of the fire. He slipped her shoes off, then reached for the garter circling her thigh and rolled it and the stocking down her leg and over her instep. His hands were calloused and warm against her night-cooled skin, and she jumped, wiggling backward.

"It's all right, really." She was breathless, trying to pull her leg free of the soothing magic of his fingers.

"Be still." He set her foot firmly against his thigh and continued to massage the calf from knee to ankle. "You're not used to riding. It'll be worse tomorrow unless you let me work out the soreness now. And I can't afford to let you slow us down."

"Oh." She closed her eyes for a moment and swallowed hard. Her foot flexed in response to his ministrations, and she tried not to think of how close it lay to the bulge of his manhood. Her best defense against the seductive wizardry of his touch was anger, and she groped for it with desperation, her voice waspish. "If you hadn't insisted I come with you, I wouldn't be slowing you down."

"You aren't—yet. And I don't intend that you will. You did well today."

"What if I can't keep up tomorrow? What if you're wrong? Innocent people will suffer because of your stubbornness. There's no point in this. Why, I know Pandora is half-crazy with worry this very minute. She'll think something awful's happened to me. It's cruel to use an old woman so."

His hands paused, and he lifted his head to meet her eyes. "Calm down, Sara. I took care of that."

"What? How?"

"I paid the livery owner in Lone Jack to deliver a letter I wrote. She'll get it in a day or two when he returns the buggy and Nubbin."

"What kind of lie did you tell her?" Sara demanded, sitting up straighter. "What could possibly allay her fears?"

"The truth—of sorts."

"Will you stop talking in riddles."

The corner of Johnny's mouth lifted and devilish laughter glinted in his eyes. "I told her we eloped."

Her shriek of rage he expected, but her heel in the pit of his stomach caught him off guard, doubling him over with a swift, grunted exhalation. She drew back her foot with the obvious intention of delivering a more telling blow to an especially vulnerable area, but he had the presence of mind to grab her. She retaliated with another shriek of pure fury, and her small fist caught his jawbone just under his ear, making his head ring. With a growl, he rolled over her, grappling for her wrists, his legs tangling in her skirts.

"Dammit, Sara!" he roared. "Cut it out!"

"You—you despicable, irresponsible bastard!" she screeched, fingers curled into claws.

He caught her hands and held them over her head. "It's the truth, isn't it? Yves will verify we're man and wife."

"No one was to know. I'm ruined! I'll never be able to show my face again!"

"The whole thing was your idea. Why whine about it now?"

"It wasn't supposed to be real!" She struggled against him, panting.

"But it is. Very real."

Sara froze, stopped by the slow, sensuous hooding of eyes that gleamed in the flickering darkness. "No!"

Holding her wrists with one hand, he dragged at her skirts, reaching to caress her thigh and rounded hip through her thin drawers. His mouth hovered over hers. "You can't deny what's between us, Sara. *This* is why you're here with me."

His mouth covered hers in a drugging kiss, a tantalizing sweep of lips and tongue that took her breath. Raising his head, he gazed deeply into her eyes, his voice thick. "Did you think I would stop wanting you?"

Bewildered, heart pumping madly, her body alive with feelings that made everything else immaterial, she whispered, "I don't know."

"You're mine now, and I haven't had enough of you."

He buried his nose in the fragrant curve of her neck and shoulder, and his voice was ragged. "Oh, God. I may *never* have enough of you."

His words made her shudder, the melting rush of desire heating her blood, setting her on fire. The weight of his body was a delicious pressure, and she moved against him in unconscious invitation. With a low groan, he took her lips again, releasing her hands and gathering her close, kissing her hungrily again and again until her mouth was swollen and damp.

Her hands clasped his neck, threading through his silky hair, following the cords of his throat to the top button of his shirt, then slipping the disk free, and the next, wanting to feel the crisp hairs of his chest against her fingers. He helped her, pulling the tail of his shirt free, shrugging out of his jacket. The shirt was open then, and she ran her hands over the flat, muscular planes of his chest, glorying in the texture of skin and hair against her palms, rubbing the bronze coins of his nipples into puckered nubs.

He feasted insatiably on her lips, tasting and exploring, then rolled her over on top of him, his fingers frantic at the line of buttons down her back. The chilly air made her gasp against his mouth when he pushed the gown down her shoulders and arms, pooling it at her waist until, impatiently, he released the tapes of her petticoats and pushed everything down and off. She shivered in the cold with only her chemmie and pantalettes to protect her, but his skillful hands were warm, so warm. Caught up in the bright flame of passion, she was only aware of his heat, his maleness, his need for—her.

The thought brought her to a heady, dizzying realization of her power, and her response was sweet and wild, her hands entreating, her lips soft and yielding. He touched her everywhere, stroking, inciting elemental need, fondling her breasts, thumbing the rosy crests to pulsating life. His hands moved down the curve of her spine to cup her firm bottom, pulling her hips intimately against the hard evidence of his arousal beneath his trousers. She moaned and twined her tongue with his.

Instantly, he rolled with her, laying her gently on her back. He knelt between her raised thighs, fumbling with the fastening on his pants, his gaze avid. The thin material of her lace-edged underthings was nearly transparent in the flicker of the campfire and so no impediment to his searching gaze. His breath caught. Her pantalettes, split for convenience's sake from front to back, revealed the dark delta at the juncture of her legs to his full, appreciative perusal. His smoldering gaze tangled with hers. Sara's eyes were glazed with passion, and her hair had tumbled from its combs and fell in lush, vibrant waves around her face. He saw her shiver.

"Are you cold?"

She shook her head.

"Afraid?"

"No."

His hands lightly smoothed the sensitive flesh of her inner thighs. "Then what?"

Her breath shallowed, and her glance flicked to the open V of his trousers. "You know."

"Tell me."

"Johnny, please," she whispered.

He leaned over her, tongued the indentation of her navel and felt her inaudible gasp. "Say it."

"I—I want you." There was an ache in her voice that matched the ache in his loins. "I want you now."

He took her then, powerfully, his trousers pushed down about his hips but his need too urgent to remove them completely. He plunged into her silky warmth, and his growl of satisfaction was deep, primeval, the primitive, exultant sound of mating.

Sara gasped and arched against him, reaching, stretching. Her thick lashes fluttered against her flushed cheekbones, and she clung to his shoulders, writhing in ecstasy beneath him, filled with him and nearly sobbing with the splendor of their joining. He lifted her legs around his waist, pulling her even closer, as close as thought. His thrusts were powerful, deep and overwhelming, and—mind shattering.

Sensation exploded, and Sara cried out, pleasure flooding every atom of her being, radiating from her center like a disintegrating star. She spiraled into fulfillment, trying to take all of him, her head thrown back as the rapture consumed her again, and her soft whimpers undid him, catapulting him over the brink after her.

There weren't any words—nor any need for them. They lay for a long time, still entwined, while their ragged breathing steadied, stunned anew by the power they had found together. Finally, Johnny tucked her under his arm, pulled the blanket around them, and let exhaustion and surcease lead them together toward sleep. And Sara knew she was lost, irrevocably.

It became the pattern of the next days—the long, arduous hours of travel, followed by the long, tender hours sharing a bedroll. Fatigue was a constant companion, yet Sara went into Johnny's arms each night knowing herself incapable of denying either of them the release they found together. He took her as his right, bringing her to unbridled fulfillment in the tenderest of ways, shouting his own joy to the heavens in the moment of completion. She was captivated, drugged with newly unleashed sensuality, her addiction for him growing to overpowering proportions. When he wasn't touching her, she was frightened by her inability to refuse him. It was demoralizing and confusing to know she was no longer her own woman, but in his arms it didn't matter. She was much subdued, uncertain of herself and her future, when they finally arrived in Baxter Springs, Kansas late the fourth day.

The town was hardly more than a crossroads, but a sign over one saloon did advertise itself as a "hotel." Sara's eyes lit up at the prospect of a hot bath, a real bed, and a hearty meal. She was disheveled and travel-strained, and Johnny's four-day's growth of beard made him appear sinister and villainous. She was dismayed when he rode her straight through the town.

"Can't we stop?" she asked, weariness making her voice tremble. "How will we find the others?"

"Don't fret," Johnny said dryly. "They'll find us."

And they did, an hour after sundown, all four of them stealthily creeping into the campsite Johnny had chosen a mile out of town. Sara was resting, sitting with her back braced against a saddle, and she jumped when Cole su denly materialized on the other side of the campfire. Je and the others appeared behind him.

"I see you're right on time, Tuck," Jesse said.

"I said I'd be here, didn't I?" Johnny's voice was even. He stirred the bubbling, aromatic contents of a stewpot hanging over the fire between two notched sticks. "Grub's ready. What kept you?"

"What the hell's *she* doing here?" Cole snarled.

Johnny handed Sara a plate of camp stew, his stubbled face impassive, but Sara noticed the whiteness around his knuckles. His tone took on a quiet, deadly note. "She belongs with me."

"We knew we could count on you," Jesse said, smirking and blinking rapidly. His sly smile was conspiratorial, and he winked at Frank and Jim. "Even love-sick."

There was a round of laughter, and Sara's cheeks burned. She stared at the congealing brown gravy and lumpy potatoes on her plate, feeling nauseous.

Johnny frowned at her downcast head, then pointed to the pile of saddlebags. "There it is, if you want to count it."

That proved a diversion, and the four newcomers carefully inspected the saddlebags, proving to their mutual satisfaction that Tuck had come through for the cause. Watching them examine the gold, Sara drew a heartfelt sigh of relief. Her people were safe.

Johnny's thoughts were not as composed. Instinct told him that mixing a large amount of gold with these unscrupulous characters was going to lead to trouble. He had serious doubts whether they actually intended to hand the Calf over to Maximillian, but it was a chance he couldn't take. If they wanted to continue to San Antonio on the pretense of taking up the Emperor's cause, then he'd have to go along with it, at least until he found a way to extricate the gold, Sara, and himself from the clutches of these bloodthirsty boys.

With the gold accounted for, Jesse and his band relaxed into a high good humor. They squatted around the fire, helping themselves to the stew, and launched into a spirited rendition of their various escapades since leaving Lexington. The discussion turned eventually to their next move and which route to take south through the Indian Territory into Texas and on to San Antonio. The Texas Trail curved through the eastern edge of the territory and followed a track blazed by the Shawnee to their summer hunting grounds, but it was widely traveled, even served by a stage line. Cole remained adamant that his tour in Texas during the war gave him more expertise in the matter, and recommended a more westerly route across the prairie following a course used by a half-breed trader called Chisholm. Eventually, they decided a combination of the two routes would be best, following the Texas Trail and crossing the Red River at Colbert's Ferry, then to Fort Worth and south to San Antonio.

Johnny said little during the discussion, but his regard kept coming back to Sara, sitting quietly and a little to one side, listening intently. What was she thinking?

Cole walked up beside him, his mouth drawn down in a scowl. "You must be going soft in the head, Tuck, bringing her along. A woman will just slow us down."

"She's done all right so far," Johnny drawled.

"The Indian Territory is rough country. Get shut of her, I say."

"She stays with me." Johnny allowed a small smile. "Sara wants a big *hacienda* when we get to Mexico, right, sugar?"

Sara set aside her plate, her appetite gone, replaced by a growing sense of humiliation and unease.

Cole's rusty voice was filled with disgust. "Thought you had more sense than to settle for just one woman—and one you can't trust, at that."

Johnny took Sara's hand and pulled her against his chest. Staring at Cole, he let his knuckles brush the underslope of Sara's breast in a blatant gesture of possession that made her gasp. His smile hinted at the hidden intimacies between them. "It has its compensations."

He turned and led her away to where their combined bedrolls lay spread apart from the others. Sara flushed with shame and mortification. She was hurt and angry, and frustrated by her helplessness.

Her voice shook. "He's right. You don't need me anymore. Let me go home."

"Don't tell me what I need," Johnny said between his teeth, his face cast in stark, savage lines.

"But . . ."

"Hush up, woman, and lie down." His tone was gruff. "I'm tired."

She cast him a swift glance, but there was nothing of the tender lover she'd come to know in his expression. Hesitantly, she lay down in her clothes. He knelt and pulled off her shoes, then his own boots. He lay down beside her and tugged her close, pulling the blanket over them. His warmth seeped into Sara's bones, but when he turned to her and his mouth sought hers, she placed her fingers against his lips in supplication and denial.

"Johnny, please." She closed her eyes for a brief moment, and when they opened again they were bright with unshed tears. "Don't shame me in front of *them.*"

"They have to know you belong to me. That if any man dares touch you, I'll kill him."

"You've made me your woman and a wanton, too, and you know I can't deny you." Her words were choked. "But I couldn't bear it if you take me now and they hear . . ."

"Shh, love." He kissed her fingertips, and then her lips, lightly. The stubble of his beard was scratchy but not unpleasant. "I wouldn't sully what we share in that manner. Rest now. It's a long way to Mexico."

He curled on his side, his back to the campfire, and pulled her against him, spoon-fashion. Wondering, but too grateful to question his self-denial, she snuggled into the curve of his body. He stifled a moan.

"Be still, honey. Just because this is neither the time nor the place doesn't mean I don't want you."

"Oh!" Her single word was a soft gasp. She felt the hard ridge of his arousal pressing against her bottom and shrank away. His hand splayed across her middle and pulled her back.

"Not so fast. I like you close. Just don't wiggle."

"Yes, Johnny." She couldn't contain the soft laugh that burst from her throat. His answering chuckle rumbled beside her ear.

"You like making me suffer, eh, wench? Well, let me tell you, a man likes a wanton in his bed, and if that's what I've made you, then I'm glad of it. Don't worry. I'll make it my business to find plenty of right times and places between here and Texas.''

His words sobered her, and she lay still and silent. She knew he would fulfill that promise. And she would be helpless to deny him, being so completely at the mercy of her own desires. He had only to look at her, and she burst into flames. But what would become of her when he tired of her? She was more than a simple whore, more than a camp-follower. He wanted her, but not out of affection, and he'd discard her without a second thought. In spite of their paper marriage, there was no commitment or fidelity between them, merely an overwhelming physical attraction that had made her forget for a time all the ill will between them. She had nothing but pride to sustain her now, so how could she follow him so docilely, allowing him every liberty? She knew she couldn't.

Her duty was discharged. She'd seen that Jesse and the rest had that dratted gold, and now there was no reason for them to threaten either her or her family. Why, Johnny would probably be glad she was gone—after he got over being angry. A nebulous plan took form. She had to escape from Johnny and the insidious seduction of his loving. Her self-respect demanded it. There would come an opportunity to slip away, and she would take it. She must!

"What's made you so quiet all of a sudden?" Johnny murmured into her hair.

Sara suppressed a startled movement. He must not become suspicious, at all costs. She tried to make her voice drowsy.

"Just thinking."

"About what?" he asked, nuzzling her ear and making her shiver with pleasure.

Shifting uncomfortably, she tried to ignore the familiar stirrings of desire centered low in her core. "Are we going to see many Indians in the Territory?"

"It's likely." His voice was dry. "It's been home to the Five Tribes for over thirty years."

"Are they—dangerous?"

He laughed softly. "Sure. They eat little white women like you for breakfast."

"You're making that up."

"Better stick close, just in case a naked Cherokee brave tries to carry you off to his lodge and make you his squaw." He chuckled again, but there was no answering murmur, and she was very still. He lifted his head, trying to read her expression in the darkness. "Sara?"

"That's not funny, Johnny."

"Why not?"

Her trembling voice was low and etched with a bleakness that cut into his soul. "Because it's too close to what you've already done to me."

Chapter 14

"Just what the hell do you think you're doing?"

They'd stopped to water the horses at the edge of a small stream, and the noonday sun beat down on them. The March wind blowing over the prairie lands was redolent with the fragrance of budding grasses, and the air was unseasonably warm, making their jackets unnecessary.

Sara gave Johnny's puzzled face a quick, annoyed glance, then turned back to her task. The scalpel she wielded sliced through the travel-stained fabric of her skirt, splitting it easily. "I refuse to ride another mile in that sidesaddle."

"Should I order milady a coach?" he asked snidely.

Sara's temper flared, and she jerked the knife through the hem and began on the other side. The rigors of overland travel in the company of five men were telling on her. She was tired, dirty, and frustrated by a lack of privacy and the fact that Johnny had hardly let her out of his sight for the past six days. Not that he'd had the opportunity to make love to her since leaving Baxter Springs due to the killing pace and a natural fastidiousness. That might account for his own ill temper. They'd been snapping and snarling at each other like cats and dogs, and Sara was fast coming to the end of her tether. He wouldn't let her go, and she couldn't escape. She ground her teeth and glared at her captor, tormentor, demon-lover.

"Just be good enough to adjust the stirrup on my saddle so I can ride astride."

"If you think I'll let you show the blisters on your butt to every saddlebum and redskin in the Territory—"

"My blisters are my concern." She wrapped the scalpel in a piece of cloth and jammed it angrily back into the saddlebag. Grabbing the hem of her petticoat, she pulled it between her legs and twisted it into her waistband. "You see? Bloomers and at least an approximation of a split riding skirt. I'm perfectly decent."

"Hell's bells! You look like a rag-picker."

"And whose fault is that?" She knew she looked a fright, with her hair in a ragged braid, a sunburnt nose, and circles of fatigue under her eyes making her look every one of her years. "I don't want to be here. I didn't ask to be dragged through this God-forsaken countryside by a bunch of thieving outlaws!"

Johnny shot a look at Jesse and the rest down by the creek bank. "Keep your voice down," he warned, but the dam of restraint had burst, and Sara was in a high rage.

"I'm sick to death of the mud, and the dust, the taste of hardtack, and the smell of horses! I want a real bath!"

"You know why we've avoided the towns."

"All I know is that I'm sick of this!" Her brown eyes glittered, coppery and molten with aggravation. "I'm sick of *you!*"

His expression was hidden under ten days' worth of sandy stubble, but his voice softened. He caressed her cheek with his callused palm and smiled. "Poor baby. It's been rough on you, I know."

"You don't know a damn thing, you thick-headed slug!"

He laughed, his green eyes sparkling, and put his arms around her. "Maybe you're just missing me, hmm? I know I'm ready to burst with wanting you. Sharing a bedroll and not being able to love you is about to kill me."

"You're obsessed," she retorted tartly, pushing at him, but her heart beat double-time. "And uncivilized."

"What if I find us a private place tonight? I'll even shave."

"Don't do me any favors."

"You can pretend to be cold, but I know better." He bent closer, whispering in her ear. "I know the little sounds you make when your blood is hot. They drive me crazy."

She closed her eyes, fighting a wave of dizziness. Desire ran like rich wine through her veins. "Stop it. I just want to go home."

"Your only home is with me, wife-of-mine. When are you going to realize that?"

Opening her eyes, she stared up at him. "That doesn't make any sense."

His answer was slow in coming, perplexed and even a bit rueful. "No, I guess it doesn't. But it doesn't matter." Then his lips found hers, sealing his possession. When he lifted his head, his voice was thick. "Tonight."

She watched him adjust her stirrup, her mind and body in turmoil. The promise in his voice meant there would be no reprieve tonight. Without a doubt, he'd weave his sensual spell on her again, taking her out of herself, sucking her dry of all defiance and self-will. She lost her identity in his arms, and that frightened her more than any physical danger, more than taking her chances alone in the wilderness. She knew she would give him everything in the end—body, heart, and soul—and that could only lead to heartache. Even though her traitorous body clamored for his touch, she couldn't afford to indulge her obsession for him again. She had to leave, elude Johnny somehow, before tonight. But how? How?

Toward evening, they came across a group of drovers with a herd of longhorns headed for the Missouri stockyards, fording a shallow branch of the Canadian River. By mutual consent the men agreed to camp together to share companionship and whiskey while the herd grazed and watered along both sides of the river. As always, Jesse set a close watch on the valuable saddlebags, safeguarding them not only from the drovers, but also from his own partners. He kept a blinking vigilance that gave no opportunity for anyone to so much as sneeze on the Calf, much less make off with it.

Johnny set their bedrolls apart from the main group, in the privacy of a small cluster of stunted trees. Sara watched his actions with growing trepidation and a sense of inevitability. It wasn't until after supper when he gave her a present that Sara knew what she had to do.

"Here," he said, pushing a bundle of clothes at her.

"If you're going to ride like a man, you can dress like one, too. You'll be more comfortable, and so will I."

Sara unfolded the clean shirt and faded trousers and looked at them in wonder. There was even a broad-brimmed hat and a pair of boots. "Where did you get these?"

He nodded toward the drovers' campsite. A fire burned near a rattletrap chuck wagon in a circle of bedrolls. The lonesome sound of some cowpoke's harmonica drifted mournfully over the lowing of the cattle. "Bought them off of a kid. Don't worry. I gave him enough to buy new duds when they reach Sedalia."

"I'd like to wash before I put them on." A germ of an idea took form in her mind. Could she carry off a subterfuge, lull Johnny's suspicions long enough to make an escape? This was the only opportunity she was likely to get. She had to try.

"I'll bring you a bucket of water," Johnny offered.

"No, I mean wash—all over."

"The river's cold as a witch's—well, it's cold. You'll freeze."

"I don't care. I'd do anything to be clean again. Please, Johnny." She gave him a tentative smile and felt a blush creep up her neck. Let him think it was from embarrassment and not the lies she must tell. "After all, I'll have you to make me warm again."

"You can count on that," he said, then laughed. "Eager, huh, Doc? Me, too." He rubbed his palm across his jaw, making a rasping sound. "I guess I can get rid of this, too."

"I'll just go upstream a little way, around that bend, if you'll keep watch here?" She tried to make her tone beguiling and was relieved when he agreed. "I may be a while," she warned, taking soap and a change of under-things from her meager assortment. "I want to wash my hair, too."

Around the bend of the river, out of sight of the encampment, Sara gave one envious thought to her planned bath, then quickly stripped off her coat, the soiled and mutilated dress, and her petticoats. Holding everything in a ball over her head, and gritting her teeth against the frigid water, she waded across the shallow river. Shivering violently from the cold and the possible consequences if her plan failed, she hurriedly blotted the water from her body and donned the boy's clothes. She turned her short coat inside out and rubbed dirt into it, pulled on the boots, and stuffed her hair under the hat. Her dress and petticoats disappeared under a pile of bracken. Her only hope was that, in the failing light, her disguise would suffice. She knew she didn't have much time.

She circled wide, skirting the outer edges of the herd, hoping her footprints would be obliterated by the milling cattle. Her heart slammed against her ribs in a chaotic rhythm, and her throat was tight with tension. Over the lowing of the longhorns, she could faintly hear laughter from the campsite. Now that she had gotten this far, she hesitated. Her initial plan had been to steal a horse and head north toward Fort Gibson, but how was she to do that without garnering unwanted attention?

She crouched behind a tuffet of rough grass, scanning the herd, awed in spite of herself at the five-foot hornspan of the cattle. She tried to spot the drovers on watch around the perimeters of the herd. Could she surprise one and take his horse? It was unlikely, but desperation might force her to try. She racked her brain for other ideas. Dared she use Johnny's "under their nose" philosophy and blithely waltz into the drovers' camp, maybe even roll up in some cowpuncher's bedroll and wait until morning to slip away? Getting back to civilization didn't worry her. She'd find a way, if only she could—

A rough hand covered her mouth, and a strong arm circled her waist, pulling her backward into denser cover. Startled, flailing wildly, she felt her heart sink to her toes. Johnny! He'd found her already! Eyes wide and frightened, she craned her head back, ready to make her appeal—and froze, the breath leaving her body as though she'd taken a blow in the stomach.

Pitch-black eyes sparkled in a handsome, exotic face framed by a swatch of midnight hair. The brave was naked except for breechclout and leggins, and his smooth, copper-colored skin gleamed with an inner fire. His hand encountered the soft roundness of her breast underneath the concealing shirt, and for an instant a look of almost comical consternation crossed his features.

Then he smiled.

Johnny smiled.

It was not a pleasant sight, the wolfish baring of teeth of a hunter scenting blood. The trail ended here, and he'd find his woman or die.

He lay on his stomach in the tall grass at the crest of a low rise, surveying the scene below. The tracks of the unshod pony had been difficult to follow, forcing him time and again to backtrack to pick up the trail, but they led to this half-finished log dwelling. The homeplace was strangely quiet in the afternoon gloom. Too quiet. A hard, frantic knot of fear swelled in his chest, and he fought it back. He had to stay cool, clear-headed. Sara's life depended on it.

Her disappearance the evening before had at first enraged him, but then he'd found the signs of struggle, the marks of moccasined feet, and he'd nearly gone wild.

"We ain't waiting while you and that bitch play hide and seek," Cole had said. The others had nodded agreement, and Johnny knew he'd find no help from them. The choice was to go after Sara or stay with the Golden Calf. It was no choice.

"Fine," he said, mounting his horse and catching up the reins of Sara's mare. "Go to hell."

"You get done with her, Tuck," Jesse called, "you can catch up with us later. You know where we'll be."

Johnny's eyes bored into the boy, and his words were a grim promise. "I'll find you. Count on it."

His message was clear: Double-cross Tuck and they'd pay the price.

Now there was another price to exact. He knew little of Indians, but if that sonofabitch had so much as harmed a single hair on Sara's head, he'd kill him. Rage burned like wildfire and, clenching his jaw, Johnny drew and cocked the Enfield. He just might kill him anyway.

He crept cautiously down the knoll, crossed the yard, and took shelter against the rough-hewn log wall. A couple of spotted ponies in a corral behind the house nickered softly. The front door hung slightly open on leather hinges, and he moved cautiously toward it. A soft mewling of distress erased his every thought of caution. He kicked open the door, leveling his gun menacingly at the group clumped around a tin washpan.

Sara bent over the basin, sleeves rolled above her elbow, her dark hair falling in wisps around her strained face. Her head jerked up at his crashing entrance, and relief lit her coffee-dark eyes.

"Oh, it's you. Thank God."

Johnny tried to assimilate the scene, the dark-skinned man and his worried, broad-faced wife, the belligerent young man taking a threatening step toward him, and the naked, whimpering child Sara held in her arms. The reality was so different from the disaster he'd imagined that he was stunned. Sara lifted the boy, a child of no more than two years, from the water-filled pan, wrapped him swiftly in a piece of cloth, and hurried toward Johnny.

"Did you bring my things?" she demanded. She shot a quick, repugnant glance at the gun he held. "And put that away."

"Are you all right?" he demanded in a ragged voice.

"Certainly. I need my medicine vials, the bismuth and salol. Little Samuel has been convulsing."

"Miss Sara?" the older man questioned.

"It's all right," she reassured him over her shoulder. "This is John Tucker, my—my husband. Johnny, the McIntosh family of the Creek Nation, Benjamin and Grace and Roly. Please, get my medicinals, quickly."

Johnny stared at her a long second, then holstered the gun. "I'm going to strangle you for this," he muttered under his breath.

She shrugged, unrepentant, rueful humor quirking her lips. "Later."

Minutes later, he watched her coax a dose of medicine into the exhausted child, crooning to him while his mother rocked him.

"It is fortunate for us, sir," Benjamin McIntosh said with innate dignity, "that Roly came across your wife when she became separated from your party. She has undoubtedly saved my second son's life."

"Yes, fortunate," Johnny echoed. He frowned slightly. He might be conversing with any educated white farmer. The McIntosh family, with their civilized ways, their mixture of calico and traditional Indian dress, the bits of decorative china over the mantlepiece, and their obvious industry, hardly fit his preconceived notions of "savages."

"Roly was out trying to round up our scattered cattle. He gave Miss Sara a fright at first," Benjamin explained. "The mission school did not teach him manners, I'm afraid."

"I wondered why Little Sister wore a boy's clothes," Roly said. He smiled. "We are great friends now."

"You have a fine place here," Johnny said evenly. "I'm sorry for the way I busted in like that. I guess I went a little crazy, worrying about my wife."

"You could not know." Benjamin shrugged. "The war was hard on everyone, white and Indian, and still there is much evil. We've only recently returned to our home. There is much to rebuild."

"The fever's broken," Sara said quietly. She rolled her sleeves down and buttoned the cuffs in an efficient manner. "I think Samuel will be all right now."

"The Old Ones sent us a gift in you. We will offer prayers each day for your happiness," Benjamin said. "Will you and your husband stay the night? Our home is yours."

"No." Johnny tempered his abrupt answer. "Thank you, but we need to rejoin our friends as soon as possible."

He felt Sara's anxious regard on him, but was so consumed by the upheaval of emotions she'd caused him, he dared not look at her. Relief, anger, even reluctant admiration at her medical skills and undaunted spirit, warred with a primitive urge to vent his wrath on her slender person. His face was calm almost to the point of impassivity, but inside he boiled like a volcano on the verge of eruption.

Johnny shook hands with McIntosh, while Sara said goodbye to Grace and Roly and checked the child one last time. They mounted up and rode away, Johnny still not trusting himself to speak. The horses cantered several miles over the lush grassland dotted with early blue larkspur and purple cohosh. After a while he slowed the pace, following the edge of a small creek. They stopped near a group of stunted cottonwoods to let the horses drink. He didn't look at her, or say a word, merely sat in the saddle and stared at the distant horizon, his jaw working with tension. Finally, Sara broke the uncomfortable silence.

"If you intend to beat me, I wish you'd get it over with."

He swung down from the saddle and jerked her off her mare in a series of swift movements, unmindful of the water covering his boots. Setting her on the bank, he grabbed her shoulders. He was amazed to find that his hands were shaking.

"I ought to," he said. "I ought to beat the hell out of you for scaring me like that."

"I thought you'd be glad to be rid of me."

"Jesus Christ! You thought I wanted to find you raped or dead on the prairie? I've been through hell!"

Contrition softened her mouth. "I'm sorry," she said softly. She lifted her hand and touched his jaw, smooth-shaven again, then let her fingers trace his upper lip and the mustache he'd left on a whim. "You look different. Rakish. I like it."

"You like—Dammit! Don't try to sidetrack me." He threw his hat to the ground in disgust and glared at her. She was as slender as a lad in those ridiculous pants and so damned fragile it could break a man's heart. "You were running away, weren't you?"

Her chin tilted at a pugnacious angle. "Yes. Is that so surprising?"

"What's surprising is that you didn't get yourself killed. How'd you end up with Roly McIntosh, anyway?"

"It was an accident. I think he was going to relieve those drovers of a stray beef if he could, but I stumbled into his plans, and once I figured out he wasn't going to scalp me, he offered me a ride to his folks' place—"

Johnny slapped his forehead in sheer disbelief. "And you went? You wanted to get away from me so badly that you'd take a chance like that?'' His face clouded. ''Why, Sara?''

She looked away. ''You've taken me from my family.''

He took a step toward her. ''That's not enough to risk your life. Why?''

''You're holding me against my will.''

''Am I? What else?'' He cupped her nape in his hand and forced her to look at him.

''I'm afraid.''

''Of me?''

''Of what you do to me,'' she whispered, her breath ragged.

''What do I do to you, Sara, love?'' he asked, moving closer. His mouth hovered tantalizingly.

''You make me forget about home, and family, everything I ever thought was important. Everything—except you.''

''And that's what made you take such a damn fool chance?'' His tawny brows drew together in a formidable line. ''My God, woman,'' he said with a groan, pulling her close, ''you'll be the death of me!''

His mouth was hot on hers, staking his possession. He make a low, hungry sound in his throat and pulled her down with him. She was dizzy, spinning with vertigo, and didn't even know she was falling until her back sank into the soft, newly-sprouted grass lining the bank. His knee moved between her legs, and she gasped, dragging her mouth free.

''Stop! What are you doing?''

''Making up for lost time.'' He nuzzled the V of her neck and began to unbutton her shirt.

''It's daylight! And—and anyone could ride up.''

''There's no one within miles, just you and me. And I can't wait for you any longer.'' His hands found her breasts and kneaded and stroked the soft flesh while his mouth ravaged hers again, leaving her weak and breathless. His deft fingers plucked at the combs securing her hair, letting them fall carelessly into the sweet-smelling grass and white-blossomed bloodroot. She made a small sound of protest, twisting and reaching for the combs.

''Be careful,'' she said.

"What?" He pulled back slightly, his face taut with need.

"My combs. Don't lose them."

"The hell with them," he muttered, fumbling with the hem of her chemise.

"No." She struggled to her knees, searching through the tender shoots of grass in frantic haste. A glad cry escaped her lips when she found the combs, and she pressed them against her heart. "Will gave them to me."

Johnny went a little mad then. Snatching the combs from her hands, he threw them away with all his strength, spiraling them into the prairie. Sara gasped in shock and shrank back. He stood over her, feet braced apart, fists clenched, eyes ablaze with fury.

"God damn your precious Will!" he roared. "It's time you forgot him! You hold onto the memory of that old man and make it some kind of shrine. He never gave you anything!"

"You're wrong! He loved me and I loved him," she cried. The tortoiseshell combs had been a treasured gift from a kind husband. Knowing they were gone was like breaking the last thread between her and Will, and it hurt terribly.

"You never loved him. It was nothing but gratitude for what he'd done and guilt because you never cared for him like you thought you should. How could you? You never became a woman until I made you one."

"Shut up," she cried, stunned by the brutality of his words, stung that they struck too near the guilty truth. She surged to her feet, fists clenched white-knuckled at her sides. "He was my husband. You don't know anything about marriage."

"What makes you think I've never been married?" He laughed harshly at her shocked expression. "No, Sara, you didn't make me a bigamist. She's dead."

"What? How?" White-faced, she pressed trembling fingers to her lips. He turned away, and the rigid line of his shoulders told her more than his words.

"She died in childbed."

"And—and the baby?"

"Was another man's whelp. While I was killing myself

making the fortune she thought she needed, my lovely socialite bride was betraying me with another man.'' He faced her again, and his lips curled. *''That's* what I know of marriage.''

"I'm so sorry," Sara whispered. "You must have loved her very much."

"I was sick with it—until I found that Gwendolyn was as false as she was beautiful. Deceiving females seem to be my lot."

He glowered at Sara, and she winced, her own guilt eating at her. No wonder he was so cynical and secretive. Experience had made him a loner and destroyed his ability to trust. "What did you do?"

"What could I? The families insisted on keeping face, and by then I didn't care enough to fight. And she laughed at me, even as she lay dying, knowing she'd delivered the final insult—another man's bastard to raise as my son."

"The baby lived?"

"Unfortunately."

"Don't say that!" She was appalled. "An innocent child! Where is he?"

"Looking for another charity case, Saint Sara?" he said with a sneer. "Don't worry. Gwendolyn's brat got everything I'd meant for her. I sold it all and left him with her parents before I went to war. Of course, they didn't want him, either, but the trust fund makes up for any inconvenience."

"The poor little boy. How could you? How could you desert an innocent baby?"

"I couldn't stand to look at him."

"So you went to war?" She stared at him, disappointment and disillusionment straining her features. "Did it help? Did the killing make up for what she'd done to you?"

His eyes were suddenly bleak. "I didn't go to war to kill, Sara. I went to war to die."

Shock paralyzed her, and an icy chill raced through her veins. A shaky laugh rocked her, and she hugged her arms around her suddenly shivering body. "Well, it didn't work, did it, Johnny? Is that why you're so determined to follow that gold all the way to Mexico? Are you still looking for a way to punish yourself for deserting that baby? And for whatever it was you think you did to deserve a faithless wife?''

''You know nothing about it.''

''I know that while you're trying to punish them, you're punishing me.''

''No, Sara, no.'' His features were stricken with the force of an enormous pain. He reached for her, tugging her struggling form into his embrace. ''You don't understand. It's not you. It's unfinished business. God, it's complicated!''

''Make me understand,'' she pleaded, nearly frantic.

''There are things you don't know about me, things you wouldn't believe now even if I told you. And anything you knew could put you in jeopardy in this mess I've made. I don't want to do anything to make it worse.''

She wept quietly against his chest, and her words were tortured. ''If only you'd trust me. You're like a shadow. I can see you, but I can't touch you.''

''Oh, honey, you touch me,'' he murmured, kissing her damp temple. ''If only you knew.''

After a while she quieted, and her breathing slowed to shuddering gasps. Gently, Johnny pressed her to sit on the ground. He squatted in front of her, holding her cold hands in his own to warm them, a look of deliberation on his face. When he spoke, his voice was rough with suppressed emotion. ''I know you have no reason to believe me, but there is one thing I'd like to tell you.''

Her watery gaze was wary. He drew in a deep breath.

''No matter what you heard before, I was not responsible in any way for your husband's death. In fact''—he paused and cleared his throat—''I tried to stop the slaughter. I failed.''

''But you rode with Quantrill . . .'' She trailed off, confused but wanting to believe. His admission was an offering. In a flash, she knew she *had* to believe. Studying his earnest expression, the glint of desperation in his eyes, she knew she did. She nodded. ''I believe you.''

His hands tightened briefly, then he rose and walked away. Sara buried her face in her hands and tried to think. It was hopeless. She was too bewildered, too raw, her emotions throbbing like an exposed nerve. She no longer knew what was right, or even what she wanted. But he had reached out to her by sharing a painful piece of his former life. Was it a start toward something deeper between them?

"Here." Johnny's gruff voice broke into her chaotic thoughts. She lifted her head to find him offering one of her combs on the palm of his hand. "I couldn't find the other one," he said. "I'm sorry."

She took it, turning it over and over in her hands as though it were a magical talisman that held the secrets of everlasting happiness. "Why—" She swallowed and began again. "Why did you come after me?"

"I told you before. I felt responsible for you. And you're my wife."

She looked up at him, her brown eyes liquid with emotion. "Am I? That was a lie, and you know it. You've made me your mistress, but I don't feel like a wife. A wife knows she has a future with the man she loves. I have no future. All I have is uncertainty."

"I don't make promises I can't keep. I've got business to finish, starting with Jesse and the Calf, and ending God knows where." He stood looking down at her, gently tracing the curve of her cheek with his knuckle. "You know I want you, but there's no future in it. And it's better that way, believe me, Sara. Haven't I already proved I'd never bring a good woman like you anything but misery?"

"That's not true." Her lips trembled. "You were my friend when you were just Johnny. And you've given me passion as Tuck. That isn't very far from love."

"Don't love me, Sara." His voice was harsh. "I can't love you back."

"Oh." A single tear slid from her eyelid. She dashed it away and rose to her feet, facing him bravely. "So all we have is now?"

His face twisted, then his jaw hardened. "Not even that. I'm taking you to the nearest stage depot and sending you home." He turned toward the horses.

"Johnny!"

Her call halted him in mid-stride. He glanced over his shoulder, his face stony. "What?"

She lifted her chin, raised her hand, and deliberately

threw the comb back into the prairie grass with its lost mate. Her eyes held a challenge, and her voice was firm. "I'll take now. For as long as it lasts."

Then she went into his arms. He groaned and caught her to him, his lips on her brow, her eyelids, the corner of her mouth.

"I don't want anything else to happen to you," he said. "I should put you on the first stage back to Missouri. It would be safer for both of us. I should send you home."

"You can't. I won't go."

He caught her face between his palms, studying her intently. She believed he was an outlaw, knew him for a ruthless user, a coldhearted taker, yet she was willing to throw her lot in with him without even so much as a word of commitment. She was willing to give up everything she knew, risk everything she was, to be with *him*. The magnitude of her sacrifice awed and humbled him. Her eyes were wide and the color of fine brandy. A man could lose himself in them forever, Johnny thought in wonder. He felt a surge of desire so powerful it made him dizzy, and he fought for sanity. She deserved better than this. She deserved better than *him*.

"You're a damned changeable female. I could make you go," he said hoarsely.

"I'm a stubborn woman, John Tucker. Don't you know that yet?" Her lips curved into a smile. "Besides, I've never been to Mexico."

He laughed helplessly. "Then God help us both!" He sobered, and his arms tightened around her. "I'm a selfish bastard, and I can't let you go. Not just yet. Not until I have to."

His mouth covered hers in a searing kiss. She responded wholeheartedly, opening her mouth, allowing him complete access, meeting his tongue with her own. With a groan, he sank with her into the sweet grass. She was lost again, she knew, and this time she did not fight it, or him.

Because it was all suddenly, perfectly clear. Whether or not he ever admitted it to himself, he needed her. She'd seen the fear and the need in his eyes when he'd burst in at the McIntoshs', heard the anguish in his voice when he told of his dead wife, known the truth for what it was when he spoke of Will. Hard he was, but there were vulnerable spots that she alone had seen, and they touched her innermost heart. He belonged to her, and had from the moment she'd first come to the aid of a dying warrior.

She gave herself to him gladly under the open skies, knowing that whatever he was, or had been, or would ever be—she loved him. She had the present, and, if she were lucky and persistent, someday he would admit he cared, and maybe they would have the future, too.

Chapter 15

The sob and wail of Spanish guitars from the Main Plaza held Sara enthralled. An unseen troubadour sang a Spanish love song, and she hummed along, wishing she could understand the emotional, evocative lyrics.

The second floor room of the St. Leonard Hotel overlooked the heart of San Antonio, the dusty square lined with flat-topped adobe buildings, clapboard saloons, tall modern brick hotels, and an ancient cathedral. She leaned against the iron balcony railing and drank in the fragrant night air and the romance of the exotic music while she waited for Johnny.

A week in San Antonio luxury had done much to restore her after a month's hard travel. She smiled to herself. Now that she was rested and her persistent headache brought on by too much sun had eased, she could look back on the sojourn with something less than repugnance. In fact, the time with Johnny had been very sweet, indeed, despite the physical hardships. In those moments on the creek bank, they'd reached an understanding that went beyond words. Bound by mutual passion and circumstances, they accepted the inevitability of their relationship. There were no words of love—Sara knew he would not welcome them from her—but there was tenderness. And for Sara, accustomed to being patient, it was enough.

They'd caught up with Jesse and the others at Colbert's Ferry on the Red River, and although Johnny had not voiced it, she'd known he was relieved. She sensed his distrust of his partners, which made his determination to stay with them all the more puzzling to her. She knew they planned to join other former Confederates in the service of Maximillian, but it was the treasure in gold coin that bound them, not high ideals. Greed and avarice were not commendable virtues, but in Cole and the rest she could understand them. Somehow, with Johnny, they rang false, but she could not tell if that were merely wishful thinking on her part, nor was she sufficiently brave to question him about it.

Jesse and the others had accepted her return with no comment. Only Cole had given her one disgusted, virulent look, then ignored her. She was grateful then that she was "Tuck's woman."

They had traveled south through Denison, then to Fort Worth where Sara had dispatched a vaguely worded letter to Pandora, saying she was safe and not to worry. Then they headed south toward Waco, and finally to the bustling southwestern city of San Antonio.

It was easy to be fascinated by everything she saw, and Johnny indulged her, settling them first in a comfortable hotel room, then taking her on rounds of shopping, replenishing her depleted wardrobe and seeing that her trousers were consigned to the trashbin. They might have been a successful rancher and his wife, come to the "metropolis" for a vacation.

Jesse and the rest took up roles as "businessmen," frequenting the saloons and gaming halls, but playing the part with surprising circumspection. The five men had placed their valuables in the hotel safe with such casual aplomb that no one would ever guess the fortune contained in the dusty saddlebags. Sara knew they waited for contact from the mysterious Señor Gonzales, but it was the present that was all important. She tried not to think ahead but instead lost herself in the heaven she found in Johnny's arms each night.

During the day, they strolled the Alameda, exploring the town, taking in the sights and scents of a culture half-American, half-Latin. Oxen pulled *carreta,* high, two-wheeled carts loaded with produce or firewood. Johnny bought her *pepitorias* and cactus candy from the *dulce* vendors, and they licked the sweets from their fingers, laughing like children. The San Fernando parish church beckoned them from the corner of the Main Plaza, and they explored its dim, incense-scented interior, even climbing the narrow stairs to the tower where Alamo defenders had sighted Santa Ana's legions in '36. The Alamo itself was now a quartermaster's warehouse for the U.S. Army, and wagons pulled by army mules unloaded supplies where Texas martyrs had died. Canvas bathhouses lined the riverbank, and sheep bleated in pens directly behind the plaza.

In the stores and markets they found champagne and gunpowder, Cholula blankets, *rebozos,* agave thread, and heavy bars of sweet chocolate from Mexico next to silk stockings from France, saddles made by local leatherworkers, bullet molds, cedar churns, and "nervous chewing tobacco." In an exclusive establishment Johnny found a pair of carved ivory combs. Though he made no comment when he gave them to her, Sara's heart swelled with hope, and she wore them daily, endowing them in her mind with nearly the same mystical quality as her wedding ring. In the evenings, they ate tamales from the chili stands at the open-air tables served by dark-eyed "chili queens," or dined American style in the hotel restaurant.

The pleasant routine had continued for seven days, but this evening had been different, bringing the long-awaited summons. At a stately *hacienda* with carved doors and thick sandstone walls, she and Johnny and his uneasy partners, decked out in their new finery, had dined with Gonzales himself, his wife and family, at the powerful man's invitation.

The talk over the meal had been of Maximillian and the schemes of disfranchised Confederates to emigrate to Mexico. The idea was being promoted by Generals Price, Magruder, Maury, and others to entice elements of the defunct Confederacy to form a colony at Cordova.

"Great opportunity is there, should a man be bold enough to take it in both hands," Señor Gonzales said. He was a short, rotund Spaniard with a pencil thin mustache and a jocular manner. Behind his good humor and sparkling black eyes Sara sensed a man of shrewd, calculating intelligence.

"Do you think such an immigration scheme can succeed?'' Jesse asked politely. An unobtrusive manservant cleared the used dessert plates.

Cole leaned his elbows on the table and scowled. "How can it, since that pipsqueak General Sheridan now requires a permit before anyone can sail for a Mexican port from Louisiana or Texas? The Cordova Colonization Plan doesn't stand a snowball's chance in hell."

"Not at all, my young friend," Gonzales said, smiling. He sipped dark red wine from a crystal goblet. "After all, there are still those courageous enough to make the journey overland. And such rewards! Grants of land from the Emperor, the reinstitution of peonage, even titles of nobility. Why, a man could be a king in his own right—if his support of Maximillian is staunch."

Sara caught Johnny's eye across the table. Would such temptations as these persuade him and his friends that a new life awaited them in Mexico? And would she be a part of that life?

When Johnny spoke, his expression was bland and his words lazy. "Word is there's a build-up of American troops along the Rio Grande."

Gonzales made a dismissive gesture. "There was panic in the fall on the other side of the border, but it was a shadow, mere feint and withdrawal by the American forces. They dare not invade Mexico to aid Juarez. By the President's own orders there must be a strict neutrality. Anything less, and the legions of the French would descend on them. The United States cannot field another war so soon after the recent 'rebellion.' " He smiled broadly and stood, pushing back his heavily carved chair. "But I fear we bore the ladies with such talk. Let us retire to discuss your—er, business proposition."

Johnny gave Sara a level look as she withdrew with the other women. She bit her lip and tried not to worry. Later, in the carriage taking them back to town, he'd squeezed her hand reassuringly, but then he'd gone off with Cole and the others rather than to the room they shared. Sara knew instinctively that he was preoccupied with his "unfinished business." Now, she felt a sudden chill of premonition and turned away from the balcony, closing the door and drawing the drapes as if to ward off some miasma of the night. She had no way to hold him, no ties but the love she felt.

Take destiny in one's own two hands, Gonzales had said. Even a woman could have ambitions, and all of Sara's now centered in her desire for a life with Johnny. There had to be a way for them to be together. Desperation made her bold. Her new taffeta petticoat rustled as she moved, and she smiled to herself, busily twirling her wedding ring while her thoughts whirled.

She knew she was desirable, and desired. Johnny had proven that often enough. That gave her a confidence she'd never known before. Tonight, she'd tell him her true feelings. She'd *show* him how much he meant to her. She knew he cared for her, and it was time he admitted it, so that they could plan a future together. Smiling to herself, she began to sing the old Spanish serenade.

It was going to be tricky, but he just might pull it off, Johnny thought, striding down the hall toward his hotel room. Gonzales had agreed to discount the fifteen thousand in gold from the Liberty holdup. Jesse was to withdraw that amount from their stash in the hotel vault at eight o'clock in the morning and then meet Gonzales. That's when he'd take the Golden Calf.

Instinct said the time to move was now. He'd seen the growing dissatisfaction in Cole's eyes and sensed that the closer they got to the border, the less this group of Missouri boys wanted to end up in Mexico. There was something downright stupid about handing over a fortune, even for the nebulous returns of a French title. Even Jesse, normally so calm and coolly decisive, seemed finely stretched by a growing tension.

Johnny paused outside the hotel room door, patting the crisp sheaf of papers in his coat pocket and frowning. Yes, it was going to be tricky—and dangerous. And if anything went wrong, he didn't want Sara caught in the middle of it. That's why he was putting her on a stagecoach first thing in the morning. He'd been selfish long enough. He ignored the knot of protest that stirred in his heart and steeled himself to inflict the hurt he knew was inevitable.

She wouldn't want to go, but he had to make her, even

at the risk of being cruel. He knew the softness in her, how wonderfully giving and loving she'd been to him, and knew he'd miss her like hell. But if he fouled up, Cole would cheerfully slit her beautiful throat just to get back at him. He couldn't risk that, any more than he could risk letting her get any closer to him. There wasn't much left inside him to give to a woman, and she deserved more than a burnt-out soldier. The truth about his past wasn't even that important. Let her continue to suspect the worst. It would make it that much easier for her to forget this episode of her life, chalk it up to experience or bad luck, and go back to what she'd been. It was more than he'd be able to do.

And if his conscience ate at him for what he'd done to her, well, that was nothing new. His cheeks tightened in a self-mocking scowl. Maybe the wad of greenbacks he'd included in the stage tickets wasn't much of a settlement, but it was all she'd expect from a sorry bastard like him, anyway.

It was time to get it over with. He raised his hand to rap on the door, then paused, hypnotized by the faint, sweet warbling of a song. He couldn't make out the words, but the melody was sad. It squeezed his heart, bringing back memories of all the good times they'd shared around Pandora's old upright piano singing and laughing the evening away as a family. He knew that more than anything, her voice would haunt him. His jaw clenched. Almost angrily, he knocked.

"Sara?" He heard her soft answer and entered, then jerked to a stop at the sight of her propped up in the tall poster bed.

She wore a brightly embroidered chemisette of white lawn so sheer it enhanced rather than concealed the rosy-brown tips of her proud breasts. Her hair fell in lush waves over bare shoulders made creamy by the warm glow of the burning lamp. But most surprising was the brilliant crimson petticoat that spilled over her legs and knees, stopping short to display the shapely turn of her delicate ankles and bare feet. She smiled at him in welcome, then laughed softly at his expression.

"What's the matter, Johnny?" she asked, her tone husky. "Don't you recognize the wanton in your bed?"

"Where did you get that get-up?" His voice sounded strange to his ears.

She drew her knees up and shook the satiny folds, making the fabric rustle. "I wanted a red dress, but this was the best I could do." She looked up at him with amused guilelessness. "Don't you like it?"

He approached the bed, swallowing hard. "I like it fine, but we have to talk."

She knelt on the mattress, her hands folded demurely in her lap, her breasts thrusting impudently against the thin cotton garment. Her lower lip drooped in a provocative pout. "Not now."

"But . . ."

Raising up, she crooked her arm around his neck, brushing him enticingly with her thighs, her belly, her breasts. Her lips wafted lightly over his; her breath stirred the thick brush of his newly-grown mustache. "I said, not now."

Heat flooded his groin, and his cheek creased with amusement. "If I didn't know better, madam, I'd say you were trying to seduce me."

Her laugh tugged at his heartstrings and sent desire rocketing through his system. She pressed against him, rubbing against his rising tumescence.

"If I didn't know better, sir, I'd say I was succeeding."

He groaned and caught her to him, wrapping his arms around her slender form and capturing her lips.

"I heard you singing," he muttered against her mouth.

"Did you?" She clung to him, soft as velvet, her hands agile in a thousand tempting places.

"Pretty song." He nipped at the corners of her mouth, tasting her like a gourmet savoring an especially pleasing morsel.

Her breathy reply was sweet on his face. "I'll sing it for you any time."

He drew her even closer, but the papers crackled in his jacket pocket, reminding him with force of what he meant to do. He drew back, breathing heavily, but the lambency in her eyes undid his resolve and inflamed his passion past

all bounds. She was so soft and pliant and wonderful, and
soon he'd lose her forever.

The hell with it, he thought as recklessness consumed
him.

"Sing for me, Sara," he said, his arms tightening
around her as if he'd never let her go. "Sing for me now."

They fell back onto the bed, limbs tangled, mouths
seeking. Sara's laughter was filled with joy and mischief,
but his answering groan was heavy with desperation.

"Once more," he muttered, and lost himself in her for
the last time.

"Ever thought about being a king, Jess?" Cole Younger
stared down into the depths of his glass, then took another
swallow of the amber whiskey.

"Cain't say that I have," was the lazy reply. Jesse was
propped in a chair in the corner of the smoke-filled saloon,
watching Cole with slit eyes.

"Well, it can't be all it's het up to be, that's what I
think."

"What are you sayin'?"

Cole reared back and pulled a hand down his mustache.
"Dammit! We didn't aim to be farmers back home, Jess.
Why the devil do we want to farm in Mexico? None of us
even knows how to parlay the talk down there."

"I guess we both been thinkin' pretty much on the same
lines. Seems to me Maximillian ain't as strong as some
folks want to believe, and he's got trouble aplenty with
the U.S. government supporting the Liberals." Jesse
blinked rapidly. "I'd sure hate like hell to be on the losing
side twice."

"You think Gonzales could discount the Calf for us,
too?"

"No reason to let that slimy thief cheat us more than
once. Nine thousand in greenbacks for the Liberty gold
will set us up for a spell. We'll save the Calf for later."
He paused in brief reflection. "Might as well make it a
four-way split though."

Cole grinned. "You want I should kill Tuck, Jesse?"

"Naw. I figure four against one ought to convince him."

Cole looked disappointed. "If you say so." He brightened. "Say, I could wing him. Slow him down a bit."

"That woman of his'll do that for us. Ain't never seen a man so moonstruck. He'll think twice about leaving her, and then we'll be long gone. Where you want to head?"

Cole thought a moment. "You remember Bud Shirley?"

"Wasn't he killed somewhere around Sarcoxie back in '63?"

"That's the one. His paw took the family to Sycene, little place east of Dallas. I'll bet we'll get plenty of hospitality there."

Jesse shrugged. "Good a place as any. Or is there something special about Sycene?"

Cole's smile was lecherous. "There's plenty special about little Myra Belle Shirley. And there's nothing like a man with money in his pocket to bring out the best in a woman."

The warm breeze stirred the curtains in a fitful rhythm, and lovers' whispers joined the night murmurs. They'd loved, then dozed, and loved again. Now, naked and spent, they rested, clasped in each other's arms, listening to the world awaken. Sara's head lay on Johnny's shoulder, and her fingers made slow, contented circles through the thatch of sandy hair on his broad chest.

"Johnny?"

"Hmm."

"Are we really going to Mexico?"

He didn't answer for a moment. "No."

She raised up on an elbow and gazed down at him. "But I thought . . ."

"Shh." He cut her off. "It's not important right now." His fingers threaded through the tangled skein of her dark hair. Gently, he pulled her back down against him. "Go to sleep."

"If you could go anywhere in the world, where would you go?"

He sighed. "Sara . . ."

"Tell me, or I'll never let you rest," she teased, licking his flat nipple like a kitten. He jumped, then wrestled her, laughing, into subjugation. "Tell me," she demanded again.

"All right, let me think. Out west to the Rockies, I guess."

"Why?"

"It's open country, big sky country. I love mountains; the rocks and minerals fascinate me. There might be work I could do, though I don't suppose I'll ever be able to work in mining again."

"Maybe when the memories of—of prison fade, it won't be so hard. Maybe you'll be able to control the claustrophobia then."

"Some things you never forget." His arms tightened on her. "Never."

"Well," she said, snuggling against him, "it's good to dream."

"And where would you go, doctor? To Paris to study at the Sorbonne? London?"

She shook her head, and there was a catch in her voice. "Don't you know? I'd go anywhere you are. I love you, Johnny."

Cold reality slapped him in the face, shattering the fantasy of warm contentment. Selfishly, he'd chosen to hold her one last time, and now look what that delay had cost him. He had no right to accept her love, and guilt made him angry. She couldn't stay with him, but he knew her strong will and tenacious nature. There would be arguments and tears, and he couldn't afford the time or the consequences if her pleas swayed him. His only recourse was to drive her away with hurtful words.

Sara held her breath. Her profession of love had come from the heart, but he was so tense and still. "Johnny? Did you hear what I said? I love you."

Abruptly he released her, sitting up on the side of the bed, his back to her, his head in his hands. "You'll get over it," he said harshly.

She shook her head, though he couldn't see it. "No," she whispered, fighting the pain, "some things you don't ever get over."

She touched the valley of his spine, and he jumped up as if scorched. He reached for his clothes and began pulling them on, his movements jerky. "It's time to end it, Sara."

Fear trickled down her backbone, and her breath came short. "Why?"

He swung around, stuffing his shirt into his waistband, his face a savage mask. "I don't want you anymore, that's why."

Her laugh was incredulous. "You're a liar."

"That's right." His hard fingers caught her chin, and he glared down into her white face. "I'm a liar, and a cheat, and a double-dealing bastard. I've used you and now I'm through with you. So get dressed, you've got a stage to catch."

What was he trying to do? Sara wondered. A man couldn't change from tender lover to scathing stranger in the blink of an eye. Or could he? Her certainty faltered. This was Tuck again, repudiating their relationship, but for what purpose? She could hardly believe he'd grown tired of her so soon, especially after what had just occurred, yet he was ever the consummate actor. Had he been acting all this time? She could scarcely countenance the thought, and it made her shake her head. "I don't believe you."

"Believe this." He threw the stage tickets onto the bed with a contemptuous flip of the wrist.

Sarah stared at them in mute horror, and something inside her died. He'd planned this! Even when he'd held her so ardently he'd been planning all along to send her away. She couldn't think, couldn't reason it all out. For whatever reason, he didn't want her anymore and that was the only thing that mattered. She wouldn't debase herself further by begging. Fighting down the hurt that lashed her, she let anger be her strength, unconsciously lifting her chin in an attitude of pride.

Johnny grabbed his gun and holster and buckled them around his waist. He paused at the door, and his gaze raked her naked form with such searing distaste that she automatically reached for the sheet to cover herself. "You've got ten minutes to get packed."

Mechanically, numb with pain, she dressed in a plain, comfortable riding habit, did her hair, and neatly folded her bits and pieces into a new portmanteau. She was careful to leave the ivory combs on the dresser. She was careful about everything, her movements fussy, as if having time to think might wreck her tenuous control. And that she would not do.

There would be no undignified scene, no tears, no begging. If he were so anxious to be rid of her, then she would not thwart him, no matter what it cost her. Let him see the kind of woman he was giving up. Let him see—and remember—and one day regret.

The sky was rosy with the first streaks of daylight when they arrived at the stage depot. The busy station on Carcel Street was loud with the jangle of harnesses, the stamp of horses, and the strident shouts of the station master for passengers for Victoria to please board.

"You're booked on a steamer from Port Lavaca to New Orleans," he said. "Then you can—"

"I can take care of myself." She took the tickets from him and stuffed them unread into her bag, her face as pale and emotionless as a marble statue. "You needn't concern yourself further."

"Ready, ma'am?" asked the impatient driver.

"Yes," she said. The driver took the portmanteau from Johnny and dropped it into the rear carrier. Two men waited inside the coach. Head high, she turned toward the open coach door, only to be stopped by Johnny's hand on her arm. She lifted eyes apprehensive and hurt, and suddenly she was pulled into his arms, his mouth hard on hers. He broke away as abruptly, and the muscle in his jaw twitched.

"Damn you, Sara," was all he said. Then he lifted her into the coach, slammed the door, and beat twice on the side of the stage. The driver whistled and shouted, and the team leapt forward. Sara didn't see anything after that because of the tears.

The obsequious Mexican clerk fussed with the dial on the hotel safe as everyone looked on.

"Cain't you hurry that up, man?" Cole grumbled. "We got business to tend to."

"Uno momento, señor." The clerk spun the wheel, muttering Spanish imprecations under his breath.

Johnny leaned casually against the edge of a desk and watched Jesse and Cole from beneath his lashes. Outside in the street, he knew Jim and Frank had their horses ready for the ride to Gonzales' *hacienda*. His arms were folded across his chest, his movements as deceptively lazy as a waiting rattler, holding himself in check until the moment to strike.

Sweating and grunting, the clerk shoved open the heavy safe door, then hauled out the sets of heavy saddlebags and laid them with a thump on the desk top. Circles of moisture stained his white shirt. He smiled and wiped his damp forehead. *"Madre de Dios!* The *señors* carry bricks made of lead, no?"

"None of your business, *amigo*," Cole snapped.

"We'd like a bit of privacy now," Jesse said to the clerk. The mildness of his request did not disguise the venom in his voice, and the clerk shot him an anxious glance.

"Certainly, *señor*." The little man slammed the safe door, twirled the dial, and stepped to a door at the rear of the room. "Knock when you wish to return your possessions to the safe."

The clerk disappeared through the doorway, and Jesse unbuckled a flap of one saddlebag and rummaged inside. He pulled a sack free, testing its weight by hefting it in his palm. "Still seems a shame to pay Gonzales this fifteen thousand and get back only nine."

"We got no choice," Cole said, and suddenly his big Colt pistol appeared in his hand, aimed directly at Johnny's navel. "And neither does Tuck here, by the looks of it."

Johnny froze. "What the hell's the meaning of this?"

Jesse rapidly stuffed the sack back into his coat pocket, then rebuckled the saddlebag. "Ain't nuthin' personal, Tuck. We ain't goin' to Mexico is all. Don't figure the Emperor needs the Calf, neither. Better hand Cole that there hogleg."

"Easy." Cole grinned, holding out his hand. "Wouldn't want to have to plug you one."

Grim-faced, Johnny slowly pulled his Enfield free of the

holster with two fingers. Cole snatched it out of Johnny's grip and shoved it into his own waistband. A gloating expression turned up the straggly ends of his mustache.

Johnny's voice was icy with rage. "Aiming to cut me out, are you, Jess?"

Jesse shrugged, his pale face emotionless. "You know what they say about blood and water. Seein' as Cole's almost kin, a four-way split makes a lot more sense."

Johnny took a step forward, his fists clenched. "You little bastard!"

Cole caught Johnny on the side of the head with the flat of his pistol. Stunned, Johnny crashed to the floor. Black and silver spangles blurred his vision, and he fought determinedly for consciousness.

There was a shuffling of boots and leather bags. Johnny tried to press himself up, but he couldn't feel his arms, and his stomach lurched with a wave of nausea. He lay still, gathering his strength for another try, cursing his weakness and his stupidity. They'd beaten him at his own game. He should have been ready for something like this.

". . . out of here 'fore he comes to," Cole urged over his head.

"Not so fast, *amigos*," the obsequious clerk warned, his voice now hard and cold with purpose. "Señor Gonzales requests I relieve you of your oh-so-heavy burden." The ominous click of a gun being cocked reverberated through the room, punctuated by Cole's brief, pithy obscenities. "Drop your weapons, and the one in your belt, too," the man barked. "Now!"

Three pistols clattered to the floor beside Johnny. From under slightly parted lids he could see the cold blue steel of the nearest one only a foot or so from his hand. With the greatest stealth, he inched his hand toward the weapon.

"You can't get away with this," Jesse warned in a low, furious voice. "Our pards are right outside."

"That is why we shall go out the back way to take a short ride. How kind of you to simplify my duties by eliminating one of your own. Is he dead?"

Johnny froze, then nearly gasped aloud as the toe of a boot found a spot on his unprotected ribs. It was only by the most stringent of efforts that he held himself immobile, his molars grinding to hold back a groan of pain.

There was a smile in the clerk's voice. "Just as well. The fewer to deal with, the better. It is unfortunate two visitors to our fair city will meet with such a terrible accident." He laughed with chilling congeniality. "But then, it is well known that the *banditos* slit throats for the pleasure of it. Come. We go."

A boot crossed Johnny's field of vision. He couldn't let this thief depart with the Calf! To hell with Jesse and Cole, it was the Calf that mattered. He focused on the gun, ignoring the throbbing in his head and side. Almost there. Almost . . .

The office door rattled, then burst open. "Where is he?" Dr. Sara Cary demanded. "I've got a thing or two to say to John Tucker—oh!"

Sara's scream was the final disconcerting element of a rapidly deteriorating situation. Johnny lunged for the gun, scooped it up, and rolled. A gunshot thundered, and a bullet splintered the wooden floor where he'd lain only moments before. Johnny fired from the hip, and a crimson blossom stained the Mexican's shoulder, flinging him backward against the wall where he fell in a groaning heap. The room was thick with the smell of cordite. Jesse and Cole scrambled in frantic haste toward their abandoned guns.

"Johnny!" Sara yelped, starting forward, her reticule and portmanteau across her arm, unmindful of danger, of anything except that Johnny was hurt.

Half-blinded by his own blood, Johnny charged, crashing into Jesse with his shoulder, then catching Cole on the tip of his jaw with a left-handed haymaker. They sprawled in a stunned pile in the middle of the floor. Almost by instinct, Johnny grabbed the abandoned saddlebags, holstered his gun, then jerked Sara's arm, dragging her toward the door.

"Run!"

She took one look at his savage, blood-stained visage, picked up her skirts, and ran. They pushed through the converging crowd in the lobby.

"Someone get a doctor," Johnny shouted at large. "There's been a hold-up!"

Excited shouts and scurrying activity surrounded them, but Johnny bulled his way through, out the frosted-glass entrance into the Plaza. He spotted Frank and Jim waiting anxiously with the horses and gave a spine-shivering Rebel yell.

"It's Jesse and Cole," he hollered. "Gonzales double-crossed us! Hurry!"

Startled by the gunshots and Tuck's bloody countenance, they took off toward the hotel at a dead run, drawing their pistols. Johnny half-carried Sara to the nearest horse and tossed her bodily into the saddle.

"What the *hell* are you doing back here?" he shouted.

"Don't you dare yell at me!" she returned, struggling to right herself in the saddle. She dropped the portmanteau across the saddle horn and glared at Johnny. "I pulled your fat out of the fire again, didn't I?"

He threw the saddlebags onto the backs of the two extra horses, grabbed their reins, and vaulted into the saddle of his own big bay. "God damn it, woman! This is exactly the kind of mess I was trying to avoid!"

"I can't help it if you're a born troublemaker," she snapped. Her angry tone eased into concern. "Are you all right?"

"I'll live. At least until Jesse and Cole catch up with me. And thanks to you, that could be any second."

She sniffed her disdain. "I should have known there was no honor among thieves."

"Hell, they tried to kill me." He looked briefly to the heavens in total exasperation. "Good God, Sara! Why'd you come back?"

"I—" She hesitated, then lifted her chin in the belligerent manner he found irresistible. Her words were prim. "I forgot to say goodbye."

He whooped with laughter. "Well hell, woman, it's too late now!" He whirled his steed around, slapping her mount's rump. The horses jumped forward into a gallop.

"Ride, Sara! Ride for your life!"

Chapter 16

"They're still behind us."

Johnny's bald statement made Sara bobble the canteen, splashing some of their precious water supply over her cracked and parched lips. She licked the moisture greedily, staring at him in dismay. "How do you know?"

He scanned the distant horizon, his face grim. "I know."

Johnny took the canteen from her and sipped a judicious quantity. Sweat trickled through the dust on his face, making streaks that disappeared into the bandana he wore knotted at his throat. His white shirt was grimy and sweat-stained, the cuffs turned back over his forearms. The small dark patch of caked blood on the side of his head bore mute evidence to the damage Cole had inflicted. Sara's skilled fingers had probed that wound, and to her relief it was no more than a goose egg and some scraped skin. It was a dark reminder of violence against his blond curls, curls that seemed to grow lighter almost hourly, bleached by the unrelenting sun.

April on the semi-arid chaparral held more than a hint of the coming summer heat. Tough grass and stunted sage scrub sent forth new shoots, and to the observant eye there was great beauty to be found in the patches of hardy yellow daisies, bluebonnets, and orange and red Indian blankets that struggled for existence in the crevices and gullies along with cholla and prickly pear. It was beautiful in a stark way, but harsh, and that harshness was taking its toll on Sara.

Her head ached with fatigue, and her joints protested at

the abuse incurred in their wild two-day ride out of San Antonio. She was past being hungry due to a nagging stomachache, but worse, their water supply was nearly gone, and just knowing that made her mouth feel as dry as cotton. They hadn't left the city supplied for such a trek, and Johnny had been merciless, pushing both them and their horses, taking only short rests, then moving on. He'd just awakened Sara from a hour's nap that she'd taken beneath a dwarfed pinyon tree, but the brief rest had only made her realize how utterly exhausted she was.

"I don't think I can go much farther," she said faintly.

Johnny looked at her sharply. "You have to, Doc." He caught her shoulders and turned her, pointing toward the north with his finger. "See that?"

She strained her eyes, but all she could make out was a distant smudge, a tiny cloud blurring the horizon. "I don't see anything . . ."

"It's them. Jesse and Cole."

"How can you be certain?"

"If it's not them, then it's Gonzales' men. Either way, they're coming. After that." He pointed to the saddlebags holding the Golden Calf. "And they'll be after blood, too. Yours and mine. I can't leave you behind. And we're almost to the border, honey."

She leaned against him, her eyelids fluttering tiredly. "What good will it do? They'll just follow us over the border, too. We'll have to keep running, keep moving to stay one jump ahead of them. It's not worth it. Let them have the gold, Johnny. Please."

"No. I can't." His face was as hard as granite.

She pulled away from him, feeling the sharp weight of disillusionment pressing down on her. With trembling hands she smoothed back her hair and tried to brush some of the dust from the split skirt of her riding habit, unconsciously setting aright her appearance in preparation for this new trial, like a gladiator girding his loins before entering the arena.

She wondered again if she'd made the right choice coming back to him. She'd been no more than thirty minutes out of San Antonio before her tears had dried, replaced by anger and a growing determination to prove him wrong.

Maybe she'd scared him off with her declaration of love. Even if he didn't want the words, he cared for her, she was certain, and he'd lied to free her from a life tied to an outlaw. She admired him for such honorable motives, even while she cursed him for depriving her of the chance to make her own decision. The only way to right the situation was to go back and make him listen. Fortunately, she was able to get off the coach at the first way-station and return by another stage. She'd never guessed she'd be walking into the middle of a double-cross and a shootout!

She sighed to herself, kneading the throbbing pleat between her eyebrows. He'd wasted no time going after the thing he cared about most—his idol, that damned gold. Now their lives were in jeopardy from the men he'd once called partners, as well as from the law. She knew she was a fool to be enamored of an amoral villain like John Tucker, but she was helpless against the feelings he evoked in her most secret heart. Only time would tell if the price she was being asked to pay was worth it.

Raising her head, she looked again at the tiny cloud of dust on the horizon. She felt so wretched she knew her presence was a handicap Johnny could not afford. "They're getting closer. You'll never outrun them with me along. You should go ahead and I—"

"No. We stay together."

She swung around to face him, her eyes tortured and fearful. "I'm slowing you down. I couldn't stand it if anything happened to you . . ."

"Nothing's going to happen," he said gruffly. He helped her mount, then swung a leg over his own horse. "They won't follow where we're going."

"Where's that?"

The corner of his mouth lifted, and his cheek creased with grim humor. "Straight into the clutches of the Union Army."

"What! Johnny, no!"

"It's a beautiful plan. There ought to be patrols riding out of Fort Ringgold. And we're nearly there, so just hang on, sweetheart."

"It's too dangerous." She shook her head in disbelief.

"Are you mad? An ex-guerrilla like you, with such a sum of gold in his possession? They'll arrest you."

"If I'm lucky." His smile widened in anticipation. "God, I'd give anything to see the expression on Jesse's face when he realizes."

She fingered the reins nervously, swallowing back the impulse to rave at him. "What about me?"

"You'll be fine. Trust me." He looked away from the reproachful expression in her eyes, and his stubbled jaw hardened. "We have no choice, Sara. It's the way it has to be."

They ran into a federal cavalry patrol a scant two hours later, a dusty and trail-weary group returning to their camp. Johnny hailed the leader, a young captain named Callahan, and quickly availed himself of their escort, explaining they'd been harassed by a group of desperados. The captain, sensing an opportunity for heroism, dispatched a group of blue-uniformed troopers back north to investigate. By this time, Sara was too tired and apprehensive to appreciate the grin of wicked amusement Johnny wore as he watched them ride off to confront his former partners.

They camped that night within the security of the troop. Utterly fatigued, Sara was too uncomfortable to sleep, light-headed and increasingly apprehensive about her own worrisome malaise. She hoped they would soon reach a place where they could truly rest, but she was too sick at heart to question Johnny about their next move, though he was couched in earnest conversation with Captain Callahan for a long time. They rode into the stockade at Fort Ringgold on the Rio Grande late the next evening.

Johnny helped Sara down from her horse in front of the main building. A stocky, strong-featured man in shirtsleeves stamped out on the board walkway, and the young captain hurried forward, throwing a smart salute, then giving his report. Even through her haze of fatigue, Sara felt Johnny stiffen, his attention diverted, focused on the newcomer, a man in his mid-thirties whose face was already etched with a lifetime of experience. She glanced apprehensively at Johnny's inscrutable countenance, then toward Captain Callahan and his superior. The captain gesticulated rapidly, pointing in their direction, and Sara's fears returned in full force. Was Johnny going to end this adventure in another prison cell?

The older man's bushy brows drew together in a fearsome frown, and his chin thrust out at a pugnacious angle. He stepped off the porch and strode toward them. Instinctively, Sara took a protective step closer to Johnny. Her head swam at the sudden movement, and she swayed, but he seemed oblivious to everything but the bulldog of a man bearing down on them.

"You've got a hell of a nerve, sir," the officer barked. "Claiming amnesty. Talk of Juarez and Maximillian, demanding immunity. Only the President has that power. What's the meaning of all this balderdash?"

"It's good to see you again, General," Johnny said simply.

Brows cranked up the officer's forehead like a windowshade, and he gave Johnny a piercing look from head to toe. Suddenly his face went slack with surprise. The only word Sara could think of to describe it was "thunderstruck."

"John!" the General cried.

Johnny grinned and saluted. "Phil."

The General caught Johnny's hand and pumped it vigorously, beaming. "By God, man! I thought you were dead!"

"I was—for a while." Johnny clasped Sara's shoulder, pulling her closer. "I guess you could say Sara brought me back. My wife, Sara. Sara, this is General Philip Sheridan."

"Madam, it's a pleasure," the General said with a courtly bow that did not conceal his sharp, inquisitive appraisal. Now it was Sara's turn to be completely speechless. The General's gaze raked Johnny again. "My God! I can't get over this! Appearing like a genie out of a damned lamp. Well, don't just stand there. Come in, come in!"

Johnny retrieved the saddlebags holding the Calf. "I've brought you a present—from Tuck."

Sheridan chuckled, leading the way toward the building.

"Tuck, you say. My God, you rascal. I've got to hear it all."

The young captain indicated the way, then followed them. Johnny placed his hand in the small of Sara's back to guide her forward. She went unresistingly, stupefied. Philip Sheridan, the famous Union commander, knew Johnny? And Tuck? How? Why?

Inside the spartan office Johnny dropped the heavy saddlebags on the top of Sheridan's scarred wooden desk. Rolls of maps and untidy stacks of dispatches littered the worktop and floor. A print of Lincoln in a gilt frame hung on a nail behind the desk.

"Corporal, get Mrs. McCulloch a chair," the General barked to an aide.

Mrs. McCulloch? Sara echoed inwardly, her head spinning. Gratefully, she sank down in the proffered chair. Cold sweat broke out on her forehead, and she gripped the chair arms with white-knuckled hands.

"What is all this? And what the hell are you doing in the bowels of Texas after all this time?" the General demanded.

"Just following orders," Johnny said. He manipulated the buckles on the saddlebags and withdrew two sacks, tossing one to the general, another to Captain Callahan.

The General dumped his sack, spilling fifty-dollar and twenty-dollar gold pieces into a shimmering pile. "Good Lord, John. You found it."

Johnny nodded. "Quantrill's Golden Calf. It was bound for Maximillian's coffers. I had to retrieve it from some former friends. Your being here is a stroke of good fortune. Maybe my luck's changing for the better—finally."

"Juarez can say the same thing. This is going to go a long way to help the cause of independent Mexico." The General stuck out his hand again. "Well done, Major."

Sara gasped softly. Her thoughts felt as slow and thick as molasses, and she struggled to assimilate all the particles of information that flowed around her. Suspicion and distrust raised spectral heads in her consciousness, and with them came pain of body, mind, and soul.

"I don't understand, General," Captain Callahan said, a puzzled expression on his smooth face.

"Quinlan, my boy, meet a God damn hero," the General said. "Major John T. McCulloch, the best damn agent the Union ever had!"

A small, agonized cry ripped from Sara's throat, and she struggled unsteadily to her feet, her face as white as alabaster. Johnny swung around, a flicker of regret shadowing his green eyes. He took a step toward her, but she backed away, her gaze dark with a terrible inner turmoil.

Their voices mingled, intertwined.

"All this time," she accused. "You let me believe . . ."

". . . couldn't tell you . . ."

". . . it was a *Confederate* prison . . ."

". . . wasn't safe for you to know about . . ."

". . . a spy, the most dangerous . . . to *die,* you said . . ."

". . . there was no good time . . ."

". . . you rode with those murderers . . . and Will . . ."

". . . stayed on that stage, you'd never have had to know . . ."

". . . why didn't you *tell* me . . . ?"

The mortal anguish of this ultimate betrayal, this final, fundamental deception, pierced her like a surgeon's blade. It *hurt.* After everything they'd been through together, everything they'd been to each other—it hurt so much she was afraid for an instant she was losing her mind. Then the rage came, a cleansing, burning fire that she welcomed as the only means of self-preservation and sanity. With the last dregs of her strength, she poured that rage into a stinging slap, smacking her palm against his cheek with a contemptuous blow that echoed like a shot in the small office.

Johnny's mouth tightened, and the muscle in his cheek pulsed while the red outline of her hand bloomed across his jawbone. He rubbed it gingerly. "I guess I deserved that."

"You are the lowest, the most vile creature that ever crawled from the pit," she said, enunciating each word carefully, painfully. Tears glittered in her eyes but did not fall. Her voice was cold and haughty and scornful. "I never want to see you again as long as I live."

The General and Callahan watched, astounded, taken aback by her sudden eruption of fury. She turned away from Johnny and, grasping the edge of the desk for support, leaned toward the General.

"Please, sir," she said. "I want to go home to Missouri as soon as possible."

General Sheridan harrumphed and stirred uncomfortably. "Well, of course, ma'am. That is, we'll do what we can—"

"Sara, listen to me." Johnny touched her elbow, but she shook him off, her pinched face focused on Sheridan. She swayed, forming her words with the utmost effort.

"I must go home to my family, sir. As soon . . ." She lurched, and all three men made abortive movements toward her, but she caught herself. Her expression was pleading. "As soon as I can. If I could just rest a while. I'm afraid I must impose on your hospitality, General."

"No imposition at all, madam," he spluttered, accustomed to warfare but not to a defenseless female with dark, suffering eyes.

"I'm not well, you see," Sara said. Her voice sounded far away, and her knees were like water. "It would be wise to quarter me well away from your troops. I think it may be—" Dizzy, almost too weak and sick and wounded to utter the words, but coerced by duty to warn the General, she murmured, "It's typhoid."

Her knees buckled, and she felt herself sliding to the floor. Curiously outside of herself, she watched Johnny move toward her, but his features were distorted, as though she was seeing him through the wrong end of a telescope. Then he faded away altogether.

"Here, John. You look like you could use this," Philip Sheridan said.

Johnny raised his bowed head from his hands and stared unseeingly at the proffered glass of amber whiskey for a long moment. Then he accepted the tumbler. "Thanks."

The commander settled in a chair across the table from Johnny and poured another drink for himself. The dining hall was empty except for the two of them, and a single lamp burned low in a wall bracket near the door. Johnny had washed, and a blue uniform shirt and regulation trousers and suspenders graced his massive form.

"How is she?" the General asked quietly.

"The fever's up." Johnny sipped the fiery liquor and grimaced. "She's a bad patient. Pitched a basin at your surgeon's head when he tried to bleed her."

Sheridan laughed and shook his head appreciatively. "Damn, that's some kind of hellcat you've got yourself tied up with this time."

"Yeah." Johnny glanced up at his friend. "I feel so damned guilty, Phil. I forced her to come with me. She didn't want to at first. If only I hadn't—"

"Don't torment yourself. She'll be all right."

"Will she? It's going to get a lot worse before it's better."

Sheridan sighed. "I know. Typhoid's a tricky thing."

"She won't see me."

"Rosa and the other women will take care of her. She's got a right to be angry." The General swirled the contents of his glass, then cocked a bushy eyebrow questioningly. "Hasn't she?"

"Yes. Hell, it's complicated." Johnny pushed an agitated hand through his thick curls. "I suppose the only thing I can do now is to take care of her whether she likes it or not."

"She'll get over it. They all do." Sheridan grinned. "You know women. They'll pout and make you pay, but in the end they forgive you. Can't help themselves, especially with a handsome devil like you."

"Maybe." Johnny downed the remainder of the whiskey in one gulp. "Sometimes I wish I'd never heard of the Golden Calf."

"It's quite a feather in your cap. Should earn you a hefty promotion."

"All I want is my back pay. I've had enough. I'm resigning my commission as soon as I can. I don't want to end up fighting Imperialists like you."

"Aw, it's not so bad," Sheridan drawled. "We're here for moral support."

"That's not the way I heard it."

"Well, if covertly supplying Juarez's Liberals with arms and ammunition isn't moral support, what is?" Sheridan's mouth curved in a small smile of satisfaction. "We cache supplies on this side of the Rio Grande. Who's to say who ends up with them? It keeps the Washington bigwigs satisfied, and they can lie to the French ambassador about our strict neutrality with perfect honesty. Why, so far we've been able to turn over nearly thirty thousand muskets from the Baton Rouge Arsenal alone.''

Johnny whistled appreciatively. "Impressive."

"Juarez has reorganized a pretty good sized army. I expect by midsummer he'll be in possession of the whole line of the Rio Grande, maybe nearly the whole of Mexico down to San Luis Potosi. Maximillian's empire is toppling. It's only a matter of time."

"That should please Grant."

"Absolutely. You know that he felt the French invasion of Mexico was so closely related to the Confederate rebellion as to be essentially a part of it. It's ironic but fitting that Quantrill's gold will go to oust the Europeans and serve an independent nation. I'd say you discharged your final orders with great honor and imagination."

Johnny stretched out his legs, crossing his ankles, and folded his hands behind his head. He gazed up at the beamed ceiling, his face bleak with self-mockery. "Honor had nothing to do with it. It was revenge, pure and simple, and I didn't care what innocent parties I took down with me. Only I still didn't get that bastard, Moses."

"From what you've told me, he's still in operation."

"Seems to be."

Sheridan hesitated. "You realize, of course, that part of the Calf is missing?"

Johnny's boots hit the floor with a thump. "What!"

"That shipment was reported to be around eighty thousand. There's only sixty in it now. Could Quantrill have hidden the rest somewhere else?"

"Christ, I don't know!" Johnny frowned. "Probably not. There wasn't time." His thoughts raced, reviewing his own near-fatal ambush, Alex Thompson's murder, Moses' interest in the Calf through contact with Jesse, then his apparent collusion with the law—and it all began to make peculiar sense.

"What if Quantrill gave Moses a portion of the Calf?" Johnny speculated. "Then something went wrong. Maybe he was suspicious, smelled treachery of some kind. That's why he buried it in the Sugarloaf and left behind a treasure map in his Bibles. He didn't trust Moses anymore.''

"That would explain a lot of things." The General poured another round of whiskey, then sat back, assessing Johnny with a practiced eye. "Well, Tuck? Want to go after the rest of the Calf and Moses, too?"

"Go to hell, General," Johnny returned affably.

Sheridan laughed. "We'll see."

Johnny scraped back his chair. "I'm going to check on Sara. As soon as she's able, I want her to go home."

"Certainly. If that's what she really wants."

Johnny's features were suddenly haggard. "That's all she'll want from me now."

A few minutes later, he peeked in the door of the room she'd been assigned, only to find her alone and sitting up on the side of the bed, holding her stomach, muttering to herself.

"You shouldn't be up," he said.

Startled, she jerked the sheet over her gown-clad body. Her face was flushed and dry, and her eyes were bright with fever. "I told you I don't want to see you."

He came forward, lifted her feet back onto the narrow cot, and began to rearrange the twisted covers. "Since when have I ever done anything you wanted?"

"You love forcing your will on helpless women, don't you, *Major?*" She made the title sound like an insult.

He was unmoved. "It's one of my favorite pastimes, madam. Not that I've ever considered you all that helpless. How do you feel?"

"Hot. It's typhoid for certain." Her voice was curiously emotionless, as though she were talking about a case history in one of her textbooks. He sat down uninvited on the edge of the cot.

"How can you be sure?"

The look she gave him was scathing. "I'm a doctor. And appendicitis doesn't produce rose spots on the patient's torso like I've got."

"Let me see." He reached for the edge of her gown.

"No! I—" She broke off, too weak to fight. "Oh, what difference does it make?"

He rolled the hem upward, revealing the rash on her stomach. "It's a pretty shade, don't you think?" he asked, trying for lightness, but his voice shook. She pushed the gown down abruptly.

"It's not pretty. It won't be pretty, not by the time the brown crust forms on my lips and tongue, and I'm out of my head with the fever."

She's scared, Johnny realized. Underneath the bravado was a scared little girl. "What can I do?" he asked, holding her hand.

"Don't let that man near me again with his dirty knife! Cool sponging is all I want done for the fever."

"I won't let him within a mile. What else?"

"If—" She bit her lip and looked away. "If I die, let Pandora know. And I want Yves to say a Mass for me."

"You're not going to die."

"You don't know . . . a lot can happen. Hemorrhage, perforation."

"You're too strong and stubborn to die, Sara. As soon as you're better, we'll go to New Orleans by steamer. You'll like that." He tried to smile. "No more horses."

She drew her hand away. "No. I won't go anywhere with you ever again."

The pain and humiliation of his treachery rose in her throat like gorge, and she rolled to her side, facing the adobe wall so that he couldn't see her face, couldn't guess the hurt that flowed through her veins, a hundred times more devastating than any fever.

For a time she'd thought, hoped, *believed* that he cared for her. Now she knew better.

Major McCulloch. The name was bitter on her tongue. She'd never understand why he'd kept that most important, most intimate secret from her all this time. Again and again, he'd proven that he was utterly amoral. The fact that he was a hero rather than a villain was irrelevant. He was too elusive, too demanding, too passionate, too dishonest, just *too much* for her to deal with anymore. Whatever his private code of behavior, honorable or not, she could not fathom it, nor him.

He'd taken everything from her—home, family, virtue, pride—and she should hate him for it, *had* to for her own salvation. She could not live with him any longer, so she must learn to live without him, wean herself from the obsession, the hunger that twisted her insides even now when she looked at him. Her love was a fraud, a mere shadow, for neither Johnny nor Tuck were real men, and she wasn't even sure about the Major. How could she tell who was substance, who was shadow? So she turned her face to the wall and prepared for a life without John Tucker McCulloch.

His voice was low. "You're never going to forgive me, are you?"

"No."

"That's not a very Christian attitude, ma'am," he chided with gentle humor.

Her answer was muffled. "I've given all I can give. I don't have any more for you, for myself, for anyone."

He felt a pang of guilt that he'd made her this way, she, who'd been the most giving of all women. He rubbed her spine, his head hanging. "I told you I was a selfish bastard."

Her shoulders shook, and her words were choked. "I believe you now."

He reached for her, turning her on her back so he could look into her fever-flushed visage. "Sara, you have to understand I had my duty to perform. Everything I did was necessary."

"Everything?"

A rush of high color stained his cheekbones, and he gazed like a starving man at the petulant thrust of her lower lip. "Perhaps not everything. But it wasn't all bad, was it? There was pleasure there for you, too. I tried to warn you not to love me."

"I didn't know anything about love, but you've taught me a lot about hate." She glared at him.

He sighed, pushing her hair from her face, trailing his fingertips over the delicate indentation of her temple. "Are we back to that again?"

"What do you think?"

He leaned over her, forcing her to return his glance. "I think a lot of what we have is good."

"We have nothing!" A tear trickled from the corner of

her eye. "It was only a dream. Now, go away and leave
me alone. I want to die in peace."

"Dammit! You are not going to die!"

"No." She laughed. "You'd hate to have my death on
your conscience. Oh, I beg your pardon. You have no conscience."

"Maybe not." He stood. "But I know my duty when I
see it. And that's to get you well."

"You're not responsible for me. I'll take care of myself."

"You're still my wife."

She sat up, flushing darkly with the effort. "Only until
I can arrange a divorce."

He clamped down on the anger that swept through him
like a hot wind. "You take a lot for granted, Sara."

"Like what?"

"Like thinking I've stopped wanting you."

She gasped, outraged. "You presume too much, sir.
You can't believe I'd allow you a husband's rights. Not
after this."

"If you weren't burning up with fever, I'd show you
just exactly what I believe."

"You—you slimy toad! You—" She spoke incoherently,
almost speechless with fury.

"Calm yourself, love." He went to the chipped china
pitcher on the twig table and poured water into its matching bowl, wringing out the cloth he found there, then returning to sit at her side. "You're getting yourself all
worked up. Let's wash that hot face of yours."

She batted at him feebly, but he would have his way,
laying her back down and smoothing her heated skin with
the cooling cloth, wiping her forehead, her wrists. "Did
you ever do this for me?" he asked.

She quit struggling against his ministrations, thrown
back in time, the vision of him unconscious and burning
with fever a powerful, evocative memory. "Y-yes."

"Then let me return the favor. I'll take care of you, the
way you did for me." He rubbed the cloth between her
fingers, his tone conversational. "And I'll tell you something else. I like having a strong-willed, hot-blooded

woman at my side. You began this marriage, but we'll dissolve it only when I say so.''

Her head felt muzzy, and his hands on her were soothing, but she still had a spark of defiance left. ''You've got a lot of nerve, Major, handing down ultimatums. I'll make you regret the day you laid eyes on me.''

He laughed softly. ''You can't drive me away, Doc, so you might as well stop trying.'' He bent, pressed a chaste kiss to her forehead. ''Rest now. No matter what, I'll be here.''

Her eyelids fluttered, and sleep surrounded her. She tried to tell him something, but she was too tired. She wanted to tell him that from a man who proclaimed an inability to love and a refusal to accept ties of any kind, his promise sounded strangely like a commitment. Curiously comforted, she let sleep overtake her, knowing that if the typhoid stole her life now, she'd go content.

Chapter 17

The crisis came on suddenly.

Sara was right. What the disease did to her wasn't pretty. But John stayed by her, sponging her down, trying to spoon fluids past her crusted lips, listening to her ravings when the delirium was upon her. It finally occurred to him that despite everything he could do, she might die. That's when he began to pray.

During one of her few quiet periods, he sat beside her cot, elbows on knees, forehead propped on his clenched fists, wondering what kind of God would visit such tribulation on a good, decent woman like Sara. She didn't deserve it, nor anything else that had happened. Was he part of God's retribution against Sara's sins? Or was the torture he felt at watching her suffer penance for his own crimes? The philosophical convolutions of the question made his mind reel. Whatever, it was hell.

Light fingers feathered over his hair, and he looked up to find Sara watching him, her eyes sunk deep in her wasted face, but with the first sign of lucidity in many days.

"You look awful," she whispered, her voice raspy. "Did I do that to you? I'm sorry."

She was worried about *him*? The enormity of her goodness made him swallow harshly. He caught her hand and tried to smile. "Watch it, Doc. I'm not the one who's sick. How do you feel?"

"Thirsty."

He brought her a drink, lifting her shoulders and helping her. She fell back, exhausted by the effort.

Her gaze wandered around the chamber, then caught on the potted yellow cactus rose resting on the table at her bedside. Sharp thorns protruded from the green flesh of the plant, but the golden blossom was gossamer and as delicate as chiffon.

"How pretty," she murmured.

John glanced at the flower, his expression diffident. "It's not a nosegay of violets, but I hoped it might cheer you up."

She blinked at him, and he could have kicked himself for reminding her of that other existence. What right did he have to bring her flowers? He reached for the plant. "I'll take it away."

"Don't. I like it very much." She watched him closely, and her voice was a whispering rustle, like the wind over the prairie. "You've been here the whole time, haven't you? Every time I woke up, I saw you."

"I had nothing better to do."

"You're a devil with green eyes, Major McCulloch, and you fight so hard to hide from yourself." She sighed. "You can stop worrying. I'm going to be all right. Look." She touched her hairline and extended her fingers to show the dampness of sweat.

"The fever's broken." He caught her hand and pressed it to his cheek. "Thank God."

Her small palm was warm on his face, the edge of her thumb unconsciously testing the velvety texture of his mustache. Connected, eyes locked, the rush of awareness between them was as new as the dawn and as old as time. It flashed like summer lightning, taking their breath, singeing lungs and hearts with its heat. Despite her weakened state and his fatigue, despite their muddled and turbulent history, despite inclination or will, it was there between them, undeniable, potent, and eloquent.

He felt her withdrawal even before she removed her hand. Shutters dropped over her expression, and she retreated behind an emotional barrier, an invisible wall he knew he'd built brick by brick with every perfidious act, every lie, every betrayal. Frustration and regret charged through him, making him feel vulnerable and raw, and he took refuge in anger and primitive male possessiveness.

Hate him though she undoubtedly did, now she was *his*, to protect, to desire, and to bed. And when she was stronger, he'd show her that nothing essential had changed between them.

Sara's convalescence was a slow process. Despite Johnny's impatience, it was a week before she was allowed up and another before she was strong enough to contemplate leaving Fort Ringgold. There had been no signs of Jesse and Cole, but then Johnny hadn't expected any trouble once they reached the haven of the fort. Still, he was anxious to take Sara away from Texas, and he chafed at the delay. She was subdued and lethargic, and although physically she was recovering, her lack of spirit distressed him. Invariably polite, she was so distant and apathetic he wanted to shake her, kiss her silly—anything to bring the life back into her. But the blank wall she kept between them, and her prevailing weakness, prevented his trying any such tactics. Finally, General Sheridan announced he was preparing to return to his headquarters in New Orleans, and Johnny knew he could not put off the trip any longer.

They left from Brownsville aboard the steamer *Henry Lee* on a brilliant May morning with the sun sparkling on the blue-green Gulf of Mexico and illuminating the white sand beaches. The voyage across the Gulf was a comfortable one, but by the time they reached the mouth of the Mississippi and journeyed upriver to the Crescent City, Sara's small reserves of strength were again depleted.

Rather than taking up residence in a hotel, Sheridan arranged for them to occupy a home located on St. Charles Avenue, and it was to this imposing edifice of Doric design and luxuriant gardens that Johnny took her. Mama Sadie, the sturdy Creole housekeeper who'd been at *L'Etoile* longer than any of its owners, took one look at Sara and promptly whisked her into bed, muttering promises of good food and plenty of rest to "fatten up this little chicken."

Sara found it was pleasant to be waited on hand and foot. Mama Sadie plied her with New Orleans delicacies with strange names like "gumbo" and "jambalaya," fresh fruits—imported bananas and plums and melon—and veg-

etables from the French Market, plus blood-building ton-
ics of rich Madeira wine. The hot southern sun was a
blessing, baking the typhoid chill from her bones, and she
spent many pleasant hours in the flower-filled gardens,
relaxing on a wicker lounge or cautiously exploring the
gravel paths underneath oak trees festooned with Spanish
moss.

She'd had no will or strength to protest Johnny's—the
Major, as she now thought of him—plans for her, but now,
as her vitality returned, she knew she could no longer
allow herself to continue to acquiesce in such a limp-spined
manner, to float like a thistle in the wind, borne mind-
lessly by the wind's currents to some unknown destina-
tion.

It was time to regain control of her life. It hurt too much
to think about what she'd almost had with Johnny, but she
knew it had been merely a dream. There was nothing here
for her any longer. It was time to go home.

The quill scratched across the paper, then paused. Sara
hesitated, chewing her lip, searching for the words she
needed. So much had happened. What should she tell Pandora? How much could a letter convey?

Her gaze roamed over the graciously appointed parlor
with its high cool ceiling and stark white walls. The *es-
critoire* where she sat was delicately made of cherry. Summer drapes of sheer muslin graced the floor-length
windows, setting off the rose-carved mahogany and satin
settees and matching chairs. A curved glass mirror of the
Federal period hung over the fireplace, and a pair of
Sèvres porcelain urns balanced the white marble mantle.

L'Etoile had been the home of a cotton merchant before
the war, but he, along with a great many of his country-
men, had lost everything. At least the occupying Union
forces had preserved it intact, Sara reflected, rather than
burning it to the ground or quartering their horses in it. A
lot of people, herself included, would never entirely forget
the war. Even a year after Lee's surrender, the repercus-
sions continued to dominate her life. Her attention caught
on the handsomely dressed figure watching her from the
open doorway.

"You're very pensive, my dear," Johnny said, coming

forward. He offered her a single creamy rose with a blush-pink center.

His tawny hair gleamed, and his shoulders looked very broad beneath the tailored frock coat. The muscles in his thighs bulged under the close fit of his fawn-colored trousers, and his calf-high boots shone with polish. He looked every inch the successful businessman, urbane and finished, charming and likeable. And totally unknown. Major McCulloch, the third facet of Johnny's personal trinity, and she was again at a loss to deal with him.

As she accepted the rose, her head filled with its sweet fragrance, and she felt more alone than she ever had in her life. "Thank you," she murmured.

"I'm glad the roses are blooming in your cheeks again," he said. "It will be good to see you back to your normal, cheerful self. I've missed those little songs of yours."

She glanced away, unnerved by his sudden appearance, striving to maintain the façade of indifference she'd so assiduously cultivated. "There hasn't been much cause for singing lately."

She cringed at the plaintive sound of those words. She was not begging for sympathy, not from him. It was imperative to preserve the illusion of distance, her only defense against the pain and shameful flutterings of recognition low in her belly. Chagrined that her traitorous body knew him, though her heart and mind did not, she made her voice cool and prim. "But I'm feeling much better, thank you."

He inspected her averted face, then lifted her chin with his forefinger. "Why do you look at me as though we were strangers?"

"You are a stranger to me, Major."

He made a sound of annoyance. "My name is John."

"Is it?" Her tone was too sweet.

"You know it is. Use it." He suppressed a smile. It was the first time she'd crossed swords verbally with him in weeks. It was a good sign that her recuperation was nearly complete.

He studied the elegant lines of her face, the weighty mass of sienna-highlighted hair in its intricate roll that made her neck seem too slim to bear its weight. A heaviness grew in his loins. He'd kept his distance, though his hunger for her was undiminished, and God, he'd missed her sleeping next to him. Perhaps tonight he'd join her in the huge poster bed where she'd slept alone since coming to *L'Etoile*. The soft, rosy outline of her lips beckoned him. Slowly, he dropped his mouth toward hers.

She drew away before he made contact, biting her lower lip, looking everywhere but at him. Breathless, she asked, "Have you finished your business in the city?"

Amused, he allowed her to escape—for now. His smile was lopsided as he straightened. *Let her flutter,* he thought. He was more than willing to pursue her, if that was what she wanted. They both knew how it must inevitably end, and the waiting made the act all the sweeter. So he indulged her shyness.

"As a matter of fact, I have to meet with Sheridan later. There are lots of loose ends and unanswered questions."

"Have you decided to stay in the Army, then?"

Crossing his arms over his chest, he shrugged. "I've been offered my choice of assignments, but I don't know."

"Have—have you sent word to your family that you're all right?"

His jaw tightened. "Not yet."

"I'm sure they'll want to know."

"I doubt it. My resurrection isn't likely to be anything but an awkward inconvenience."

"I refuse to believe that." She sat back in her writing chair, a delicate shell-pink hue washing her cheekbones. "It is too callous of you to deny them the knowledge that you're alive, no matter what bitterness lies between you. And what of the child? Shouldn't you check on his welfare?"

"Gwendolyn's brat is well cared for, rest assured," he said, an Arctic chill freezing his words. "You needn't concern yourself. I've done my duty."

"Duty!" She straightened indignantly. "Your notion of duty leaves me cold, Major."

"I suppose you'd like me to take the little bastard to my breast?"

"No, though it would be the selfless thing to do. But I wouldn't wish that kind of hostility on anyone, much less an innocent child. Your wife did a terrible thing to you, but you've done worse to that babe. A child deserves parents who love him." Her lower lip quivered. "Any child."

"What the hell do you know about—" He broke off, stunned. Squatting, he dropped to her eye level, grasping her clasped hands urgently. "What are you saying, Sara? Are you with child? My, God, I never thought—"

She gazed over his head, her expression stony. "I can't have children. It's just as well, considering our situation. A child would only complicate things."

He rose slowly, scraping fingers through his hair. "I'd do right by you, you know that."

"Another duty, Major?" she asked, her tone scathing. "No, thank you. I've had all of that overworked virtue I can stand."

His angry retort faltered unspoken as his gaze snagged on her letter. Frowning suddenly, he slid the creamy sheet of paper off the desk top. "What's this?"

It would be too undignified to resort to a tugging match, she decided, so she merely held out her hand. "A letter to Pandora. Unlike you, I am anxious to assure my family that I am safe. May I have it, please?"

He scanned the even lines, his features drawing together in a scowl. His fist closed around the sheet, crumpling it violently, then he tossed it disdainfully at her feet. "You're not going anywhere yet, Sara, so put that out of your head. You're still too weak from the typhoid."

"I'm the best judge of that," she said evenly. "I want to go home. If you'll advance me money for the passage, I'll return it to you as soon as I can."

"Shut up." A dark flush rose under his deep tan, and he looked as though he'd like to slap her. "You're my wife, God damn it. No matter how it happened, I'll take care of you."

"The way you took care of Gwendolyn? And that little boy?" Her laugh was mocking. "No, thank you, Major."

"Have a care, Sara," he warned.

"Poor man, you really don't know what it is you want, do you? Unless it's to hurt others as badly as you've been hurt. I'm sorry, Major, I'm not so self-destructive that I intend to wait around for another dose of your brand of morality.''

He plucked her from the chair before she could take a breath. "This is what I want from you," he said harshly. Holding the back of her head, ignoring her squirmings, he ground his lips against hers.

"Stop." She gasped at the bold invasion of his tongue, pulling away in panic. "You have no right."

"Wrong. I have every right to make love to my wife." His mouth traveled across her eyelids, kissing them shut, then nipped her nose and nuzzled the sensitive spot between her ear and jawbone. She shuddered uncontrollably, as if revisited by the typhoid chills, but she knew this disease, this hunger was more dangerous than any physical sickness, for it was an obsession of the soul. She whimpered helplessly, then his mouth claimed hers, and she melted against him, greedy for him, flinging all her brave resolutions to the wind.

His tongue was lascivious, the kiss deep and wild and wonderful, bringing forth all the freedom and delight they'd enjoyed in each other before Sara knew her love was a lie. The enormity of her loss crushed her frail defenses, and she sobbed for the tragedy of losing a love she'd never really had. He drew back.

"Sara?" His voice grated like broken glass. "Sweet, don't cry."

She buried her face in her hands, but her eyes were dry, her despair too deep for mere tears.

The rattle of dishes on a tray intruded upon the strained silence. Mama Sadie sailed into the parlor, a loaded coffee tray outstretched like an offering to an idol, as regal as a goddess in her madras *tignon*.

"Madelaine done fixed you her special sponge cake this evenin', Missus McCulloch," she said. Catching sight of Johnny, she widened her smile. "Didn't know you'd come in, Major. Set yourself, and I'll fetch another cup."

Reluctantly, Johnny released Sara, stepping away from her with difficulty. "I won't be staying."

Mama Sadie glanced curiously at Sara's pale face, then the Major's implacable expression. Wisely, she forbore saying anything. If there was one thing Mama Sadie knew, it was her place. She busied herself setting the tray on the low table, chattering to fill the oppressive silence.

"You be missing out on some fine sponge cake, Major. Got that marmalade fillin' you so fond of . . . ." She raised curious eyes to find him gone, and Sara staring bleakly into space. "Now, you jest come rest a spell, Missus," she urged, touching Sara's arm.

Sara came aware with a start. "Oh, of course. Thank you, Mama Sadie," she said, trying to smile.

The Creole poured coffee, added thick cream and a dollop of brown sugar, and pressed the cup into her mistress' hands. "Don't worry, honey-lamb. All dem men folks gets riled once in a while. But even a blind man can see that the Major, he dotes on you fer shore."

"Oh, Mama Sadie," Sara said sadly, "if only that were true." Then she began to cry, and Mama Sadie held her and patted her and thought to herself that sometimes white folks acted mighty peculiar.

"And to the best of your knowledge, Major, this 'Moses' was responsible for the majority of the intelligence that Quantrill received?"

"That's correct." John McCulloch sat across the table from the officers who formed the inquiry board, General Sheridan, General Baird, two aides-de-camp, and a stenographer.

General Baird scribbled rapidly on a sheet, then frowned and threw down his pen. "It rankles that such a traitor should still be at large, and according to Major McCulloch, very busy with matters that threaten national security."

"I agree," Philip Sheridan replied. "I suggest we take the matter under advisement and keep the file on Moses the Prophet open until we can make a final decision regarding the disposition of the problem."

"Let the record so state," General Baird intoned. "Also let the record reflect that Major McCulloch is exonerated of all charges, civil or otherwise, incurred in the discharge of his orders pursuant to the subject of Quantrill and the shipment of gold known as the Golden Calf. This board is adjourned."

Chairs scraped backwards, and the officers filed out of the room. Philip Sheridan fell into step beside John. "Don't you want to see that bastard Moses get what's coming to him?" he asked, his bushy eyebrows lifted in inquiry.

"Sure. He eliminated Alex Thompson, and he ambushed me, but I can't prove it. And then there's the problem of finding out just who Moses really is."

"You could start with that fellow Moody."

"Wait a minute, Phil." John frowned. "I haven't agreed to anything. You seem to forget I've lost better than a year out of my life. And before that it was a tightrope walk with Quantrill. I'm entitled to a breather before I decide if the Army is still in my future. Remember, I'm no West Pointer."

Sheridan snorted. "Hell, what difference does that make? You've got enough experience and savvy to outthink two-thirds of the Chiefs of Staff. We need men like you. There's unrest in the seceded states, not to mention the atmosphere on the Rio Grande and the Indian problem in the western territories. The Army can always find a place for a good man."

"Thanks, Phil," John said, slapping his friend on the shoulder. "I appreciate your confidence, but I've got things to sort out."

"Starting with that wife of yours, no doubt." Sheridan shrugged. "Can't say I blame you. How is Sara, anyway?"

John's mouth tightened. "Better."

"Will she mind if you go have a drink with an old friend?"

"No," John said, his expression glum, "she won't mind at all."

The dream was piercingly sweet. His hands were upon her, knowing and pleasurable. The taste of him, potent and faintly whiskey-flavored, was in her mouth, familiar and inflaming.

"Johnny," Sara murmured, drugged by sleep and a seductive warmth that made her ache with need.

"Come to me, sweet." His voice was thick with desire,

and she responded with all her heart, giving herself totally to the man she loved.

The mists of slumber receded, and dream and reality blurred, shifted, reformed. The hand that stroked her hip through the thin lawn gown was no ghostly image. The lips that wooed her belonged to no phantom conjured by her wayward imagination. She gasped against his mouth, and he took her breath inside him, deepening the kiss, stealing her thoughts, so that the moment of resistance faded as if it had never been, and she lifted her hands to pull him closer.

With trembling fingertips, she discovered he was naked against her. He felt wonderful, his weight and bulk welcome. She gloried in the texture of his skin, his unique male scent, the soft bramble of chest hair, the hard muscles of his flanks. With a groan, he dragged her gown upward, and unerringly his hand cupped her feminine mound. With infinite care, he stroked the dewy folds of sensitive flesh until she trembled and gasped, and sensation exploded with a magical unreality that spun her toward the stars.

Limp with the cataclysmic release, she could offer no assistance as he urgently tugged the gown over her head, throwing it to the floor. His face was taut with need in the shadowy darkness. Kneading the soft mounds of her breasts, he dipped his head, taking an aching tip deep into his mouth and sucking strongly. She cried out, grasping his shoulders, hardly down from one plateau before he began her ascent to the next. Her fingers twined through his thick tawny hair and stroked the strong cords at the back of his neck. She watched him move over her body like a supplicant, teasing and tantalizing, the shadowy outline of his broad shoulders and his strong profile in gray relief against the filmy drapes of sheer mosquito netting that marked the boundaries of enchantment in the big bed.

It was as if he wanted to savor every inch of her skin, and he sought out every secret place to pay his homage, until she was wild with need, and desperate to know him just as intimately. She explored the corner of his mouth with the tip of her tongue, thumbed the aroused nub of his nipple with audacity, and finally, when she knew she could not bear to be without him a moment longer, stroked the hard, hot shaft of his arousal. With a low guttural cry, he pulled her beneath him, and his entry was hard and fast and exactly what they both wanted.

He braced himself on his palms, holding the moment, drinking in the sultry look on her face, the pouty pearllike tips of her nipples, the place where they joined, light and dark, hard and soft, male and female. The pleasure was so intense, so exquisite, he wondered why he did not die of it. But the need was upon him, and his hips moved, plunging and withdrawing into the wet velvet heat of his woman.

The conflagration of senses took them to new, unparalleled heights. In the moment of completion, her soft cries rippled over him, and the contractions of her body pulled him under in a whirlpool of ecstasy, lost to sight, and sound, and thought, and everything but the unspoken certainty that he'd never needed anything as much as he needed this, and he'd never deserved it less.

She came awake by degrees, conscious first of the raucous shriek of a blue jay just outside the window and the faraway chants of the black Cala women, peddling their sweet rice cakes down St. Charles Avenue in the cool of early morning. A sense of well-being permeated her, and she stretched like a cat, almost purring, rubbing against the warmth and solidity that supported her back, the lazy stroking of a broad, callused hand over the subtle protrusion of hipbone and the silky length of her thigh. Reality intruded, and her eyes popped open. This was no dream!

"Morning, love," he murmured, and his hand slid possessively to the indentation of her waist. In his beard-stubbled face, eyes the color of a new spring leaf caressed her with knowing thoroughness.

She gasped and rolled away, a moan clogging her throat. Mortified, she buried her face in a pillow, dragging her knees up as though in pain. His mouth traveled over her bare shoulder, his lips warm and firm, delineated by the velvety brush of mustache above and the prickles of a night's growth of stubble below.

"Don't," she moaned against the pillow. "Oh God, don't."

There was humor and lazy satisfaction in his drawl. "I can't help myself. You taste so good."

She erupted from the bed in a flurry of white bed-clothes, reaching for her robe and defensively pulling it over her nakedness. Her eyes burned, their copper gleam an indication of her fury. "Damn you! You had no right to sneak in here like a thief and . . . and . . ."

"And make love to my wife?" he asked, one eyebrow lifted in mockery.

He raised up on his elbow, the opposite arm propped on an uplifted knee, a blatant and unselfconscious speci-men of virile masculinity, every particle of him, every muscle and sinew, beautiful to her eyes. She tore her gaze away, whirling around so that his magnetism could not capture her again, and steadied herself on the edge of the dressing table.

The image of the woman in the mirror behind the table shocked her. Well-kissed, slightly swollen lips, and sleepy eyelids heavy with satiation mocked her. Her dark hair tumbled in wild, glorious abandon, giving her the sensual air of a woman who was certainly no lady. She grabbed up her hairbrush and dragged it through the thick locks, working furiously to control the mass as any decent woman should. It gave her something to do, something to think about besides the man lounging in her bed and what had passed between them in the night.

She had her hair twisted up and was reaching for her hairpins when John stepped into the reflection behind her. "Wear these again for me," he said softly. His large hands were awkward as he slid the ivory combs into place on either side of her head.

Stunned, Sara turned to him, lifting tentative fingers to trace the delicate carving. A faint glimmer of hope shone in her eyes. He'd kept the combs, when he'd had no reason to think he'd ever see her again. Dared she believe he cared for her? She could forgive him everything, if only he loved her.

"Why?" she asked shakily. "Why should I wear them?"

He studied the tilt of her nose and the curve of her sweet lips, and his hard mouth softened. "Because it gives me such pleasure to take them out again. And I intend to do it often.''

Crestfallen, her fragile hopes dashed like a crystal goblet in careless hands, her lips trembled and her eyes filled. "Let me go.''

Startled, he stared. "What?''

"I can't stay with you any longer," she whispered. "Don't be so cruel as to force me.''

"After last night, I think it's very clear that we can be together.'' He turned and snatched up his pants from the floor, stepping into them with jerky movements. "This is just more of your damned foolishness, woman, and I won't stand for it.''

"You don't want me.''

"Hell's bells! How can you say that?''

Tears slipped from her eyes and spilled down her cheeks. "You don't want me in the way I *need* to be wanted. I was wrong. *Now* isn't enough for me. It never was.''

"I don't believe you.''

"You take everything and give back nothing. You're eaten up with bitterness and hatred for what the war and your wife did to you, but until you're able to put them behind you, you'll only go on hurting yourself—and me. Oh, you can make me want you,'' she admitted bitterly. "You strip me of all pride because you know I cannot deny this physical thing between us, and you use it against me.'' Her hands clasped under her breasts, pressing at the pain that smote her heart. The cold circle of her wedding band bit into the flesh of her finger, and her voice twisted with anguish. "Don't you understand you're destroying me?''

That brought him up short, but his features turned glacial. "Melodramatics don't become you, Sara. Let me ring for coffee. You'll feel better.''

"I don't want any damn coffee!'' she shrieked, pushed past all endurance. She jerked the combs from her hair and threw them at him. He dodged the frail projectiles easily, but then she started on the contents of the dresser top, hurling her brush, powder box, hand mirror, porcelain pin dish, and hair receiver in rapid succession to crash against the floor and wall.

"God damn it, woman!" he roared as the heavy silver lid of the powder box smashed onto his bare toe. He closed the distance between them and grabbed her arms, shaking her hard enough to spill her loose hair down her shoulders again. "Get hold of yourself!"

Her fury dissolved in a flood of tears, harsh sobs racking her slender form. With a muttered exclamation, he pulled her against his bare chest, supporting her swaying form with his strong arms. "Shh, Sara. Don't weep so," he begged.

But she was past comprehension, past comfort, and her tears splashed hotly against his skin and trickled through his chest hair like fiery brands that seared his soul. He'd seen her cry before, but never like this, with such absolute despair. It tore at him with scaly claws, his guilt and misery lacerating his conscience.

He'd never felt so helpless, so wretched. From the very first time he'd touched her, deep down he'd been waiting for this moment, for when he finally drove her away and lost her for good. It wasn't such a surprise. He knew he was a damn bastard, his soul bound for perdition. He'd known all along that he didn't deserve Sara's love.

Maybe that was the real reason he'd never confided the truth about himself. Oh, there'd been plenty of other, logical, sensible reasons, of course. He'd seen to that. But way down deep, in that dark, scorched place in his soul, he'd known that he had to drive her away, to convince her there was nothing worthy of love in John Tucker Mc-Culloch—because in his heart of hearts he knew *that* was the only truth that mattered.

And now he'd done it. He'd broken her completely. She knew now what he'd known all along. Well, he was a bastard, all right, but he had one spark of decency left in him. He wasn't so completely base that he'd continue to hold her simply for his own selfish pleasure. He'd die to lose her, but what was a little more misery to him anyway? He knew he was going to hell eventually. There was no way he was going to drag Sara down with him.

Her sobs had subsided, but her breath moved in and out in painful shudders. John tightened his arms around her, holding her as gently as a precious, spun-glass angel.

"I tried to warn you. I tried to tell you I was no good for you," he murmured brokenly. He blinked rapidly, surprised by the sting of tears in his own eyes. He traced the wet paths down her cheeks with his fingers, then tilted her chin upward. Her eyelids fluttered helplessly, and her mouth was rosy and unbearably vulnerable. Groaning softly, he kissed her, mingling their breaths, tasting her for the last time. He set her away from him gently, and with infinite regret.

"You win, Sara." His voice was hoarse. "You're right. I'll only hurt you more if I keep you with me. And whether you believe me or not, that was something I never meant to do."

"Johnny." His name was a plea on her lips.

"Go home, Sara, love." His handsome features twisted with pain so real it hurt her to look on him. "Go home," he repeated, "while I can still bear to let you."

Chapter 18

The high shriek of the steamship whistle made Sara cover her ears. She leaned against the railing, a picture of slender impatience in a gray poplin traveling dress. A lilac silk bonnet perched atop her severely upswept hair, and the flirtatious loveknot of violets that trimmed the hat bobbed as she scanned the busy Lexington wharf. Tall, billowing clouds cast fleeting shadows through the June sunshine, and the white spire of the Court House glistened above the bluff.

Home! She felt as though she'd been away for three years instead of only three months. Had they come to meet her? Her gaze snagged on a familiar face.

"Dorie!" Sara yelled, waving frantically. "Dorie, here I am!"

The silver-haired matron pushed through the clump of onlookers, her face a wreath of smiles. She gaily flogged a lace-edged handkerchief against the river breeze. With a cry of gladness, Sara hurried with unladylike eagerness to the gangplank, tripping down its length and flinging herself into her sister-in-law's welcoming arms.

"Oh, Dorie," she cried, "it's so good to be home!"

"Bedbugs and blueberries, Sara Jane! How you do carry on." Pandora laughed, but her pale blue eyes were suspiciously bright. She gave Sara another quick, fierce hug, her confidential whisper for Sara's ears only. "I couldn't believe such a tale. Eloping with the hired man, indeed! Father Yves told us how those terrible men forced you and Johnny to help them. I knew you were doing something brave and foolish, so when your letters came, and I knew

278

you were safe, I told everyone you had taken Johnny to a medical conference.''

''Why Dorie!'' Sara was astounded. So Pandora didn't believe she'd married Johnny. That changed the complexion of things.

''Well, it saved awkward explanations,'' Pandora muttered. ''So mind what you say. How did you come to be in New Orleans?''

''It's a long story.'' Sara hesitated. She'd thought she was finished with deception, but Pandora's tale had already placed her in the thick of it. If another fib and a series of half-truths appeased Pandora's sensibilities about the situation, what harm would there be? ''By the time we'd eluded those men, we were in Texas, and then I fell ill. It was simpler to travel back by way of Louisiana so I could recover.''

''Hardly a situation where you could observe the proprieties, was it? How fortunate you had Johnny to look after you. Are you all right now?''

''Perfectly well, Dorie, but glad to be home.''

Pandora looked over her shoulder. ''But where is the boy? Isn't he with you?''

''No.'' Sara's heart hurt, and it was all she could do to keep from placing a hand over it. But she was all cried out. Saying goodbye to John for the final time had been an agony. She pushed the pain determinedly to the farthest corner of her mind. At least in the end John had had the decency to let her go. He'd even offered to attend to the legalities of ending their marriage, promising to send the necessary documents later.

The river voyage back to Missouri had given her plenty of time to think and to grieve, and after days of self-pity, she'd wiped her red eyes and decided to rejoin the human race. After all, she was on her way home, to a family that needed her, and she promised herself she'd shed her last tear for John Tucker McCulloch.

''Pandora,'' Sara explained tightly, ''Johnny remembered. He has his memory again, and he chose to stay in New Orleans.''

''His memory! Well, thank the merciful Lord!'' Pandora exclaimed. ''It's a miracle.''

Before Pandora could demand details, the crowd surged
and suddenly a phalanx of familiar faces surrounded Sara,
all talking at once. Father Yves, grinning from ear to ear;
Lizzie, her angelic face beaming; even Ambrose, less morose than usual, reaching for her bags. Sara gave hugs all
around, laughing and talking and drinking in the affection
radiating from them all.

"Miss Sara! Miss Sara!" Clem was there, too, bobbing
up and down like a fishing cork, impatiently demanding
her attention. Sara dropped to his level, reaching for his
hands.

"Oh, Clem, I swear you've grown a mile," she said.

"Look, Miss Sara! I got a surprise for you." He turned,
his smile brilliant in his chocolate brown face, gesturing
to the neatly-dressed Negro couple waiting behind him.
"They found me, Miss Sara! My Mam and Pappy. They
came!"

"Oh!" Sara stood, her mouth hanging open, then joy
at Clem's good fortune lit her eyes.

"I just had faith, like you said, Miss Sara," Clem
crowed. "And here they stand."

"I'm Ella Washington," said the tiny black woman in
a head kerchief and apron. "This here's my man, Joe.
Lord bless you, ma'am, for what you did for our boy."

"I'm so glad to meet you both," Sara said, shaking
their hands in turn. A flicker of apprehension crossed her
face. "Will you be taking Clem away with you?"

"That's where I come in, my dear," a deep voice said.

"Menard!" Sara turned and smiled in amazement at the
handsome, thickset judge. "What are you doing here?"

Plunket bowed over Sara's hand, hesitated, then grabbed
her shoulders and greeted her with a brief, smacking kiss
on her surprised and flustered mouth. He stepped away,
his voice rough like worn velvet. "You've been away too
long. I don't intend to let you out of my sight again."

"You don't?" Sara croaked inanely, a high flush of color
staining her cheekbones.

"Not at all, and I don't care how important and fascinating your next medical conference is." He smiled, his
thick side whiskers quivering, apparently satisfied with her
reaction to his salutation. "But about the Washingtons. At

Miss Cary's suggestion, I've settled them on a piece of my property, much to everyone's mutual satisfaction.''

"I'm gonna learn how to be a farmer, Miss Sara," Clem piped up, and everyone laughed. Joe Washington, a tall, spare man with sad eyes and a kind but unsmiling demeanor, clamped a hand on Clem's thin shoulder.

"We need to go now, son," he said.

"But where's Johnny? I want to say hello to Johnny," Clem protested.

Sara swallowed and touched Clem's shoulder. "He's not coming back, Clem."

The boy's eyes went wide. "Not ever?"

"No." She licked her dry lips. "He remembered, you see, and he had to go back to his old life." Clem looked so stricken that she hurried on, letting her heart make up the lie. "But he told me to tell you—all of you—that he thanks you for being his friends and—and he loves you all."

Pandora dabbed her handkerchief at her nose and sniffed delicately. "We're all going to miss that boy."

"Perhaps not all of us," Plunket murmured in an aside to Sara. "I don't mind admitting I had my reservations about that charity case of yours."

"He wasn't at all what you feared, Menard," Sara replied, just as softly. It seemed right to defend Johnny to the most powerful man in the county, to explain Johnny's true role in the late war. "He wasn't a Confederate at all, but a Union soldier assigned to spy on Quantrill's activities. The irony of it all is that he was nearly killed by his own troops. He's got family in Pennsylvania, and I think he'll probably return to them. I wish him well, and so should you."

Menard frowned, his heavy features momentarily perturbed, then an impassive mask slid into place. Pandora took a final swipe at her nose with the embroidered square, stuffed it into her cuff, and straightened her shoulders. "Well, what are we waiting for?" she demanded. "Let's take our prodigal home."

Ambrose brought around the buggy hitched to the dappled gelding that had once belonged to Zee Mimms' father. Everyone clambered into the vehicle. Judge Plunket offered Sara a hand to steady herself, and she paused, asking politely, "Will you come, Menard?"

He shook his head, forcing a smile. "I'm afraid the press of business down at the bank . . ."

"I understand. It was good of you to come to greet me."

"I intend to take up all of your time now that you're home again," he said, his dark eyes nearly black with sudden seriousness. "Sara, you can't know how much I missed you."

She was discomfited by his regard, yet her battered pride was soothed by the warm balm of his attentions. Perhaps this was just what she needed to bring her life back into focus after the intensity and chaos of her relationship with John McCulloch. The affection and respect of a nice man whose goals and ideals matched her own could restore the balance that she so sorely needed. She gave the judge a tentative smile.

"I'm home to stay, Menard."

He squeezed her hand a final time and smiled broadly. "My heart is glad to hear it."

Sara mulled over his words on the ride home, but then she was practically carried into the house by Pandora and the rest, and she had no time to think, not when there was punch to drink and a beautiful cake with real buttercream icing to admire. There was a great deal of laughing and chattering, and a holiday atmosphere prevailed all during the evening meal. Finally, pleading exhaustion, she fell onto the overstuffed sofa in the parlor, smiling, her hands fanning her flushed face.

"Oh, I'm all talked out. Play something for us, Dorie," she begged.

Pandora obligingly plopped her considerable bulk onto the piano stool and plunged into a spirited rendition of "Blue-tailed Fly," her fingers bouncing energetically over the ivory keys. Lizzie brought Ambrose another plate of cake, smiling shyly at him, then took a place beside the piano, gently tapping her foot and patting her hand against her calico skirts in time with the snappy song. Sara beckoned Father Yves, who deposited his slight form beside her, his fey, freckled face alight with affection.

"Ah, we've missed you, Sara-lass, that we have," he said.

"Tell me everything. Have you been well?"

"The crone bedeviled me unmercifully after you left. Punishment for my careless tongue, I know." He shuddered.

Sara chewed her lip. "Yves, the drinking—"

"Nary a drop, m'dear, I swear."

"Then the visions have stopped?"

"Young men will see visions, the Good Book says. Old men only dream dreams." He shook his head sadly. "I've stopped keeping company with John Barleycorn, but the dreams are still with me. Am I possessed or just mad?"

"You're neither," Sara said firmly.

"I wonder."

"The mind plays tricks. Perhaps through this crone your mind is trying to tell you something. If you open yourself to the message, anything might happen. Why, look at Johnny's recovery. We never dreamed he'd regain his memory."

"Aye, that's a marvel all right." His voice dropped to a confidential murmur. "I hope the lad wasn't too angry. I didn't mean to tell him about the marriage ceremony. That should have been your right."

"He would have had to know sooner or later. He—he's arranging to dissolve the marriage."

"Sara, *petite,* you and the boy—"

"It's all over, Father Yves. I'd rather not talk about it. Now, tell me about the mission. Have we had any more trouble from Mr. Cavendish?"

Pandora pounded out the last chord with a flourish, then spun around on her spindly stool at Sara's question. "We've closed the mission," she stated baldly.

"What? Why?" Sara demanded. "Has that wretched Cavendish—"

"No, no, nothing like that," Pandora soothed. "It's just that, well, there aren't any people."

"No one?"

"An occasional drifter looking for a handout, but the local churches can handle that need easily enough," Yves said. "Judge Plunket arranged for work for all the able-bodied men, and their families went with them. I suppose many are staying in the countryside for the growing season. Perhaps when winter comes again . . .''

Sara felt disoriented, as though someone had tugged the rug from under her feet. She'd counted on the mission to give her purpose, but she couldn't argue with the success that had led to empty beds and closed doors. Perhaps now, a year after the war, the nation was finally getting back to normal. She ought to be glad, but she felt lost. ''It's really wonderful,'' she said slowly. ''Who'd have thought we'd be out of business like that?''

''I've an idea, Sara Jane,'' Pandora ventured. ''Seeing Clem and knowing he'll need an education in order to support himself got me to thinking. We could turn the building into a school for the children of freedmen.''

Sara perked up. ''Why, Dorie, that's a wonderful thought. What about teachers?''

''What's wrong with me?'' Pandora demanded. ''I'm not so old and useless that I can't still be of service. I'm tired of inactivity, and it's a worthy cause. Besides, if I have to give Regina Whitaker another excruciating piano lesson, I think I'll die.''

The two women regarded each other closely, then burst into giggles.

''I could help,'' Yves offered when their merriment had subsided. ''We're all God's children, black or white.''

''You're both amazing,'' Sara said. Her brow puckered. ''You know, I'd hate to see children of any race in that neighborhood if we can help it. Maybe we should try to sell the warehouse, Dorie. If you're willing, we could apply the proceeds toward a proper school in a more suitable location.''

''Seems sensible,'' Pandora said. ''Otherwise, we'll have to put some money into repairs. Ambrose says the roof will need work soon.''

''Won't last the winter,'' Ambrose mumbled around a final mouthful of cake. He set the delicate china plate on Pandora's piecrust table.

''Yes, but who'd be willing to buy it?'' Sara wondered.

Ambrose scratched his chin thoughtfully. ''Brass Bull?''

''Old Cavendish?'' Yves hooted.

Sara laughed. "He might buy it, at that. Just to get us 'Bible thumpers' off his back doorstep."

"Then we'll offer it to him first," Pandora said decisively. She twirled around again on the stool, and her fingers tinkled the piano keys. "Come sing for us, Sara Jane."

"Only if everyone will join in."

They gathered around the piano, voices blending to "Old Black Joe" and "Camptown Races." Then Pandora swept into the sweetly melancholic "My Old Kentucky Home."

Emotion swelled in Sara's breast. To be home, to be with family, even a motley and assorted family such as hers, was her only solace. Although she'd never fully understand the enigmatic man whose triad of personalities encompassed Johnny and Tuck and the Major, she knew she'd always love him. She grieved deeply that she had not been enough for him, nor possessed the ephemeral quality he'd needed to heal his hurts. Sorrowfully, she accepted that it was her failure, that she lacked something essential that could have made him take the risk of loving her back.

Despite everything, he *had* given her something precious—a new identity as a woman. He'd once accused her of substituting her human strays for a man's love, but at least she'd risked it all, heart and soul, while he'd held something back. She was able to love and to hurt as only a complete woman could, and she accepted the pain because, thanks to him, she'd experienced the joy.

She would endure. She would go on. She would forge her life in a new shape. Perhaps there would come a time when she could share her life with another man. Maybe she would adopt a child. If not, then good works and alleviating the suffering of humanity through her medical skills would have to be enough. And someday she would be able to remember John Tucker McCulloch without pain, as no more than a sad, sweet memory. Until then, she had her family to sustain her.

She let her gaze roam over the group, Pandora swaying slightly as she played, Ambrose and Father Yves bent forward to follow the words on the sheet music, and Lizzie—

Startled, Sara's song died on her lips. Lizzie, her blue

eyes filled with love, was focused on Ambrose, and her
lips moved in time with the music. Straining, every nerve
receptive, Sara listened—and heard the faint, raspy whisper. Lizzie was singing!

Sara was afraid to move, afraid to disturb the miracle
that was happening before her eyes. Something of her tension must have reached Yves, for he glanced curiously at
her, then, with a sudden frown at Lizzie. His voice died
away, too. In the second it took for Ambrose and Pandora
to realize they had lost their harmony, they faltered—just
long enough for all to hear Lizzie's sweet, breathy words.

" . . . Old Kentucky home so far away . . ."

The piano chords became a discordant clash, and Pandora gasped. "Oh! Oh, my dear child." She grasped Lizzie's hand.

"Lizzie? Stay calm, dear," Sara urged, placing an arm
around the girl's suddenly quaking shoulders. "Did you
hear yourself? You were singing. There's nothing wrong
with your voice. You can use it. Do you understand?"

Lizzie's lips trembled. Her eyes, wide and frightened,
never left Ambrose's face. Her mouth moved, but only a
breath whistled.

"You can do it, Lizzie. Just try," Sara said.

Lizzie bit her bottom lip and drew a deep breath. Her
voice was weak and rusty from disuse, but the words were
unmistakable. "Wha—what should I say?"

Cries of delight and exultation surrounded the girl, but
Sara was shocked by the awful pain that twisted Ambrose's features. He turned and rushed from the room,
jarring them all into stunned silence. Only Lizzie's anguished call floated after him.

"Am-brose!"

Nothing in the Cary home was the same after that.

Sara's office was dusty with disuse, for her practice had
suffered from her protracted absence, and even an adver-
tisement placed in the *Missouri Valley Register* brought
few patients to her door. The mission lay empty and silent,
and the house was different, quieter, with both Clem and
Johnny absent. Ambrose was withdrawn and taciturn, and
Lizzie silent and unhappy despite her new-found voice.

Father Yves and Pandora were often engrossed in their plans for a freedmen's school, and Sara felt left out, isolated. She was at loose ends, lonely and restless, and the satisfaction she'd thought would be hers if she could only come home again seemed flat and empty.

Inactivity gave her too much time to think and remember, too much time to relive the moments with Johnny and wonder if things could have been different if she had made other choices. Sometimes she felt as though fate had pushed her through her life, and she had little control over her own destiny. She fought against these feelings and the depression that threatened by filling her waking hours with mundane tasks, making work to keep busy.

The Cary house smelled of lemon oil and vinegar, for the heavy furniture had never seen such a polishing, nor had the windows ever sparkled quite so brilliantly. Jars and jars of preserves and jellies were "put by," and the straggly rose beds were grass-free and pruned to within an inch of extinction. The stacks of medical journals diminished and vanished one by one as Sara caught up on her reading. But still the long summer days were endless, and even though she worked until she was physically exhausted, the nights seemed even longer.

At first, she accepted Menard Plunket's invitations because she could find no reason not to, and they filled the time. Then she went out with him because he was an enjoyable and often diverting companion. As the summer progressed, people grew accustomed to seeing them together. They attended the Fourth of July picnic and concerts at the Turner Society Hall. They took long drives in the countryside and dined together at the town's best restaurants. Sara knew that many times it was her presence that elicited invitations from the old scions of Lexington society, for there were still some reservations about Plunket as a political appointee of the Radical state government. But just as often, *she* was accepted because she was on *his* arm, her "scandalous" profession overlooked due to his prominence. It was a pleasant arrangement.

Yes, Menard's company was undemanding and enjoyable, and she took advantage of his kind invitations in an effort to fill the lonely hours of each day, but she was not prepared for the question he posed one evening in her parlor.

"I—I don't know what to say, Menard." Sara's jaw hung slack, and her eyes were wide and startled. The stereoscope she'd been sharing with the judge lay forgotten in her lap, the vistas of Italian gardens and villas dissolving before her eyes.

"Say you'll make me the happiest man on earth. Say you'll be my wife." Menard's face was earnest, and his hand pressed hers fervently. Pandora had just left the parlor, giving them an approving smile as she went, and Menard had taken advantage of their privacy to press his suit.

Sara's thoughts tumbled and rolled, flitting across her consciousness. The warmth of Menard's broad hand pressed against hers, a vivid reminder that he was flesh and blood, possessed of feelings, too, and not just a convenient escort. He was attractive in a dark, burly way. His thick hair grew back from his wide forehead, and his deepset eyes were intelligent. And he treated her with perfect courtesy. Why had she not foreseen this proposal? She felt guilty, for she'd offered him only friendship, and now it appeared he wanted much more.

She dropped her flustered gaze to their clasped hands. "It seems very sudden."

"I need a wife, Sara, my dear, and you're the one I want. You know I hold you in the highest regard, and we rub on well together."

"Surely that isn't enough on which to build a marriage," she hedged.

His smile was kind. "We're both well past the first hot blood of youth. Mutual respect and similar interests and ambitions will hold us close through the years. The desperation of romantic love isn't for us. We'll have something better."

Sara bit her lip. She knew well the pain of loving a man who didn't love her. She experienced it vicariously every day in the dark blue misery of Lizzie's eyes. Since Lizzie had regained her vocal powers, Ambrose had for all practical purposes repudiated their friendship. He wouldn't come near Lizzie if he could avoid it, and he spoke to her, his monosyllables unexpectedly curt, only when forced to do so. And Lizzie was suffering. When Sara had offered to intervene, however, Lizzie had been quick to decline, saying in her still quiet manner that Ambrose had to work things out for himself.

Yes, Sara thought, from her admittedly limited experience she'd learned that passion and love often brought a high price in pain. The security and companionship Menard offered was tempting, but she knew it was impossible. She had not yet received a decree of divorce from Johnny and could not in good conscience offer Menard any encouragement until she did. She had to refuse him and only hoped that since his emotions were not seriously engaged, he could accept her decision with equanimity. Besides, there was another matter.

"I'm sincerely flattered, Menard, but I cannot accept. You should seek a young wife," she murmured, vainly trying to tug her hand from his.

He refused to release her, his dark eyes liquid with determination. "Why? I think we suit very well."

"I—I'm not able to bear children. You'll need heirs and—"

His laugh interrupted her. "My dear, your ability or lack of it to breed children doesn't enter into my thinking at all. We'll let things work out of their own accord in that area. But I want a strong woman at my side, to run my home and be my helpmeet in all things. Just think, Sara. I'm a wealthy man. I could keep you in comfort. Anything you want. Why, together we'll set this town on its ear! People will look to *us* as the new elite. Would you like to take our honeymoon in Italy? We'll buy statuary for the gardens, carpets for my house, wardrobes of clothes—"

"Oh, stop, Menard," Sara cried, distressed. "You must not press me so. How can I think sensibly?"

His white teeth flashed in his swarthy face. "I don't want you to think. I want you to say yes."

He leaned nearer, then pressed his lips against hers in a tentative kiss, the first he'd given since that day on the dock. Startled, Sara froze, and she accepted the kiss passively. It was a tolerable experiment, even vaguely pleasant, but there was no fire, and she was disappointed, wishing he'd taken her strongly, pressing his body close and tasting her with a blatant sweep of his tongue, wiping out of her memory the feel of another man's passionate kisses. She knew that if he could, she would have been tempted to accept his proposal with no hesitation despite the impediments. But when he drew away, the hope of the moment was dashed.

"Say yes, Sara," Menard urged in a deep voice.

She looked down at her knotted hands, and the dull glint of gold winked on her finger. "I cannot. I'm very sorry."

"Sara, please! No maidenly show of reluctance," Menard ordered firmly. "We have scarce time to waste on a series of proposals and refusals before you finally deign to accept me. So no coy displays, for I find I have small patience on this topic, so eager am I to make you a part of my life."

"Menard, please understand," Sara begged, upset by his refusal to take her answer seriously. "I treasure your friendship, but that is all I can offer you at present."

"Then I may hope in the future your answer will be the one I want?"

"No, that's not what I meant," she said with growing frustration.

Menard sat back, his mouth twitching in a patronizing smile. "Oh, I see. Well, I can understand that a woman must play her games. All right, Sara, I'll dance to your tune if that's the way it must be. I realize a lady is expected to gracefully decline an offer for her hand at least half a dozen times before she relents. I'll not deny you that pleasure, so I'll woo you as you wish, my dear."

Horribly uncomfortable, Sara wondered desperately how to make him understand she was completely serious. And why had she never before noticed that streak of arrogance in his nature? She tried again.

"I deeply regret any pain or inconvenience, but you must accept my decision."

He waved his hand placatingly and gave her a smug wink. "Of course, my dear, as you wish. Now, we'll say no more, shall we? And you'll still allow me to escort you to the Taylors' dinner party, won't you?"

"Oh, but—"

"You wouldn't be so cruel as to deprive me of the pleasure of your company, would you?"

"Perhaps it's not wise." She bit her lip. "I should not presume to take advantage of your friendship in that fashion."

"Let me be the judge of that." He chuckled at his own wit. "A little joke, my dear."

She smiled weakly. "Of course."

Menard rose to take his leave, giving her a pat on the shoulder and placing a brief, dry kiss on her brow. "I'll play the ardent suitor, my dear. Just don't keep me waiting too long."

When Menard was gone, Sara went to her room to sort out her tumultuous thoughts. His refusal to take no for an answer made her angry, yet in another way, it was a balm to her pride. Just for a moment she considered the possibilities of his offer, the prospect of a pleasant companion, a relationship based on a logical decision and a commitment with no false promises. She wasn't free, but perhaps soon that problem would be rectified. What then? If Menard still wanted her, what would hold her back then? What would be fair to Menard? To herself?

Biting her lip, she crossed to her dresser and slowly pulled open the top drawer. There among her handkerchiefs and gloves lay the pair of ivory combs John had given her. She picked one up, tracing the carvings across the back, and her gaze turned inward. Involuntarily, her hand curled around the comb until the prongs stabbed into the soft flesh of her palm. She hardly felt the pain, for the memory of John's hard, passionate mouth rose in her, poignant, sweet, and strong.

The memory of her soft mouth was so sweet and strong it hurt.

John McCulloch splashed another three fingers' worth of sour-mash whiskey into the chipped government-issue mug and poured half the burning liquor down his throat, exhaling sharply. The bare room was typically austere officer's quarters, and he scowled at the narrow iron cot that had been his torture rack since leaving *L'Etoile*. A man as big as he was shouldn't be expected to sleep in such, but maybe what kept him awake nights, tossing and turning on the over-stretched springs, wasn't the narrowness of the cot, but the fact that he slept alone. He gave the leg of the bed a vicious kick, then sprawled in the straight wooden chair at his table-cum-desk-cum-washstand and poured another drink.

"It's a bad sign, drinking alone."

John peered over the edge of the mug at Philip Sheridan. The General stood in the open doorway holding a sheaf of papers, his blue uniform crumpled, his bushy eyebrows lifted in wry mockery. John reared back in the chair, balancing on two legs. He waved the mug in a gesture of invitation.

"Come in, General. Have a drink. I hope to hell that's my mustering out papers you've got. I had no idea it was such an ordeal to get shut of this man's army."

"What are you complaining about? You've been busy enough," the General said.

John laughed. "Yeah. Nothing like a race riot and forty dead to keep you occupied, is there? Martial law in this town is a barrel of laughs."

On the thirtieth of July, Mayor John T. Monroe had employed city police to suppress a meeting of delegates intent on remodeling the state government. The result had been a bloody encounter.

Sheridan grimaced and sighed tiredly. "You've been a big help during the unrest this summer, and you know I needed all the active officers I could get. Jesus! How does Grant expect me to be everywhere at once? Congress is boiling over the massacre, and I'm supposed to keep the civil population of New Orleans under control here while I fight renegade Mexican rancheros across the Rio Grande." Sheridan shut the door and came forward. He picked up the whiskey bottle, sniffed it, then took a pull. His voice was hoarse when he spoke again. "How can you drink this rotgut?"

"Practice, Phil. Lots of practice."

Sheridan shot at sharp glance at John, then propped his rump on the corner of the table. "Word is you're doing more than your share."

John squinted at the bottom of his empty mug. "It passes the time."

And time was an enemy. It griped like a bitch to admit he missed Sara. Whiskey kept the piercing misery at a dull ache. He'd even visited Madame Toinette's in the hope that another warm body was all he needed, but he hadn't been able to touch one of the whores, luscious and inviting though they'd been. No, it was a certain scrappy snippet of a woman, a special laugh, and dark coffee-brown eyes alight with copper sparks that haunted his days and nights. New Orleans was the "City that Care Forgot," but— dammit!—all he'd been able to do since Sara left was admit to himself that he *did* care. A hell of a lot.

But she was better off without him, he reminded himself. That's why he'd let the General use him. Having some objective, even if it was the U.S. Army's, kept him from going after her. That was the last thing she needed. He stirred now, looking down his nose at the General.

"Well, if you haven't brought my discharge papers, to what do I owe the pleasure of your company?"

"I thought you might be interested in this." Sheridan tossed a slim folder down on the table. John flipped through the file with mild curiosity, then straightened abruptly, his negligent demeanor slipping away like a false skin. His face darkened ominously.

"Moses!"

"Sources in St. Louis think the gold that just surfaced was used to bribe a Radical leader. Gold from Quantrill's cache."

Green eyes as cold as glacial ice scanned the information before him. "That son of a bitch! I want to nail that bastard, Phil. Can you cut me some orders?"

"You really want to go after him?"

"Jesus Christ! What do you think?" John raked a hand through his hair.

"I had a feeling you'd say that." Sheridan took an official paper from his inside coat pocket and flipped it open. "Your discharge."

"Sonofabitch! You've been holding out on me."

"Shall I tear it up?"

John's teeth snapped together, and his eyes narrowed.

The General held John's freedom in his hand. The army had once been his refuge, but now he wanted to put everything behind him, head for open country, seek a new life and the forgetfulness he'd once enjoyed. But his commission gave him power, and the business with Moses remained unfinished.

And then there was Sara. John glanced at the report again. It contained familiar names, people in Lexington she had dealings with. And she knew a lot about Moses, simply because she'd been privy to all those conversations around the campfire with Jesse and the boys. What if she made the connection? She could be in peril because of the things he'd forced her to witness, doubly so if whispers of Moses brought the James brothers back to her vicinity with thoughts of revenge on their minds. He owed it to her to remove any threat, didn't he? *And for once in your life, McCulloch, be truthful, at least with yourself,* he thought with mocking self-derision. *Admit you want to see her again. Admit you have to.*

Because the months separated from her had taught him something essential. Whether or not he wanted it or admitted it, she was a part of him. She made him a whole man. Even when she believed the worst, she had loved him. And somehow, her belief in him eased the separateness and bitter self-contempt that had returned the day he'd remembered his name. Always, it was her love and compassion that sustained him. If Sara loved him, even a little, then there *had* to be something worthy within him. He knew he had to find out if that was true, and to learn if salvation was possible for him. Only Sara could tell him, and Sheridan, for all his manipulation, was offering him the means and the excuse to go to her.

"Well, John?" Sheridan asked.

John's gaze snapped back to his friend. "Tear it up."

Menard Plunket made a final careful notation on the border of a Lafayette County survey map and closed the thick folder of geological findings and railroad extensions with a satisfied sigh. After a false start in the spring, now a summer's calculated work was on the verge of culmination, and he was hard pressed not to feel the tiniest bit smug. A dry September breeze blew through the windows of his newly-renovated library and rustled the edges of the map. Despite the lateness of the hour, the heat of the day still penetrated the book-lined room, and his fine linen shirt felt unpleasantly damp with his perspiration.

He went to the hinged mahogany cabinet and poured a brandy from the imported cut-crystal decanter. The spirit was smooth and fiery against his tongue, and he savored it as he admired the room, from the deep red Turkish carpet to the rows and rows of leather-bound books to the English hunting scene over the mantel. The library was his favorite place in the house, for it was here that he most felt the aura of his own growing respectability. *Not bad for a wharf rat from East St. Louis,* he thought with satisfaction.

The portly figure drowsing in the Cordovan leather wing chair beside the hearth stirred, snorted, and scratched his bushy mustache. "Well, eh? Is it there?"

Plunket nodded. "Yes. It's perfect. You may congratulate me on two counts."

"Two?"

"First, there's enough coal on that tract to make me a very rich man, especially with my railroad contracts."

"You're already a rich man," the fat, balding man grumbled.

"When is it ever enough?" Menard laughed. "But as I was saying, I can mine it commercially for the first time in this region and—"

"I been buying coal to burn for years," the man interrupted.

"Not like this, my friend. High grade bituminous. Perfect for steamboats, railroads, new factories, and even municipal gas plants. In unbelievable quantities."

"If you can buy it. You tried once . . ."

"That is the second reason you may congratulate me." Menard smiled. "I've decided to get married."

"What!"

"You can see the wisdom of it. A man in my position needs a respectable wife at his side, and if she comes to the marriage dowried with such a rich inheritance, all the better."

"You're loco."

"On the contrary, Earl."

Earl Cavendish levered himself up out of the chair and scratched his protruding stomach. "I know you been squiring Sara Cary around all summer, but why tie yourself permanent to that whey-faced harpy?"

"Because she'll be grateful, for one thing, and that is an excellent quality in a wife. She's known for her good works, another commendable attribute, and her family by marriage is of the old guard, ensuring my acceptance in Lexington society. And"—Menard paused and thumped the fat folder with the back of his hand—"because on our marriage, *I* get control of the Sugarloaf."

"We been partners a long time, and we've made a right pretty penny together, but I think you're crazy," Earl muttered. "She waltzed her fanny right into the Bull again last week, just like she was the Queen of Sheba. Says make me an offer or she might sell her place to the Temperance Society and then I'd have revival meetings goin' on *all* the damned time! How's a man to run his business with a bunch of hymn-singing do-gooders across the alley?"

Menard laughed. "She's shrewd, and not afraid to stand up for herself. That's why I like her. You'd better buy it before she does what she says."

"I still think you musta took a hard lick to the back of the skull."

"A genius is just a madman who's made good. You'll see, Earl. Let's drink to my soon-to-be fiancée."

"She ain't said yes yet?"

"No, but she will." His features settled into lines of sly complacency. "She will, indeed."

Cavendish shrugged and raised his glass. "It's your funeral. Here's how."

"To Sara." Menard swallowed the remainder of his drink, smiled, and pitched the empty snifter into the cold fireplace. Cavendish jumped at the crash of shattering glass. Menard laughed again and went around his desk. "Be sure to let yourself out the side door, Earl. Have to keep up appearances, you know."

Cavendish's piggy eyes squinted malevolently at Plunket, and his mustache twitched, but he carefully set down his glass and left the room. As the door shut behind him, he heard the faint, whistled strains of "The Wedding March."

What if Menard wanted a real wedding? Sara wondered. In a church? Complete with flowers and music? She'd never had a real wedding. It had merely been a swift mumble of vows with Will. And you'd hardly call the way she'd pried the words from Johnny a real wedding, although the marriage was genuine enough.

Dust motes floated through the shafts of pale yellow sunlight pouring through the windows of the deserted mission. She folded another curtain and stuffed it into the half-filled packing barrel, then wiped her damp face on her sleeve. She sighed wearily and arched her spine, hands pressing into the gingham-covered small of her back. Bending, she picked up her turkey feather duster and went back to work on the grimy window sills.

Cavendish had finally made an offer, and as soon as Menard prepared the papers, the warehouse would no longer belong to the Cary family. Now it was only a matter of packing up the memories along with the old shipping ledgers and boxes of invoices from her father-in-law's business, and the miscellaneous bedding and cooking utensils left over from the mission work.

Reaching up, she released another curtain panel. The fabric fell, limp and dusty, into her hands. Impulsively, she draped it over her head, then turned the duster bottom up, forming an imaginary bride's bouquet. Ever since Menard's amazing proposal, she'd found her thoughts turning again and again to the possibility of accepting him. It was like a sore tooth she couldn't leave alone. The idea was always *there,* and under Menard's determined assault, she knew she was wavering. Loneliness was his most powerful ally.

What would it be like to march down the aisle of a church? she mused. To know that at the end of that aisle waited a man who *wanted* to make a lifetime's vows with her? Trying to picture Menard, she took a tentative step, then another, practicing the hesitant walk thought proper for *real* weddings.

Why was she holding back? Didn't her head tell her that life with Menard Plunket would be comfortable? She knew without doubt that he'd be a doting husband who'd cosset her against life's trials. Menard had enlisted Pandora's aid in his suit, and she was enthusiastic about the proposal, encouraging Sara daily to accept the judge. And wasn't Menard's ardency flattering? He pressed her, not ungallantly, for an answer every day, and every day she refused him because she had no alternative until her divorce decree arrived. She knew that when it did, she was pragmatic enough to admit it would be foolish not to accept Menard immediately. Why then did she feel this stubborn, unreasonable reluctance?

Wizards and washtubs, Sara Jane! she chided herself. *You know why. You don't love Menard Plunket, that's why!*

But what difference did that make? She'd had her one great love of a lifetime, and it had been a fraud. Her "family" was disintegrating about her, and she was no longer needed as she had once been. Her medical practice was almost nonexistent, and she felt a distant panic as all the moorings of her life were loosed, one by one, casting her adrift on a sea of loneliness.

Wasn't companionship and security all she wanted now? It was time to grow up, to stop reaching for the stars and settle for a good, solid, if unexciting, reality in the here and now before Menard changed his mind.

Nodding to herself, she took another practice step. Yes, she'd do it. When she was at last free of John McCulloch, not only emotionally but legally, then she'd make the mature and logical choice and not throw away what might be her last chance for contentment.

Her skirts swished around her ankles.

Step—pause—step.

Her hands tightened on her feather bouquet.

Step—pause—step.

She lifted her chin regally. Step—

Her gaze careened headlong into a pair of laughing eyes, eyes the color of a new spring leaf.

Chapter 19

She couldn't help the jolt of sheer joy that immobilized her, nor could she contain the sudden suspicious wariness that made her voice cold.

"What are you doing here?"

He "tsked" softly between his teeth, and a mocking smile twisted his mouth. "Hardly the welcome I was hoping for."

Suddenly she realized how ridiculous she must appear and hastily dragged the makeshift veil from her hair, glaring at John.

Oh, God, he's a handsome scoundrel, she thought in an agony of recognition. Tall and lean, dressed in a well-tailored suit, his pale hair a shining halo, the sandy bush of eyebrows and mustache a counterpoint to his sculpted cheeks, he still had the power to move her unbearably. Her heart thumped double-time, and she cursed her involuntary reaction.

Lord, she's lovely, he thought, drinking in the sight of her. Even dusty and disheveled, she was adorable, her life and vibrancy drawing him. And the feisty glints of copper in those luscious brown eyes! She was ready to scrap, and he felt like laughing out loud.

Her eyes narrowed, and her elegant features became stony. Abruptly, she turned away, slamming the duster down on the countertop. "Whatever it is you want, get out."

He reached for her wrist. "Not so fast."

Jerking her hand free, she whirled around with a feline snarl. "Don't!"

His hands went up in mock surrender. "Sure, Sara. Anything you want."

"I want you to tell me what you're doing here."

"I've some unfinished business to tend to here in Lexington."

"We said our goodbyes, Major." Her chin tilted at a haughty angle. "Or had you forgotten?"

"No, Sara, I haven't forgotten anything." His eyes burned. "But this is official. Sheridan sent me. There's new information on Moses the Prophet, and I'm going to hang that traitorous bastard."

Sara felt a stab of dismay. So his reappearance in her life wasn't personal. She quickly squelched her unreasonable disappointment. Her lips tightened with disdain. "The war's over, Major."

"Not for me."

Her mouth softened, quivered with sudden vulnerability. "I know. But that's your problem, not mine. Not anymore."

He steeled himself against the raw pain in her voice. Damn! He felt as guilty as sin for all the rotten things he'd done, but he had his duty to perform. "I'm going to need your cooperation. You're involved, whether you like it or not. You can't refuse an official request of the U.S. government."

Her eyes smoldered with resentment. "Just watch me. I've had enough of your connivings. I don't care what you're about. Just get out and stay away from me."

"I'm afraid that's not going to be possible, not if I'm going to prove my suspicions about Moses."

"I don't know any Moses. Who are you talking about?"

"The mastermind who directed Quantrill and nearly got me killed. From the information we have, it looks like he's your old friend and neighbor, Earl Cavendish."

"What? That nauseating little man?"

"Don't judge a book by its cover. Moses ran a shrewd operation. That's why I've got to move cautiously in this investigation. And you're going to help me."

"Oh, no." She took a step back, shaking her head. "We're selling the mission to Mr. Cavendish. I don't care what you believe, I will not become involved in any of your schemes.''

She cast about desperately for a defense against John's presence, against his appeal to her senses. She caught upon a lie that was nearly a truth, and that in some unexplained measure might, at worst, assuage her pride, and at best, hurt John as she'd been hurt.

"I've got my own life to live, my own future to consider," she said defiantly. "When I marry Menard—"

"Marry Plunket!" His brows drew down in a thunderous line. He glanced askance at the discarded curtain and feather duster. His mouth compressed in a grim line. "Is that what you were playing at when I came in? Make-believe wedding games? God damn it, woman! Are you crazy? I think that bootlicker Plunket is involved, too!"

Dumbstruck, Sara stared. Then she understood, and rage clouded her vision. "Oh, no. I'm not going to let you do this to me," she said between clenched teeth. "I know what you're trying to do, but it won't work. This is just some kind of villainous ploy to destroy any happiness I've found. You're still trying to punish me for what I did. But I don't believe a word of it, so take your poisonous insinuations and go straight to hell."

"You can't be involved with that pompous ass."

"You have no right to dictate to me. Menard has high standards. Respectability is important to him. He would never stoop to any questionable activity."

"Oh, no?" John laughed snidely. "Then take a look at the Court House records. He and Cavendish are linked to any number of shady land deals. At the very least he's a thief and a swindler."

"And you're a liar! Why should I believe you? Can you prove it?"

"Not yet . . ."

"Ha!" She sneered, vindicated. Snatching up the duster, she waved it threateningly. "Not another word against the man I intend to marry, do you hear? Now get out."

He dodged her thrust, but there was no humor softening the grim line of his mouth. "Mighty fickle in your affections, aren't you, Doc? Not long ago you were sure you

were in love with me. But maybe you've developed a taste
for things of the flesh. How far have you let him go? Has
he discovered how hot you are in bed?''

With a shriek of outrage, she charged like a banty hen,
trouncing his head and shoulders in a flurry of turkey
feathers until a cloud of loose plumage surrounded them.
He ducked and feinted, his hands and upraised arms taking the brunt of the fluffy but unrelenting attack. Loose
feathers littered his tawny curls like an Indian headdress,
and he puffed and spit, trying to remove clinging bits of
downy fluff from his lips. Finally, fed up, he wrenched
the weapon from her hand and grabbed her by the upper
arms.

''Cut it out, you hellcat.''

''You have no right to speak to me that way! Menard's
a gentleman, something you'd never understand.''

''Well, the more fool him,'' John muttered. ''But aren't
you forgetting something? Like the fact that we're still
man and wife? Makes planning a wedding a bit complicated.''

''I should have known not to trust you. You haven't
done anything you said you would, have you?''

''So what?'' He shrugged as jealousy clawed at his gut.
''I certainly never thought you'd have been so eager to leap
into matrimony again. Especially with that piece of—''

''John! I'll thank you to keep a civil tongue in your
head.''

''I can think of lots more interesting places to put it,''
he muttered, his heavy lids dropping to half-mast. She
drew in an outraged breath, but he swooped, capturing her
surprised mouth, plunging his tongue past the slightly
parted barrier of her lips.

She tasted wonderful, fresh and uniquely Sara. One
hand stole up to cup the back of her head, and he moved
slightly, sealing their mouths even tighter, twining his
tongue with hers in a jolting, elemental joining. He filled
his palm with her breast and inhaled her soft moan. There
was nothing in the universe but the two of them, and he
wondered dazedly how he'd ever thought he could survive
without this, without *her*.

Love seemed too tame a word for what he felt. He

wanted her and needed her beyond hope or thought, and he loved her more than his own life. She *was* his life, the dream that had saved him physically and emotionally from death in all its heinous forms. Her sweetness, her goodness, her passion—he was only going through the motions of living without those things. He lifted his head to tell her, and his voice was thick.

"Sara, I—"

"No!" She wrenched away, leaving him bereft. She pressed fingertips against her mouth, and her eyes shone bright with tears. "Not again. I won't let you use me again."

"It's not that."

"Stay away from me." She backed away, skittish and tearful. "I don't care what you do, just stay away from me."

"You're my wife, and—"

"Not for a minute longer than I can help it. I'm going to have divorce papers drawn up today."

"How can you think of marrying another man?" he asked, his anger growing apace with her obstinacy. "After what we've shared? Didn't we just prove that?"

"It means nothing except that you're skillful in the art of seduction, but that's not what I want in my life."

He laughed harshly. "You hypocrite. You'd offer yourself to Plunket, knowing how you feel about me?"

"I hate you."

"Yeah, but you love to hate me, don't you? We shoot sparks off each other every time we touch. How do you propose to explain that to the judge? Or haven't you told him you spent all those weeks on the trail sleeping with an outlaw?" At the stricken look on her face he chuckled mirthlessly. "He doesn't know, does he?"

"You—you wouldn't tell him?" Her face fell. "Of course you would. Anything to hurt me."

Her words pierced him like the blade of a knife. The muscle in his jaw worked with tension. "Our so-called marriage is no one's business but ours," he snapped. "It's our sordid little secret. At least until I decide differently."

Her shoulders slumped in relief, then he saw her visibly

gather herself together, lifting her chin and robing herself with the tattered shreds of her dignity.

"I'd like you to go now," she said. "Please don't come back."

Her display of fortitude moved him, made him ashamed, even while he cursed her for her stubbornness. Well, he could be stubborn, too, and things weren't over between them, not by a long shot.

"All right, Sara, I'll go for now. But we aren't finished."

"I have nothing more to say to you, now or ever."

His mouth twisted. "Well, you'd better think of something, or it's going to be damned awkward sitting across the dinner table from you tonight."

She gawked.

"I've been by to visit Miss Pandora, and she kindly invited me to dinner."

Wild-eyed, Sara spluttered. "You—you can't! Menard's coming tonight."

"Then I'd say things are liable to be downright entertaining," he drawled. "And by the way, when Lizzie opened her mouth and said hello, it was one of the sweetest sounds I've ever heard. You made a miracle for that girl, Doc." His lips twisted. "Maybe you can make another one tonight." He gave her a mocking, two-finger salute. "See you at seven."

Aghast, Sara could only stare in silent shock long after the door had closed behind him. Finally, open-mouthed horror galvanized her into action, and she whipped off her apron.

"Frump and Wimple, Frump and Wimple." She whispered the name of her local law firm over and over like a litany. There had to be some way to free herself from John McCulloch, and she intended to find it today, no matter what the cost to her reputation or finances. She must cut the ties once and for all, and her lie to John must become the truth if she were to have any hope of resisting her obsession for the man who was the instrument of her own destruction. Once she was promised to Menard, then she'd no longer be so vulnerable. Menard could protect her from herself. He would be her haven of security and trust. Be-

hind the boundaries of a proper engagement, even a man
such as John McCulloch dared not trespass.

But as she locked the mission door and hurried down
the board sidewalk, Sara wondered with fear if she were
running *to* Menard, or merely *away* from John.

Lizzie carefully cut the slices of roast beef on Ambrose's plate, as she had countless times before. She dished
stewed tomatoes and green beans beside the meat and
turned to the handyman, her winsome face soft with confusion.

"It seems so strange, having Johnny back," she said
in her quiet, rusty voice. "He's still the same, but—
different."

"Ain't a kid no more," Ambrose said, tapping his temple. "Up here."

A concerned frown puckered Lizzie's angelic face. "He
and Judge Plunket don't like each other. The air's so thick
around that table you could cut it with a knife."

"Two roosters courtin' the same hen. Feathers bound
to fly."

"Well, it's upsetting Miss Sara. She's trying not to show
it, but I can tell."

Ambrose made an abrupt, impatient sound. "Gonna
make me wait all night for that grub?"

Lizzie glanced down at the forgotten plate in her hand
and blushed, a peachy shade that turned her frizzy hair to
pure gilt. "Oh. I'm sorry." She placed it on the kitchen
table, but Ambrose scooped up his fork, dropping it into
the pocket of his chambray work shirt, then picked up the
plate and turned to leave.

"Don't you want to eat in here?" Lizzie asked in a
plaintive tone. "I've got buttermilk."

Ambrose didn't look at her. "Naw. Things to do."

Hurt, and feeling unaccustomed anger, Lizzie cinched
her cherubic mouth like a pursestring. "Wait, Ambrose,"
she said, catching the fabric of his empty shirt-sleeve to
stop him. Off-balance, he slewed around, and the plate
spun out of his hand, landing upside-down with a sicken-
ing crash.

"Dang-nab it! Now look what you done," he roared.

"I'm sorry," Lizzie quavered. They both went to their knees, reaching for the mess. Lizzie's fingers grazed Ambrose's knuckles, and he jerked away. She bit her lip, and her voice shook. "Why don't you like me anymore, Ambrose?"

Startled, he looked up, his hazel eyes locking with her troubled blue ones. He glanced away, swallowing, and his Adam's apple bobbed up and down. "You talk junk. I like you fine."

"No, you don't. You used to talk to me, tell me things, make me laugh inside. Now . . ." She trailed off, sniffing, and wiped her nose on the back of her hand. "Sometimes I wish I'd never found my voice again."

"Hush up! Dang blathering females!" He scraped the broken plate into a pile. "Always crying over somethin'."

"Why shouldn't I?" Lizzie hiccoughed. "I thought maybe you l-loved me a little. But I don't guess you could, 'cause I'm s-soiled." She buried her face in her hands and sobbed.

"Don't talk foolish. I don't care about that," he said harshly. "You're so pretty, and—and sweet and all. Anybody who counts knows the past don't matter. Pretty soon you'll end up with a husband and a passel of kids."

"I wanted 'em to be your kids, Ambrose." She choked, tears streaming down her face. "I never knew a man as kind and good as you."

Helplessly, Ambrose stared at her, a muscle twitching in his grizzled cheek. "You ain't thinking, Lizzie-girl," he said, his voice losing some of its edge. "What would you want with an old cripple like me, anyway?"

"You aren't old!"

He sighed. "I'm thirty. Too old and ugly for the likes of you."

Her cupid's bow mouth curved, and she gave him a watery smile. "I like the way you look, though I wish you'd shave more often." Her fingertips trailed across his stubbled jaw. He drew back, raw pain making his eyes go dark.

"It's hard to shave one-handed." He shook his head. "You see, I ain't got anything to offer you."

"Oh, Ambrose, you're so wrong," she whispered.

"You know so much and can do so many things. And besides, I could shave you. Or you could grow a beard. Sharing and compromise. Ain't that what loving is all about?"

"Lizzie, stop." He struggled to his feet, his voice hoarse. "I'm trying to do what's best for you. Someday you'll thank me."

She rose and studied him with flooded eyes. Her voice cracked and wavered, but her words were brave. "Don't you understand I'd rather have the man I love with one good arm around me than anyone else with two?"

Ambrose paused for the space of two heartbeats. "Aw, Lizzie-girl," he said gruffly, "you're somethin'. I reckon I can't help but love you, too." His lips quivered in a tentative, hopeful smile, and he lifted his good arm in invitation. "If your mind's made up, then maybe you'd better come over here and let me practice holdin' you."

She gave a small, glad cry and flung herself against his chest. Sighs and murmurs were all that disturbed the tranquility of the kitchen for quite a long time.

Major John McCulloch flipped through the latest stack of dispatches, then tossed them on the desk. Crossing to the window, he pulled aside the frayed drape and looked toward the river, the view being the only redeeming quality to this nondescript room in the Lexington Eagle Hotel. Two weeks of painstaking investigation, and what did he have, besides bunions and an empty wallet? Nothing, that's what.

Well, what did you expect? he asked himself. *For Moses to drop into your lap?*

He shook his head and let the curtain drop. Sprawling on the iron bedstead, hands behind his head, stockinged feet crossed at the ankles, he gazed sightlessly at the fly-specked ceiling.

Not that he hadn't been busy. But information in this town was as scarce as hen's teeth, despite the fact that he'd greased many an outstretched palm. He'd even slipped a few greenbacks to Eustace, the skinny young bartender at the Brass Bull, but he hadn't gotten more than a stammered thanks before that big bastard Moody appeared, putting an end to any confidences. He'd been to Kansas City to the federal authorities, even visited with Sheriff Ramsey, savvy old lawman that he was, but no one had any answers. The trail of gold pieces, minted in Colorado, which had turned up in St. Louis and sent him on this wild goose hunt, had dried up as if it had never been. Visiting every area bank and savings establishment in search of coined gold had been less than fruitless. "No one has gold these days, mister," he'd been told time and again.

Of course, his efforts hadn't been entirely wasted. John grinned to himself. He'd managed to irritate Menard Plunket to no end, disrupting his courting of Sara by appearing at inopportune moments, using his guise of old family friend to drop frequently by the Cary home. There was no doubt in John's mind that Plunket was a penny-ante crook, like so many post-war politicians, and it made him queasy to see that oily rascal with Sara. Instinct told him that Plunket wasn't genuine. Why couldn't she see through him?

John frowned, chewing the inside of his cheek. He had to be careful he didn't push her too hard, too fast, or she'd rush into Plunket's arms for sure. At least, for all her threats, she hadn't promised herself to that slimy politician yet. That meant something, didn't it? Still, it was hard to be patient. It was comforting to know that she couldn't do anything rash while they were still legally joined. That was another important reason to get this business with Moses settled. Once his assignment was completed, he fully intended to make Sara realize that they belonged together.

So now what?

Maybe the direct approach was the only way. It was time he bearded Cavendish in his own den. He wouldn't admit anything, of course, but at least John could rattle his cage. It might be interesting to see which way he'd jump. The thought made him smile. Reaching for boots and gun, he made ready to leave. If it didn't take long, he might even drop in on Sara. He liked to see her jump, too.

"What did he want?"
"What do you think?"

"Moses."

"Sure, what else? The damn fool thinks *I'm* you."

Two figures, one short, one of medium height, both imposingly thickset, stood in the dark of night under a crooked elm near the isolated Eighteenth Street entrance of Machpelah Cemetery. No passerby would notice the waiting buggy and horse, and only the silent tombstones across the ravine could bear witness to the whispered conversation.

"What did you tell him?"

"Not a blamed thing—yet."

The deep voice was a sinister growl. "What do you mean—yet?"

"Seems to me, keeping such an important secret should be worth a bigger cut. Seeing how you cherish your good name and all. It'd be a shame if the railroad agents got wind of it, too. Likely spoil everything."

"You're a bigger fool than I thought."

"A businessman, just like you, friend."

"You'd destroy all we've worked for, everything I've accomplished in this town, for more money?"

"Look, I know you got plenty, stashed away safe and sound in that bank vault. That'd be mighty interesting to the right people, too. All I'm wanting is a fair share," the second voice wheedled. "I take all the risk. The settlement should be more—what's the word you use?—equitable. Oh, and one other thing."

"What?"

"I use the front door from now on."

"The hell you will."

A shot cracked. The pistol's orange flare was a brief flicker of illumination that revealed Earl Cavendish's surprised expression and the gaping wound in the center of his chest. He fell before the sound ceased vibrating between the stone grave markers, and his last word bubbled obscenely from his blood-filled throat. "Moses . . ."

Menard Plunket looked at the dead heap of human flesh at his feet and pocketed his gun, contempt twisting his features. He pushed the body over the edge of the ravine with his foot, and it rolled and thumped sickeningly to the bottom.

''Stupid, Earl. Very stupid. Don't you know Moses is dead?''

Sara wiped the dust from a cobalt blue vial of ammonium carbonate and thought about missionary work in China. She counted the brown bottles of mercury pills and wondered if a woman physician would be accepted among the tribes of the Indian Nations. She stacked unused instruments and thought longingly of her Quaker friends in Philadelphia. Would they consider a convert?

Don't be a fool, Sara Jane, she scolded herself. *Only a coward runs away.*

Oh, but the thought was so tempting. She adjusted the wick of the lamp and examined the label on a bottle of quinine, then wrote it on her inventory list. Taking stock of her office and her profession—or current lack of it—was time consuming but necessary. Unfortunately, it also gave her too much opportunity to think.

Her life was in a jumble, and it was all John McCulloch's fault. Why couldn't he have stayed in New Orleans? His presence had destroyed her hard-won peace of mind, and every time she turned around, he was taking malicious pleasure in promoting anything that might further confound and confuse her. She knew his allegations against Menard were absurd, but it took real effort to ignore the seeds of suspicion he'd planted that first day. His return to Lexington as John Tucker was also cause for comment from the entire town, and she was tired of making up explanations about how he'd recovered, what he was doing, and why he no longer stayed at the Cary house.

Menard was also understandably perturbed by the situation, scarcely understanding Sara's apparent tolerance for a man he still found suspect. She nearly groaned aloud at the memory of the ghastly dinner they'd shared: John, with his wicked grin and insolent manner; Menard, puzzled and hostile; and herself, caught in the middle.

Since then, Menard's demands for an answer to his proposal had become vocal and vehement. As desperately as she needed his protection, she still had to refuse, because Frump and Wimple moved as fast as two ancient snails. She was tempted to accept Menard without the proper papers and then select a wedding date sufficiently far in the future to accommodate the necessary legalities, but she had not fallen so low in her integrity that she had to stoop to such tactics yet.

In some ways, Menard was already acting as though she had agreed to marry him anyway, advising her on business matters and making suggestions she was too harried to protest. She felt guilty for continually putting him off with excuses, but she needed him as a defense, a buffer between herself and John.

She chewed her lip thoughtfully, and doubts assailed her. There were so many things about Menard she didn't know. Perhaps she was allowing circumstances to rush her into a decision that she might regret later. And then there was her disturbing visit with Clem's parents and Daisy Wiley to consider. The former slaves weren't as pleased with their benefactor as Menard had led her to believe.

"Why is it you're always working your sweet tail off when I come to call?" John McCulloch grumbled from the doorway.

Sara jumped and forced a look of annoyance to her features before she turned. "Perhaps if you'd visit at a decent hour, or with someone who cares to see you, you wouldn't have this problem," she suggested tartly.

The corner of his mouth lifted, and he chuckled wryly. "That's what I love about you, Doc. I can always count on you to put me in my place."

He looked tired, she thought. His hair was rumpled, his open collar revealed the crisp froth of sandy chest hair, and his coat was draped languidly between the crook of his wrist and his lean hip. She tried to fight the surge of gladness that tightened her chest. Fool! she chided herself. He's not what you need. But her body disagreed, contracting and swelling in all her secret places at the mere sight of him. She turned back to her work, re-counting bottles but making no sense of them.

"Is there some reason for this visit, or have you merely come to annoy me?" she asked. He sauntered over, leaning a broad shoulder against the glass case.

"Maybe a little of both." He trailed the tip of his finger down a tendril of hair dangling in front of her ear. She tried to ignore him, but she'd lost count again and had to start over. He smiled and folded his arms across his chest. "Actually, I came to see Yves."

The bottle in her hand hit the glass shelf with enough force to shake the whole case. "I told you once before not to involve my people in your schemes. I won't have—"

"Pax, Sara. Can't I visit a friend without your attributing ulterior motives to it?"

"Oh." She bit her lip in embarrassment. "Sorry."

"Not that he wasn't a help. You'd be surprised what that man can learn on the streets."

"John, please! Keep Yves out of it. He's done so well this summer."

"No heavenly visitations, no trances or snake handling, no visions of the pit?"

"Don't laugh at him."

John's features were suddenly solemn. "Honey, I'm not laughing. I've been there, too, and but for the grace of God—and you—I'd be there still. I don't think I ever thanked you for that."

She looked away. "There's no need."

He snorted. "I wish it were that easy."

Fingers trembling, she slammed the display case doors shut, turned with a whirl of dark blue skirts, and busied herself tidying an already tidy desk. "Your business—how does it fare?"

"Slowly."

"I mean, how much longer do you expect to be here?"

"As long as it takes."

There were levels of meaning in his words she tried to ignore. She stiffened when his hands caught her shoulders from behind, and her pulse jumped in her throat.

"Sara, when this is over, we have to talk."

She stared straight ahead. "It's all been said."

"Not everything," he murmured. His warm lips touched the tender nape of her neck.

"Don't start," she begged raggedly, but he turned her, his mouth traveling across her neck, dampening the lace edge of her high collar.

"I have to," he said thickly. "I'm sick with wanting

you. Nothing matters to me but this. Not revenge, not Moses—I don't care anymore.''

His lips nibbled sensuously on the underside of her jaw, and she arched her neck, unconsciously allowing him greater access. His large hands cupped her face, and she clasped his wrists, hanging weakly to his strength while he dropped kisses across her brow, the curve of her cheekbone, the corner of her mouth. "God, I've missed you," he said.

She was slipping again, her will not her own, knotted up with longings that made a mockery of all her logical, sensible plans. Oh, Lord, she *wanted* to believe he was sincere, but her trust had been shattered more than once, and she was heart-shy. What was he offering her now except more heartache? From far away, she heard knocking, voices, and with the greatest difficulty pulled back, shivering and blinking like a newborn plunged into the cold world.

"Someone's here," she said, groping for the back of her chair and easing into it as though she might break with the first sudden move. And so she might, for her heart was full to overflowing, a chalice made too fragile by shattered trust to hold the overwhelming love and desire that she felt for this man.

The office door burst open, admitting a flustered Pandora, followed by Menard Plunket and Sheriff Ramsey.

"Treacle and trapezoids! I'm sure I don't know what the world is coming to!" Pandora complained. "Comings and goings at all hours of the night. Here he is. Johnny, these men want to see you."

"Thank you, Miss Pandora," John said. He lifted an eyebrow. "Well, gentlemen?"

"All right, Sheriff," Plunket barked. "Do your duty."

Sheriff Ramsey, waistcoat and duster covering his lean cowboy's frame, darted an uncomfortable glance at Judge Plunket, then cleared his throat. "Son," he said, addressing John, "we got to ask you a few questions."

"Go right ahead. Always happy to cooperate with the law." He caught Sara's eye and winked. His insouciance filled her with dread.

"You were seen earlier this evening with a man name of Cavendish. You goin' to deny that?"

John shrugged. "Why should I? It's the truth. Why?"

"They found Earl Cavendish half hour ago down in the ravine at Machpelah with his chest blown in."

Sara gasped and clapped a hand over her mouth to keep from crying out. Pandora stared, her chatter stilled for once.

"It was a cold-blooded killing," Plunket said. There was a chilly gleam of triumph in his black eyes, and his fleshy lips curled upward.

John straightened, his eyes narrowing, swift calculations going on behind the hard implacability of his expression. "Sorry to hear it, but what's that got to do with me?"

"We got two witnesses say you done it, son," the sheriff said, almost sorrowfully. "John Tucker, you're under arrest for the murder of Earl Cavendish."

Chapter 20

"I was afraid they'd hang you."

John McCulloch froze on the threshold of his hotel room, taken aback by Sara's quiet statement. After four days in the Lafayette County Jail, they'd had to release him, as he'd known they would, for lack of evidence. The two witness had mysteriously failed to materialize, and it hadn't been necessary to reveal his full name and rank—yet. To all observers, John Tucker had merely been in the wrong place at the wrong time. But finding Sara waiting in his room was a surprise, albeit a pleasant one. His weary features twitched with the beginnings of a smile, and he shut the door, leaning against it and crossing arms and ankles in a typically arrogant, male stance.

"You know I'm too tough to kill."

"Maybe the seventh man is just lucky." She shrugged. "Or maybe you're too clever to get caught."

John frowned, studying her. She was perched with lady-like precision on the rickety straight-backed chair in the corner, her spine straight under the tight bodice of her gray-striped dress. Her hands were clasped in her lap, and her face was pale in the waning light. There were plum-colored smudges under her eyes, but her visage was calm and purposeful.

"You think I killed him, don't you?" he stated flatly.

"I—" She broke off, shaking her head. "You came here for revenge on Moses . . ."

"I came for justice," he said, gritting his teeth.

"Justice, revenge—I don't care what you call it. I know what you wanted and what you're capable of—" Some-

315

thing flickered in her dark eyes, then died. "No, I don't believe you killed Earl Cavendish."

"How very loyal of you," he said. "I'm obliged."

"Well, why shouldn't I have doubts?" she asked angrily. "All I heard from you was revenge. All right, you've gotten what you wanted. Moses is dead."

"Is he? I can't help but think Cavendish's death is just a little too damned convenient."

"He was the kind to have lots of enemies. Why should you care? Your work is done."

"You and Sheridan agree on that." His mouth tightened, and he pulled a folded square of paper from his breast pocket. "My traveling orders. The case of Moses the Prophet is officially closed and I'm to report to Fort Leavenworth."

She looked down at her fingers, twisting the gold band on her left hand, realized what she was doing, and stopped, deliberately smoothing her skirts over her knees. "I knew you'd be going soon."

He pushed away from the door and went to the washstand. Dubiously eyeing the scummy water in the pitcher, he shrugged to himself, poured it into the chipped bowl, then began to unbutton his dirty shirt. The jail hadn't been the worst he'd ever visited, but he was tired of his own stink. He tugged loose his shirttails and peeled off the garment. Reaching for the soap, he cast Sara a wry glance, amused at her disapproving frown.

"Is that why you didn't come visit me, wife-of-mine?" he said mockingly, lathering his hands.

"I sent Mr. Wimple to help you, didn't I? Coming myself would have been—awkward." She glanced away from his ablutions.

"No more awkward than visiting my hotel room." Vigorous splashing punctuated his words.

A rose tint highlighted her cheekbones. "I was discreet."

"Then whatever it is you've got to say must be important." He turned toward her, rubbing his face and damp chest with a length of linen toweling.

"It is. I'm taking Pandora to visit her cousin in St. Genevieve for a few weeks, but I wanted this done first."

She dug into her reticule and pulled out a set of folded papers. Rising, she handed them to him.

"What's this?"

"Your freedom. And mine."

He draped the towel over his neck, then flipped through the papers, scowling at the contents.

"It's just the separation papers, of course," she said with a nervous tremor. "Mr. Wimple assures me everything is in order, though, and the final divorce decree will come through in six months. If you'll just sign . . ."

"Damn." He folded the sheaves carefully, his chest rising and falling with deep, shuddering breaths. Turning, he walked stiffly to the washstand and laid the papers there, then braced his arms on the edge, gazing sightlessly into the bowl, his future as murky as the soapy water. He didn't look at her when she came hesitantly to his side, but he heard her swallow.

"When I forced Father Yves to say the words over us, I never dreamed it would become so complicated. Things got tangled up." She paused, gulping. "I meant no harm. Please believe that."

"You did what you thought best. And I never meant to hurt you, Sara," he said, then made a sound of disgust. Lifting his head, he stared into the mirror at his own green-eyed reflection. "No, that's not true. I meant to hurt you plenty of times. But I regret doing so now."

"I know," she whispered. "Let's not hurt each other any more. I need order and peace in my life. I want this thing between us finished for good, with no loose ends to trip us up again. I want a real home, a family, and a man who can make a commitment and keep it."

She turned away, clutching her elbows to contain shivers that had nothing to do with the warm October sunshine outside. "That's why I'm going to marry Menard Plunket when the divorce is final."

He staggered, dizzy with a sense of having lived through it all before. First Gwendolyn, now Sara. Rejection and betrayal from the women he loved filled him with wild anguish. "The hell you are!"

She whirled to face him, startled at his livid countenance. "John, please! If you care about me at all, you'll accept my decision."

"Care about you!" His fists clenched at his sides, and his voice was rough with emotion. "My God, woman, are you blind? I love you!"

The words echoed in the silent room.

"Why?" she whispered at last, her voice tremulous. "Why would you lie about that now? What can you possibly hope to gain? I thought we were through hurting."

He caught her cold hands and pressed them against his naked chest. "I mean it."

"No, you don't. You think I need to hear that because of guilt or because you think you owe it to me, but you've deceived me too many times. Don't try to manipulate me this way." Her laugh was bitter. "Oh, no, Major, you can't cry wolf and expect me to come running anymore. You have nothing I want. I don't think you ever did."

"Sara, believe me. I do love you."

"You don't know what love is, you're so eaten up with deceit and bitterness," she accused, her tone scathing. "You can't love anyone until you learn to love yourself, but you can't because you're separated from yourself by all those roles you play. Are you Tuck now? The Major? Did the part of you that was Johnny die when Tuck woke up again? I've been as close to you as a woman can be, but I still don't know who you are."

He caught her low on her rounded hips. "You know I'm the only man for you."

She gasped, struggling against him. "You conceited ape! What can you offer me? Security like Will did? Prestige and comfort like I'll have with Menard? Or more lies? More uncertainty and misery? Everything but the truth, I'll wager. Well, no, thank you!"

He pulled her nearer, his eyes narrowing, his mouth quirked in reckless enjoyment. "What about excitement? What about life?" He pressed his lower body against her stomach, letting her experience the force of his desire, then murmured in her ear. "Feel that, Sara? Tell me you've forgotten how good we are together, and then I'll tell you who's the liar."

"I don't want you to do this," she said with a moan.

His mouth hovered over hers, dropping quick, unsatisfying kisses. "Don't you? Sweet, sweet Sara, and such a little liar." He plucked at the buttons on her bodice, then placed his lips at the base of her throat, counting her pulsebeats with his tongue. "This is what I give you, love. We've always had it together."

Her eyelids fluttered at the moist warmth of his mouth on her skin. His scent, warm and musky and male, filled her nostrils. "It's not enough anymore," she said desperately.

His answer was husky. "It's better than nothing."

"You're despicable." Her words were weak.

"I know what I want."

He nibbled on her earlobe, pushing her back until she was pressed between the cold iron pipe of the bedstead and the hard, hot length of his body. His fingers worked on her chignon, dropping hairpins, then freeing the thick mass of her hair. He pulled his fingers through the fine strands, laying them over her shoulders and smoothing them down over her aroused breasts. His palms rubbed the whiskey-dark silk over the rounded mounds in slow, circular motions as he gazed deeply into her dazed eyes.

"You brought me back from the dead. We woke each other up. How can you turn your back on that? Is it so easy?"

"No," she whispered in an aching voice. "It's so very hard."

"Then don't," he said simply.

She gave a small, helpless moan, and her hands came up, knotting in his thick, tawny hair, urgently tugging him down to meet her mouth. His kiss was hot, wet, thoroughly carnal, a mating of tongues that drew sensation from every extremity to lodge low and demanding in the core of her being. Then she was truly lost, the quickening of her body overruling all coherent thought in the fever heat of his touch.

Months of deprivation exploded in an instant, hungry combustion of the senses. He was the quintessential male, hard muscle and sinew, questing hands and sensual mouth. She was everything that was female, velvety soft and fragrant, offering herself in complete and perfect submission, her very weakness the strength that gave her victory. Her reluctance forgotten, she was all eagerness, pushing aside the restrictions of clothing, falling with him on the iron bedstead, their bodies tangled and dewy.

Familiar but new, he tested the texture of her skin in a thousand places, murmuring praise at the hard rosy pearl of her nipple, the satin smoothness of her thigh. She measured each length of muscle in his arms, counted the hard ridges of his belly, caressed the firmness of his lean buttocks. When neither of them could bear the waiting a moment longer, they came together, but it was with a sense of desperation, of things unspoken.

Of ''I love you'' and ''goodbye.''

Of ''trust me'' and ''I can't.''

Of ''don't leave me'' and ''I must.''

The plunging fulfillment was a moment's revelation, another universe glimpsed only for that single shining instant of intense pleasure, then lost in the hard crush of reality where nothing was solved and no answers magically appeared. Afterwards, they lay side by side in the darkness, not touching, failure hovering between them like a dark angel.

Eventually, his voice rasped across her shattered nerves. ''You can't deny what we have together.''

When her words came, they were heavy with tears. ''It doesn't change anything.''

''No.''

He left the bed, striking a match to light the lamp, then reaching for his pants. Behind him, he heard the soft rustle of clothing being adjusted.

He hadn't convinced her, or maybe she hadn't wanted to be convinced, too wary of past failures to risk one more. He supposed he couldn't blame her. After all, what had he offered her besides physical pleasure? He was still the same burnt-out soldier in search of answers.

He'd found those answers in Sara, only to realize that in the process of discovery he'd destroyed her ability to believe in him. He was the method of his own destruction, and he would have laughed at the irony if only it didn't hurt so much.

There was nothing he could offer Sara. He could never

compete with the sacred, saintly memory of old Will Cary. He thought Plunket was pompous and possibly venal, but perhaps underneath there was something in him that could make her happy. If true love was sacrifice, then the least John McCulloch could do was not stand in her way.

Crossing to the washstand, he unfolded the legal papers, rummaged through a drawer for his pen, then signed his name. In the wavering orange light the ink looked as dark as blood, and his mouth tightened in grim humor. Maybe it was his heart's blood. Better to spill it on this document for Sara than on some forgotten battlefield, but either way, he was just as dead.

"I'll see you home," he said quietly, turning to find her watching him with wide, solemn eyes, modestly gowned, hair back in place, all signs of their loving gone except for the faintly swollen, well-kissed look of her lips.

"No." She swallowed and reached for her reticule. "I'd rather you didn't. Please."

He nodded his acquiescence, the muscle in his jaw jumping. Reluctantly, he handed her the legal papers. He tried to smile. "I don't suppose I'll get an invitation to the wedding."

"No, it wouldn't be wise." She pushed the document into her reticule without looking at it.

"The judge would take exception to an Outlaw Reb at his wedding, I guess."

"He knows you're not," she said earnestly. "I told him, months ago."

"Oh. Sara . . ." he began.

"Please!" Her voice wobbled. "Don't say anything."

Again he nodded, dying inside. Hands shoved into his trouser pockets, fists clenched, he stared at a spot somewhere over her shoulder. She moved past him and paused.

"Johnny," she whispered, "remember me."

Then she was gone, leaving behind only the faint scent of rosewater and a man whose tears fell unchecked.

"The . . . cat . . . is . . . black."

Father Yves O'Shea nodded. "Good. Keep going, Clem."

Clem bent over the *McGuffey Reader* he and several

other students shared. His brow knit with concentration as he pulled his finger across the line of type.

"The . . . cat . . . caught . . . a . . . rat!"

"Huh! I'd like to see our old tomcat do that." Little Archie Munson grinned, proudly showing off the space left by a missing tooth. "Last time he tried, old rat liketa chawed his ear loose."

The class sitting on benches in the front office of the old Aid Society Mission dissolved into titters and guffaws at Archie's witticism. Yves hid a smile and "harrumphed" sternly. Twelve freedmen's sons and daughters quickly came to order again.

"Thank you, Archie, for sharing that with us," Yves said, blue eyes twinkling. "On that note, I think we'll call it a day. Class dismissed."

Yves bade his students goodbye and collected the tattered readers. It wasn't much of a school yet, but it could be. Of course, Earl Cavendish's death just two weeks ago had put an end to the sale of the warehouse, so Pandora's plans to purchase a new location for the school had been placed on hold temporarily. But Pandora seemed to thrive on adversity, for no sooner had those plans fallen through than she'd decided to visit her rich cousin Mathilde in St. Genevieve. She'd assured Yves that Mathilde would be making a substantial donation to the school—and soon. Yves' smile faltered. It was just as well Pandora had taken Sara with her.

He sighed. Poor child! What a muddle. Johnny's arrest had upset Sara greatly, but his release and subsequent departure hadn't brought her any joy, either. He wished he knew what troubled her, but she hadn't confided in him before they'd left for St. Genevieve any more than Johnny had when he'd come by to bid Yves a final farewell. As an observer of the species, Yves had recognized the same bleakness in both their eyes, but all his offers of help had been gently rebuffed.

"I guess I'm done for good in Lexington," Johnny had said. "Moses gone, the Golden Calf recovered—or most of it, anyway. There's nothing left for me to do here."

"We'll miss you, son," Yves said.

"Just watch over Sara for me, will you?" he asked,

voice gruff. "I owe her a lot. I want her to be happy with Plunket. But if you need me . . ."

"Yes, I understand."

Yves sighed again and stacked the last reader on his desk. Sometimes young people could be so foolish. Or was it wishful thinking on his part, hoping he could undo his guilt over their unusual joining if they should decide to keep their vows intact?

That didn't appear possible with Johnny gone, Sara off visiting, and Judge Plunket planning a Harvest Ball as a surprise to announce their engagement as soon as she returned. Yves hoped the judge knew what he was doing, because he was fairly certain Sara hadn't given Plunket a formal answer to his proposal. Yves knew there were legalities involved, but not exactly what she'd told the judge. He hoped Plunket wasn't setting himself up for disappointment, not after all the trouble he'd gone to. Why, he'd even enlisted Lizzie's help to prepare for the feast.

Now, there was a happy pair, Yves thought with a grin. Ambrose and Lizzie, billing and cooing like two turtledoves. Who'd have thought Ambrose had the heart of a romantic? They were planning a Christmas wedding and looking for an inn to run, knowing that Lizzie's cooking would set them up just fine. Yves was almost glad Sara wasn't home to be an uncomfortable witness to their delight, and that was another reason to feel guilty.

Yves grimaced. As usual, guilt in all of its manifestations gave him a powerful thirst. He'd taken to drink after young Brother Mathias' death, a death Yves believed he could have prevented, or at least should have shared. If only he'd had the courage to stand up to the mob accusing Mathias of rape. But the blood-scent had been upon them, and Mathias had died a martyr's death, while Yves, sobbing and trembling under a broken wagon, had suffered his Judas' guilt every day of his wretched life.

Sometimes he wondered if his life were a waking vision, the penance for his cowardice, and those terrifying dreams the true reality. Even absolution from the vicar hadn't brought him peace. He'd been near death and almost insane when he first came to Lexington. Thank God for Sara Cary. She'd brought him purpose and a renewed

sense of salvation. Lately, for her sake he'd even been
willing to face his crone without the benefit of alcohol. If
only he could help her now in the same way.

A faint scratching caught Yves' attention. When he
opened the door, his face lit up at the sight of the young
man waiting nervously on the threshold.

"Come in, come in," Yves said. "Eustace, my boy,
where have you been keeping yourself, lad?"

The bartender from the Brass Bull raked skinny fingers
through his thinning blond hair. "I been around, Father
Yves. You ain't been by to sip a beer with me lately."

"No. Temptation bedevils me, but I dare not risk even
a dram." His eyes narrowed thoughtfully on the young
man's harrowed countenance. "Come in for a wee spell.
Though I mustn't drink, it doesn't mean I cannot visit with
my friends."

Eustace ducked his head and wiped his damp brow, took
a last look outside at the mild October afternoon, then
sidled through the door. "I—I gotta talk to somebody."

"Certainly. Come, sit," Yves invited, concern etching
his puckish features. "What is it, lad? Are you in trouble?
Is it about poor Mr. Cavendish?"

Eustace's lower lip quivered, and his brown eyes grew
bright with moisture. "You know, you're the only one
that's called him that. Everyone else says he was a bully
and a crook, and the world's well rid of him."

"I'm certain he had his faults, but he didn't deserve
murdering, I'm sure," Yves soothed, pulling Eustace
down on the bench beside him. "A poet said: 'Every man's
death diminishes me,' and I know it's true."

"That's the way I feel."

"I guess Mr. Cavendish was a friend to you," Yves
suggested kindly. To his surprise, Eustace's face crumpled, and he began to sob into his hands.

"He was more than that. He was my father."

"Ah, poor laddie," Yves consoled, laying a comforting
arm on the young man's shoulders.

"Nobody knew, you see. He wasn't married to my ma,
but when she died, he took me in. Whatever he was to the
rest of the world, he was good to me." Eustace sniffled

and vainly wiped his flowing eyes on his soggy shirt-sleeve.

"What a tangle," Yves muttered. "There, now, boy. It's perfectly all right to grieve for your father."

"I want to get the lousy bastard that killed him, that's what I want!"

Yves straightened, startled. "Do you know who shot him? Eustace, that's a job for the law, not you."

"You don't understand. I can't prove anything. And Earl, well, he had some pretty shady dealings, so the law don't really care who killed him. But he left me a letter, in case anything happened to him." His sobs returned in force. "Only I never thought it would."

"Calm yourself, son. What kind of letter?"

Eustace wiped his nose on his sleeve and dug into a voluminous trousers pocket. "Here. See for yourself."

Yves gingerly opened the creased and stained paper, then scanned the contents. His eyes grew wide as he read, and his mouth dropped open. When he was finished, he thoughtfully refolded the letter.

"Well, Father? What should I do?" Eustace asked.

"The hand of Providence was on you, boy, when He brought you to me," Yves said carefully. "There's only one man who can help you, and I know where to find him."

"What do you suppose Ambrose is so happy about to-night?" Pandora asked in a low voice.

Sara tugged the edge of her black lace mitts and glanced toward the front seat of the covered buggy. Ambrose whistled cheerfully between his teeth and occasionally clicked to the trotting horse. Light from side lanterns splashed into the darkness, illuminating the road leading to Menard Plunket's house. Sara shrugged, settling her satin mantle over her square-necked aubergine dinner gown. In two day's time it would be All Hallow's Eve, and a giant yellow moon hung low over the horizon while woodsmoke and dried leaves perfumed the crisp night air.

"He's got a lot to be glad about," Sara said absently. "He and Lizzie have found an inn not far from Watkin's Mill."

"Yes, I know, but look at him," Pandora demanded. "He looks like the cat that swallowed the canary."

Sara obediently studied Ambrose's smooth-shaven jaw and neatly trimmed hair. Even his carriage was straighter, prouder. Love had given him back his youth and his drive. And, Sara had to admit, there was a disconcerting twinkle in his eye tonight.

"Well." Pandora sniffed, folding her arms over her considerable bosom. "Whatever it is, he can't be half as pleased as I am. I had no idea Mathilde was in that big house all alone. I'm so glad she's agreed to come stay with us at Christmas."

"Her donation toward the school was most generous, too," Sara agreed.

Their three week visit to St. Genevieve had been a respite Sara welcomed. The dissolution of a marriage, even so strange a one as hers, and the final bittersweet farewell to a lover were things that took a terrible emotional toll. Pandora's acerbic and witty cousin Mathilde, demanding though she'd been, had helped take Sara's mind off her aching heart. The gentle routine of desultory days gave her time to evaluate her situation and think deeply about her future. The answers hadn't been easy, for there was so much to consider and, after a couple of weeks, serious and even startling conclusions to draw.

Sara tried to contain a shiver of trepidation. She dreaded what she had to do this evening, what she could no longer put off. As gracefully as possible, she must refuse Menard's offer of marriage. And this time she'd make him understand she meant it.

She wished she could have seen him sooner, hating to delay the distasteful task, but ever since their return three days ago, he'd been unable to call, sending her flowers and notes of apology, citing the urgent press of business at the bank. The newspaper had reported that Judge Plunket, along with other city fathers, had been meeting daily with representatives of a railroad conglomerate, and there was much excitement over this project. A railroad link from Lexington to Sedalia or Macon would ensure the city's continued growth, providing the vital rail link to eastern markets for Texas beef and beating that upstart,

Kansas City, in the competition for shipping supremacy. Sara understood, but chafed impatiently, for once her decision was made, she abhorred the delay.

So when Menard had invited her and Pandora to his home for dinner, Sara had known she could not risk losing the opportunity. Surely she could beg a few moments of private conversation. Her reasons were valid, and the sooner she shut the door on this chapter of her life, the sooner she could go on to the next challenge.

She nibbled the fingertip of her glove, turning something over in her mind. "Dorie, what would you think about asking Clem's parents to help out after Lizzie and Ambrose leave?"

"Do you think they would?"

Sara glanced into the darkness, hiding her troubled expression. She'd been to visit with the Washingtons and Daisy Wiley again, and she'd seen for herself their miserable living conditions and the crushingly high terms demanded by their landlord. Though the Emancipation Proclamation was a reality, they had merely traded one form of slavery for another. Sara was vastly disturbed that she'd had a part in it through her championship of Menard. Even if he were unaware of the policies of his overseers, such laxness was deplorable and could not be countenanced.

"Yes. I'm almost certain the Washingtons would be glad to come work for us," she said.

"Then let's ask them. I declare, I do miss Clem."

"Won't be long now," Ambrose called over his shoulder. He grinned, a sight so unusual that Pandora and Sara stared. "Judge Plunket's place is just around the curve."

The windows of the Plunket mansion were ablaze with light when Ambrose turned the buggy up the long drive. Numerous teams with buggies, shays, wagons, and even a carriage or two stood parked on the wide, sloping front lawn.

"My goodness," Pandora exclaimed. "It looks as though the whole town is here."

"Ambrose, what's going on?" Sara asked.

Ambrose drew the buggy to a halt at the base of the wide front steps and vaulted down. He offered her his hand, his face wreathed with a smug smile. "You'll see, Miss Sara. Something special."

"Oh, dear," Sara murmured in dismay, hanging back.

"Don't just sit there, Sara Jane," Pandora urged, and Sara reluctantly climbed down from the buggy. Heart beating nervously, feet leaden with reluctance, she mounted the steps with Pandora puffing beside her.

The wide double doors swung open, and a smiling man-servant ushered them into the brilliantly lit entrance hall and took their wraps. Music and the muted hum of conversation buzzed in her ears, then Menard was there, coming forward with outstretched hands, his beefy face ruddy with good humor and excitement.

"Ladies, good evening. Miss Pandora, welcome." He turned to Sara, grasping her cold hands. "Sara, my dear, you look stunning." His heated gaze brushed over the creamy flesh revealed by the square-cut neckline of her gown. Sara drew a sharp breath, conscious of the constriction of the tight bodice and the tender voluptuousness of her bosom.

"Menard, what is all this?" she asked. "I thought we were to share a quiet dinner."

He laughed, throwing back his head. "Just a little surprise in the way of a welcome home party. Come," he said, placing her hand in the crook of his arm. "Come and greet our guests."

"Menard, please, I must speak with you," she said under her breath.

But he was already leading her forward, threading their way through the crush of women in brightly colored gowns and men in dark, conservative suits. Pandora was immediately hailed by her friend Minerva and went to speak to her. Familiar faces, neighbors and acquaintances, all nodded approvingly and called greetings to Sara and Menard. The large parlor and dining room had been thrown open to form one big reception area, and it was a bower of fall leaves and gold and yellow chrysanthemums, wicker cornucopias spilling colorful squashes and dried corn, even several pumpkins and cornstalks in the corners. Menard took her to a long table laden with a bounty of food and drink.

"You're positively glowing tonight, my dear," Menard commented. He smoothed his sidewhiskers with his knuckles, studying her with blatant and heated approval. "Would you care for a glass of champagne?"

"Yes, please." Though hot and flustered, she sipped the cool beverage with scarce enjoyment. "You've outdone yourself. Everything looks sumptuous. You've gone to so much trouble when you really shouldn't have."

"What's the use of having anything if you can't show it off once in a while?" he asked jovially. He bent closer. "I enjoy the envy of others, especially those snobs who look down their noses at a self-made man. And I've always thought a Harvest Ball quite an elegant occasion, certainly a fitting framework in which to announce our engagement."

Sara's heart lurched, and she nearly dropped her glass. "Menard! I must talk to you!"

He relieved her of the drink, smiling widely. "Afterwards, my dear. All our friends are waiting for—"

"You don't understand! You can't do this!" She was frantic.

Menard's brows drew together, and he grasped her hand so hard that she gasped. His voice was low and forceful, the full weight of his powerful personality behind his words. "No, *you* don't understand, my dear. I've waited all my life for this moment. A gracious home, and a beautiful and accomplished wife—the envy of all, a pinnacle of success and respectability—and you're part of it."

"Please don't do this, I implore you. We must talk first."

His expression softened. His grip eased, and he lifted her bruised hand to his lips. "Ah, I understand. A case of pre-nuptial nerves. But I've been very patient."

"Yes. Yes, you have," she agreed eagerly. "If you could just wait a little longer—"

"Such nervousness is understandable, Sara, but you'll feel an enormous relief once the announcement's been made. Just wait and see." He tugged her hand, striding with her in tow until they stood under the arbor-draped casement between the two rooms.

"Menard, no!" The humiliation to come clogged her

throat and made tears prickle behind her eyelids. He ignored her, merely squeezing her hand in warning.

"Friends," he began, "if I could have your attention for a moment, please."

The guests turned toward them, and Sara's cheeks burned crimson as all gazes fell on her. Frantic thoughts of escape whirled through her brain. She didn't know what to do. Menard was intent on announcing their engagement, and to cause a scene went against the grain. If only he would listen! Maybe the best she could do was brazen it out. Afterwards Menard would have to listen to her, and in a few weeks they could quietly break it off. But the humiliation! Menard was so sensitive to the nuances of shame. He would never forgive her. Her stomach heaved, and she regretted drinking the champagne intensely. She had to try again, anything to stop this farce from becoming a disaster.

"Menard, please," she insisted. "I—I think I'm going to be sick."

He grabbed her by the waist, pulling her against him and burying his nose in the hair beside her ear in a convincing imitation of fondness. "Pull yourself together," he said harshly. He looked up with a smile for all the curious guests.

"She's a little nervous, folks," he said, his voice indulgent. There was a titter of appreciative laughter. She made a slight movement toward escape, but his hand bit painfully into her waist, controlling her. "As I was saying, Sara and I would like to—" There came a loud crash from the front of the house and a babble of excited protest. "What the devil?"

A tall figure resplendent in Union blue and gold appeared in the doorway, striding into the room and parting the assembled company as easily as a hot blade through soft butter. Sara felt a wave of dizziness nearly overtake her. It was the devil, all right, and this one had leaf-green eyes!

A wicked half-smile touched John McCulloch's mouth. "Pardon the intrusion, Judge Plunket."

Menard's eyes grew black and lusterless with rage. "What is the meaning of this?"

"Major John T. McCulloch, at your service, sir," John said, sweeping a mocking bow. Then his eyes narrowed, and his voice became deadly. "Now, if you don't mind, I'll thank you to take your damn hands off my wife."

Chapter 21

If the earth had opened at that moment, Sara would gladly have leaped into the inferno. Instead, she had to endure the hot, curious stares of every guest licking over her like flames. Menard's face was a mask of naked fury, his grasp on her waist crushing. John's thin smile was an icy contrast, chilling and dangerous.

"Just what the hell are you trying to pull, Tucker?" Menard demanded.

"I've come to claim what's rightly mine," John replied, taking Sara's arm. His hard jerk freed her from Menard's hold, and she stumbled against his blue-coated chest. "And the name's McCulloch."

"You have no rights here!" Menard caught Sara's other arm, and she was bound between the two angry men, shackled by hard, unforgiving hands. "Sara, I want to know what's going on."

"Menard," she managed weakly, "I tried to tell you."

"Ask Father O'Shea," John interrupted. "He married us over a year ago."

"What?" Menard's countenance took on a purple bloom, and for a moment there was a flicker of panic in his black eyes.

"We're separated," Sara interposed desperately. "We're getting a divorce."

Menard jerked, and his ruddy features relaxed into flaccid relief at this reprieve. "Why didn't you say so, darling? Then there's no problem really," he said, tugging her arm possessively. "You're still mine—"

"Not by a damn sight, Plunket," John said, snatching her back.

Something snapped inside Sara. She twisted, tearing loose of both men, backing away. "Stop it, both of you! I won't be growled over like a bone between two mongrels." She pointed a finger at Menard's nose. "You! I kept trying to tell you, but you wouldn't listen. No, you had to go ahead with this pretentious party, to announce something I hadn't agreed to, and without my consent. I was trying to tell you I couldn't marry you. It didn't have to be this way, but your stupid pride did it."

Menard's visage paled. "But Sara . . ."

She turned her back on him and glared at John. Giving him a hard shove on his blue-uniformed chest, she pushed him backward with her insignificant weight and towering rage. "And you! How could you? How dare you barge in here like this? Airing our private affairs before the whole town! I'll never forgive you. Never!"

"Now, honey . . ."

"Don't say another word," she shouted, magnificent in her fury. "I'm through with the both of you, and if I ever see either of you again, it'll be too soon!"

With that, she picked up her skirts, lifted her chin, and marched from the room, slamming out of the front door. The stunned guests immediately began to murmur, and in one corner Pandora swooned on a settee while Minerva Haskett frantically waved smelling salts under her friend's insensible nose.

"I should have had them hang you when we had the chance," Menard said furiously.

John's lip curled. "That's always been your style, hasn't it, Moses?"

Plunket froze, and his stillness was that of a coiled rattler waiting to strike. John knew then that it was true. His mouth twisted. All this time. He should have known. Judge Menard Plunket—alias Moses the Prophet.

It was all there in Cavendish's own hand. John had arrived in town only an hour earlier in response to Yves' urgent summons, and he'd tarried just long enough for Yves to give him the damning evidence. Cavendish had put it all in the letter he'd left his son—the details of his partnership with Moses, their ring of spies during the war, the profiteering, even the murder of Captain Alex Thompson. And it all made perfect sense. As Deputy Provost Marshal, Plunket had had access to vital military information to pass to Quantrill. In the final hectic days of the war, Thompson must have carelessly revealed John's role to Plunket, and to protect himself Plunket had Thompson killed and sent unsuspecting Union troops out to murder Tuck the guerrilla raider. Moses was worse than a traitor; he was a scabrous parasite, selling out both sides for profit. The knowledge that he wanted Sara made John's blood run cold.

"Well, Moses?" John taunted in a low voice that carried no further than the scowling judge. "Isn't that your trademark? Letting someone else do your dirty work. Except once. Did you really have the guts to kill Cavendish yourself, or did one of your hired thugs do it?"

"Get out!" Menard ordered. "I won't tolerate these insane insinuations from the likes of you. Get out of my home!"

"With pleasure," John said, his nostrils flaring. "The stench is getting a bit thick. But we aren't done, Plunket. I'll be back. You can count on that."

John strode from the room, oblivious to the avid stares that followed him, pausing only to retrieve his hat from the stupefied manservant. Outside, he paused on the top step, then caught sight of Ambrose scratching his head and gazing down the drive in amazement.

"Ambrose? Did Sara come this way?" John vaulted down the steps, reaching for the riding gloves tucked neatly into his belt.

Ambrose gave him a sharp glance, his face puckered with confusion. "Did she ever! Stormed out there and climbed into the buggy without so much as a fare-thee-well, then lit outta here like her tail was on fire!"

John mounted a big bay with a government saddle, barely resisting the urge to go after Sara. The thought of her involved with Plunket made his stomach roll and his blood boil. When Yves had told him about this so-called engagement party, he'd known he'd do anything to keep her out of the clutches of that murdering slime.

It may have been foolhardy to accuse Moses in his own home before insuring his arrest with the local authorities, but when Sara was involved it was hard to stay rational and cool. After Yves' revelations, nothing could have kept John away from her tonight. No matter what she thought, no matter what it cost him personally in terms of her regard, he was determined to halt the proposed match once and for all. He loved her, whether she believed it or not, and nothing as evil as Moses was going to threaten her if he could help it! He groaned inwardly, knowing his interference had likely sealed his fate forever in Sara's mind. Lord, he'd made a mess of it, but what the hell was a man supposed to do? If only he could go after her and explain!

But the letter Yves had given him was burning a hole in his pocket. Like an ass, he'd let a show of temper forewarn his sworn enemy.

Well, let the bastard try to run, John thought grimly. Nothing would give him greater pleasure than to bring Plunket back to pay for his crimes face down over the back of a horse. Missing that, he was going to bring Moses the Prophet to justice legally, by-the-book, so the slippery devil couldn't slide through their fingers. Sheriff Ramsey was the only lawman he could trust. It was time to enlist his aid.

"I guess she'll be all right when she cools off," John told Ambrose. "But I have a feeling Miss Pandora is going to need you."

"I'll get Lizzie from the kitchen, but I ain't so sure I know what the hell's goin' on." Ambrose gave John a thorough once-over, from the crown of his blue hat to the soles of his polished boots. "You're just full of surprises, ain't you?"

"Yeah." John grinned and kicked the horse into a gallop. "And I'm not finished yet!"

Menard Plunket stormed into the library, his face as black as a thundercloud. God damn that bitch! She'd let him court her, knowing full well she wasn't free. And after all he'd done for her, she had the nerve to turn him down, and in front of half the town, too. His reputation was in shreds. She'd made him look like a fool. Well, she wasn't going to get away with it scot-free. There was just too much riding on his marriage to Sara Cary.

His gaze fell on his desk, on the stack of signed and notarized contracts. Contracts that were going to make the rest of his fortune, contracts with the railroads for coal from the Sugarloaf, contracts signing over to him all rights to the holdings of Mrs. Menard Plunket. He ground his teeth together. With those contracts, and the capital he'd managed to accumulate, including a piece of Quantrill's Golden Calf now resting safely in the vault of Alexander Mitchell and Company, he was going to take his place as one of the first western rail tycoons. It was so close he could almost taste it.

Damn the bitch! And damn that black-hearted bastard, Tucker or McCulloch or whatever he called himself! Plunket cursed the opportunities he'd missed to rid himself of that sonofabitch. A look of shrewd calculation narrowed his black eyes. There were others besides himself who had reason to hate John McCulloch. A thin, feral smile split Plunket's swarthy face, and he slowly drew his knuckles down his sidewhiskers in an attitude of deep thought. There was still a way to snatch victory from the jaws of disaster.

Plunket crossed to a door and pounded on it with his fist. "Moody!" he barked. "Where the hell are you?"

The door opened, and the big, burly cowboy entered, rubbing his face in a sleepy fashion. "Yeah, boss?"

"Wake up, you clod! We've got work to do. But first, go get me our two visitors. You know who I mean."

"Yes, sir." Moody paused at the door, jamming his greasy slouch hat down over his bushy black hair. "You want I should bring them here?"

"No, you fool. Have them meet me at the bank." Plunket's hands gripped the stacks of contracts. He seemed to draw strength from the reams of papers, and his expression suddenly cleared. Picking up a pen, he sat down and drew the inkwell to him, then began scribbling rapidly.

"Anything else, boss?" Moody asked.

Plunket didn't look up, his fingers scratching out line after line of official-looking jargon. "Yes. Meet me at the bank, too. And, Moody, I want you to bring me a preacher."

* * *

Sara slammed into her office. The drive from Menard's house had done little to cool her ire. She impatiently peeled off one black lace mitt, then the other. The delicate mesh ripped, and with a soft, angry exclamation, she threw them down on her desk with her reticule and began to pace back and forth, back and forth. She pressed her clenched fist against her trembling lips, and her thoughts and emotions churned in turmoil. Her gaze flitted across the office, seeing items one by one—her new doctor's bag, Will's framed sketch of the Sugarloaf, her discarded mitts—as if to glean some answer to the messy scene she'd been party to earlier. But there were no answers, nor even any comfort. She groaned wretchedly and began pacing anew.

When someone rapped in a peremptory fashion on the front door, she jumped, her gaze startled and wary. The knock came again. Knowing Yves was dozing over his newspaper in the parlor, she went to answer the summons, hoping it was a medical call, anything to take her mind off the disastrous evening. But her hopes were not to be realized. Waiting on the porch, hat in hand, was Judge Plunket. She nearly slammed the door again, but that was a coward's way out. She lifted her chin and composed her face.

"Menard."

"Sara. May I come in?"

She bit her lip. "That's not a good idea."

"Surely the least I deserve is an explanation?"

The hurt look on his face softened Sara's resolve. "I suppose you're right." She sighed, opening the door wider. "Come in, but just for a minute."

They stood in the foyer, awkward and silent. Sara nervously rotated her wedding band. "I'm sorry for what happened, Menard."

He cleared his throat. "It was unfortunate. Why didn't you tell me?"

"I tried, truly I did."

"I mean before tonight."

"Oh." She shrugged. "It was a—a marriage of convenience, and by the time you and I began spending time together, I'd already taken steps to dissolve it."

"So at some point you will be free to accept my proposal."

"Free, yes. But not to marry you. Menard, I'm sorry, but my answer has to be no. I've thought about it very hard."

"If it's about the way I behaved tonight—"

"No, I'd already made my decision. We haven't the bonds between us necessary to make a good marriage."

"And you did with Tucker—er, McCulloch?"

"No." She glanced away. "We didn't either."

"Sara, reconsider," he begged, grasping her hands. "We will be splendid together, I know it."

She shook her head, flustered and uncomfortable. "There are other considerations. You must accept my decision."

"What? Tell me. We'll work it out."

"No, really, there's no need. My answer will be the same."

"I demand to know the reason." His hands tightened on hers, and she made a small murmur of pain.

"Menard, you're hurting me!"

His grip hardened relentlessly. "Tell me."

"My career means a lot to me."

"What career? You've had only a pitiful handful of patients recently. I could offer you financial security. You'd never have to worry again about dealing with the sordid ills of the riffraff."

Sara tugged her hands free, feeling a growing anger. So that's how he really felt about her role as a female physician. She clasped her hands behind her back and massaged the bruised places.

"I don't want to go into it," she muttered. "It will only make things worse."

"You're being deliberately obstructive, failing to see all I can offer you. And you haven't given me one good, solid reason for refusing me, Sara." He caught her shoulders and glared down into her face.

"All right!" she snapped, goaded. "I don't think you're the honorable man you want me to believe you are. I heard the whispers, but I couldn't believe it until I saw with my own eyes. The schemes you're using to hold freedmen on your farms is slavery all over again, forcing them to buy their house plots from you, then pay you nearly all of their wages for the privilege of living in those hovels. It's indecent, Menard.''

His dark brows laced together. ''Who's come crying to you with this sad tale? The Wiley woman? Or your friends the Washingtons? You know you can't believe a lying, thieving nigger! Besides, that's business. Man's work, and none of your concern.''

Sara's features became haughty and cold. ''It would be if I became your wife. And what other wickedness are you hiding? I can't attach myself to a man who'd do such a thing.'' She tried to pull away, but his grip hardened. Her voice had an arctic chill. ''I'm sorry for everything, Menard, but I think you'd better go now.''

''Dammit, I'm not going to let you throw this all away!''

''You don't have a choice.''

His laugh was harsh, and it sent chills down her spine with the scaly menace it conveyed. His inky eyes glittered with a cold, reptilian rage. ''Oh no, Sara, my sweet. There are always choices, and I'm going to help you make the right one.''

''What do you mean?''

''I want you, and I intend to have you, my dear, whatever the cost.'' He grasped the back of her neck in a painful grip and ground his mouth against hers. She shuddered with shocked revulsion at the feel of his fleshy lips and pushed against his chest, but he took her reaction as response and laughed softly at her struggles.

''You see? You want me, too.''

''You conceited donkey!'' she snapped, furious. ''Let me go!''

''There's no time for you to play the coy maiden. I've got a decree of divorce in my pocket and a special marriage license. We're going to settle this once and for all.''

''What?'' Sara couldn't believe her ears.

''Where's your wrap? We mustn't keep the preacher waiting.''

The wild, harried light in his eyes frightened her nearly as much as his words. ''You're mad,'' she protested, gasping. ''I'm not going to marry you. I can't.''

"That's easily remedied, my dear. Now come along." He grabbed her mantle from the hall tree and thrust it around her shoulders, then hauled her toward the front door.

"Stop, Menard." She dug her heels in, but she was no match for his superior strength. Her voice rose. "This is absurd—"

"What's the ruckus, I say?" Yves stood blinking owlishly in the parlor doorway.

Sara was so relieved she could have sobbed for joy. "Yves, make him stop!"

"Release the lass, Your Honor," Yves ordered, his tone heavy with irony and his gray eyes brilliant with outrage. "It's clear she doesn't want to go with you."

"You drunken lunatic." Menard sneered. "You're the cause of this mess. If only you hadn't married her to that half-wit."

Yves bristled. "If it's a donnybook you're after, I can give it to you. Now, let the girl alone."

"Get out of my way, old man." A steel-blue pistol appeared in Plunket's meaty fist, pointing directly at Yves' narrow chest. All the air rushed from Sara's lungs in a single burst of horror.

"What are you doing?" she cried, frantically trying to pry Menard's fingers loose from her upper arm. "Yves, get back!"

"That won't solve anything," Yves said. He took a step toward Plunket.

"Move aside, before I blast you to hell and gone," the judge warned, dragging Sara toward the front door.

Yves held out his hand and took another step. "Give me the gun, Your Honor. Haven't you got enough trouble?"

Menard's laugh was harsh. "None I can't handle, old man."

"Leave Sara out of it." Yves moved relentlessly forward, his gaze never wavering.

"I said get back!" Menard cocked the hammer, and the sound echoed ominously. Sara bit back a whimper of fear.

"Yves, don't," she pleaded. What was he doing? Why was he risking himself like this? She couldn't understand such foolhardiness. But he acted as though he were invincible, girded like a young David with the power of the Lord. What was he trying to prove?

"You'll lose every chance of redemption if you don't lay down that weapon now, son," Yves said. "Don't compound the sins of Moses the Prophet by doing this to Sara."

Menard choked. "Moses? I don't know what you're talking about."

"Aye, you do indeed. But you may not know Cavendish had a son, and he gave his son a letter. And Eustace Cavendish gave it to me. The days of Moses are numbered. Now give me the gun."

"No!" Plunket's voice was hoarse.

"Dear God," Sara gasped. "You're Moses?" She sank her nails into the back of Menard's hand. He grunted in pain, releasing her and slamming the back of his hand across her unprotected cheek all in one movement, sending her staggering to one knee. Yves gave a cry of protest and moved, but not fast enough. Menard fired the pistol.

The force of the bullet tearing through Yves' upper body hurled him backward like a toy tossed by a giant's hand. Blood splattered on Pandora's flower trellis wallpaper, and Sara screamed. The red-haired priest sprawled in a heap, still and silent. She scrambled forward, but a heavy hand caught in her hair, jerking her to a painful halt. Roughly, Menard dragged her to her feet, hauling her toward the front door.

"No," she cried. "Let me go. He may be dying! I've got to help him!"

"Let him rot," Plunket muttered harshly. The barrel of the pistol poked her ribs, and the hot metal burned through her satin gown. "Come on! And don't give me any more trouble, or you'll get the same."

Ashen-faced with terror, Sara looked back over her shoulder as Plunket pulled her from the house, but there was no movement from the frail body on the rug. Every instinct told her Yves was dead, and grief tore through her, paralyzing and shocking. She was hardly aware that Menard shoved her into a buggy, only partly cognizant of their furious drive through the nearly empty streets of Lexington. When Plunket pulled the lathered team to a halt at the rear of the Alexander Mitchell and Company Bank, then dragged her from the buggy and up the dark alley to the back entrance, she began to come to her senses. Fear was still present, but with it came the hot trickle of fortifying anger.

Plunket pushed her ahead of him down a corridor and into a meeting room furnished with a long wooden table and chairs. Roughly, he shoved her into one of the chairs.

"Now, my dear, on with business," he said, pulling papers from his inside coat pocket. He unfolded them, set them in front of her, and pulled a silver-plated pen and inkstand into position. His half-smile was cruel and cunning. "Sign them."

Sara stared mutinously at the meticulously written lines, then touched the pages distastefully. Decree of divorce, marriage certificate, power of attorney. With barely leashed violence, she shoved the papers off the table. "No. I won't."

He slapped her again, delicately this time, hard enough to bring tears to her eyes but not hard enough to damage her. "You'll do it. You'll do it because you have no other choice. Don't make me hurt you again, Sara."

Her eyes glittered with hatred. "Murdering filth! You think I'll do anything you want, after what you did to Yves?"

"That interfering cleric got what he deserved." He grabbed the papers from the floor, slamming them back down in front of her. "Now sign!" he roared.

Sara cowered in the chair, her eyes wide, her face white except for the rosy mark of his handprint. "Why? Why is it so important to you?"

He grabbed the arms of her chair, leaning over her, his body coiled with menace. "Because I need the Sugarloaf, that's why, and marrying you is the perfect way to get it." He laughed at her confused expression. "You still don't get it, do you? I'm meeting tomorrow to sign a deal that will make me the richest man in Missouri. It's a perfect plan, my dear, but don't worry, you'll reap the benefits as my wife. Wealth, respectability, prestige—it's all within our grasp."

"You want the Sugarloaf? Will's land?" she asked dazedly. Her eyes danced unseeingly over the room while she tried to make sense of his revelation. A thought struck her, and she drew in a sharp breath. "The coal. Of course! Johnny said it was there."

"McCulloch?" Plunket's tone was sharp, his black eyes watchful. "How did he know?"

"He—he saw it," she faltered, "when we went to the cave after the—the—" She broke off, biting her lip. Menard laughed.

"The Golden Calf?" He laughed again. "Yes, I know all about it. Damn near had my hands on the rest of it, too, except for his interference."

"Then you *are* Moses," she whispered, aghast.

His brows drew together, and he glowered fiercely. "Moses is dead. They found him in Machpelah Cemetery. The sooner you realize that, the better." He pushed the papers toward her. "Do it."

"I can't," she protested, seizing on a new argument while her brain whirled. "Half of that land is Pandora's. You can't just take it and—"

"Let me worry about that. Enough arguing, Sara. Let's get this over with."

"No." Her brown eyes glinted with triumph. "I refuse to go through with such a farce."

"You little bitch! I'll show you . . ." He raised his hand again, but she didn't flinch.

"Do your worst," she spat. "But you can't kill me because then everything I have will revert back to Pandora."

His eyes narrowed, and he rubbed his thick sideburns thoughtfully. "Very astute of you, my dear. But there are methods to secure your cooperation."

"Threats, Menard?" she taunted. "What more can you do?"

"I can kill John McCulloch." Her breath caught on a harsh note, and he laughed. "I thought that would get your attention. You care for him, don't you? I suppose I should have realized that before now."

Her chin tilted at a belligerent angle, and she feigned

mocking astonishment. "I'm surprised you'd have the courage to fight the Major."

"I've associates who want him dead even more than I do. All I have to do is say the word. So if you want your Major safe . . ." He trailed off, shrugging, and silently offered her the pen.

She ignored it, sniffing disdainfully. "You'll have to do better than that."

He gave a long-suffering sigh, shaking his head in regret at her stubbornness. "Ah, Sara, you try me sorely. Now you force my hand." He went to an opposite door, opened it, and bellowed, "Moody, get in here! And bring the others."

Sara stared apprehensively, chewing the inside of her cheek, hoping whoever it was might offer her some assistance. She recognized Moody as the big cowboy from the Brass Bull, but the skinny old man wearing a clerical collar around his scrawny neck who came after him was a stranger. She swallowed uncertainly and got to her feet, words of appeal ready on her tongue. The preacher looked around myopically, his head swaying like a praying mantis, his sly features avaricious and irreverent. She knew she'd find no help there.

"The Reverend Greely, Sara," Menard introduced. "He's agreed to perform the ceremony."

"A blessed occasion, I'm sure," Greely said, folding his hands piously. His jaw hung slack, and he admired Sara's low neckline with lascivious appreciation.

She shuddered uncontrollably, aware of his gaze as though something alien and slimy had touched her flesh. She could not help pulling her mantle modestly over her shoulders.

"I'm not going to do it," she said, backing away. Menard grabbed her arm, and his black eyes bored through her with the force of a lightning bolt.

"You are," he retorted. "You're fortunate to have friends to act as witnesses. Agree, or I'll loose them on your precious Major."

"You can't—" A sharp gasp broke her tirade.

"Well, if it ain't the female medic," Cole Younger drawled. He swaggered into the room, his spurs clinking against the wooden floor, his red horseshoe mustache curling up in wry mockery. "Good to see the little lady again, ain't it, Jess?"

"How do, ma'am?" Jesse James blinked rapidly at Sara, and the icy expression in his blue, protuberant eyes chilled Sara to the bone.

A wave of dizziness clouded her vision, and she swayed drunkenly. Menard supported her, almost gently. She gulped and fought the surge of sickness that pressed against her breastbone.

"Aren't you going to say hello to your old friends, my dear?" Menard asked maliciously. "We had quite a long association during the war, but when Moody brought word these young men were down on their luck, having been swindled out of quite a sum of money, I thought it was time to meet face to face at last and offer them a chance at a job. Boys as handy with firearms as they are will be mighty useful when we begin mining your coal."

"Yeah, can you beat that?" Cole drawled. His eyes were wary, but it was clear he knew Menard was both powerful and useful to them. "We got what you call regular employment. Might even turn us into upright citizens like the judge here."

"Have I mentioned I ran into your old friend Tuck this evening?" Menard asked conversationally. Both Jesse and Cole stiffened, their attention suddenly focused and deadly.

Cole sucked air through his teeth and blew it out. "Been a long time since we seen ole Tuck. Reckon we got a score to settle."

"Something you want us to do, Moses?" Jesse asked in his soft, malignant voice.

Menard's brows lifted in kindly inquiry. "Well, Sara? Do I? Your choice."

"N-no." Her voice cracked. They'd kill Johnny, she knew. They couldn't forgive him for outsmarting them and taking the Golden Calf. These vicious young men would track him down and kill him, with no warning, no chance to defend himself. She couldn't stand the thought. If he died, she was partly responsible, she wouldn't be able to go on. The urge to protect him was ingrained, a part of her. How could she abandon him now?

Maybe Menard could control Jesse and Cole, at least. for a time. She didn't care about the Sugarloaf, or even about another farce of a marriage, if only she could buy some time for Johnny. She lifted her gaze to find Menard watching her closely, and she shuddered, repulsed by the idea of linking her life with this sinister man.

"You can have the Sugarloaf," she said. "I'll sign everything over to you."

"No. I want it all. The land and you."

"I can't be any kind of wife to you."

He shrugged. "You'll come around."

"But—"

"Mr. James, you can find Tuck—"

"All right! I'll do it," she cried. "Just—don't."

Menard stroked her jawbone with his blunt fingers and smiled. "Very wise of you, my dear."

It took only a few moments for Sara to affix her signature to the appropriate documents, then she stood before the Reverend Greely, her cold hand clasped in Plunket's thick paw. The words flowed over her.

"Dearly beloved, we are gathered together . . ."

Greely's unctuous voice slithered over her nerve endings, and she tried to control her trembling limbs. Only one mental picture kept her on her feet, her responses low but adequate. It was an image of Yves as she'd last seen him, with Johnny's imagined prostrate form beside him. What she was doing was insane, but she would make any sacrifice for the man she loved.

" . . . pronounce you man and wife."

Menard's lips were as hot as coals on her cool mouth when he kissed her. Sara had to force herself not to turn away. He patted her shoulder.

"There, you see? Things are better already."

She didn't answer, afraid she would vomit at his feet, appalled by the vows she'd made and the terrible secret she carried. Menard could have the Sugarloaf. He could have everything. She only wanted to get away.

Plunket gave Moody orders to return the Reverend Greely to whatever slimy hole he'd crawled from, and pushed greenbacks into the minister's outstretched hand. Greely praised God for his generosity as Moody hauled him from the room. Jesse watched silently, his eyes blinking in that annoying, sinister fashion of his, but Cole seemed consumed with jocularity.

"Always knew cats landed on their feet," he remarked, walking around Sara, eyeing her with an appreciative light in his eyes. "You must be somethin' else in bed, honey. Too bad I never got a taste."

"That's my wife you're talking to, Younger," Plunket snapped. "Have some respect."

"Oh, I got plenty of that for the Doc." Cole laughed, lounging in the loose-boned way of a seasoned horseman. "Yessir, she always lands on her feet. 'Cept with Tuck most of the time she was on her back."

"That's enough." Menard jerked his thumb toward the back door. "You know what to do. Get going."

"Thankee, Mr. Moses, sir," Cole said insolently, tipping his head and backing away. "Don't worry. We're going to get that bastard, but good. I'm gonna take him apart piece by piece till there ain't nothing left of ole Tuck but his gizzard."

"What!" Sara cried. Her fingers twisted in Menard's coat sleeve, but he shook her off. "But you promised—"

Menard ignored her. "He shouldn't be so hard to find," he said with a complacent smile. "Big fellow, blond hair, in a Union uniform."

"We'll do a good job. Tidy. No mess," Jesse said.

"You lied," Sara accused hoarsely. "I did what you wanted, but you lied."

"You're altogether too trusting, my dear."

Sara laughed, a sound high with near-hysteria. "So are you. You think I'll keep silent about this? You think I'll forget about Yves? I'll see you in hell first!"

A chuckle rumbled from Cole, and Menard scowled, unwilling to lose face before the two ex-guerrillas.

"A wife can't testify against her husband," he said. "Not that you would." He walked toward her, his gaze avid and hot. His thick forefinger trailed over her exposed collarbone, staking his possession. He flicked aside her mantle and watched the gooseflesh creep over her satiny skin. "Not after I've had you a few times."

"You're vile. You think I'd ever let you touch me after

I've known heaven in John McCulloch's arms?'' she demanded haughtily. She pointed at Jesse and Cole, contempt and hatred radiating from her words. "You'll send these men to kill him, and you think I'll meekly submit to you? You're a bigger fool than I thought. I'll kill myself first. I'll kill *you* first!"

Plunket turned to the two men grinning at this exchange. "I thought you had a job to do," he snapped.

"Keep your shirt on. We're gittin'," Cole drawled. They moved toward the door, pausing when Menard turned back to confront his defiant new wife.

"You're overwrought, but you'll soon learn nobody calls me a fool without paying the price," he said, his hands clenching.

Sara's laughter tinkled gaily, grim amusement twisting her mouth. "Soon the entire town will know you for a fool, Menard Plunket." Her voice was contemptuous and scathing. "Just as soon as everyone realizes the child your *wife* carries isn't yours!"

"What!" His hands seized her throat as though he would throttle the life from her, but she stood proud and uncowed, smiling with perfect defiance. "You're lying," he said harshly.

She laughed. "I'm a *doctor*. I know these things. Well, Menard? Do you let me go, or shall we carry this farce to its end?"

His eyes glittered, and his hands eased, sliding to the base of her throat to test her pulse. "Poor Sara, such an amateur at these things. Don't you realize you've just handed me the weapon that will keep you next to me all of your days?"

Her eyes widened with sudden trepidation, and he laughed. "Yes, my dear. McCulloch's brat, you say? No matter. I'll raise it as my own. What better revenge could I take than that? And a mother willingly sacrifices herself for the wellbeing of her babe, doesn't she? I trust you'll keep that in mind at all times."

"You're insane," she whispered, terror looming with razor-sharp talons to shred her future and her unborn child's. "You wouldn't!"

"I will."

"No!" She broke free, making a desperate break for the door, but he caught her again. The seams of the gown ripped. She turned on him, reaching for his eyes with hands curved into claws, but his massive fist caught the tip of her chin and everything went . . .

. . . black.

Why was it so dark? She was cold all over, and it was dark. Was she still asleep? No, her eyes opened and closed. She couldn't move her hands, her feet. But where . . . ?

A match spluttered, and Sara gasped. Menard calmly lit a stubby candle and set it on the low ledge. Overhead, the rocky ceiling of the cave disappeared into darkness.

"Awake at last, love?"

"Where—where is this?" she asked, but she knew.

"Don't you recognize your own Sugarloaf?" He brushed the rock dust from his jacket. "Had a hell of a time getting you here."

"Why?"

"I needed someplace safe to leave you until you come to your senses."

"No." The word was a whimper.

"You'll be all right," he said, his deep voice the essence of reassurance. "What could harm you? It's cozy, if a bit chilly. When you're ready to see reason, there's a nice warm home and a loving husband waiting for you."

"Menard, don't do this, please."

He squatted before her, briskly checking the scratchy hemp ropes that bound her hands and feet. "I love it when you beg. My guess is you'll be doing a lot of begging before much longer. Well, I've got to go. It'll be morning soon, and I've got to meet with the railroad agents." He pulled her light mantle over her shoulders, kissed her forehead, and stood.

"Don't you dare leave me here like this, you despicable jackass!"

He smiled. "That's very good, Sara. Shout all you want. No one can hear you. When I come back, we'll have a long talk." He picked up the candle.

Her eyes widened with incredulity. "You—you're taking the light?"

''You have no need of it, do you? Anyway, I think you'll see reason a bit faster this way.'' He turned and started up the cavern, and the glow of the candle followed him like a halo.

She couldn't believe he'd actually do it, but the blackness closed in, relentless and merciless. Her scream of terror echoed like the wail of a lost soul.

"You have no need of it, do you? Anyway, I'll
see you a bit faster this way." He turned
up the collar of his . . . .

Chapter 22

Sheriff Ramsey didn't take kindly to being disturbed in the middle of the night. In fact, he was mad as hell. He stood in his boardinghouse parlor, barefooted, trousers hastily pulled on over his red winter underwear, suspenders hanging past his knees. He especially didn't take to having been hoodwinked by a certain Major John Mc-Culloch.

"Why the hell didn't you tell me you were Army before?" he demanded. He shook John's identification papers and Cavendish's letter under John's nose. "This beats all I ever seen."

"It was a delicate situation, Sheriff. Sorry I couldn't be more forthcoming at the time, but as you see, patience has paid off." John shifted impatiently.

"My God, the Judge himself," Ramsey mused. His sharp-eyed gaze caught John. "Godalmighty, Major! This is a damned ticklish situation. You realize I'll have to go before the grand jury with these allegations before we can draw up the arrest warrants."

John grimaced. "Just as long as you move fast. I'm afraid I tipped the bastard off, and I don't want him getting away."

"I know my duty, youngster. Hell, guess I might as well go on down to the Court House. You be there first thing in the morning, and I'll see you testify before the jury first, but we can't move without those warrants."

"I'll be there." John stuck out his hand. "And thanks, Sheriff."

Ramsey shook hands, his grip rock-hard, man-to-man.

"Hell of a story, McCulloch. And a hell of a nerve you got, too."

"I'm just anxious to see justice done."

John left the boardinghouse feeling better. At last the wheels of justice were grinding, and he sincerely hoped Plunket would soon find himself grist for the mill. Now for Sara. God, he hoped she'd be willing to listen! He chuckled to himself. She'd been in a royal, flaming temper when she'd stormed out of that party. Well, maybe her ire had cooled a bit. Even if it hadn't, he was too anxious to see her again to postpone a visit any longer.

He kicked the bay into a trot and headed for South Street. He knew something was wrong the minute he saw the house. The front door stood wide open. He was halfway up the front steps when he heard Pandora's wails.

The scene in the entrance hall was one of chaos. Ambrose and Lizzie were kneeling on the floor beside a heap of limp clothing, and Pandora was wringing her plump hands, tears streaming down her wrinkled cheeks.

"Oh, dear God!" she wept. "Yves! Who could have done this?"

John's heart pounded, and he hurried forward, his nostrils twitching as he caught the scent of fresh blood. It was everywhere. Pooled on the threadbare carpet, splattered on the walls, staining with crimson the rags Lizzie pressed to Yves' chest. John grabbed Pandora's shoulders, turning her face into his chest. She clutched his sleeves and sobbed uncontrollably.

"Sweet Jesus!" he muttered. "What happened?"

Ambrose glanced up. "Dunno. Just got here. Miss Dorie found him like this."

"Is he alive?" John asked.

"Barely," Lizzie said softly. "Oh, Johnny! Just barely. We need Miss Sara."

"Sara! Where is she?"

"Dunno that either," Ambrose said. Yves moaned then, a sibilant whistle. John released Pandora and moved to help.

"Let's get him into Sara's office."

Yves' slight form, as brittle as a bag of sticks, was no challenge to John's strength. He scooped up the wounded priest and strode into Sara's office, stretching him out on the examination table, then stripping back the bloody remnants of his shirt. Lizzie went to work with water and gauze, competent and calm despite the tracks of tears down her pale face. John started to move out of her way, but surprisingly, Yves' scrawny hand knotted on the hem of his coat. John bent over him.

"Father Yves, can you hear me? Who did this?" he asked urgently.

The priest's eyelids fluttered weakly, and his mouth looked blue in his ashen face. His lips moved, and John moved closer to catch the barely audible wheeze.

"Judge . . . he took . . . Sara. Help her . . ."

John straightened as though rammed by a hot poker. Plunket! And he had Sara! Self-recrimination clawed at his gut. What had he done? By losing his temper with Plunket and confronting him, he'd given the bastard a hand-delivered warning. And look what that madman had done! Yves was still trying to speak.

"Don't talk anymore. I'll find Sara," John promised. He glanced at the obscene wound still oozing blood, then squeezed Yves' shoulder. "Don't worry, old friend, everything will be all right."

That seemed to satisfy the priest, and he lapsed back into unconsciousness.

"Ambrose, ride for another doctor," John ordered tersely. "Then find Sheriff Ramsey at the Court House and tell him what's happened."

"Here, Ambrose, let me do that," Pandora said, taking the wad of gauze from him and sliding into his place beside Yves' still form. She was once more in control, indomitable and determined. Ambrose was gone in a flash.

"Will you be all right until he gets back?" John asked.

"Of course, God willing," Pandora snapped. "Now you go find Sara."

John needed no second urging. He raced through the house, vaulted the steps, hurried to his waiting horse. There were only a few places Plunket could have taken her. If he hurt her . . .

"Hold it right there!"

The ominous click of cocking pistols made John's hands

freeze on the saddle horn. He didn't need to turn around to identify the voice that came out of the darkness. The itchy place between his shoulder blades said this wasn't a social visit, either.

"Nice and easy now, two-finger that hogleg and drop it on the ground."

John did as he was told, cursing inwardly. Cole Younger! Why'd he have to show up now, of all times? Frustration surged, and fear for Sara, but he contained them, reaching for the icy aloofness of a trained warrior. He knew his life, and maybe Sara's, depended on his keeping his wits about him now.

"You boys enjoy the ride back from Texas?" he drawled over his shoulder.

"Can the crap, Tuck," Cole snapped, picking up John's Enfield and shoving it into his waistband. "This ain't no tea party. Now, let's take a little walk toward the barn. Slowly. Jesse don't like no sudden moves. Makes his trigger finger squirm. Ain't that right, Jess?"

"That's right," Jesse replied softly.

Jaw clenched, John took the bay's reins and walked down Sara's drive toward the dark barn. The door creaked on its rusty hinges, and a rat rustled across an overhead beam, making shadows flutter in the pale moonlight. John turned the bay into an empty stall, then faced his former allies.

"Well, boys? What's on your minds?"

"He makes a helluva fine figure, don't he, Jess?" Cole remarked, waving the barrel of his big Colt at John. "Right pretty, he is, in that Yankee getup. I guess he was a blue-belly all the time he rode with Quantrill."

"That's right," John acknowledged. "Quantrill ran the Union Army ragged. I just evened up the odds a bit."

"Moses sent us," Jesse said.

John shrugged. "I'm not surprised."

"We aim to kill you, Tuck." Jesse's young voice was flat, unemotional, deadly.

"Thought as much." John lifted a tawny eyebrow. "Well, have at it, son."

"You're right calm for a sonofabitch about to meet his maker," Cole said.

"At least I'm not jumping to Moses' beck and call like a couple of lick-spittle hound dogs."

"What the hell's that supposed to mean?" Cole asked, his temper flaring.

"Shut up, Cole. He's just trying to rile you," Jesse said mildly.

"Sure." John chuckled. "But once you kill me, Moses will be in the clear. He'll have won it all. Talk about the last laugh."

Pale blue eyes blinked rapidly. "Don't try to sidetrack us, Tuck. You took the Calf, and you're going to pay."

"Yeah. Don't blame you for having hard feelings." John folded his arms, and a wry grin tilted his mouth upward. "Hell of a good game, wasn't it? Especially since you intended to double-cross me first."

Cole laughed. "By God, you turned the tables on us, though. I had enough of Texas to last me a lifetime. Don't suppose you could still put your hands on the Calf, could you? Might be worth your life."

"Unfortunately, the Army lost the Calf again. Rumor has it some Juaristas got their hands on it."

"Well, damnation! That was stupid," Cole said sourly.

"No." John's voice was soft. "As you once told Sara: That was war."

"What you tryin' to say, Tuck?" Jesse asked.

"I've got nothing against you boys. You were good partners and worthy enemies."

"You want us to forgive and forget, is that it?" Cole laughed. "Jesus, Tuck! You're a funny bastard."

"We thought we knew who to count on," Jesse said sadly. "Guess 'tweren't you."

"No? Remember that last day? Who pulled you out from under that horse?"

Jesse looked away, his cheek twitching. "You did. Guess you saved my life."

"I took two bullets that day, too." John's eyes narrowed. "You'd sent word you were coming in to surrender, hadn't you? Well, I'd sent word, too, to my contact. I had Quantrill's Bible, and hell, the war was over, wasn't it? But Moses didn't see it that way. Don't you understand? Moses—Plunket—was Deputy Provost Marshal then, and he and Cavendish were still playing both sides against the middle. He had my contact murdered, then sent that patrol out to meet us, Jess. With orders to shoot to kill. You, me, everyone. He covered his ass. We were both duped like a couple of greenhorns.''

For a long moment Jesse's involuntary blinking stilled, and his blue eyes grew wide. Then his breath hissed inward on a whispered snarl. ''That stinkin' sonofabitch!''

John's lips twitched. ''Yeah. Something like that. His partners don't tend to last long. I'm certain he shot Cavendish himself. You see, boys? It was Moses I wanted all along, and you just got in the way. Nothing personal.''

Jesse advanced, pistol leveled at John's belly, his face gray with rage. ''Personal, hell!''

The punch Jesse landed rocked John backward onto his butt. He palmed his throbbing jaw, surprised at the power of the slight man's blow. Astonishment changed to amused admiration, and he chuckled softly, looking up from his seat on the hay-strewn floor into Jesse's glowering expression. ''Hell, Jess! What was that?''

Jesse's young-old face creased with a faint, surprising shimmer of a smile. ''I'd call that just about even.''

Jesse shoved his pistol into its holster and offered John a hand. John stared at it for a moment, then grasped it firmly and levered himself to his feet. He gingerly fingered his chin. ''I think you loosened a couple of teeth.'' He cocked a mocking eyebrow at Cole. ''What say, Cole? You want a chance at working on the other side?''

Cole grinned and scratched his mustache. Shrugging, he dragged John's Enfield out of his belt and passed it to him butt-first. ''Most times, Jess speaks for the both of us. Guess this is one of them.''

With an inner sigh of relief, John accepted the gun. He put it away, his expression thoughtful. ''Seems to me you boys might be thinking of taking your own revenge on Moses now.''

''Moses used us like a couple of whores,'' Cole said. ''You got any suggestions?''

''Would you be interested in what's left of the Golden Calf?''

''What?''

"We didn't have it all. Quantrill passed part of it to Plunket, and he used it to buy his way into the judgeship. But there's a lot left, and my guess is he's got it stashed in the vault at that bank of his."

Jesse began to laugh softly. "You suggesting we rob a bank? Upright citizen like you? A damn Yankee Major?"

John smiled. "There's justice, and then there's justice." His smile died. "You hit him where it hurts, and I'll see that the law turns a blind eye to this one. But only this one. And no killing, of course. Then I advise you to get out of the bank robbery business before you wind up on the short end of a rope."

"Won't be a noose that finishes us," Cole drawled. "They can't catch us."

"A bullet might," Jesse warned. He blinked and shivered, as if in premonition, then rubbed his jaw. "And what about you, Tuck?"

"I'm going after Moses. He shot the priest in cold blood, and he's got my woman."

"Yeah, we know."

"What! Jesus Christ! Is she all right? Where are they?"

Jesse and Cole looked at each other, then at John. He felt a sharp thrill of fear trickle up his spine.

"He made her sign some papers, then a preacher married them," Cole said. "Don't appear she's your woman no more."

"Good God! What's that bastard up to?" John groaned. "Then what?"

"It ain't good," Jesse muttered.

"Yeah, they were having a helluva fight," Cole agreed. "He slugged her, Tuck. Knocked her out cold."

The rage John had been holding in exploded in a white-hot fireball. "I'm going to kill him! Where is he?"

"He said something about hiding her—"

"Where, goddamnit?" John roared.

"The Sugarloaf. Down in the caves."

John's stomach lurched, and he felt the blood drain from his face. "Aw, hell!"

". . . flow, sweet river, flow . . ."

Sara's soft voice floated eerily in the enveloping dark-

ness, strange and unearthly to her own ears, but better in
all ways than the oppressive silence of the cave. She sawed
at the bonds around her wrists with a sharp sliver of rock,
the lyrics of the song punctuated with gasps and grunts of
effort.

Dear God, how could Johnny stand this? she wondered.
Time had lost all meaning eons ago. Her mind floated
somewhere above herself, objectively observing the hud-
dled figure blindly severing the ropes thread by thread, her
hands raw, her voice a frightened warble as she sang to
keep the demons away. Terrified though she was, she knew
she had not experienced even a tenth of the horror she'd
seen Johnny suffer. Yet he had survived, and so must she.
The memory of his success kept her courage from faltering.

She felt another thread give way and rested again, her
breath rasping in her throat and the blood hammering in
her ears. Was it her imagination, or were the ropes a fraction looser? It was awkward, trying to hold the rock steady
while she rubbed it back and forth, but it was the best
system she'd found. Not that she was certain what she'd
do once she was free. After all, she'd completely lost her
sense of direction. If she started out exploring in the darkness, she could just as easily head deeper and deeper into
the caves where no one would ever find her. Then the
Sugarloaf would be her tomb for eternity. She shuddered
and pressed her joined hands low against her belly. She
had to survive. Another life depended on her.

It was a miracle, that life growing within her womb, a
blessed miracle. She hadn't wanted to believe at first, but
all the classic signs were there, and her monthly flow was
never late—until now. In St. Genevieve, she'd had to accept it. The last time she'd been with John, his seed had
found fertile ground. Wonder filled her, even now. Johnny's child. How could she ever regret that? And how could
she allow Menard to use that innocent babe against her?
Like a she-tiger, her maternal instincts were aroused. She
would protect her baby at any cost. Determinedly, she began to saw on the ropes once more.

Two more threads popped before her hoarse, whispered
song faltered again. Her head fell back against the rocky

wall behind her, and she gasped for breath. In spite of the chill, sweat dewed her upper lip and dampened the hair at her temples. Then she heard it. A rattle of rocks and shale, as if the hill itself trembled, and then the distant sound of her name.

Menard! Was he back so soon? She pushed awkwardly to her feet, bracing her back against the wall. Oh, God, what should she do? How could she pretend to be docile and cowed when her hatred of him rushed so strongly through her veins? She strained mightily at the ropes, tearing at the ragged strands with her teeth. There! Something slipped. Nearly sobbing, she twisted and pulled one hand, scraping gouges in the delicate flesh. Ignoring the sting of blood, she worked with all her strength, and the blood made her skin just slippery enough . . .

Free! Frantically, she pushed aside the ropes and grasped the knife-sliver of rock, her only defense. Hobbled as she was, her only hope was to take him by surprise. She smiled grimly into the pitch black cave. He wouldn't expect to find anything but a broken woman. Maybe a wildcat could catch him off guard and make escape possible.

Reaching out her hands, she explored the uneven wall, seeking and finding a shallow indentation. Hopping, she pressed herself into the depression, praying she'd be hidden. Holding the knife-sliver in her teeth, she bent and tried to decipher the snarl of knots binding her ankles. The low sound of muttered curses jerked her upright. Swiftly, she transferred the knife to her hand and flattened herself against the wall.

Light dazzled her eyes, and she squinted, focusing on the blurry silhouette behind the upraised lantern. It was enough. She launched herself, every atom intent on burying her weapon hilt-deep into Menard's evil throat. But the feeble blade slid harmlessly across his upraised forearm, and she knew she'd failed even as she plunged helplessly forward.

"Sara!"

Strong arms caught her, broke the dizzy fall, but she thought she was either crazy or dead because the voice sounded like . . .

"Johnny!"

He cradled her across his lap, hastily setting the lantern aside. "Jesus, woman! What were you trying to do?"

Sara's voice was faint, the shock of going from hell straight into heaven almost too much for her strained mind to grasp. "I thought you were Menard coming back."

"And you were going to subdue him with this?" He dropped her ineffectual rock-sliver with casual contempt and shook his head in amazement. "Trying to carve him while you're trussed up like a Christmas turkey. Good Lord, Doc. What will you try next?"

She opened her mouth to defend herself, but he shushed her. "Don't answer that. Just—come here."

With a deep groan, he pulled her close, kissing her ardently. The brass buttons on his uniform dug into her through the purple satin of her ruined gown, but she only pressed closer, seeking his warmth and fire. His big hands trembled on her face. "Are you all right? Did he hurt you?"

She shook her head dazedly. "No. I'm fine. But you? How can you be here? You hate this place so much . . ."

He looked surprised, then lifted his eyes and let his gaze roam over the rocky tunnel. "Yeah, I do, don't I? But maybe not so much anymore." His expression changed, and a great tenderness softened his rugged visage. "Look at you, alone in this hellhole for hours, and still worried about *me*. My God, can't you see I was more scared for you than of being in a mine ten miles deep?"

She fought back a surge of joy, holding his words in her heart to examine later, but anxious for him to understand everything that had happened. "But, Johnny . . . Menard . . . I think he's lost his mind."

"He's a crazy bastard, all right," he said, his tone grim. He worked on her ankle bonds, finally loosening them enough to free her. Pulling her to her feet, he grasped her hands, then his face twisted savagely. "God damn it, he did hurt you! I'm going to draw and quarter that bastard!"

Sara looked down at the bloody streaks and deep scrapes on her hands and wrists. "I—I did that to myself, getting the ropes loose."

"I swear he's going to pay for everything he's done."

"He said he'd kill you if I didn't do what he said. He wants the coal in the Sugarloaf for some railroad deal." She was babbling, trying to assimilate the facts herself, and her voice rose higher and higher. "He—he made that disgusting Reverend Greely marry us."

"We'll get it straightened out," he soothed.

"I didn't want to, Johnny, but he made me. He was going to send—" She broke off with a gasp of recollection, her fingers curling into his lapels. "Jesse! And Cole! They're here and out to get you. You've got to be careful, Johnny!"

"Easy, Sara, love. That's all taken care of."

"You've seen them?" Her eyes went wide. "You didn't—"

"No. Wasn't a shot fired. In fact, they told me where to find you. Let's just say we've come to a mutual understanding now that they know the truth about Moses. If those two were a gun, they'd be aimed at Moses' head this very minute."

She trembled with relief. "Thank God."

There was a soundless vibration of earth settling, a faint tremor felt only through the soles of their shoes. John gave another glance at the cave walls. "You know, this still isn't my favorite place to be, and I swear there's some instability. Let's get the hell out of here."

"I don't know where *here* is," she said plaintively.

"Don't you know this part of the caves?"

"No. Will considered some sections too dangerous to explore."

"Well, he was right. It's almost like a labyrinth, the way some of these holes keep looping back on themselves. I've been going around in circles down here." He shrugged and grinned. "Should have brought your string, I guess."

"Can you find the way out?"

"I think so. I noticed some landmarks." He retrieved the lantern and took her arm. "Come on."

They picked their way over the uneven surface, passing the dark and gaping maws of auxiliary tunnels, making their way toward the surface. A haze of rock dust in the cool, musty air made Sara cough. She clung nervously to

John's supporting arm, jumping at the occasional shift and crawl of loose rock.

"Almost there," John said.

"Not quite," a mocking voice contradicted. Menard Plunket appeared suddenly in front of them, waving a pistol in silent menace.

Sara gasped, clutching John's coat sleeve. "Menard!"

"Well, well. Isn't this a touching sight?" The words were slurred almost as if he were drunk. Plunket's normally impeccable garb was crushed and dirty. His cravat hung crookedly, and his shirt was stained. The coat he wore had lost a button and was spattered with mud. But it was the wild, insane light in his black eyes that caught Sara's attention. Here was a man on the edge, more dangerous because he was losing control, and Sara froze, hypnotized like a rabbit under the spell of a snake's eyes. John felt no such paralysis.

"Get out of the way, Plunket. You're done here."

Plunket laughed harshly. "Mighty big talk from a dead man. God damn you, McCulloch! You've interfered with me for the last time. Ramsey's poking around soured my railroad deal, and you're to blame. You're *both* to blame, but, by God, I'm going to make something of it yet. Now drop that gun."

"It's beyond salvage, Moses," John drawled. "Haven't you realized that?"

"Just drop the gun," Plunket said shrilly. The pistol swung, pointed directly at Sara's head. "Drop it, or I'll blow her brains out where she stands."

Silently, his jaw working, John pulled the Enfield free and carefully placed it on the rocky ground.

"Now back away," Plunket ordered. When they did, he came cautiously forward and kicked the weapon into a dark, distant corner. The leveled barrel of his gun never wavered. He reached into a crevice for his own lantern, rolled up the wick until the globe glowed orange, then gave a slight, faintly reptilian smile. "That's better. Now we're going to go back down. Turn around and start walking."

"What's the purpose of this?" John demanded, but he did as Plunket said. He held his own lantern high in one hand and Sara's wrist with the other, speaking over his shoulder as they began slowly retracing their steps. "Ramsey's got the evidence. You're finished, Plunket."

"Not if it's only my word against theirs. That's why you two are going to conveniently disappear. Everyone will assume you've run off together again. Oh, yes, I realized Sara's story of a medical convention was merely an excuse, but it didn't matter to my plan. Now, on the day of her marriage to me, when the fickle doctor flies with her lover, I, of course, will be heartbroken. But I'll recover." Menard's voice had become almost conversational. "It's really a pity I have to kill you, Sara, my dear. Too bad we haven't had the opportunity to share conjugal rights during our brief marriage. I'm almost tempted . . . well, perhaps not."

Sara felt John stiffen with rage and dug her fingers into his hand in warning. "You can't expect anyone to believe that tale of yours," she said in a shaky voice.

"There'll be no one to refute it. The priest is dead . . ."

"No, he's not," John said. "He was alive and talking when I saw him at Sara's house. Grievously wounded, but he knew damn well who'd shot him and taken Sara at gunpoint."

"Oh, thank the Lord," Sara breathed.

"You're lying!" Plunket growled.

"And then there's Cavendish's son," John continued. "He'll be doing some talking, too. He wants the man who killed his father to hang."

"A court will never believe a little snot like Eustace. Not over a leading citizen." But Plunket's tone was becoming more uncertain. "Besides, there are ways to deal with him."

"You plan to shoot Eustace, too? Or slit his throat like Alex Thompson?" John chuckled his disdain. His steps slowed, and he squeezed Sara's wrist, hard.

Biting her lip, she stumbled, her brain spinning. Eustace was Cavendish's son? She risked an anxious glance at John. His gaze flicked toward a dark opening in the tunnel wall, and he squeezed her wrist again. She nodded, just a little dip of her chin to show him she understood. Her heart thumped in her chest, and her mouth went dry. She didn't know what he would do, just that she had to be ready.

John continued to taunt Plunket. "Where's it going to end, Moses? After you've murdered the entire town?"

"Shut up! Don't you realize what money and position can do for a man?"

"What makes you think you've got either one?"

Plunket laughed, something of his old cocky self again. "You're shooting in the dark now, McCulloch."

"That patrol you sent out to meet me nearly cost Jesse his life, too. He figures you owe him. That's why he and Cole robbed the Mitchell Bank this morning. Reckon they got what was left of the Calf, too. You're not only a traitor, you're busted."

Plunket's howl of rage was the savage cry of a mortally wounded animal. John swung the lantern in an arc and gave Sara a shove toward the auxiliary corridor. The lantern caught the barrel of Plunket's pistol, deflecting his shot, then crashed to the ground as John disappeared into the tunnel after Sara.

The gun blast reverberated against the cave walls. Rocks and pieces of shale slid from the ceiling and bounced against the floor in a peckerwood attack of noise and dust. Another shot zinged past John's ear and ricocheted into the darkness ahead of Sara's retreating figure. He cursed and positioned his body as best he could between her and the gunman behind them.

"Stay against the wall!" Another shot whizzed over his head, and more rocks splintered and clattered down to crash on the uneven floor. "Dammit! He's going to bring the whole place down on us!"

"I can't see!"

"Keep going!" He caught up with her, grabbing her from behind and bodily lifting her ahead. "Now, where is that damn—ah, here."

He turned them into a right-angled offshoot, coming up short, Sara pressed between him and the wall.

"Ouch! You bumped my head," she protested.

"If that's the worst you get out of this, we'll be lucky," he said grimly.

"John McCulloch, I'm never going to forgive you if you get us killed!"

He threw back his head and laughed into the blackness, loving her with every atom of his being. "Me either, honey."

Her teeth were chattering. "What are we going to do now?"

"Can you stand it if I leave you here? I've got to try to work my way around. I think this opens back up in the corridor above him."

"But he's got a gun. Couldn't we just wait him out?"

Another shot echoed, and more rock descended on them. "We don't have time. Stay here and keep your head covered. Here." He pressed a small object into her hand. "Don't light one until you hear me call you." His hand cupped her chin, and he kissed her, rather lopsidedly, then scrambled off into the black void. She felt the bundle. Matches.

She heard Menard's bellow of rage echoing amid the clatter. Crouching against the wall, she strained her ears, praying. Could Johnny disarm him? Could he find his way through the darkness? At least there hadn't been any more shots, though Menard's threats and curses still floated down the tunnel. She inched closer to the opening. She flinched as another shot rang out, then—nothing. No curses, no screams, no calls from Johnny—nothing.

Biting her lip, she peered around the aperture. A faint glow illuminated the jagged opening into the main tunnel. She couldn't stand it. Had that shot found a target? What if it had hit Johnny? She had to help him! She hurried down the narrow passage, nimbly sidestepping stones and debris in an agony of haste. The soft sounds of a near-silent but mighty struggle greeted her. She slid to a halt and gasped.

In the wavering lantern light, the two men rolled over and over, each seeking possession of the pistol clenched in Menard's hand. Blows thudded, skin smacked, skulls cracked against the rock-littered earth, but neither man would give ground.

John's face twisted in a fierce grimace. His hand wrapped around Menard's wrist, then slammed the gun against a rocky outcropping, once, twice—the pistol flew free, skidding past Sara's feet. John hooked one hand in Menard's once-immaculate shirtfront, using his other fist on jaw and nose and chin in a punishing barrage. Blood ran from Plunket's nose, and his head lolled in near-insensibility as John reared his hand back for more of the same.

Sara made a small sound and dashed forward, catching John's arm. "Stop. It's enough." He glared at her as though he didn't recognize her, his face contorted by the pleasure of revenge. "Johnny," she said softly, "stop. You're killing him."

He blinked and drew in a sharp, shuddering breath. Lowering his hand, he looked at the vanquished Moses, then released him, dropping him to the earth with a sound of disgust. "You're right. He isn't worth it."

John caught Sara to him and buried his face in her rose-fragrant hair. He drew air into his lungs in great gusts and felt an oppressive weight lift from him forever. No longer was he bound by a lust for revenge. By God, Plunket deserved to die, but it wouldn't be at John McCulloch's hand. His war was over at last.

"Can we go now?" Sara pleaded, her voice thick with relief.

"Yeah, we'd better, before this roof decides to fall." He lifted his head and gave her shoulders a bone-crushing squeeze. A low groan drew his attention to Plunket struggling groggily to all fours, and John's expression grew savage again. "What I'd like to do is leave this sonofabitch here buried alive like he did you."

"You can't."

"No. He's got to face the music." His voice was grim. "Don't worry, Sara. We'll let the law hang him."

"No!" Plunket roared like a mortally wounded bull and lurched past them, scrambling in the opening of the small tunnel. He came up fumbling with the forgotten gun, backing away. "Stay back!" he rasped, his face streaming with a mixture of blood and sweat.

John hesitated, cursing under his breath at his own stupidity. Why had he let his guard down with this viper even for a moment? He pushed Sara behind him. "Give me the gun, Plunket."

"No." The judge staggered, caught himself on the wall. Behind him in the darkness more rock tumbled and crashed. He jumped, and the gun tilted erratically. His voice grated with a terrible, hysterical rage. "You've done it. My position, my wealth—you've taken it all."

"Make it easy on yourself. You'll have your day in court. Maybe you'll even figure out a way to outsmart the law again," John said in an even tone, steadily advancing.

"You don't understand. The disgrace . . ." Plunket's black eyes were harried, and he shuddered. "I've seen the way the mob howls at a hanging. It's undignified . . . for a man of my station . . ." His brow furrowed, and his wandering attention focused on John again. He raised the gun. "You did this to me!"

Sara gave a small, frightened cry behind him, but John held firm. "You've only got one shot left. You think you can get me with it? One more blast and the whole damned place is going to cave in on all of us. Don't risk it, Plunket."

The man who'd been Moses the Prophet hesitated, looking around frantically as if seeking answers in the cold stone walls of the Sugarloaf.

"Give it up, Moses," John urged softly. "The day of reckoning is come."

A wild and terrible light burned in Plunket's eyes. "For both of us." His smile was chilling, the same defiant grimace that Lucifer himself perhaps had on his lips when he was cast into the pit. He raised the gun toward John, but his gaze caught on the pale, pure oval of Sara's face.

"Menard, for heaven's sake," she whispered, throwing herself against John McCulloch with such a look of naked love that Plunket's gut twisted with a terrible sense of loss. Something flickered in his expression—resignation, regret, and perhaps even a plea for forgiveness.

"No, Sara," he said. "For your sake."

He turned and stumbled into the maw of the tunnel. A final shot rang out. The earth trembled—above them, below them, everywhere—and the Sugarloaf shifted, began to collapse. Slabs of rock fell in slow motion from the ceiling and slid down the walls. Sara watched, horrified, as the earth closed over where Menard Plunket had stood only moments before.

"Sweet Jesus!"

John's hoarse exclamation mingled with the growling rumble of moving earth. He caught Sara roughly around the waist, dragging her away, and his words rasped in her ear.

"Run, Sara. *Run!*"

Chapter 23

They stumbled out of the black bowels of the Sugarloaf blind and deaf, expelled, newborn, into a world of light and air by the death throes of the caverns. The impetus of their dash for life took them through the opening of the cave, down the slope of the abutment to the relative safety of the bank of the Little Sni, gasping for breath, battered, torn, and bleeding.

John came to a halt beside the stream and loosened his death-grip on Sara's arm, supporting her as she sank, weak-kneed, to the sandy bank. Her gasps were almost sobs as she hung her head and tried to breathe. Neither one of them could speak. John sucked great draughts of air into his lungs, combatting the suffocating thickness of rock dust and fear. His eyes were streaming, and his heart thudded painfully in his chest.

He knew without a doubt that after this, he'd never fear the darkness of a cave again. There'd been no time for thought, for hesitation, or for the paralysis of terror, and he felt a return of confidence and pride that he'd led them both unerringly to the surface. If he could survive this, he could survive anything, *do* anything.

He threw back his head, blowing, stretching, and looked up through the winter-stripped branches to the blue vault of heaven. It was barely mid-morning, and the air was crisp and fragrant with fall odors. The sun shone warm on his upturned face. It was a beautiful day.

The thought came like an echo from the past.

I'd do it differently.

He went still, swallowing harshly, remembering that

long ago promise to himself. A promise he'd failed to keep.
Oh, he'd kept it for a time, during that happy interval when
he'd been just Johnny, but then Tuck had come back into
his life, and the Major, and everything had gone to hell
again. His throat tightened. He'd been brought close to
death once before and had been given a chance to make a
change, but he'd blown it. Now once again, he'd teetered
on the brink of extinction and damnation, only to be
dragged back by some unseen hand. It seemed the Lord
wasn't done with the seventh man.

He closed his eyes, sending heavenward a wordless
prayer of thanks for second chances. But he had to do it
right this time, from the very beginning. No mistakes. It
wasn't every day a man was re-born, and he had a lot to
make up for, to Sara and to himself.

He squatted beside her, his hand gentle on her tangled
hair. "Honey, are you all right?"

She shook her bowed head, her uneven breath shaking
her slender form with convulsive shudders. Tears stained
her dirty, beloved face. "I—I don't know. It was—"

"Close," he finished. "Much too close. But it's over.
You're safe now."

She raised her head, her face working with a confused
mixture of emotions—shock, elation, fear, anguish. "Oh,
Johnny, why'd he do it?"

"Plunket?" He shrugged. "Greed, ambition, power—
who knows?"

"No. Why did he take his own life?"

"Doc, he was trying to kill *us.*"

She shivered violently, crossing her arms over the ruined remains of her gown. "At first, but not in the end."

John made an annoyed noise and shrugged out of his
uniform jacket. He wrapped it around her shoulders and
pulled her into his embrace. "He couldn't face the public
disgrace of a hanging, but he damn well wasn't going to
let us get away either."

"I don't believe he meant to cause that cave-in."

"We'll probably never agree on that," John said. He
shook his head. "Not that it matters any longer."

"He was so troubled." She spoke into his chest, her

forehead pressed wearily against him. "Did—did I do that to him?"

"Don't you try to take responsibility for that, too, do you hear?" he ordered fiercely, his hands hard on her shoulders. He shook her, forcing her to meet his stony gaze. "Moses was bound for perdition long before you came into the picture. Somehow the ambition in him became insanity, and it made him a killer."

"I can't help feeling sorry."

His mouth tightened, clamped together in a thin line that expressed his disapproval of her pity. "You're too damned forgiving, Sara."

She swallowed and looked away. Her voice was barely audible. "Yes, perhaps I am."

John frowned, pricked by the double meaning. "Have you forgotten what he did to Yves?"

She gasped and began struggling to her feet. "Dear God! Yves!" Her fingers curled urgently into John's shirt-front as he rose with her. "Johnny, take me home."

It was three days before Yves regained consciousness. Three anxious days for Sara as she hovered over her patient, hardly leaving his room to eat or sleep, despite Pandora's protestations. She ignored everything, everyone, focusing on Yves as if to instill some of her own life-energy into his still form. He'd risked himself so courageously for her, she could do nothing less, and so she missed the tumult that swept the town following the daring daylight robbery of the Alexander Mitchell Bank and the revelation of the fantastic story of Judge Menard Plunket's death.

Somehow John took care of all the questions, dealing with Sheriff Ramsey, the lawyers, the curiosity-seekers, and she was grateful. She knew that soon she would have to face John and the question of their relationship, but she refused to concern herself with that or anything else while Yves' life wavered in such delicate balance.

He was so weak from loss of blood and the trauma of the wound that Sara found it a miracle he held onto life at all, much less that he slowly began to rally. And when he opened his wide gray eyes and gave her a small fey smile, she knew her prayers were not in vain. Yves' thin form made barely a lump under the blanket, and his face was white beneath the dusting of orange freckles, but when he spoke his voice was steady.

"Sara, lass," he said, lifting a feeble hand. "Praise be you're safe."

She took his hand, checking his brow for fever. It was cool at last, and she smiled in relief. "I'm fine, Father Yves, thanks to you. And I think you're going to be fine now, too."

"I had a dream . . ."

"Shh. You should try to rest."

His skinny fingers tightened around her hand. "Such a dream, lass. I know who the Lady is."

"What?" Sara was startled. Had his visions returned to disturb his mind? Was he delirious after all?

"All this time. And to think I was afraid of her." He laughed weakly.

"Yves, you mustn't—"

"Margaret of Lauthecourt. No witch or devil-crone. A saintly French nun she was. Sara, she was trying to make me understand, all this time."

"Understand what?"

"That the bleeding heart she held wasn't mine, but our Blessed Savior's. She was trying to tell me that our Lord's Sacred Heart has room for everyone, and peace and forgiveness even for drunken, cowardly sinners like me."

Sara's expression softened. "But you knew that, didn't you, Father?"

"I think I'd forgotten until the Lady nun made me see." His sigh was tired, but he seemed strangely content for the first time since Sara had known him. "I will be able to do His work again."

How could Sara argue against such conviction? Whether he'd truly been visited by a heavenly personage or somewhere deep inside himself found the answers he needed, Yves was again at peace with his faith. Sara squeezed his hand. "I'm so glad for you, Father. Do you feel well enough to eat something? You'll need your strength."

His nearly transparent eyelids fluttered sleepily. "Some

of Lizzie's nice soup? In a little while, lass. I think I'll
just rest now . . .''

"I'll get it for you," she began, but he was already
asleep. She smiled, straightened the covers, and tiptoed
from the room. Pulling the door shut, she smoothed her
sedate blue-sprigged day gown and touched her hair, automatically checking the pins. She hadn't been brave
enough to wear Johnny's combs, but perhaps soon . . .

Uncertainly, she bit her lip. There hadn't been time or
opportunity to talk seriously to Johnny since the awful day
at the Sugarloaf, and oh, she longed to be held again! She
loved him, this man of many parts, and once, he'd said
that he loved her. Was it possible to forge a commitment
between them? She knew she had to tell him about the
baby. She had no idea what it would mean to him, but
above all else she had to be with Johnny, on whatever
terms he chose. Her only hope of happiness resided in that
fact.

"How is he?"

Sara spun around to find John watching her from the
end of the hall. He looked impressively tall and handsome
in his bright blue uniform, and her heart skipped a beat.
She drew a deep breath and gave him a tentative smile.

"He's much better. Out of danger, I think."

"Good." He did not return her smile, and his mouth
was a straight, solemn line under his golden mustache.

She looked at him, saw the seriousness in his leaf-green
eyes, and felt a frigid hand touch her heart. Icy fear ran
up her spine, and a sudden, bitter frost withered her bur-
geoning hope.

"You're leaving," she said, praying he would deny it.

"Yes."

"When?"

"In a few minutes. I had to say goodbye."

John watched the hope drain from her sweet face along
with every vestige of color, and cursed himself for what
he had to do. For an instant, he saw her naked despair,
and her pain pierced him through. He wanted to explain,
to make her understand. Their tempestuous relationship
had seen too many farewells, but this one was different.

"There's something I have to do, Sara, before . . ." He

broke off, and his jaw hardened. It was impossible. "There's something I have to do."

Her voice was brittle, mocking. "More 'unfinished business,' Major?"

"You could say that."

"I see."

There's no future for us, Sara, love, he thought, anguished, *not until I finish what I began. How can I promise you forever when I'm still not sure I have today?*

Second chances weren't for the faint of heart. There were obligations that had prior claim on him, responsibilities he'd neglected for too long. He'd thought himself a courageous man, but the prospect that these duties might prevent his returning to Sara filled him with the starkest terror. Despite everything he could do, things might not work out as he planned.

The day the earth had disgorged him, whole and new, he'd known the only way he would ever be worthy enough to claim Sara Cary as his own was to come to terms with his personal demons. Until he did, he'd never be the kind of man she needed and deserved. And he'd surely end up driving her away. And that would be the bleakest desolation of all.

So he made no promises.

How could he, when he didn't know whether he'd be able to keep them? It would hurt her a thousandfold more to believe an easily spoken assurance and then find herself betrayed yet again. How could she believe him anyway, when he'd broken his word countless times? If he told her now how dearly he loved her, and promised to return, those words would be just for him, as a salve to his conscience, glittery words, all dross and no gold. They would make things easier for him, not her, and for once in his miserable life, he was determined to do the selfless thing. At least this way she would have her dignity. God willing, someday she might have more.

Ah, Sara, my love, he thought, feeling her anger and hurt keenly. *Believe me, it's better this way.*

Her fists twisted against her skirts, and he saw her force her features into lines as unrevealing as a marble statue. He could see what the effort cost her.

Her hopes died, painfully. He hadn't changed after all, she thought, despite all that had passed between them. Whatever dark forces still drove him, she would be no part of them. She realized to her despair that if he could leave her again so easily, then there'd been nothing there to hold him in the first place. She would not cling or plead, nor would she try to tie him unwillingly to her with the knowledge of his unborn child. He might stay for a while, but in the end he'd go all the same. And that would kill her.

She battled for composure. Pandora's training reasserted itself. Even in a crisis, a lady maintained a gracious demeanor. She forced the polite words through her constricted throat. "I'll wish you a *bon voyage,* Major, and thank you for all your help."

"I wish I didn't have to leave you like this, Sara." His tone was low and strained. Against his will, the words of atonement spilled from his lips. "I'm sorry, Doc. You know if I can, I'll come back."

"John, don't." She grew even paler. "Please spare me your good intentions. I don't think I could stand that."

The muscle in his jaw flexed. "Yes. You're right."

"Now you must excuse me, Major. I've got to prepare some good strong broth for Yves. I'll tell him you asked about him." She went to sweep by him, her chin held imperiously high.

His hand on her arm stopped her. Unable to prevent himself, he turned her to take one last look at her face. His hand traveled lightly over the soft wisps of hair at her temple.

"Sweet Sara." He bent to kiss her, but she turned away at the last moment, and his lips brushed her cool cheek. His sigh was heavy. "Just . . . take care of yourself." Then he was gone, tromping down the hall in his heavy boots, leaving behind an echo of masculine footsteps.

She stood alone in the empty hall.

As the days passed, Sara missed Johnny desperately. Her yearning was an ever-constant presence that shadowed her days and made a mockery of her nights, and she knew that the loss she felt would always be with her. She also knew that for the sake of her child, she had to get on with her life.

She refused to let bitterness become her sole reason for being. She was honest enough to take responsibility for her choices. The risks of loving had been hers to take or reject, and she'd grasped them with both hands. And she had much to be grateful to Johnny for.

Thanks to him, she'd experienced the full range of human emotions, from the heights to the depths and every plane in between. Somehow, fighting and laughing and loving with the man had changed her, completed her. She was no longer barren in either body or soul, but truly a woman in all ways. Though her heart ached, she could not regret a single moment. He'd challenged and stretched her abilities, her senses, and her emotions. She was no longer dependent on her menagerie of misfits to bring purpose to her life. She could find it within herself, and knew herself confident and capable of loving and rearing John's child. It was a center of quiet joy that sustained her even during the darkest times.

There was little time for moping. Surprisingly, she found that Menard's machinations had been perfectly legal. She'd been divorced, married, and widowed in the course of twenty-four hours, and in the eyes of the law, she was Mrs. Menard Plunket, the late judge's only heir. Although Menard's monetary wealth had been wiped out by the holdup of the Alexander Mitchell bank, his estate still consisted of many acres of land as well as the mansion. Horrified at first, Sara soon realized that some good might still come from this development, and she worked diligently to see that it did.

She made equitable adjustments with the sharecroppers he'd sought to swindle, and, in many cases, including Daisy Wiley's and her husband's, made provision for them to own the land outright. Some land she sold, and with the proceeds reimbursed the innocent people who'd held savings in the Mitchell Bank. She even offered to make a settlement with Eustace Cavendish, but the young man refused, saying his father had provided for him well enough. Coal negotiations with the railroad people fizzled, disappointing a number of city fathers, but Sara was just as glad that the Sugarloaf and Menard's tomb would remain undisturbed. Disposal of the final piece of Menard's property took a little more thought, but when she announced her decision, Pandora was ecstatic.

"Sara Jane, that is the most generous gesture I ever heard," Pandora said. They sat in the parlor, where a cheerful fire crackled in the grate. An early December chill had swept in from the river that evening. "Are you certain you want to donate Judge Plunket's home to the Freedmen's Society?"

"I'm positive, Dorie." Sara bent over the yarn in her lap, laboriously knitting another row.

"Not many women would give up a mansion like that," Pandora continued, popping her needle in and out of her own hoop of embroidery, every stitch perfect. "No matter what the circumstances."

Sara shrugged. "You know I don't feel right about keeping anything that was Menard's. This solves the problem nicely."

Sara looked up as Ella Washington brought in a loaded coffee tray. Clem's parents were welcome additions to the household staff. Clem hobbled in behind his mother, bearing a dish of gingered walnuts, and Sara smiled her welcome.

"And with a new school, Clem won't play hooky so often, will you, Clem?" she teased.

"Aw, Miss Sara," Clem protested, grinning. "You know I like school. Father Yves says if I study hard, I might even go to college."

"I'm sure you will," Sara replied. She took the cup Pandora offered her, but her stomach lurched uncertainly at the rich aroma. Cautiously, she stirred the brew, pretending to let it cool. She hadn't yet told Pandora about the baby, but she knew the changes that were taking place in her body would not go unnoticed much longer. She hoped by that time she would have decided what to do.

"Where is Father Yves?" Pandora asked.

"Mr. Ambrose and Miss Lizzie took him for a ride in the buggy," Ella volunteered. "Come on, Clem. You still got studying to finish."

"Oh, dear," Sara said, biting her lip after they'd left. She set aside her cup. "I hope Yves doesn't overdo it."

"Will you quit fussing like an old biddy?" Pandora scolded. "You know Ambrose will take care of him. Besides, an outing will do him good, now that he's feeling so much better."

"Yes, he is, isn't he?" Sara went to the window, drawing aside the heavy drape to stare into the darkness. "He'll be fit enough to perform the nuptials for Lizzie and Ambrose in a few weeks. He's talking about going back to New Orleans after that."

"It will be quiet here if he leaves after Lizzie and Ambrose move to Watkin's Mill. I'm glad Cousin Mathilde is coming soon. Do you think we could prevail on her to stay for a while?"

"I think she's lonely by herself. She'd be good company to have around permanently."

"My thoughts exactly. She has such a sharp tongue." Pandora giggled. "I can't wait until I get her and Minerva Haskett together."

Sara smiled wanly and dropped the curtain. "There's sure to be fireworks. And you'll love every minute."

"You know, it's not Yves I've been worried about," Pandora remarked. "It's you, Sara. You're so pale and peaked. Are you all right?"

"Of course, Dorie," Sara answered, too quickly. She managed a little smile. "I'm just tired tonight."

"That's understandable. You've been so busy with these awkward business matters, and, after all, it's only been a month since your ordeal."

"Yes, that's it, I'm sure."

"All of it?" Pandora probed gently.

Sara was quiet for a long moment. When she spoke again, her words were low with misery. "I miss him so much, Dorie."

They both knew who she meant. Pandora nodded. "Yes, I know."

"Sometimes I don't know how I'll bear it."

"You will. You'll survive this just as you have every other trial. After a while, you'll even get over it, after a fashion." Pandora's faded blue eyes looked back on a memory, and her voice was husky. "Though you won't ever forget."

Sara looked questioningly at her sister-in-law. "Dorie? Did you . . . ?"

Pandora came back to herself, and her gray chignon bobbed as she laughed lightly. "Oh, yes, there was once a young man in my life. I was quite the belle back then, but Papa was a Tartar and his family didn't approve . . ." She shrugged. "We all have our regrets, Sara Jane. I've always been sorry I didn't run off with him when he asked."

Sara sat down beside Pandora and reached for her hands. "Oh, Dorie, I'm sorry."

"Now, child, there's no need for that. I've got my memories, and so do you."

Sara bit her lip. "Yes, you're right." And soon, she thought, she would have more than that. It was a perfect time to tell Pandora about the baby, but Sara didn't. Somehow it made her feel closer to Johnny to keep the secret just a while longer. She sighed and got up.

"It's late and I'm tired. I think I'll go to bed." She kissed the older woman's wrinkled cheek. "Good night."

As she prepared for bed, Sara worried about her choices. She had no doubt Pandora would support her wholeheartedly when she learned about the baby. But the prospect of the disgrace, the old gossip and scandal that would be dredged up once her condition was apparent, was more than daunting. And her medical practice was almost nonexistent now and would remain so with her reputation in shreds. Perhaps the time had come to consider leaving Lexington.

Sara brushed her hair with vigorous strokes, leaving it loose, spilling in crackling waves about her shoulders.

She hated the idea of leaving Pandora, but she wanted the best for her child. If Mathilde stayed on with Pandora, Sara knew she wouldn't worry about her sister-in-law. Somewhere there had to be a place where she could earn a living as a physician. After all, she would have a child to support, as well as herself. She knew she could do it, but oh, why were life's choices always so hard?

She put away the brushes in her dresser drawer, then

hesitated, spying the combs John had given her an endless age ago during their wonderful time in San Antonio. She touched them lingeringly, as she'd done each evening since he'd left. The ritual was vaguely comforting, but tonight she had no patience with herself. Did she think to conjure him back into her life with such a talisman? She'd need more than magic to accomplish that feat!

Annoyed at herself for hanging on to the past when she needed to move into the future, she grabbed the combs and rushed to the window. Throwing up the sash, she pitched the combs into the darkness, then stood, shivering, as the cold night air wafted over her thinly-clad form. She was chilled in body and soul when she finally climbed into the high carved bed.

Her dreams were especially troubled that night, playing over and over the scenes of parting and separation. She knew she wept.

"Don't cry, darling," came the whispered plea in her dreams. Lips tenderly brushed hers, and she sighed, her heart swelling with poignancy and sadness.

"Johnny," she called through the mists of slumber, aching for him.

"I never meant to make you cry."

"Yes, you did," she told this dream-Johnny sorrowfully. "You left me."

"I'm back." His mouth nuzzled the curve of her jaw, and she felt the whisper-tickle of his silky mustache. She could almost feel the warmth of his skin and smell his uniquely male scent.

She shook her head, reluctant to believe the unspoken pledge in his husky, tantalizing voice. "You'll only leave me again."

"I'm staying this time."

It was too much. She groaned and tossed restlessly. A tender dream-lover full of sweet but false promises was worse torture than no Johnny at all. "Go away."

"Why?"

"You're only a dream."

A low chuckle rumbled in her ear. "Why don't you wake up, Doc, and find out for sure?"

She shook her head again, more vehemently, keeping

her eyes tightly closed. This dream-Johnny was as bossy as the real thing. "No."

"Then I'll have to rely on my powers of persuasion."

The bed dipped, and strong arms closed around her. Then she was being kissed, expertly and ardently. His tongue gently probed the ribbon of her lips. With a sigh, she opened for him, reveling in the taste and heat of him. If this was a dream, she never wanted to wake up. Her hands stole upwards over broad shoulders to caress his thick neck and the silky hair at his nape. Oh, he felt so wonderful! How could she bear to open her eyes and have him vanish like a wisp of smoke? She held on tighter, kissing him back with the strength and fervency of all her pent-up desires.

"Sweet Sara." There was laughter and passion in his voice. "Are you awake yet?"

"I don't think so."

"I'd better try harder then."

"Umm, please."

His lips were masterful, and his hands moved over her with the old familiarity, learning her anew through the thin stuff of her gown. She arched against him and sighed, eyelids fluttering. Her dreamscape was fast becoming a reality she never wanted to leave.

Her hands found the flat, faintly-stubbled planes of his face, then sank into the thick curls she loved so well. Had she conjured him forth with the power of her wishes? But no, he was warm and solid, exciting and dangerous. Her fingers twisted in the starched cotton of his white shirt. Suddenly, she had to know if this splendor were real, and she forced her eyes open.

"I'm awake," she murmured in wary disbelief. John's strong features were barely visible in the pre-dawn light seeping through her window curtains. "What are you doing here?"

His voice was thick. "I believe . . . I'm making love with you."

"Tell me why—"

"Because you're beautiful and I want you so much it's killing me."

"—why you're here."

"I couldn't wait until morning to see you." He dipped his head and nuzzled the cleft between her breasts, making her gasp and wiggle.

"How did you get in?"

His soft puff of laughter heated her skin. "I used to live here. I know where Pandora keeps the key."

"Old habits die hard with you."

There was a grin in his voice. "Right. I slipped into your bed once before when we were on the outs and it worked. Thought it was worth another try."

"That depends."

"On what?"

She palmed his broad shoulders, her neck arching as he blazed a trail along her throbbing pulse points. "On what you've got to say to me."

"What do you want me to say?"

"That you were a fool to leave me."

His voice was a rumbly growl. "I was a fool to leave you."

"That you love me desperately."

He lifted his head, and his tone went deadly serious. "Honey, I love you desperately."

"You do?" Her lower lip trembled.

"I do, indeed."

"Then come here. It worked again."

He laughed, kissed her hard, then pulled away, groaning. "No. Dammit. No."

"What?" She was bewildered. "Why?"

He hauled her to a sitting position. "We're going to do it right this time. From the very beginning."

She dimpled and blushed. "It felt all right to me."

His chuckle was appreciative. "You're a helluva woman, Doc." Pulling her across his lap, he held her in the crook of his arm. "Jesus, I missed you!"

"Then why did you leave?" she asked softly, her eyes velvet-soft with hurt.

"So that this time, when I came to you, I could do it honestly."

A pleat appeared between her brows. "I don't understand."

"No, of course you don't, but you're still willing to let

me love you, right here, right now, with no explanations.''
He explored the curve of her stomach and the full, tender
thrust of her breasts.

She shivered with the pleasure of his touch. ''You—you
said everything I need to know.'' She was too glad to see
him to quibble about details.

''I said you were too forgiving,'' he said against her
lips. ''You should scream and throw things at me for pulling something like this again.''

She reached for him, pulling his head down to hers.
''Remind me later.''

He groaned, hungrily delving into her mouth with his
tongue, sweeping the secret sensitive places, asserting his
power and his need. His hand moved, stroked, sought out
all the well-known curves, then suddenly he faltered. He
drew back, breathing heavily, a look of puzzled consterna-
nation on his face. Pulling the soft stuff of her gown tight,
he measured her with his hand.

Sara watched him anxiously, biting her lip. He checked
the extra voluptuousness of her bosom, the slight thick-
ening of her belly, and a look of wondrous amazement
made his jaw go slack. Stunned, he raised his gaze to her
anxious face.

''Sara.'' His hands bracketed her cheeks, and his mouth
worked with emotion as the enormity of his discovery hit
him. ''You weren't going to tell me, were you?''

''I couldn't try to hold you that way,'' she whispered.
''I'm selfish enough to want you for myself first.''

''Well, you've got me, honey. Oh, God, how you've got
me!'' His strong arms gathered her close, and he pressed
his forehead against hers.

''And the baby?'' she murmured.

''How could I not love a part of you? God, I can't wait
to hear you singing lullabies and playing patty-cake. A
child of our own makes everything perfect.''

Their kiss was sweet with homecoming, and when John
raised his head he was breathing gustily. ''You make me
forget what I'm here for, Doc.''

''Isn't that me?'' she asked guilelessly.

''Yes, but—'' He broke off. ''Here, I'll show you.''

Taking her hand, he led her out of the room, padding

through the silent house, down the stairs into the parlor. Sara shivered in her ankle-length nightdress and looked at John with a question in her eyes. His regard shifted to a small bundle on the parlor divan, and Sara followed his gaze, then stifled a gasp.

The little boy asleep on the divan had thick, straight hair the color of ripe corn. His pudgy cheek rested against his folded hands, and in repose his breath was sweet and even with the untroubled sleep of innocence. He was covered with one of Pandora's afghans. Sara moved on tiptoe, kneeling beside the sleeping child. He looked about five years old.

"Oh, Johnny," she breathed, barely touching the silky head. "He's . . ."

"Todd. His name is Todd. My son." He said the word with a touch of defiance and a great deal of pride.

"That's where you were. You went home." Tears glittered on her eyelashes. "That was your unfinished business."

John's voice was gruff. "I knew I couldn't start over until I'd made peace with my family."

"And did you?"

"I think so. They love me, in their own strange way. They had grieved to think me dead all that time. I think we reached an understanding."

Sara rose and went to stand in front of him. Taking his hands, she lifted her chin so she could see into his eyes. "I'm so glad for you. And Todd?"

John's gaze flicked to the sleeping child. "God knows I made mistakes with Gwendolyn. She was so young and I was gone a lot . . ." He took a deep breath. "I can't hate her anymore. And the boy, well, her parents tried, but they couldn't give him the kind of family, the kind of love he needs. They were happy to let me take him off their hands. He's a good kid, Sara." His voice was earnest, and he squeezed her hands. "I took one look at him and knew he needed you as much as I do. I guess you could say we're a package deal. If you'll have us."

Sara's throat felt thick at this rare and wonderful acceptance by John, not only of Todd but of himself. Only a man at peace within himself, with all his varied personalities finally meshed into a cohesive whole, could make such a gesture of love. Here was a man worthy and honorable and most adored.

"Yes." Her voice was tremulous. "I'll have you both."

He pulled her into his arms. "Brave lady."

She shook her head, clinging to him. "I'm scared to death of life without you."

"Sara . . ." He couldn't get enough of her. If he had a hundred lifetimes, he'd never grow tired of this woman. He stroked the tangled skein of her hair and cupped her face, needing to tell her all that he felt. His voice was hoarse with feeling.

"From the very first, you were the only one who really knew me. You saw past all the hurt and anger and fear down to the man who needed you so badly. You healed me, Sara, body, soul, and heart. You took that burnt-out shell of a man, put him back together, and taught him how to love again. I hope you're ready for me, because I'm not ever letting you go again."

She turned her head, kissing his palm. "I've been ready for you all my life, only I never knew it. You had to break me out of my shell. I was afraid to live and afraid of love until you forced me to feel."

"I was a damned bastard to you."

"Maybe you were what I needed. I can't help myself. I love you so much, Johnny."

His fingertip tenderly stroked the curve of her cheekbone. "I know you were what *I* needed, though I fought it every step of the way. And I'll grow old needing you. Sara, I hear they're begging for geologists and doctors and families in the Rockies. The Army's done with me, and I've got a stake from back pay and Todd's trust. I'm ready to try my hand at mining again. I think we can build a life together. Will you come with me?"

"Of course."

He grinned, exultant. "And I want Father Yves to marry us again. Only this time, I'm going to be wide awake and know exactly what I'm doing. Does that suit you?"

Her smile was joyous, but she answered demurely. "Yes, it suits me fine."

"You don't fool me a bit, Doc," John said mock-sternly,

laughing a little. "I know I'm going to have my hands full with you."

"I'll be a model wife, a perfect helpmeet, a—" A look of horror crossed her features. "Oh, no!"

"Sara, what is it?"

But she had slipped from his grasp and dashed through the entrance hall. Flinging open the front door, she flew down the porch steps, barefoot in her nightdress, her hair streaming behind her like a dark flag as golden streaks of daylight broke over the Lexington rooftops. Alarmed, John followed her to the porch, frowning as she kicked through the damp grass under her window. She gave a cry, bent to pick up something, then clambered up the steps again, smiling in triumph. "I found them!"

"What?" He swept an arm around her and dragged her back inside. She unfolded her hands.

"Your combs. Oh, I couldn't bear to lose them."

"What the hell were they doing out there?"

She blushed, and her expression was sheepish and appealing all at once. "I threw them there. I guess I was trying to prove something."

"Didn't work, did it?" He grinned, then as quickly frowned. "Well, don't do it again. You're half dressed and could catch your death of cold like that."

"I'll remind you, John McCulloch," Sara said mischievously, shoving the prized ivory combs into her thick locks, "that you shouldn't chastise a woman in my delicate condition."

John gathered her close and bent his head to kiss her. "I can think of other ways to tame you," he murmured.

Pandora's slippered feet were silent on the staircase. She came up short at the sight of the blond boy sitting patiently on the bottom step. He looked up at her curiously, lifted his stubby forefinger to his lips, then pointed toward the couple locked in an ardent embrace in the hallway. Stunned, Pandora sat down shakily beside the child.

"That's my papa," the boy said in a whisper. "And my new mama. There's going to be a wedding."

Pandora's glad cry rang to the top of the house.

"Hotcakes and honeymoons! It's about time!"

Author's Notes

The Sugarloaf is purely fictional, although the James gang was known to use the caves of southwestern Missouri on occasion as hideouts. However, coal was mined in the Little Sni Creek area beginning in the 1870s. Plans for rail lines connecting Lexington with other railheads did not materialize until the St. Louis, Kansas City, and Northern Railroad constructed to a point opposite the city in 1868, but within the decade Kansas City outstripped its neighbor as a major cattle production and shipping center.

The Liberty and Lexington bank robberies marked the beginning of the James and Younger brothers' careers, which extended through the late 1870s and early 1880s. They actually made the trip to San Antonio and dealt with Gonzales. On the way back from that trip, Cole Younger began his relationship with Myra Belle Shirley, the woman who eventually became known as the "outlaw queen," Belle Starr. In 1876 Cole Younger was sentenced to life imprisonment for his crimes. He was paroled in 1903. Jesse James was murdered by Robert Ford in 1882.

"The Lost Gold of the Reynolds Gang" still lures treasure seekers in Colorado to the region of the Spanish Peaks where a portion of $60,000 in minted gold from Jim Reynolds's holdup of a wagon train was reported buried. To this day, it has not been found.

Saint Margaret Mary Alacoque of Lauthecourt was beatified in 1864 and canonized in 1920.

SUZANNAH DAVIS

SUZANNAH DAVIS has lived in the same sleepy Louisiana town for most of her life and feels that the easy pace and old-fashioned values keep her feet on the ground while her head stays in the clouds dreaming up romances. The daughter of a newspaper family, Suzannah Davis was born with printer's ink in her veins, but she never thought her tendency to fantasize would lead to a career as an author. After college at Louisiana State University, she worked as a librarian and social worker, then "retired" to become a homemaker and mother. Now, her eclectic tastes and passion for the written word keep her busy at her new vocation: exploring life's endless variety and love's many adventures through her novels. She's always believed in happy endings, and her attorney-husband and three lively children are a constant reminder that dreams do come true—sometimes in the most unexpected fashion!

Avon Romances—
the best in exceptional authors and unforgettable novels!

OUTLAW HEART Suzannah Davis
75672-2/$3.95 US/$4.95 Can

LADY MIDNIGHT Maria Greene
75563-7/$3.95 US/$4.95 Can

SILVER NIGHTS Jane Feather
75569-6/$3.95 US/$4.95 Can

TENDER CONQUEST Lisa Bingham
75734-6/$3.95 US/$4.95 Can

MOONSHADOW Susan Wiggs
75639-0/$3.95 US/$4.95 Can

FORTUNE'S BRIDE Cheryl Spencer
75725-7/$3.95 US/$4.95 Can

BRITTANY Linda Lang Bartell
75545-9/$3.95 US/$4.95 Can

BY HONOR BOUND Scotney St. James
75602-1/$3.95 US/$4.95 Can

WINDSONG Judith E. French
75551-3/$3.95 US/$4.95 Can

ROGUE'S LADY Victoria Thompson
75526-2/$3.95 US/$4.95 Can

FIRESTORM Brenda Joyce
75577-7/$3.95 US/$4.95 Can

STOLEN HEART Barbara Dawson Smith
75510-6/$3.95 US/$4.95 Can

**Everyone Loves
A Lindsey—**

**Coming in June 1989
from Avon Books**

the next breathtakingly
beautiful novel of love and passion
from the *New York Times* bestselling
author

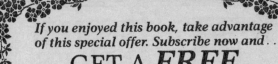